# Norine's Revenge, and, Sir Noel's Heir

# by May Agnes Fleming

Copyright © 8/24/2015
Jefferson Publication

ISBN-13: 978-1517056544

Printed in the United States of America

# Contents

# CHAPTER I.

### TWO BLACK EYES AND THEIR WORK.

The early express train from Montreal to Portland, Maine, was crowded.

Mr. Richard Gilbert, lawyer, of New York, entering five minutes before starting time, found just one seat unoccupied near the door. A crusty old farmer held the upper half, and moved grumpily toward the window, under protest, as Mr. Gilbert took the place.

The month was March, the morning snowy and blowy, slushy and sleety, as it is in the nature of Canadian March mornings to be. The sharp sleet lashed the glass, people shivered in multitudinous wraps, lifted purple noses, over-twisted woolen clouds and looked forlorn and miserable. And Mr. Gilbert, congratulating himself inwardly on having secured a seat by the stove, opened the damp *Montreal True Witness*, and settled himself comfortably to read. He turned to the leading article, read three lines, and never finished it from that day to this. For the door opened, a howl of March wind, a rush of March rain whirled in, and lifting his eyes, Mr. Richard Gilbert saw in the doorway a new passenger.

The new passenger was a young lady, and the young lady was the prettiest young lady, Mr. Gilbert thought, in that first moment, he had ever seen.

She was tall, she was slim, she was dark, she had long loose, curly black hair, falling to her waist, and two big, bright, black, Canadian eyes, as lovely eyes as the wide earth holds. She stood there in the doorway, faltering, frightened, irresolute, a very picture—the color coming and going in the youthful, sensitive face, the luminous brown eyes glancing like the eyes of a startled bird. She stood there, laden with bundles, bandboxes, and reticules, and holding a little blinking spaniel by a string.

Every seat was filled, no one seemed disposed to dispossess themselves, even for the accommodation of youth and beauty. Only for six seconds, though; then Richard Gilbert, rose up, and quietly, and, as a matter of course, offered his seat to the young lady. She smiled—what a smile it was, what a bright little row of teeth it showed, dimpled, blushed—the loveliest rose-pink blush in the world, hesitated, and spoke:

"But, monsieur!" in excellent English, set to a delicious French accent. "But, monsieur will have no place."

"Monsieur will do very well. Oblige me, mademoiselle, by taking this seat."

"Monsieur is very good. Thanks."

She fluttered down into the seat, and Mr. Gilbert disposed of the many bundles and boxes and bags on the rack overhead. He was smiling a little to himself as he did so; the *role* of lady's man was quite a new one in this gentleman's cast in the great play of Life. The grumpy old farmer, with a grunt of disapprobation, edged still further up to the window.

"Monsieur can sit on the arm of the seat," suggests the young lady, glancing up with a pretty girl's glance—half shy, half coquettish; "it is so very fatiguing to stand."

Monsieur avails himself of the offer immediately, and finds he is in an excellent position to examine that very charming face. But he does not examine it: he is not one of your light-minded, mustache-growing, frivolous-headed youths of three-or-four-and-twenty, to whom the smiling face of a pretty girl is the most fascinating object under heaven.

Mr. Gilbert casts one look, only one, then draws forth the *True Witness* and buries himself in the leading article. The last bell rings, the whistle shrieks, a plunge, a snort, and they are rushing madly off into the wild March morning. The young lady looks about her, the grumpy farmer is between her and the window, the window is all blurred and blotted; Mr. Gilbert is fathoms deep in his paper. She gives a little sigh, then lifts her small dog up in her lap, and begins an animated conversation with him in French. Frollo understands Canadian French, certainly not a word of English, and he blinks his watery eyes, and listens sagaciously to it all. The farmer looks askance, and grunts like one of his own pigs; the lawyer, from behind his printed sheet, finds the words dancing fantastically before his eyes, and his brain taking in nothing but the sweet-spoken, foolish little prattle of mademoiselle to Frollo.

He is thirty-five years of age, he is a hard-headed, hard-working lawyer, he has a species of contempt for all women, as bundles of nerves and nonsense, fashions and foolery. He is thirty-five; he has never asked any woman to marry him in his life; he looks upon that foolish boy-and-girl idiocy, called love, as your worldly-wise cynics do look upon it, with a sneer and a scoff. Pretty girls he has met and known by the score—handsome women and clever women, but not the prettiest, the handsomest, the cleverest of them all has ever made his well-regulated legal pulses beat one throb the quicker in all his five-and-thirty years of life. Why is it then that he looks at this little French Canadienne with an interest he has never felt in looking at any of the bright New York beauties he has known so long? Simple curiosity, no doubt—nothing more.

"She looks like a picture I once saw of Joanna of Naples," he thought, "only Joanna had golden hair. I hope the similarity to that very improper person ends with the outward resemblance."

He returned to his newspaper, but somehow politics and cable dispatches, and Our Foreign Relations, had lost their interest. Again and again, under cover of the friendly sheet, his eyes wandered back to that fair drooping face, that piquant profile, those long eyelashes, and the rippling black tresses falling from beneath the little hat. The hat was trimmed with crape, and the graceful figure wore dingy black.

"Who is she?" Mr. Gilbert found himself wondering "where is she going? and for whom is she in mourning?" And then, conscious of his own folly and levity, he pulled himself up, and went back for the dozenth time to the *True Witness*.

But—his hour had come, and it would not do. The low French babble to the dog rang in his ears, the dark mignonne face came between him and the printed page, and blotted it out.

"She is much too young, and—yes, too pretty to be travelling alone. I wonder where is she going; and if her friends will meet her? Very imprudent to allow a child like this to travel alone. She hardly looks sixteen."

His interest—fatherly, brotherly of course, in this handsome child was increasing every moment. It was something not to be explained or comprehended. He had heard of such imbecility as "love at first sight," but was it likely that he, a man of five-and-thirty, a lawyer, without an ounce of sentimentality in his composition should make an idiot of himself over a French Canadienne, a total stranger, a bread-and-butter-eating school-girl at his time of life. Not likely. She interested him as a pretty picture or marble Venus, or other work of art might—just that.

He did not address her. Lawyers are not bashful as a body. Mr. Gilbert was not bashful individually, but something, for which he knew no name, held him silent now. If that grumpy, overgrown farmer were only out of the way, he thought, instead of sitting sulkily there staring at the falling rain, he could no doubt find something to say.

Fate favored him, his evil angel "cursed him with the curse of an accomplished prayer." At the very next station the surly husbandman got up and left; and the mistress of Frollo, moving close to the window, lifted those two orbs of wondrous brown light to the lawyer's grave, thoughtful face, and the sweet voice spoke:

"Will monsieur resume his place now?"

Monsieur needed no second bidding. He resumed it, threw aside his paper, and opened conversation in the usual brilliant and original way:

"The storm seems to increase—don't you think so? Abominable weather it has been since March came in, and no hope of its holding up to day."

"Oh, yes, monsieur," mademoiselle answered, with animation; "and it is such a pity, isn't it? It makes one low-spirited, one can see nothing, and one does like so to see the country as one goes along."

"Was she going far?" the lawyer inquired.

"Oh, very far!" Mademoiselle makes a little Gallic gesture, with shoulders and eyebrows and hands all together to express the immensity of the distance.

"A great way. To Portland," with a strong accent on the name of that city. "Monsieur knows where Portland is?"

"Yes, very well—he was going there himself *en route* to New York. You, mademoiselle," he adds, inquiringly, "are going on a visit, probably?"

Mademoiselle shakes her pretty head, and purses her pretty lips.

"Monsieur, no—I am going home."

"Home? But you are French."

"But yes, monsieur, certainly French, still my home is there. Papa and mamma have become dead," the brown eyes fill, "and Uncle Louis and Aunt Mathilde have seven of their own, and are poor. I am going to mamma's relatives, mamma was not French."

"No?" Mr. Gilbert says in sympathetic inquiry.

"No, monsieur. Mamma was Yan-*kee*, a New England lady, papa French Canadian. Mamma's friends did not wish her to marry papa, and she ran away. It is five years ago since she died, and papa—papa could not live without her, and two years after the good God took him too."

The tearful brown eyes look down at her shabby black dress. "Monsieur beholds I wear mourning still. Then Uncle Louis took me, and sent me to school, but Uncle Louis has so many, so I wrote to mamma's brothers in Portland, and they sent a letter back and money, and told me to come. And I am going—Frollo and me."

She bends over the little dog, her lips quivering like the lips of a grieved child, and the lawyer's middle-aged heart goes out to her in a great compassion.

"Poor little lonely child!" he thinks, watching the sweet overcast face: "I hope they will be good to her, those Yankee friends." Then aloud. "But you are very young, are you not, to travel this distance alone?"

"I am seventeen, and I had to travel alone, there was no one to come with me. My Uncle Kent will meet me at Portland."

"You are Mademoiselle Kent?" he says with a smile.

"No, monsieur, my name is Bourdon—Norine Kent Bourdon."

"Have you ever seen those relatives to whom you are going?"

"Once. They came to see mamma when she was dead. There are three—two uncles and an aunt. They were very kind. I liked them very much."

"I trust you will be happy in your new home, Miss Bourdon," the lawyer says gravely. "Permit me to offer you my card. If you ever visit New York I may meet you again—who knows?"

The young lady smiles as she reads the name.

"Ah—who knows? I am going out as governess by-and-by. Perhaps I shall write to you to help get me a situation."

"What a frank, innocent child it is!" thought Mr. Gilbert, looking down at the smiling, trustful face: "other girls of her age would be bashful, coquettish, or afraid of a masculine stranger. But this pretty child smiles up in my face, and tells me her little history as though I were her brother. I wish I were her brother, and had power to shield her from the hardships of life." "Any service in my power I shall always be happy to render you, my dear young lady," he said; "if at any time you apply to me, believe me I shall do my utmost to serve you."

Mademoiselle Norine Kent Bourdon looked up into the grave, genial face, with soft, trustful eyes that thanked him. She could not have defined it, but she felt he was a man to be trusted—a good man, a faithful friend and an honorable gentleman.

The train flew on.

As the afternoon wore away the storm increased. The trees rocked in the high wind, and the ceaseless sleet beat against the windows. Miss Bourdon had a novel in her satchel, an English novel, and she perused a few pages of this work at intervals, and watched the storm-blotted landscape flitting by. She made small French remarks to Frollo, and she refreshed herself with apples, ginger-bread and dyspeptic confectionery. But, all these recreations palling after a time, and as the darkness of the stormy March day closed, drowsiness came, and leaning her head against the window, the young lady fell asleep.

Mr. Gilbert could watch her now to his heart's content, and he did watch her with an interest all-absorbing, and utterly beyond his comprehension. He laid his railway rug lightly over her, and shielded her from all other male eyes, with jealous care. What was it that charmed him about this French girl?

He could no more have told you then than he could ever have told you afterward. It was written, it was Kismet; his fate had come to him as it comes to all, in unlooked-for form. She looked, the poetic simile came to the unpoetical mind of the lawyer—like a folded rose, the sweetness and bloom yet unbrushed from the leaves.

Mademoiselle did not awake until the train stopped; then she opened her eyes bewildered. But Mr. Gilbert gathered up the boxes and bundles, drew her hand under his arm, and led her out of the cars, and up to the big noisy hotel, where they were to stop for the night. Miss Bourdon took her supper seated beside her friend, at the long crowded table, and was dazzled, and delighted. It was all so new to her; and at seventeen, novelty is delight. After supper her protector gave her into the hands of a chambermaid, told her at what hour they started next morning, bade her good-night, and dismissed her.

Were Richard Gilbert's dreams that night haunted by the vision of a dark, soft face, two dark tender eyes, and the smile of an angel? Richard Gilbert only knows. But this is certain: when Mademoiselle Bourdon descended the stairs next morning he was standing at the dining-room door awaiting her, and his calm eyes lit up, as few had ever seen them light in his life. He led her into breakfast, and watched her hearty, school-girl morning appetite with pleasure. Then, there being half-an-hour to spare before the train started, he proposed a little stroll in the crisp, cool sunshine that had followed yesterday's storm. It was very fair, there in that lovely valley in Vermont, with the tall mountains piercing the heavens, and the silvery lakes flashing like mirrors below.

It was past noon when they reached Portland. The usual rush followed, but Norine, safe under the protecting wing of Mr. Gilbert, made her way unscathed. She looked eagerly among the crowd in the long depot, and cried out at last at sight of a familiar face.

"There, monsieur—there! Uncle Reuben is standing yonder with the blue coat and fur cap. He is looking for me. Oh! take me to him at once, please."

Mr. Gilbert led Miss Bourdon up to where a bluff-looking, middle-aged countryman stood—"Down East" from top to toe.

"Uncle," cried Norine, holding out both hands, eagerly, "I have come."

And then, heedless of the crowd, of Mr. Gilbert, mademoiselle flung both arms around Uncle Reuben's neck with very French effusion, and kissed him, smick—smack, on both cheeks.

"Hey! bless my soul! it is you, is it?" Uncle Reuben exclaimed, extricating himself. "It is, I swow, and growed out of all knowin'. You're welcome, my dear, and I'm right glad to have you with us, for your poor mother's sake. You ain't a look of her, though—no, not one— Gustave Bourdon all over. And how did you manage on your journey? I tell you, we was all considerable uneasy about you."

He looked at her tall companion as he ceased, half suspiciously, half inquiringly, and Miss Bourdon hastened to introduce them.

"This gentleman is Mr. Gilbert, uncle. He has been very kind to me all the way. I don't know what I should have done but for him. He has taken care of me ever since we left Montreal."

"Thanky, sir—much obliged to you for looking after this little girl. Come along and spend the day with us at my place, Kent Farm."

"Thanks, very much," the lawyer answered; "I regret more than I can say that circumstances render that pleasure impossible. I must be in New York to-morrow, but the very next time I am in Portland I shall certainly avail myself of your kind invitation. Miss Bourdon, until that time comes, good-by."

He shook hands with her, and saw her led away by her uncle, with a feeling of strange, yearning regret. A two-seated country sleigh stood near. Uncle Reuben helped her in, took his seat beside her, tucked her up, said "Ga'lang," and they were off. Once she looked back, to smile, to wave her hand to him in adieu. One more glimpse of that brunette face, of that rare smile, of those black Canadian eyes, and the clumsy sleigh turned an acute angle, and she was gone.

Gone. A blank seemed to fall, the whole place turned desolate and empty. With a wistful look in his face he turned slowly away.

"Poor little girl!" the lawyer thought. "I hope she will be happy. She is so pretty—so pretty!"

# CHAPTER II.

**A WISE MAN'S FOLLY.**

r. Richard Gilbert went to New York, and the girl with the black Canadian eyes and floating hair went with him—in spirit, that is to say. That dark, piquant face; that uplifted, gentle glance; that dimpling smile haunted him all through the upward journey; haunted and lit up his dingy office, and came between him and Blackstone, and Coke upon Littleton, and other legal lights.

Her bright, seventeen-year old face formed itself into a picture upon every page of those mouldering, dry-as-dust tomes, looked at him in the purple twilight, in the sunny mornings, in the dead waste and middle of the night. He had become "A Haunted Man," in short, Mr. Gilbert was in love.

And so, "how it came let doctors tell," all of a sudden Mr. Gilbert found that business required his presence Down East early in July. It was trifling business, too, understrappers in the office thought, that could very well have done without his personal supervision; but Mr. Gilbert reasoned otherwise; and, with a very unwonted glow about the region of the heart, packed his portmanteau, and started for Portland, Me.

The hot July sun was blazing in the afternoon sky and the streets of Portland were blistering in the heat, as the New York lawyer walked from the cars to his hotel. That important business which had brought him so many miles was transacted in a couple of hours, and then he returned to his hotel to dress and dine. Dress!—when had Richard Gilbert in his plain business pepper-and-salt suit and round-topped straw hat, ever taken so much pains with his toilet before, ever sported such faultless broadcloth in July, ever wore a diamond pin in his snowy linen, ever stood so long before the glass, ever felt so little satisfied with the result? When had the crow's feet around mouth and eyes ever shown so plainly, when had his tall, bald forehead ever appeared so patriarchal, when had he ever looked so dreadfully middle-aged, and plodding and priggish in his own legal eyes? Ah, when indeed?

He hired a light wagon and a bony horse at the nearest livery stable, and inquired the way to Kent Farm. Kent Farm was three miles distant, he found, and the white, dusty road lay like a strip of silver between the golden, green fields. The haymakers were at work, the summer air was sweet with perfume, the fields of buckwheat waved, the birds sang in the branches of the elms, the grasshoppers chirped until the drowsy air was alive, and far beyond all, more beautiful than all, the silver sea lay asleep under the sparkling sun. Pretty houses, all white and green, were everywhere; and more than one Maud Müller leaned on her rake, and looked up under her broad-brimmed hat as this thoughtful Judge rode by. He rode very slowly, so slowly that it was nearly an hour before he reached his destination and drew up at the gate of Kent Farm.

Had he been wise to come? What was this young girl, this child of seventeen, to him? What could she ever be? Youth turns to youth, as flowers to the sun. What if he found her the plighted wife of some stalwart young farmer, some elegant dry-goods clerk of the town? What? His heart contracted with a sharp, sudden spasm, and told him what?

Kent Farm at last. Half a mile from any other house, on the summit of a green, sloping eminence, an old red, weather-beaten farm-house its once glaring color toned and mellowed down by the sober hand of Time. A charming old place, its garden sloping down to the roadside, its lilac trees in full bloom. A wide-spreading old-fashioned garden, with rose bushes, and gooseberry bushes, currant bushes, sunflowers, and hollyhocks, and big gnarled old apple trees, mixed up in picturesque confusion.

Seated in a chair of twisted branches, under one of these crooked, blossoming apple trees, the sunlight tangled in her shining hair, and the mignonne face, sat Norine Kent Bourdon, reading a novel.

He opened the gate. Her book was interesting—she did not hear. He walked up the gravelled path, and drew near. Then she looked up, then half rose, in doubt for a moment, and then—to the day of his death, until all things earthly, will Richard Gilbert remember the flush of joy, the flash of recognition, the glad cry of welcome, with which she flung aside her book and sprang towards him, both hands outstretched.

"Monsieur! monsieur!" the sweet voice cried. "Ah, monsieur! how glad I am to see you."

She gave him her hands. The lovely, laughing face the eyes of fathomless light, looked up into his. Yes, she was glad to see him, glad with the impulsive gladness of a little younger sister to see an indulgent brother, old and grave, yet beloved. But Mr. Gilbert, holding those hands, looking into that eager, sparkling face, drew no such nice distinctions.

"Thank you, mademoiselle. You have not quite forgotten me, then, after all?"

"Forgotten you, monsieur? Oh, my memory is better than that. You have come to pay us that promised visit, have you not? Uncle Reuben has been looking for you ever since the first of June, and Aunt Hester is never so happy as when she has company. You have come to stay, I know."

"Well, I'm not sure about that, Miss Bourdon. I may remain a week or two, certainly. New York is not habitable after the first week of July, but I am stopping at the Preble House. I am too much of a stranger to trespass on your good uncle's hospitality."

"You have been kind to me, monsieur, and you are a stranger no more. Besides, it is dull here—pleasant but dull, and it will be a second kindness to enliven us with a little New York society."

She laughed and drew away her hands. The golden light of the July afternoon gilded the girlish face, upon which the New York gentleman gazed with an admiration he did not try to hide.

"Dull," he repeated; "you don't find it dull, I should think. Your face tells a very different story."

Mademoiselle shook back her rippling satin hair, and made a little French *moue mutine*.

"Ah, but it is. Only the fields and the flowers, the trees and the birds, the eating and sleeping, and reading. Now, flowers and fields and birds are very nice and pleasant things, but I like people, new faces, new friends, pleasure, excitement, change. I ride the horse, I milk the cows, I pick the strawberries, I darn the stockings, I play the piano, I make the beds, I read the novels. But I see nobody—nobody—nobody, and it is dull."

"Then you prefer the old life and Montreal?"

"Montreal!" Miss Bourdon's black eyes flashed out, as your black eyes can. "Monsieur," solemnly, "I adore Montreal. It was always new and always nice there; bright and gay and French. French! it is all Yankee here, not but that I like Yankees too. Aunt Hester thinks," a merry laugh, "there never was anybody born like me, and Uncle Reuben thinks I would be an angel if I didn't read so many novels and eat so many custard pies. And, monsieur," with the saucy uplifted coquettish glance he remembered so well, "if *you* find out I'm not an angel don't tell him, please. I wouldn't have him undeceived for the world."

"I don't think I shall find it out, mademoiselle. I quite agree with your uncle. Here he comes now."

Reuben Kent came out of the open front door, smoking a pipe. He paused at sight of his niece in friendly colloquy with a strange gentleman. The next moment he recognized him, and came forward at once in hearty welcome.

"Wal, squire," Mr. Kent said, "you *hev* come, when I had e'enamost gi'n you up. How dye deow? 'Tarnal hot, ain't it? Must be a powerful sight hotter, though, up to York. How air you. You're lookin' pretty considerably spry. Norry's glad to see you, *I* know. That gal's bin a talkin' o' ye continual. Come in, squire—come in. My sister Hester will be right glad to see ye."

What a cordial welcome it was; what a charming agricultural person Mr. Reuben Kent, one of nature's Down East noblemen, indeed. In a glow of pleasure, feeling ten years younger and ten times better looking than when he had started, the New York lawyer walked up to the house, into the wide, cool hall, into the "keepin' room," and took a seat. A pleasant room; but was not everything about Kent Farm pleasant, with two large western windows, through which the rose and golden light of the low dropping sun streamed over the store carpet, the cane-seated chairs, the flowers in the cracked tumblers, and white, delf pitchers. Traces of Norine were everywhere; the piano in a corner, the centre-table littered with books, papers, magazines and scraps of needle-work, the two canaries singing in the sunny windows, all spoke of taste, and girlhood. There were white muslin curtains, crocheted tidies on every chair in the room, a lounge, covered with *cretonne* in a high state of glaze and gaudy coloring, and the scent of the hay fields and the lilacs over all. No fifth-avenue drawing-room, no satin-hung silver-gilt reception-room, had ever looked one half so exquisite in this metropolitan gentleman's professional eyes. For there, amid the singing birds and the scented roses, stood a tall, slim girl, in a pink muslin dress—and where were the ormolu or brocatelle could embellish any room as she did?

Uncle Reuben went in search of Aunt Hester, and returned with that lady presently; and Mr. Gilbert saw a bony little woman with bright eyes and a saffron complexion. Miss Kent welcomed him as an old friend, and pressed him to "stay to tea."

"It's jest ready," she remarked,—a maiden lady was Aunt Hester,—"we've ben waitin' for brother Joe, and he's jest come. There ain't nothing more refreshing, I think myself, than a nice cup o' hot tea on a warm day."

Uncle Reuben seconded the motion at once.

"We can't offer you anything very grand—silver spoons and sech—as you get at them air hotels, but sech as it is, and Hester's a master hand at crawlers and hot biscuit, you're most mightly welcome. Norry, you fetch him along, while I go and wash up."

Miss Bourdon obeyed. Mr. Gilbert did not require all that pressing, if they had but known it. There was no need to apologize for that "high tea." No silver teaspoons, it is true, but the plated-ware glistened as the real Simon Pure never could have done; and no hotel in Maine, or out of it, could have shown a snowier table-cloth, hotter, whiter, more dyspeptic biscuits, blacker tea, redder strawberries, richer cream, yellower ginger-bread, or pinker cold-sliced ham. Mr. Gilbert ate ham and jelly, strawberries and tea, hot biscuit and cold ginger-bread—in a way that fairly warmed Aunt Hester's heart.

"And we calk'late on keeping you while you're down here, Mr. Gilbert," Uncle Reuben's hearty voice said. "It's a pleasant place, though I say it as hadn't ought to—a heap pleasanter than the city. Our house ain't none too fine, and our ways may be homespun and old-fashioned, but I reckon Norry and Hester kin make you pretty tol'bel comfortable ef you stay."

"Comfortable!"

He looked across at that face opposite; comfortable in the same house with her! But still he murmured some faint objection.

"Don't mention trouble, sir," said Uncle Joe, who was the counterpart of Uncle Reuben; "you've ben kind to our little Norry, and that's enough for us. Norry, hain't you got nothin' to say?"

"I say stay!" and the bewildering black eyes flashed their laughing light across at the victimized lawyer. "Stay, and I'll teach you to milk and make butter, and feed poultry, and pick strawberries, and improve your mind in a thousand rural ways. You shall swing me when Uncle Joe is too busy, and help me make short-cake, and escort me to 'quiltin' bees,' and learn to rake hay. And I—I'll sing for you wet days, and drive you all over the neighborhood, and let you tell me all about New York and the fashions, and the stores, and the theatres, and the belles of Broadway. Of course you stay."

Of course he stayed. It is so easy to let rosy lips persuade us into doing what we are dying to do. He stayed, and his fate was fixed—for good or for evil—fixed. That very night his portmanteau came from Portland, and the "spare room" was his.

Supper over, Uncles Reuben and Joe lit their pipes, and went away to their fields and their cattle—Aunt Hester "cleared up," and Miss Bourdon took possession of Mr. Gilbert. She wasn't the least in awe of him, she was only a bright, frank, fearless, grown-up child. He was grave, staid, old—is not thirty-five a fossil age in the eyes of seventeen?—but venerable though he was, she was not the least afraid of him.

She led her captive—oh, too willing, forth in triumph to see her treasures—sleek, well-fed cows, skittish ponies, big horses, hissing geese, gobling turkeys, hens and chicks innumerable. He took a pleased interest in them all—calves and colts, chickens and ducklings, ganders and gobblers, listened to the history of each, as though he had never listened to such absorbing biographies in all his life before.

How rosy were the lips that spoke, how eager the sunny face uplifted to his, and when was there a time that Wisdom did not fall down and worship Beauty? He liked to think of her pure and sweet, absorbed in these innocent things, to find neither coquetry nor sentimentalism in this healthy young mind, to know her ignorant as the goslings themselves of all the badness and hardness and cruelty of the big, cruel world.

They went into the garden, and lingered under the lilacs, until the last pink flush of the July day died, and the stars came out, and the moon sailed up serene. They found plenty to say; and, as a rule, Richard Gilbert rarely found much to say to girls. But Miss Bourdon could talk, and the lawyer listened to the silvery, silly prattle with a grave smile on his face.

9

It was easy to answer all her eager questions, to tell her of life in New York, of the opera and the theatres, and the men and women who wrote the books and the poems she loved. And as she drank it in, her face glowed and her great eyes shone.

"Oh, how beautiful it all must be!" she cried, "to hear such music, to see such plays, to know such people! If one's life could only be like the lives of the heroines of books—romantic, and beautiful, and full of change. If one could only be rich and a lady, Mr. Gilbert!"

She clasped her hands with the hopelessness of that thought. He smiled as he listened.

"A lady, Miss Bourdon? Are you not that now?" Miss Bourdon shook her head mournfully.

"Of course not, only a little stupid country girl, a farmer's niece. Oh! to be a lady—beautiful and haughty and admired, to go to balls in diamonds and laces, to go to the opera like a queen, to lead the fashion, and to be worshipped by every one one met! But what is the use of wishing, it never, never, never, can be."

"Can it not? I don't quite see that, although the ladies you are thinking of exist in novels only, never in this prosy, work-a-day world. Wealth is not happiness—a worn-out aphorism, but true now as the first day it was uttered. Great wealth, perhaps, may never come to you but what may seem wealth in your eyes may be nearer than you think—who knows?"

He looked at her, a sudden flush rising over his face, but Norine shook her black ringlets soberly.

"No, I will never be rich. Uncle Reuben won't hear of my going out as governess, so there is nothing left but to go on with the chicken-feeding and butter-making and novel-reading forever. Perhaps it is ungrateful, though, to desire any change, for I am happy too."

He drew a little nearer her; a light in his grave eyes, a glow on his sober face, warm words on his lips. What was Richard Gilbert about to say? The young, sweet, wistful face was fair enough in that tender light, to turn the head of even a thirty-five year-old-lawyer. But those impulsive words were not spoken, for "Norry, Norry!" piped Aunt Hester's shrill treble. "Where's that child gone? Doesn't she know she'll get her death out there in the evening air."

Norine laughed.

"From romance to reality! Aunt Hester doesn't believe in moonlight and star-gazing and foolish longings for the impossible. Perhaps she is right; but I wonder if she didn't stop to look at the moon sometimes, too, when she was seventeen?"

It was a very fair opening, given in all innocence. But Mr. Gilbert did not avail himself of it. He was not a "lady's man" in any sense of the word. Up to the present he had never given the fairest, the cleverest among them a second glance, a second thought. The language of compliment and flirtation was as Chaldaic and Sanscrit to him, and he walked by her side up to the house and into the keeping-room in ignoble silence.

The little old maid and the big old bachelors were assembled here, the lamp was lit, the curtains down and the silvery shimmer of that lovely moon-rise jealously shut out. Norine went to the piano, and entertained her audience with music. She played very well, indeed. She had had plenty of piano-forte-drudgery at the Convent school of the Grey Nuns in her beloved Montreal. She sung for them in the voice that suited her mignonne face, a full, rich contralto.

She sang gayly, with eyes that sparkled, the national song of Lower Canada: "*Vive la Canadienne*," and the New York lawyer went up to bed that first night with its ringing refrain in his ears:

"Vive la Canadienne et ses beaux yeux, Et ses beaux yeux tous doux, Et ses beaux yeux."

"Ah!" Richard Gilbert thought, "well may the *habitàns* sing and extol the *beaux yeux* of their fair countrywomen, if those bright eyes are one-half as lovely as Norine Bourdon's."

He stayed his fortnight out at the old red farm-house; and he who ran might read the foolish record. He, a sober, practical man of thirty-five, who up to the present had escaped unscarred, had fallen a victim at last to a juvenile disease in its most malignant form. And juvenile disorders are very apt to be fatal when caught in mature years. He was in love with a tall child of seventeen, a foolish little French girl, who looked upon him with precisely the same affection she felt for Uncle Reuben.

"What a fool I am," the lawyer thought, moodily, "to dream a child like that can ever be my wife? A sensible, practical young woman of seven-and-twenty is nearer your mark, Richard Gilbert. What do I know of this girl, except that she has silken ringlets and shining black eyes, and all sorts of charming, childish, bewitching ways. I will not make an idiot of myself at my age. I will go away and forget her and my folly. I was a simpleton ever to come."

He kept his word. He went away with his story untold. He bade them all good-bye, with a pang of regret more keen than any he had ever felt before in his life. Perhaps the little brown hand of mademoiselle lingered a thought longer than the others in his; perhaps his parting look into those *beaux yeux* was a shade more wistful. He was going for good now—to become a wise man once more, and he might never look into those wonderful, dark eyes more.

Norine was sorry, very sorry, and said so with a frank regret her middle-aged lover did not half like. He might be unskilled in the mysteries of the tender passion, but he had an inward conviction that love would never speak such candid words, never look back at him with such crystal clear eyes. She walked with him to the gate; her ebon curls a stream in the July breeze.

"Will you not write to me sometimes?" Mr. Gilbert could not help asking. "You don't know how glad I shall be to hear of—of you all."

Mademoiselle Bourdon promised readily.

"Though I don't write very good letters," she remarked deprecatingly. "I get the spelling wrong, and the grammar dreadfully mixed when I write in English, but I want to improve. If you'll promise to tell me of all my mistakes, I'll write with pleasure."

So what were to be the most precious love letters on earth to the gentleman, were to be regarded as "English composition," by the lady. Truly, the French proverb saith: "There is always one who loves, and one who is loved."

Mr. Gilbert returned to New York, and found that populous city a blank and howling wilderness. The exercises in English composition began, and though both grammar and spelling might get themselves into hopeless snarls, to him they were the most eloquent and precious epistles ever woman penned. He had read the letters of Lady Mary Wortley Montague, but what were those vapid epistles to Miss

Bourdon's? He watched for the coming of the Eastern mail; he tore open the little white envelope; he read and re-read, and smiled over the contents.

And time went on. August, September, October passed. The letters from Miss Norine Bourdon came like clock work, and were the bright spots in Richard Gilbert's hard-working, drab-colored life. He wrote her back; he sent her books and music, and pictures and albums, and pretty things without end, and was happy. And then the Ides of dark November came, and all this pastoral bliss was ended and over.

The letters with the Down-east post mark ceased abruptly, and without any reason; his last two remained unanswered. He wrote a third, and fell into a fever while he waited. Was she sick, was she dead, was she——. No, not faithless, surely, he turned cold at the bare thought. But what was it? The last week of November brought him his answer. Very short, very unsatisfactory.

"Kent Farm, Nov. 28, 1860.

"Dear Mr. Gilbert—You must pardon me for not replying to your last letters. I have been so busy. A gentleman met with an accident nearly three weeks ago, close by our house, broke his left arm, and sprained his right ankle. I have had to take care of him. Aunt Hetty has so much to do all the time that she could not. We are all very well, and send you our best wishes. I am very much obliged for the pretty work-box, and the magazines, etc. And I am, dear Mr. Gilbert, with the most affectionate sentiments,

"Norine K. Bourdon.

"P. S.—The gentleman is greatly better. He is with us still. He is very nice. He is from your city.

"N."

In the solitude of his legal sanctum, Richard Gilbert, with frowning brow and gloomy eyes, read this blighting epistle. His worst fears were realized, more than realized.

There was a gentleman in the case. A gentleman who absorbed so much of Miss Norine Bourdon's time that she could not answer his letters. And he was "greatly better" and he was from your city. Confound the puppy! He was young and good-looking, no doubt; and he must meet with his accident, at her very door; precisely as though he were enacting a chapter out of a novel. Of course, too, it was his arm and his ankle that were smashed, not his villainous face. And Norine sat by his bedside, and bathed his forehead, and held cooling draughts to his parched lips, and listened to his romantic, imbecile delirium, etc., etc., etc. She sat up with him nights; she read to him; she talked to him; she sang for him. He could see it all.

Mr. Gilbert was a Christian gentleman, so he did not swear. But I am bound to say he felt like swearing. He jumped up; he crushed that poor little letter into a ball; he strode up and down his office like a caged (legal) tiger. The green-eyed monster put forth its obnoxious claws, and never left him for many a dreary year. It was that atrocious postscript, so innocently written, so diabolical to read. "He is greatly better. He is with us still. He is very nice." Oh, confound him! what a pity it had not been his neck.

Suddenly he paused in his walk, his brows knit, his eyes flashing, his mouth set. Yes, that was it, he would do it, his resolution was taken. He would go straight to Kent Farm, and see for himself. And next morning at 8 o'clock the express train for Boston bore among its passengers Mr. R. Gilbert, of New York.

The train whirled him away, and as the chill, murky December landscape flew by, he awoke all at once to a sense of what he was about. Why was he going? what did he mean? to ask Norine Bourdon to be his wife? certainly not. To play dog in the manger, and keep some more fortunate man from loving and marrying her? most certainly not. Then why had he come? At this juncture he set his teeth, took up the *Herald* and scowled moodily at its printed pages all day long.

He slept that night in Boston, and next morning resumed his journey. He reached Portland before noon, dined at his usual hotel, and then, as the afternoon sun began to drop low in the wintry sky, set out on foot for Kent Farm.

How familiar it all was; how often, when the fields were green, the trees waving, and the birds singing, he had walked this road beside Norine. But the fields were white with snow to-day, the trees black, gaunt skeletons, and the July birds dead or gone. All things had changed in four months—why not Norine as well?

It was four by the lawyer's watch as he raised the latch of the garden gate, and walked up the snow-shrouded path. There stood the gnarled old apple tree, with its rustic chair, but the tree was leafless, and the chair empty. Doors and windows had stood wide when he saw them last, with sunshine and summer floating in; now all were closed, and the December blasts howled around the gables. There was no one to be seen, but the red light of a fire streamed brightly out through the curtains of the keeping-room.

He went slowly up the steps, opened the front door, and entered the hall. The door of that best apartment stood half open, light and warmth, voices and laughter came through. Mr. Gilbert paused on the threshold an instant, and looked at the picture within.

A very pretty picture.

The room was lit by the leaping fire alone. Seated on a low stool, before the fire and beside the sofa, he saw Norine. She was reading aloud the lovely story of *Lalla Rookh*. He had sent her the green and gilt volume himself. She wore a crimson merino dress, over which her black hair fell, and in the fantastic firelight how fair the dark, piquant face looked, the dark eyes were bent upon her book, and the soft voice was the only sound in the room.

On the sofa, perilously near, lay the "gentleman" of her letter—the hero of the broken arm and sprained ankle, who was "very nice." And Richard Gilbert looking, gave a great start.

He knew him.

His worst fears were realized. He saw a man both young and good-looking—something more, indeed, than good-looking. The face was thin and pale, but when was that a fault in the eyes of a girl!—a tall figure in a dark suit, brown hair, and silken blonde mustache artistically curled. Surely a charming picture of youth and beauty on both sides, and yet if Mr. Gilbert had seen a cobra di capella coiled up beside the girl he loved, he could hardly have turned sicker with jealous fear.

"Laurence Thorndyke," he thought blankly "of all the men in the wide world, what evil fortune has sent Laurence Thorndyke here!"

11

# CHAPTER III.

### MR. LAURENCE THORNDYKE.

he little dog Frollo, curled up beside his mistress, was the first to see and greet the newcomer. He rushed forward, barking a friendly greeting, and the young lady looked up from the book she was reading, the young gentleman from the face he was reading at the same moment, and beheld the dark figure in the doorway.

Norine Bourdon sprang to her feet, blushing violently, and came forward with outstretched hand. It was the first time he had ever seen her blush—like that—the first time her eyes had fallen, the first time her voice had faltered. She might be glad to see him, as she said, but all the old, frank, childish gladness was gone.

"I have taken you by surprise," he said, gazing into her flushed face and shrinking eyes, "as I did once before. I get tired of New York and business very suddenly sometimes, and you know I have a standing invitation here."

"We are very glad—*I* am very glad to see you, Mr. Gilbert," Norine answered, but with an embarrassment, a restraint altogether new in his experience of her. "We missed you very much after you went away."

The young man on the sofa, who all this time had been calmly looking and listening, now took an easier position, and spoke:

"Six-and-twenty-years experience of this wicked world has taught me the folly of being surprised at anything under the sun. But if I had not outlived the power of wondering, centuries ago, I should wonder at seeing Mr. Richard Gilbert out of the classic precincts of Wall street the first week of December. I suppose now you wouldn't have looked to see *me* here?"

He held out a shapely, languid hand, with a diamond ablaze on it. The lawyer touched it about as cordially as though it had been an extended toad.

"I certainly would not, Mr. Thorndyke. I imagined, and so did Mr. Darcy, when I saw him last, that you were in Boston, practicing your profession."

"Ah! no doubt! So I was until a month ago. I suppose it never entered your—I mean his venerable noddle, to conceive the possibility of my growing tired practicing my profession. Such is the fact, however. Even the hub of the universe may pall on the frivolous mind of youth, and I've 'thrown physic to the dogs, I'll none of it,' for the present at least. My patients—few and far between, I'm happy to say, will get on much more comfortably, and stand a much better chance of recovery without me."

"Indeed! I don't doubt it at all. But your uncle?"

"My uncle can't hope to escape the crosses of life any more than poorer and better men. All work and no play makes, what's his name, a dull boy. There will be a row very likely, the sooner my venerated relative is convinced that my talents don't lie in the bleeding and blistering, the senna and salts line, the better. They don't."

"Don't they? It would be difficult to say, from what I know of Mr. Laurence Thorndyke, in what line they *do* lie. May I ask what you mean to do?"

"I shall go in for sculpture," responded Mr. Laurence Thorndyke, with the calm consciousness of superior genius. "Other men have made fame and fortune by art, and why not I? If my hypocondriacal adopted uncle would only shell out, send me to Rome, and enable me to study the old masters, I have the strongest internal conviction that—"

"That you would set the world on fire with your genius. That you would eclipse the Greek Slave. No doubt—I have known others to think so before, and I know the sort of 'fame and fortune' they made. How do you come to be here?" Very curtly and abruptly, this.

"Ah!—thereby hangs a tale," with a long tender glance at Norine. "I am the debtor of a most happy accident. My horse threw me, and Miss Bourdon, happening along at the moment, turned Good Samaritan and took me in."

"I don't mean that," Mr. Gilbert said, stiffly; "how do you come to be in Maine at all?"

"I beg your pardon. Tom Lydyard—the Portland Lydyards, you know—no I suppose you don't know, by the by. Tom Lydyard was to be married, and invited me over on the auspicious occasion. Tom's a Harvard man like myself, sworn chums, brothers-in-arms, Damon and Pythias, and all that bosh; and when he asked me down to his wedding, could I—I put it to yourself, now, Gilbert, could I refuse? I cut the shop. I turned my back on blue pills and chloral, I came I saw, I—mademoiselle, may I trouble you for a glass of lemonade? You have no idea, Mr. Gilbert, what a nuisance I am, not being able to do anything for myself yet."

"Perhaps I have" was Mr. Gilbert's frigid response. The sight of Norine bending over that recumbent figure gave him a sensation of actual physical pain. He knew what this languid, graceful, slow speaking young Sybarite's life had been, if she did not.

Just at that moment—and it was a relief, Aunt Hester entered, followed by Uncles Reuben and Joe. No restraint here, no doubt about his welcome from them, no change in the place he held in their esteem and affection. Tea was ready, would everybody please to come.

Mr. Thorndyke's fractured limb was by no means equal to locomotion, so Uncle Reuben wheeled him, sofa and all, into the next room, and Aunt Hester and Norine vied with each other in waiting on him. It comes natural to all women to pet sick men—if the man be young and handsome, why it comes all the more naturally.

Mr. Thorndyke wasn't sick by any means—that was all over and done with. He took his tea from Aunt Hester's hand and drank it, his toast and chicken from Norine and ate them. He talked to them both in that lazy, pleasant voice of his, or lay silent and stroked his mustache with his diamond-ringed hand, and looked handsome, and whether the talk or the silence were most dangerous, it would have puzzled a cleverer man than Richard Gilbert to tell. To sit there listening to Aunt Hester chirping and Uncle Reuben prosing, and see the blue eyes making love, in eloquent silence, to the black ones, was almost too much for human nature to endure. She sat there silent, shy, all unlike the bright, chattering Norine of the summer gone, but with, oh! such an infinitely happy face! She sat beside Laurence Thorndyke— she ministered to that convalescent appetite of his, and that was enough. What need of speech when silence is so sweet?

Supper ended, Mr. Thorndyke was wheeled back to his post in the front room beside the fire. Norine never came near him all the rest of the evening, she sat at the little piano, and poured out her whole heart in song. Richard Gilbert, full of miserable, knawing jealousy, understood those songs; perhaps Laurence Thorndyke, lying with half-closed eyes, half-smiling lips, did too. They were old-fashioned songs that the lawyer had sent her, favorites of his own: "Twere vain to tell thee all I feel," and "Drink to me only with thine eyes." Yes, the meaning of those tender old ballads was not for him. It was maddening to see Laurence Thorndyke lying there, with that conscious smile on his lips; he could endure no more—he arose with the last note, abruptly enough, and bade them good-night.

"What! so early, Gilbert?" Thorndyke said, looking at his watch. "What a dickens of a hurry you're in. You've got no clients in Portland, have you? and Miss Bourdon, is going to sing us half-a-dozen more songs yet."

Mr. Gilbert paid no attention whatever to this flippant young man. He turned his back upon him indeed, and explained elaborately to Uncle Reuben that it was impossible for him to remain longer to-night, but that he would call early on the morrow.

"He is very much changed," remarked Aunt Hester, thoughtfully; "don't you think so, Norry? He's nothing like so pleasant and free, as he used to be."

"Particularly grumpy, I should say," interposed Mr. Thorndyke. "'Pleasant and free' are the last terms I should think of applying to Richard Gilbert. Not half a bad fellow either, old Gilbert, but an awful prig—don't you think so, Miss Bourdon?"

"I like Mr. Gilbert very much," Miss Bourdon answered, strumming idly on the keys; "and I think him pleasant. He seemed out of spirits to-night, though, I fancy."

It was bright, frosty starlight as the lawyer walked back to town. He walked rapidly, his head well up, a dark frown clouding his face.

"Any one but Thorndyke—any one but Thorndyke!" he was thinking bitterly. Alas! Mr. Gilbert, would you not have been jealous of the Archbishop of Canterbury had that dignitary been "keeping company" with Miss Bourdon? "And she loves him already—already. A very old story to Laurence Thorndyke. Six-and-twenty years, a well-shaped nose, two blue eyes, a mustache, and the easy insolence of the 'golden youth' of New York. What else has he but that? What else is needed to win *any* woman's heart? And hers is his, for good or for evil, for ever and ever. He is the Prince Charming of her fairy tale, and she has caught his wandering, artist fancy, as scores have caught it before. And when I tell her the truth, that his plighted wife awaits him, what then? Little Norine! to think that you should fall into the power of Laurence Thorndyke."

Yes, she was in his power—for she loved him. Had it all not been so delightfully romantic, so like a chapter out of one of her pet novels, that first meeting, when Fate itself had flung him wounded and bleeding at her feet? Was it not all photographed forever on her mind, a picture whose vividness time never could dim! It had befallen in this way:

On the afternoon of the third of November Miss Bourdon had driven over in the light wagon from the farm to the city, to receive her usual, eagerly-looked-for package from Mr. Gilbert. It had been dark and windy from early morning. As the afternoon wore on, the sky grew darker, the wind higher. She got her bundle of books, visited one or two stores, one or two friends, and night had fallen before she turned old Kitty's head towards Kent Farm. A faint and watery moon made its way up through the drifts of jagged cloud, and the gale howled through the street as though it had gone mad. It was a lonely and unpleasant ride; but old Kitty could have made her way asleep, and Norine sang to herself as she drove slowly along. They were within a quarter of a mile of the house, when Kitty pricked up her red ears, gave a neigh of alarm, and shied from some long, dark object lying motionless across her path. Norine bent over and looked down. There, she saw, lying on his face, the prostrate form of a man.

Was he drunk, or was he dead? She was out in a twinkling, and bending above him. There was blood on his clothes, and on the dusty road. She turned his face over until the pallid moon shone upon it. Dead, to all seeming, the eyes closed, life and consciousness gone.

Fifteen minutes later, Mr. Laurence Thorndyke was lying in the best bedroom of Kent Farm, with Aunt Hester and Norine bending over him, and Uncle Joe scudding along on horseback for a doctor. All their efforts to bring him out of that fainting fit were vain. White and cold he lay; and so Norine Bourdon, with a great pity in her heart, looked first upon the face of Laurence Thorndyke.

# CHAPTER IV.

### THE LAWYER'S WARNING.

r. Gilbert appeared in no hurry to revisit his friends at Kent Farm. It was late in the afternoon of the next day before he came slowly along the quiet country road. He had passed the morning idly enough, staring from the hotel window, down at the peaceful street and the few straggling passers by. After his three o'clock dinner he had put on hat and overcoat, and leisurely taken his way over the familiar ground.

It was a gray December afternoon, with a threatening of coming storm in the overcast sky. A few feathery flakes whirled already through the leaden air, an icy blast blew up from the sea, the road was deserted, the dreary fields snow-shrouded and forsaken. And only yesterday it seemed he had walked here by her side, the golden grain breast high, and the scarlet poppies aflame in the gardens. His youth had come back to him with that sunlit holiday. If he had spoken then, who knew what her answer might have been. But he had let the hour and the day go by, and now it was too late.

The snow flakes were whirling faster and faster as Mr. Gilbert opened the gate and approached the house. He could see the rose light of the fire through the curtained windows, and a slight, graceful figure seated at one, sewing. The brown rattling stems of hop vines twining around it, like sere serpents, made a framework for the girlish head and fair young face. All the floss silk curls were bound back with scarlet ribbon, and the luminous black eyes were fixed on her work. They saw the tardy visitor, however, and with a bright, welcoming smile she sprang up, and ran to open the door.

"How late you are. We thought you were not coming at all. I have been looking for you all day." She held out her hand, far more like Norine of old than last night, and led the way back into the parlor. There on his comfortable sofa, by his comfortable fire, reposed of course the five feet, eleven inches of Mr. Laurence Thorndyke. Mr. Gilbert gave that invalid a nod several degrees icier than the elements out doors.

"Ah, you have come! I told Norine you would."—Norine! it had come to that then—"I know you to be one of those uncompromising sort of characters, Gilbert, who never break their word. Have you your cigar case about you? I should like a smoke."

"Miss Bourdon is present, Mr. Thorndyke."

"So she is—for which Allah be praised. But Miss Bourdon is the most sensible, as she is most charming of young ladies. She gave me *carte blanche* ages ago to smoke as much as I please. Didn't you Norry? She fills my pipe, she even lights it when this confounded shoulder twitches more than usual."

Richard Gilbert set his teeth with inward fury. To sit here, and listen to Laurence Thorndyke's insolent familiarity, his lover like—"Norry," drove him half wild.

"I have not my cigar case," he answered, more and more frigidly; "and if I had, I don't know that I should countenance such a trespass on common decency as to let you smoke one here. How long before your doctor thinks you fit to be removed?"

"Oh, not for weeks yet; it was a deuce of a fracture, I can tell you. Why, pray? My insignificant movements, as a rule, are all unworthy Mr. Gilbert's attention."

"Your uncle is my friend, sir," the lawyer replied, "and I prefer not to see him hoodwinked. I recommend you strongly to write and explain your position, or I shall take an early opportunity of doing so myself."

"Will you? How very kind you are. But isn't it a pity to give yourself so much unnecessary trouble? I believe Mr. Hugh Darcy did invest you with a species of authority over my actions, but at six-and-twenty, don't you think a fellow ought to be let loose from the leading strings? And what would you have? I couldn't help accepting Tom Lydyard's invitation. I couldn't help my horse taking fright and throwing me. I couldn't help breaking my arm, and spraining my ankle, and I can't help being in the seventh heaven of happiness and comfort with two such nurses as Miss Kent and Miss Bourdon. Don't be unreasonable, Gilbert. Norine—*ma belle*, I am utterly exhausted with all this talking. What are you laughing at? Do pray favor me with my meerschaum and a light."

The pleasant lazy voice stopped, the pleasant smile turned upon Norine.

Miss Bourdon laughing at this passage of arms arose with alacrity to obey, and the lawyer, looking unspeakably grim got up, too.

"Permit me to say good-by, Miss Bourdon. I start for New York to-night. Can I see your uncle a moment before I go?" The door opened as he asked the question and Aunt Hester came into the room.

"I heard your voice as I passed through the hall," she said. "Surely you ain't going so soon?"

"I regret I must, my business requires my immediate return. I have only time to say good-by and speak a word to your brother. Where shall I find him?"

"In the stable, most likely. I'll go with you."

"Thanks. Farewell, Miss Bourdon."

Again their hands met, she looked perplexed and wistful, but she did not urge him to stay. With a second stiff nod to Mr. Thorndyke, the lawyer strode out of the room after Aunt Hetty.

"A word to her brother," muttered Mr. Thorndyke to himself looking after them. "I think I know what that means. 'That fellow, Thorndyke, is a spendthrift, a gambler, a flirt, an engaged man. Don't let him have anything to say to Norine.' That will be about the sum and substance of it. To think of his falling in love at his time of life, when he's old enough and big enough to know better. But then middle-aged fools are the worst of all fools. And you come a day after the fair, Mr. Richard Gilbert. Your word of warning is just two weeks too late. I owe you two or three little grudges for your *espionage* of the past, and for two or three little games blocked, and I think I see my way clearly to wiping them out at last. A thousand thanks my charming little nurse." Aloud to Norine, entering with pipe and pipe-light:

"What should I ever do without you?"

Mr. Gilbert, escorted by Aunt Hester, reached the stable, where Uncle Reuben stood busily curry-combing Kitty.

"I want to speak half-a-dozen words in private to you, Kent," the lawyer began, abruptly enough. "You will tell your good sister here at your convenience, if you see fit. You must excuse my seeming rudeness, Miss Kent, and say good-by, now."

He shook hands with her cordially, and watched her out of sight. Then he turned to her brother.

"We are quite alone?" he asked.

"Quite, squire. Take a seat."

He brought forward a stool, but Mr. Gilbert waved it away.

"No, no, what I have to say will take but a minute, and then I shall be going. I want to speak to you of that young man who is your guest—Laurence Thorndyke."

"Wal, squire."

"You have not known me very long, Mr. Kent, but I think, I hope, you have known me long enough to trust me, to believe what I say, to understand I have no selfish motive. It is for"—he paused a moment—"it is for your niece's sake I speak, you can hardly take a deeper interest in her welfare than I do."

Was there ever so slight a tremor in the grave, steady voice, or did Reuben Kent only fancy it? He paused in Kitty's toilet and looked at him keenly.

"Wal, squire?" he said again.

"Laurence Thorndyke is no fit, no safe companion for your niece. He is not a good man, he is as false as he is fascinating. She is only seventeen, she knows nothing of the world, nothing of such men as he, and believe me, Kent, it won't do."

Reuben Kent looked up, a sudden flash in his eye, a sudden redness in his face.

"Go on," he said, curtly.

"I am afraid Miss Bourdon cares more for him already than—" He paused again and averted his face. "You know what I mean. He is handsome, and she is only a girl. She will grow to love him, and he could not marry her if he would, he is already engaged, and unless I mistake him greatly, would not if he could. Mr. Kent, this young man will go away, and Norine will be neither the better nor the happier for his coming."

His voice was husky. Something of the pain he felt was in his face. The farmer stretched forth and caught the lawyer's hand in a hard grip.

"Thanky, squire," he said; "I ain't a man to jaw much, but I believe *you*, and am obliged to you for this. If that young jacknapes from York tries to come any of his city games down here, by the Lord Jehosaphat! I'll lay him up with something worse than a broken arm!"

"Can you not avert the danger?" suggested Mr. Gilbert. "It may not be too late. Send the fellow away."

"Wal, squire, you see that mightn't be doing the square thing by him. It would look unpleasantly like turning him out. No, I can't send him away until the doctor says he's fit to go, but, by ginger, I'll send her!"

"Will she go?"

Uncle Reuben chuckled.

"We won't ask her. I'll fix it off. We've some cousins thirty miles up country, and they've invited her time and again, but, somehow, we've never felt—Joe and me—as though we could spare her afore. It's powerful lonesome, I tell ye, squire, when Norry ain't around. But now—I'll take her to-morrow morning."

15

"The best thing you can do. And now, before it gets any later and stormier, I will be off. Good-by, Mr. Kent, for the present."

"Good-by, and thanky, squire, thanky. You'll be along again soon, hey?"

"Well, perhaps so," replied the lawyer, coloring slightly. "Take care of your niece, Kent, and good-by to you."

They parted at the gate. Reuben Kent watched the stalwart form of the lawyer out of sight, then walked slowly and thoughtfully back to the house and the sitting-room. Mr. Thorndyke, in a deep, melodious tenor, was reading aloud "Lucille," and Miss Bourdon, with flushed cheeks and glistening eyes of light, was listening.

The reading ceased at the farmer's entrance; the spell was broken, and Norine looked up.

"Has Mr. Gilbert gone, Uncle Reuben?"

"Yes."

He said it with unusual gravity, regarding young Thorndyke. The girl saw the change in his usually good humored, red-and-tan face, and went over and threw an arm around his neck.

"What is it, uncle? Something gone wrong?"

"No—yes. Nothing that can't be set right, I hope. Where's your aunt?"

"In the kitchen baking cake. Shall I run and call her?"

"No, I'll go myself."

He left the room. Mr. Thorndyke watched him.

"It is as I thought," he said to himself. "My label is up, 'dangerous.' What has Gilbert been saying? Has he given Uncle Reuben my whole interesting biography? Has he told him I drink, I gamble, I make love to pretty girls wherever I meet them? All right, my legal duffer; you have set your forty-years-old heart on pretty, black-eyed, belle Norine, and so have I. Now, let's see who'll win."

Mr. Kent found his sister in the kitchen, baking, as Norine had said, cakes for tea, their fragrant sweetness perfuming the hot air. In very few words he repeated to her the lawyer's warning.

"We might a seen it ourselves, Hetty, if we hadn't been blinder than bats. I'll take her up to Abel Merryweather's to-morrow, and just leave her thar till this ere chap goes."

"Will you tell her, Reuben?" Aunt Hetty asked.

"No; I kinder don't like to, somehow. She'll guess without any telling, I reckon. If I told her, she might tell him, there ain't never no countin' on gals, and then he'd be after her hot foot. Least said's soonest mended. Jest call her down to help you, Hetty, and keep her here as long as you can. What with his poetry reading, his singing, his fine talk, and good-lookin' face, he's enough to turn any gal's head."

"It was very good of Mr. Gilbert to tell you, Reuben."

"Very."

They looked at each other, and smiled. Poor Richard Gilbert! Your cherished secret was very large print after all.

"Mr. Gilbert's her best friend, and sets heaps by her," said Uncle Reuben rising. "Call the girl at once, Hetty."

He left the kitchen and Aunt Hester obeyed. Norine was summoned from "Lucille," and Mr. Thorndyke—to look after the cakes, to make tea, to roll out the short-cake, to butter the biscuits, to set the table. For once Aunt Hester turned lazy and left everything to Norine. She had not breathing space until supper was on the table.

After supper it was as bad. Contrary to all precedent, instead of going to the piano, Norine got a basket of socks to darn. She looked at the heap and the rents with laughing dismay.

"All these for me, Aunty! I'll never get through in the world, and I want to practice my new songs with Mr. Thorndyke."

"Mr. Thorndyke will excuse you, I am sure," Aunt Hetty answered quietly. "You sing a great deal more for him than you darn for me. You darn very badly—it is time that you learned something useful. Here is your needle and ball, my dear, go to work at once."

Miss Bourdon made a little wry face; Mr. Thorndyke's laughing blue eyes looked knowing. Love and music were to be exchanged for cooking and darning, all thanks to Mr. Gilbert.

Aunt Hester placed herself between her guest and her niece, and kept her post like a very duenna all the evening. No poetry, no music, no compliments, no love-making, only silence and sock-darning. Laurence Thorndyke reclining on his lounge, even his efforts at conversation falling flat, saw and understood it all perfectly. By Gilbert's order the ewe lamb was to be guarded from the wolf. And his spirit rose with the resistance.

"Guard her as you like," he said inwardly,—"watch her as you will, I'll baffle the whole of you yet. If I cared nothing for the girl, and I don't care much, I would still conquer you here, if only for the pleasure of paying off Richard Gilbert. Meddling old prig! There was that affair of Lucy West, he had to bring that to light, and old Darcy was within an ace of disinheriting me. He wants to marry this little black-eyed, sentimental French girl himself—more fool he—and it shall be my pleasant and profitable occupation to nip that middle-aged romance in the bud. I flatter myself I am rather more than a match for Aunt Hetty."

But Mr. Thorndyke was yet to learn whether he was or no. At no time, well or ill, was this elegant young doctor addicted to the vice of early-rising. It was mostly noon when, half-carried in the strong arms of Uncle Reuben and Joe, he reached the parlor.

Norine, however, was up with the lark—that is to say there were no larks in December, but with the striking six of the kitchen clock. On the morning following the stocking darning, as the family assembled together for their seven o'clock breakfast, Uncle Reuben said:

"Norry, I'm a going to give you a treat to-day—something you've been wanting this long time."

Norine opened her black eyes, and held the portion of buckwheat cake on her fork, suspended in space.

"A treat! Something I've been wanting this long time! You darling old dear, what is it?"

16

"Don't ask me, it's a secret, it's to be a surprise. Have you finished breakfast? Wal, run and put on the best duds you've got, while I go round and gear up Kitty."

"Kitty! Then we're going somewhere. Now Uncle Reuben——"

"It ain't a mite o' use, Norry, I ain't agoin' to tell. Be off and clap on your Sunday fixins, while I get around the cutter."

"You're going to take me to the city and buy me some thing—a silk dress, perhaps. Oh, uncle! what a dear old love you are! I'll be ready in ten minutes."

Uncle Reuben's heart smote him a little as he received Norine's rapturous kiss, but there was no drawing back. He left the house, while Miss Bourdon flew off singing like a skylark, to make her toilet. A new silk—yes, that was it—a new wine-colored silk with black lace trimming. If Mr. Thorndyke admired her in last winter's dingy red merino, how would he be dazzled by the wine-colored silk? In fifteen minutes her rapid toilet was made, and looking charming in her holiday attire she came running back to Uncle Reuben. The sleigh was drawn up before the door; she sprang into her seat beside him. Aunt Hetty, in the doorway, was smiling good-by, the bells jingled, the whip cracked, Kitty tossed her head and darted away into the frosty morning sunshine.

"*Not* going to the city, uncle!" cried Norine "now, where on earth can you be taking me?"

"To Merryweather's my dear," calmly responded Uncle Reuben, "where you have been teasing me to take you these three months. There! ain't that a pleasant surprise?"

There was a blank silence for a moment—the silence of great amaze. He looked at her askance. A surprise beyond a doubt, but a pleasant one. Well, that was another question. Her face had changed ominously all in a moment.

"To Merryweather's?" she repeated. "Thirty miles!"

"Exactly, my dear—to stay two or three weeks, as they've been wanting you to do. I didn't tell you, because I wanted to surprise you. I knew you would be pleased to death."

"But uncle I can't!" exclaimed the girl, vehemently. "I can't go. I have nothing to wear. My trunk and all my things are at home."

"Jest so; the cutter wouldn't hold your trunk; but Joe, he's going out 'bout the end of the week, and he'll fetch. Make your mind easy, my dear; Aunt Hetty will forget nothin'."

Norine made no reply. The sunny face wore the darkest expression Uncle Reuben had ever seen it wear yet. Was Mr. Gilbert right—was the mischief done—was it too late, after all?

He drove on. The blank silence lasted. He had never dreamed the laughing face of his little Norine could wear the look it wore now. She spoke after a long pause, in a tone of sullen inquiry:

"I wish you had told me last night, Uncle Reuben. It seems very odd going off in this way. What will Mr. Thorndyke say?"

"What business is it of his?" placidly inquired Uncle Reuben.

An angry flush rose up over Norine's face.

"He will think it very strange—*very* strange; I did not even say good-by."

"I'll explain all that."

"And Aunt Hetty—how will she ever get along without me, with the house work to do, and Mr. Thorndyke to wait on, and everything."

"He won't be to wait on long, he'll be able to return to his friends in Portland in a week, and to tell the truth, I shan't be sorry to be rid of him. As for you, Norry, by the way you object, one would think you didn't want to go, after all."

Again Norine flushed angrily.

"I don't object to going," she said, in a tone that contradicted her words. "It is the manner of going I don't like. I do think you might have told me last night, Uncle Reuben."

Uncle Reuben stopped the cutter abruptly, and looked at her.

"Shall I turn and drive back?" he asked.

What could she say? The black eyes emitted an angry flash, the voice that answered was sharp and petulant.

"No—go on."

He drove on, without another word. Norine lay back in the sleigh, wrapped her cloak about her, pulled a little veil she wore, over her face, and was silent. A great fear, a great dismay, a great foreboding filled Uncle Reuben's heart. Had this girl lived with them so long, made herself so dear, and hidden the nature that was within her, after all? What lay under that sparkling surface that had seemed as clear as limpid water? Dark depths he could never fathom, depths undreamed of as yet by herself. Was she—he wondered this vaguely, with a keen sense of pain—the gentle, affectionate, yielding child they had thought her, or a self-willed, passionate, headstrong woman, ready, woman-like, to throw over her oldest and truest friends if they stood between her and the man she loved?

# CHAPTER V.

### "I WILL BE YOUR WIFE."

iss Bourdon's visit to the family of Mr. Abel Merryweather lasted just three weeks and two days, and unspeakably dull and empty the old red farm-house seemed without her. Uncle Joe had gone out with her trunk on Saturday, and with the news that everybody was well, and Mr. Thorndyke was to go for good the following Monday.

"To New York?" Norine asked, turning very pale.

"I reckon so," Uncle Joe responded, coolly; "that's to say, he's to stop a few days in Portland with his friends there; he's going to spend the rest of the winter South—so he told Hetty—down to Maryland somewhere."

Norine set her lips, and turned away without a word. She would have given half her life to be able to return with Uncle Joe, but she was far too proud to ask. Some dim inkling of the truth was beginning to dawn upon her. For some cruel reason they did not wish her to be with Mr. Thorndyke, and they had sent her here to be out of his way.

They were the dullest three weeks of the young lady's life. It was a pleasant place, too—Mr. Abel Merryweather's, with a jolly, noisy houseful of sons and daughters, and country frolics without end. Two months ago, Norine had looked forward to this visit with delight. But in two months the whole world had changed; and now, there was no sunshine in heaven, no gladness on earth, since a well-looking, well-dressed young man from the city would light her life with his smile no more.

Mr. Thorndyke did depart the following Monday. He had been considerably surprised on first missing Norine, and inquired of Aunt Hetty where she was. The reply was very brief and reserved.

"Uncle Reuben has taken her away to visit some friends."

Mr. Thorndyke fixed his large, blue eyes full upon the speaker's face. Aunt Hester, never looking at him, went on arranging the furniture.

"How long will she be gone?" he asked, at length.

"That depends upon circumstances," replied Miss Kent; "probably some weeks."

Mr. Thorndyke said no more. Aunt Hetty poured out his tea, arranged his buttered toast and boiled eggs, and left the room. It had been Norine's labor of love hitherto, Norine's bright face that smiled across the little round table, instead of the withered, sallow one of Aunt Hetty. He sat alone now over his noon-day breakfast, an inexplicable look on his handsome face.

"So," he thought, "they have gone even farther than I anticipated, they have spirited her away altogether. Poor little girl! pretty little Norry! I believe I am really fond of you, after all. I wonder if she went willingly?" he smiled to himself, his vanity answered that question pretty accurately. "It's rather hard on her, a modern case of Elizabeth and the exiles. It's all my friend Gilbert's doing, of course. Very well. It is his day now, it may be mine, to-morrow."

The intervening days were hopelessly long and dreary to Mr. Laurence Thorndyke. How fond he had grown of that sparkling brunette face, those limpid eyes of "liquid light," he never knew until he lost her. That pleasant, homely room was so full of her—the closed piano, the little rocker and work-stand by the window, her beloved books and birds. Life became, all in an hour, a horrible bore in that dull red farm-house. Come what might to ankle and arm, ailing still, he would go at once. He dispatched a note to his friends in Portland, and early on Monday morning drove away with Mr. Thomas Lydyard, his friend.

"Good-by Miss Kent," he said, as he shook hands with her on the doorstep. "I can never repay all your kindness, I know, but I will do my best if the opportunity ever offers. Give my very best regards to Miss Bourdon, and tell her how much I regretted her running away."

And so he was gone. Uncle Reuben watched him out of sight with a great breath of relief.

"Thank the Lord *he's* gone, and that danger's over."

Ah, was it? Had you known Mr. Laurence Thorndyke better, Reuben Kent, you would have known, also, that the danger was but beginning.

Mr. Thorndyke remained four days with his friends in the city, and then started for New York. Reuben Kent heard it with immense relief and satisfaction.

"He's gone, Hetty," he said to his sister, "and the good Lord send he may never cross our little girl's path again. I can see her now, with the color fading out of her face, and that white look of disappointment coming over it. I hope she's forgot him before this."

18

"Will you go for her to-day?" Aunt Hetty asked. "It's dreadful lonesome without her."

"Not to-day. Next week will do. She'll forget him faster there than here, Hetty."

It wanted but three days of Christmas when Uncle Reuben went for his niece, and it was late on Christmas eve when they returned. The snow was piled high and white everywhere. The trees stood up, black, rattling skeletons around the old house. All things seemed to have changed in the weeks of her absence, and nothing more than Norine Bourdon.

She sank down in a chair, in a tired, spiritless sort of way, and let Aunt Hetty remove her wraps. She had grown thin, in the past fortnight, and pale and worn-looking.

"You precious little Norry," aunt Hetty said, giving her a welcoming hug. "You can't tell how glad we are to have you back again; how dreadfully we missed you. I expect you enjoyed your visit awfully now?"

"No," the young girl answered, with an impatient sigh; "it was dull."

"Dull, Norry! with four girls and three young men in the house?"

"Well, it was dull to me. I didn't care for their frolics and sleighing parties and quilting bees. It was horridly stupid, the whole of it."

"Then you are glad to be home again?"

"Yes."

She did not look particularly glad, however. She leaned her head against the back of the chair, and closed her eyes with weary listlessness. Aunt Hetty watched her with a thrill of apprehension. Was her fancy for their departed guest something more than mere fancy?—had she not begun even to forget yet, after all?

She opened her eyes suddenly while Aunt Hetty was thinking this, and spoke abruptly.

"What did Mr. Thorndyke say when he found I was gone?"

"Nothing. Oh—he asked how long you were going to stay."

"Was that all?"

"That was all."

"Did he not inquire where I had gone?"

"No, my dear."

Norine said no more. The firelight shone full on her face, and she lifted a book and held it as a screen. So long she sat mute and motionless that Aunt Hetty fancied she had fallen asleep. She laid her hand on her shoulder. Norine's black, sombre eyes looked up.

"I thought you were asleep, my dear, you sat so still. Is anything the matter?"

"I am tired, and my head aches. I believe I will go to bed."

"But, Norry, it is Christmas eve. Supper is ready, and—"

"I can't eat supper—I don't wish any. Give me a cup of tea, aunty, and let me go."

With a sigh, aunty obeyed, and slowly and wearily Norine toiled up to her room. It was very cosy, very pleasant, very home-like and warm, that snug upper chamber, with its striped, home-made carpet of scarlet and green, its blazing fire and shaded lamp. Outside, the keen, Christmas stars shone coldly, and the world lay white in its chill winding sheet of snow.

But Norine thought neither of the comfort within nor the desolation without. She sank down into a low chair before the fire and looked blankly into the red coals.

"Gone!" something in her head seemed beating that one word, like the ticking of a clock; "gone—gone—gone forever. And it was only thirty miles, and the cars would have taken him, and he never came. And I thought, I thought, he liked me a little."

It was a dismal Christmas eve at Kent Farm; how were they to eat, drink and be merry with Norine absent. No she had not begun to forget; the mischief was wrought, every room in the house was haunted by the image of the "youth who had loved, and who rode away."

The New Year dawned, passed, and the ides of February came. And Norine—she was only seventeen, remember, began to pluck up heart of grace once more, and her laugh rang out, and her songs began to be as merry, almost, as before the coming and going of Prince Charming. Almost; the woman's heart had awakened in the girl's breast, and the old childish joyousness could never be quite the same. He never wrote, she never heard his name, even Mr. Gilbert had ceased to write. March came. "Time, that blunts the edge of things, dries our tears and spoils our bliss," had dried all hers long ago, and the splendor of Laurence Thorndyke's image was wofully dimmed by this time. Life had flown back into the old, dull channels, comfortable, but dull. No letters to look for now from Mr. Gilbert, no books, no music, everybody forgot her, Richard Gilbert, Laurence Thorndyke—all.

She sighed a little over the quilt she was making—a wonderful quilt of white and "Turkey red," a bewildering Chinese puzzle to the uninitiated. It was a dull March afternoon, cheerless and slushy, the house still as a tomb, and no living thing to be seen in the outer world, as she sat alone at her work.

"What a stupid, dismal humdrum sort of life it is." Miss Bourdon thought, drearily, "and I suppose it will go on for thirty or forty years exactly like this, and I'll dry up, and wrinkle and grow yellow and ugly, and be an old maid like Aunt Hetty. I think it would be a great deal better if some people never were born at all."

She paused suddenly, with this wise generality in her mind. A man was approaching—a tall man, a familiar and rather distinguished-looking man. One glance was enough. With a cry of delight she dropped the Chinese-puzzle quilt, sprang up, rushed out, and plumped full into the arms of the gentleman.

"Oh, Mr. Gilbert!" she cried, her black eyes, her whole face radiant with the delight of seeing some one, "how glad I am to see you! It has been so dull, and I thought you had forgotten us altogether. Come in—come in."

She held both his hands, and pulled him in. Unhappy Richard Gilbert! Who is to blame you for construing that enthusiastic welcome to suit yourself? In fear and foreboding, you had approached that house—you had looked for coldness, aversion, reproaches, perhaps. You had nerved yourself to bear them, and defend yourself, and instead—*this*.

His sallow face flushed all over with a delight more vivid than her own. For one delicious moment his breath stopped.

"And so you have thought of me, Norine!"

"Oh, so often! And hoped, and longed, and looked for your coming. But you never came, and you never wrote, and I was sure you had forgotten me altogether."

Here was an opening, and—he let it fall dead! He might be a clever lawyer, but certainly he was not a clever lover. He was smiling, and yes, actually blushing, and tingling with delight to his finger ends. Her radiant, blooming face was upturned to him, the black eyes lifted and dancing, and he looked down upon those sparkling charms, and in a flat voice—said this:

"We have had a great deal of snow lately. How are your uncles and aunts?"

But the young lady's enthusiasm was not in the least dampened. He was her friend, not her lover, he was a kindly gleam of sunshine across the dead level of her sad-colored life.

"They are all very well, thank you, Mr. Gilbert, and will be very glad to see you. Sit down and take off your overcoat. You'll stay for tea, won't you, and all night? Oh, how pleasant it is to see you back here again!"

Happy Mr. Gilbert! And yet, if he had stopped to analyze that frank, glad, sisterly welcome, he would have known it the most ominous thing on earth for his hopes. Had he been Laurence Thorndyke she would never have welcomed him like this. But just now he took the goods the gods provided, and never stopped to analyze.

"Perhaps I was mistaken after all about Thorndyke," he thought, "he has gone for good, and I never saw her look more brightly blooming. After all a girl's fancy for a handsome face, and a flirting manner, need not be very deep or lasting. It was only a fancy, and died a natural death in a week. How fortunate I spoke in time, and how clear and true she rings! I will ask her to be my wife before I leave Kent Farm."

He had come to stake his fate—"to win or lose it all," to lay his life at her feet, but he had hoped for nothing like this. He loved her—he knew it now as your staid middle-aged men do once in a lifetime. He had waited until he could wait no longer—she might refuse, he had little hope of anything else, but then at least, any certainty was better than suspense.

Mr. Gilbert's greeting from the Kent family was all that mortal man could look for. They had guessed his secret; perhaps they also guessed his object in coming now. He was very rich, and above them no doubt, but was there king or kaiser in all the world too good for their beautiful Norine.

He stayed to tea. After that meal, while Aunt Hetty was busy in the kitchen, and the men about the farm-yard, he found himself alone in the front room with Miss Bourdon. She stood looking out through the undrawn curtains at the still, white, melancholy winter night.

The first surprise and delight of the meeting past, she had grown very still. His coming had brought other memories rushing upon her as she stood here in that pretty attitude looking out at the frosty stars.

She was nerving herself to ask a question. Without turning round, and speaking very carelessly, she asked it.

"I suppose Mr. Thorndyke is in New York. Have you seen him lately?"

A jealous pang shot through the lawyer's heart. She remembered yet.

"I see him very often," he answered, promptly, and a little coldly; "I saw him the day I left. He is about to be married."

She was standing with her back to him, fluttering in a restless sort of way. As he said this she suddenly grew still.

"The match is a very old affair," Mr. Gilbert went on, resolutely; "he has been engaged nearly two years. His uncle, Mr. Darcy, wishes it very much. The young lady is an heiress, and extremely handsome. They are very much attached to one another, it is said and are to be married early in the spring."

She did not move—she did not speak. A blank uncomfortable silence followed, and once more poor Mr. Gilbert's heart contracted with a painful jealous spasm. If she would only turn round and let him see her face. Who was to understand these girls!

"What! all in the dark, Norry?" cried Uncle Reuben's cheery voice, as he came bustling in redolent of stable odors. "Come, light up, and give Mr. Gilbert a song."

She obeyed at once. The glare of the lamp fell full upon her, what change was it that he saw in her face? She was hardly paler than usual, she rarely had much color, but there was an expression about the soft-cut childish mouth, an unpleasant tightness about the lips that quite altered the whole expression of the face.

She opened the piano and sung—sung and played better than he had ever heard her before. She sang for hours, everything she knew—Mr. Thorndyke's favorites and all. She never rose until the striking of ten told her that bedtime had come.

The lawyer stayed all night; but in that pleasant guest-chamber that had lodged his rival last, he slept little. Was she in love with Thorndyke, or was she not? Impossible to judge these women—any girl in her teens can baffle the shrewdest lawyer of them all. He lay tossing about full of hope, of love, of jealousy, of doubt, his fever at its very climax.

"I'll endure this torture no longer," he resolved, sullenly. "I'll ask her to marry me to-morrow."

With Richard Gilbert to resolve was to act. Five seconds after they had met, shaken hands, and said good-morning, he proposed a sleigh ride. The day was mild and sunny, the sleighing splendid, and a sleigh ride to a New Yorker a rare and delightful luxury. Would she go? Yes, she would go, but Miss Bourdon said it spiritlessly enough. And so the sleigh was brought round, and at ten o'clock in the crisp, yellow sunshine, the pair started.

But it must have been a much duller spirit than that of Norine that could have remained dull in that dazzling sunshine, that swift rush through the still frozen air. A lovely rose-pink came into her pale cheeks, a bright light into her brown eyes, her laugh rang out, she was herself as he had first known her once more.

20

"How splendid winter is, after all!" she exclaimed; "look at those crystallized hemlocks—did you ever see anything so beautiful? I sometimes wonder how I can find it so dreary."

"You do find it dreary, then?"

"Oh, so dreary—so long—so humdrum—so dull!" She checked herself with one of her pretty French gestures. "It seems ungrateful to say so, but I can't help it. Life seems hardly worth the living sometimes here."

"Here! Would it be better elsewhere?"

"Yes—I think so. Change is always pleasant. One grows dull and stupid living in one dull stupid place forever. Change is what I want, novelty is delight."

"Let me offer it to you then, Norine. Come to New York with me."

"Mr. Gilbert! With you!"

"With me—as my wife, I love you, Norine."

It was said. The old formula, the commonplace words that are to tell all that is in a heart full to overflowing. He sat very pale, beyond that and a certain nervous twitching of his face there was nothing to tell that all the happiness of his life hung on her reply. For her—she just looked at him blankly, incredulous—with wide open eyes of wonder.

"Your wife! Marry *you*! Mr. Gilbert!"

"I love you, Norine. It seems strange you have not known it until I tell it. I am double your age, but I will do my best to make you happy. Ah, Norine, if you knew how long I have thought of this—how dearly I love you, you would surely not refuse. I am a rich man, and all I have is yours. The world you have longed to see, you shall see. Be my wife Norine, and come with me to New York."

The first shock of surprise was over. She sat very still, looking straight out before her at the dazzling expanse of sun and snow. His words awoke no answering thrill in her heart, and yet she was conscious of a sense of pleasure. Be his wife—well, why not? The prospect of a new life broke upon her—the bright, exciting, ever-new life of a great city. She thought of that, not of Richard Gilbert.

"Speak to me, Norine," he said, "for Heaven's sake don't sit silent like this—only to answer no. For good or evil, let me have my answer at once."

But still she sat mute. She had lost Laurence Thorndyke—lost—nay he had never been hers for one poor second. He belonged to that beautiful, high-bred heiress whom he was to marry in the spring. She would read it in the papers some day, and then—her own blank, empty, aimless life spread before her. She turned suddenly to the man beside her, with something of the look her face had worn last night when she had first heard of Thorndyke's marriage.

"You are very good," she answered, quite steadily. "I will be your wife if you like."

"Thank Heaven!"—he said under his breath. "Thank Heaven!"

Her heart smote her. She was giving him so little—he was giving her so much. He had always been her good, kind, faithful friend, and she had liked him so much. Yes, that was just it, she liked him so well she could never love him. But at least she would be honest.

"I—I don't care for—I mean I don't love——" she broke down, her eyes fixed on her muff. "Oh, Mr. Gilbert, I do like you, but not like that. I—I know I'm not half good enough ever to marry you."

He smiled, a smile of great content.

"You will let me be the judge of that, Norry. You are quite sure you like me?"

"Oh, yes. I always did, you know, but I never—no never thought you cared for— Oh, dear me! how odd it seems. What will Uncle Reuben say?"

Mr Gilbert smiled again.

"Uncle Reuben won't lose his senses with surprise, I fancy. Ah, Norry, Uncle Reuben's eyes are not half a quarter so bright nor so black as yours, but he has seen more than you after all."

And then all the way home he poured into her pleased listening ear the story of her future life. It sounded like a fairy tale to the country girl. A dazzling vista spread before her, a long life in "marble halls," Brussels carpets, satin upholstery, a grand piano, pictures, books, and new music without end. Silk dresses, diamond ear-rings, the theatres, the opera, a carriage, a waiting-maid—French, if possible—her favorite heroines all had French maids, Long Branch, Newport, balls, dinners—her head swam with the dazzle and delight of it all. Be his wife—of course she would be his wife—to-morrow, if it were practicable.

But she did not say this, you understand. Her face was all rosy and dimpling and smiling as they drove home; and alas for Richard Gilbert, how little he personally had to do with all that girlish rapture. He saw that well-pleased face, and, like a wise man, asked no useless questions. She was going to be his wife, everything was said in that.

# CHAPTER VI.

**BEFORE THE WEDDING.**

he sober March twilight lay low on the snowy earth when the sleigh whirled up to the door. The red firelight shone through the windows, and they could see Aunt Hetty bustling about the kitchen. Neither had spoken for a time, but now Norine turned to him, as she lightly sprang out.

"Say nothing of this to-night," she said, hurriedly; "wait until to-morrow."

She was gone before he could answer, and he drove round to the stable. Uncle Reuben was there, and Mr. Gilbert remained with him until Aunt Hetty's voice was heard calling them to supper. The lawyer was standing in the doorway, watching the solemn stars come out, a great silent gravity on his face. But oh, so happy, too—so deeply, unutterably happy.

The supper table was spread, lamp-light beamed, firelight glowed, and Aunt Hetty awaited them impatient, lest her warm milk biscuits and sugared "flap-jacks" should grow cold.

Norine stood leaning against the mantel, looking dreamily into the red fire. How pale she was, how strangely grave and thoughtful. Yet not unhappy, surely, for she glanced up in her lover's face with a quick blush and smile, and talked to him shyly throughout supper. Later still she played and sang for him the songs and pieces he liked best, played a game of euchre with him, and if she thought of Laurence Thorndyke, who had taught her the game, Richard Gilbert did not know it.

"She will learn to love me," he thought. "My pretty, dark-eyed darling! I will love her so much. I will so gratify her in everything. I will be so devoted, in all ways, that she cannot help it. Please Heaven, her life shall be a happy one with me."

Norine retired early. Her long drive had made her tired and sleepy she said; but she did not go to sleep.

Moon and stars shone crystal clear, pearly bright. She blew out her lamp, wrapped a shawl about her, and sat down by the window. Weirdly still lay everything, ivory light, ebony shadows, no sound but the rattling of the skeleton trees in the wintry night wind. No living thing was visible far or near. There was only the star-gemmed sky above, the chill, white world below. She could read her heart in the holy hush of the night, and look into the life that was dawning for her, by its solemn light. Richard Gilbert's wife! How strange and unreal that seemed. She liked him very much as she might have liked an indulgent elder brother, but love him—no! She might have deluded herself into thinking so, had Laurence Thorndyke's splendid image never dazzled her. She knew better now—the knowledge had come upon her all at once, transforming her from a child to a woman.

"If I had never met him," she thought, "I might have been a happy wife, but now! Now can I ever learn to forget him, and to give Mr. Gilbert his place?"

She covered her face with her hands, alone as she was. Alas for Richard Gilbert! congratulating himself at that very moment on having won for his very own the fairest, the sweetest, the truest of her sex.

Miss Bourdon sat mournfully musing there until long past bedtime, long past midnight. Moonlight and starlight paled presently, the prospect grew gloomy, the air bitter cold, and shivering and miserable, the girl crept away to bed. Even then she could not sleep—her nerves were all unstrung and on edge. She lay broad awake trying to imagine what her life would be like as Mr. Gilbert's wife. The fairy world of her dreams and her books would open to her. Costly dresses and jewels, a fine house in New York, her carriage and servants, summer travel and winter balls—all this he had promised her. And there in the midst of it all, once again she would meet Laurence Thorndyke. It would be part of the romance, she as the wife, he as the husband of another, and the weak silly heart fluttering under the bedclothes, gave a great bound. Then she remembered that it would be wicked to wish to see him—a sin to be happy in his presence; but do what she would, the hope of meeting him again, was at the bottom of her willingness to become the lawyer's wife.

When Norine descended to breakfast next morning, she found Mr. Gilbert standing in the open doorway, looking out at the frosty sunshine. He came forward to meet her, his face suddenly radiant.

"I have been waiting to waylay you," he said, smiling, "I want you to let me tell your uncle to-day."

"You are in a hurry," Norine answered, rather impatiently.

"Yes, my darling. Why should I not be? And I return to New York early next week. You say yes—do you not, Norine?"

She smiled, and gave him her hand. She had said "yes" to a more important proposition, he had been very good to her, why should she not please him?

"Do as you like, Mr. Gilbert. Tell my uncle if you choose."

"And if he consents, Norine—as I think he will—when shall I tell him our marriage is to take place? I want it to be soon, my dearest girl, very soon, for I don't feel as though I could live much longer without you. Come, my little wife! name an early day."

"Oh, I cannot! I don't know when. Next summer some time."

"That is indefinite," he laughed. "Allow me to be definite. Say early next May."

"No, no, no! that is too soon—greatly too soon! I couldn't be ready."

"Then, when? I won't be selfish, but you must be merciful, mademoiselle, and not keep me in suspense too long."

She laughed her old gay laugh.

"Patience, monsieur; patience stands chief among the virtues. Will June do—the last?"

"The first, Norine."

Aunt Hetty was coming through the hall. Norine darted away.

"Have it as you will! Don't you want me to help you with breakfast, auntie?"

Mr. Gilbert smilingly looked after his bright little prize, so soon to be his bright little wife, then turned to Aunt Hetty.

"Where is your brother this morning, Miss Kent? I wish to speak to him."

"In the stable, I think. Shall I go and see?"

"Not at all. I will go myself."

He walked away, humming a tune, in the happiness of his heart. Ah! shone ever winter sun so brightly before, looked ever the work-a-day world so paradisiacal as now! The earth and all thereon was transformed as with an enchanter's wand to this middle-aged legal gentleman in love.

Uncle Reuben, busy among his cattle, looked up in some surprise at sight of his early visitor.

"Don't let me interfere with your work, Kent," the lawyer said. "You can attend to your horses and listen, too. I must leave the day after to-morrow; my business has been too long neglected, and I have something of importance to tell you before I go. Something I hope—I believe, you will not be sorry to hear."

The eyes of the two men met. There was a peculiar smile on the lawyer's face, a happy light in his eyes, and Reuben Kent's countenance grew suddenly bright with intelligence.

"Is it about Norry?"

A smile and a nod answered him.

"Then I reckon I can guess. You have asked her to marry you?"

"Exactly. But how, in the name of everything wonderful have you found it out?"

Uncle Reuben's eyes twinkled shrewdly.

"I ain't a lawyer, Mr. Gilbert, but I can see as far into a milestone as any other man. Do you think I s'posed it was to see me and Joe and Hetty you came to Kent Hill so often? No, sir! I see you had a hankering after our little girl from the first."

Mr. Gilbert actually blushed. And he had guarded his precious secret so carefully, he had thought.

"Well, Mr. Kent, I trust I have your approval?"

Reuben Kent stretched out his big brown paw, and grasped the lawyer's white hand.

"I give her to you with all my heart, sir. I'd rather see her your wife than the wife of the President. I've been hoping this long time it would come to this. She's a good girl, as good as she's pretty, and I know she'll make you a good wife."

Not one word of the honor done them or her by the wealthy lawyer's offer—not one thought of it. In Reuben Kent's eyes no king or kaiser on the wide earth would have been too good for his beautiful Norine.

"And when is it to be, sir?" he asked.

"The wedding?" smiled Mr. Gilbert. "The first week of June. If I possibly can, I will run down here once or twice between this and then, but I am doubtful of its being possible. I have neglected business somewhat of late, and it has accumulated. You will tell your brother and sister, Kent?"

They walked back to the house together to breakfast. Norine saw in her uncle's face that he had been told, and blushed beautifully. How very, very near and real, it seemed to bring it, this telling Uncle Reuben.

Mr. Gilbert took her out for a walk after breakfast, and Uncle Reuben availed himself of the opportunity to inform his sister and brother. They were no more surprised than he had been, and equally pleased, but Aunt Hetty cried quietly, woman-fashion, for all that.

"We will miss her so much," she said; "the old house will seem like a tomb without her. He is a good man, a rich man, and a gentleman—I ought to rejoice for her sake, but it does seem hard at first to give her up for good."

"These things will happen, Hetty," said Uncle Reuben, philosophically, but sighing, too; "it's nater. We ought to think of nothing but the Lord's goodness in giving her such a man as Mr. Gilbert for a husband."

So it was settled. When Norine came back from her walk, Aunt Hetty kissed her, shook hands with the lawyer, and the betrothal was quietly over. There was no scene, and no tears, but the good wishes for both, were none the less heartfelt for that.

The day after to-morrow came. Mr. Gilbert went, and the preparations for the wedding began. Norine's "setting out" was to be on a scale of unprecedented magnificence. Uncle Reuben had money, and did not grudge spending it. Aunt Hetty took her into town, and a whole day was spent shopping—the big family carryall went home in the evening filled to repletion with dry goods. A seamstress and a dressmaker were engaged, both to come out on the following day, and Norine, in the pleasant bustle and hurry, actually forgot Laurence Thorndyke for eight consecutive hours.

The two seamstresses came to Kent Hill the following morning, and great and mighty were the measuring and cutting that ensued. The "keeping room," was given up to them and the bride elect, and all day long, and for many days after, their busy needles flew. Before the end of the week it was known far and wide that pretty Norry Kent, as she was called there, had made a great conquest, and was about to be married to one of the richest lawyers in New York.

Mr. Gilbert's letters came like clock-work every week, and Norine's replies went dutifully the day after. They were not much like love-letters on either side, particularly on hers, but Mr. Gilbert's were deeply and tenderly affectionate, better than all the rhapsodies ever written. His presents, too—and such presents, poured in, in a ceaseless stream. Jewelry that half turned the pretty bride's head with its dazzling splendor, laces that fairy fingers alone could have woven, pretty, costly *bijouterie* of all kinds.

"How good he is—how good he is!" Norine thought, in a burst of gratitude. "I ought to love him—I *will* love him—who could help it in time, and I will make him as happy as ever I can."

She might have kept her word; it would surely have been no impossible task to learn to love Richard Gilbert. She meant it in all sincerity—his generosity had already kindled a deeper feeling than mere gratitude in her heart. The dazzle of Laurence Thorndyke's image was slowly but surely dimming, and she could sing blithely once more as she bent over her work, or tripped about the rooms. Who could be unhappy in white silk and lustrous pearls, orange blossoms and Mechlin lace, with rich rings a-sparkle on every finger, and glittering bracelets clasping the lovely arms? The color came back to Miss Bourdon's cheek, the girlish brightness to her lovely Canadian eyes—once more her gay girl's laugh rang out—once more the tripping French ballads made melody through the old gray rooms. You see she was not quite eighteen, poor child, and so much is possible for young persons of eighteen.

The weeks flew by—busy dreams; March passed, April passed. The wedding day was drawing very near. May came, mellow with sweet spring blossoms and sunshine, and the first half was over. The first Thursday in June was to be the day of days, not quite a fortnight off now. The world had woke up for her wedding, Norine thought, snow and dreariness were gone, spring, in Eden-like freshness and bloom was with them. All day long the birds sang in the sunlight; the garden was gay with odorous grasses and blossoms. In three days more the bridegroom would be here to claim his bride, to leave no more until he bore her away by his side. Yes, it was a new Eden. Kent Hill in its spring-tide resurrection, but, as once before, the serpent was close at hand.

# CHAPTER VII.

### THE GATHERING STORM.

he last week came—the last night of the last week.

A radiant moonlight night. Over the blue misty hill-tops the silver half-moon sailed, and at the garden gate stood the pretty bride elect, alone, gazing with eyes of dreamy darkness at the mystic light. No sound but the "sounds of the silence" broke her reverie, the twitter of a bird in its nest, the light flutter of the cool wind, the slipping of a snake in the underbrush. Green and silvery spread the wide fields of Kent Hill; dark, cool and perfumy the pine woods, long and white the dusty, high road—over all the sparkling stars and crystal moon.

Leaning on the gate, stood Norine. A trifle thinner and paler than of old, very pale in the cold, white moon-rays, but very fair and sweet the *mignonne* face. Something almost pathetic in the pallid beauty of the night touched her, the great dark eyes looked with wistful sadness up to the starry sky. She stood there thinking of the new life to begin in a few days now—the life that seemed to recede and grow more and more unreal the nearer it came. Its novelty and brightness blinded her no more—distance had lent enchantment to the view—to-night she only knew she was about to marry a man she did not love.

The past arose before her. Laurence Thorndyke's smiling, cynical, handsome face floated in the haze like a vision, her girl's fancy returned with tenfold sweetness and power. If he were only to be the bridegroom on Thursday next! A passionate longing to see him once more, to hear his voice, filled her whole soul with unutterable desire. In the moonlight she stretched out her arms involuntarily—in the silence she spoke, a heart-sob in every word:

"Laurence!" she cried, "come back!"

The restless leaves fluttered around her, the wind touched her face and swept by. She leaned wearily against the gate.

"Laurence!" she whispered, "Laurence! Laurence! If I could only see you once more—only once—if I knew you had not quite forgotten me—if I could only bid you good-by before we part forever, I think everything would be easy after that."

Had the thought evoked his phantom?

Who was that coming along the silent road? A tall, slender figure, wearing a loose, light overcoat, strangely, bewilderingly familiar. That negligent, graceful walk, that uplifted carriage of the head—surely, surely she knew both. She leaned forward in breathless expectation—her lips apart, her eyes alight. Nearer and nearer he came, and the face she had longed to see, had prayed to see, looked down upon her once more with the old familiar smile.

Laurence Thorndyke!

She leaned against the gate still in breathless hush, pale, terrified. She could not speak, so intense was her surprise, and the voice for whose sound she had hungered and thirsted with her whole foolish, romantic heart sounded in the silence:

"Norine!"

She made no answer; in her utter astonishment and swift joy she could only stand and gaze, speechless.

"Norine, I have come back again. Have you no word of welcome for your old friend?"

Still she did not speak—still she stood looking as though she never could look enough—only trembling a little now.

"I have startled you," he said very gently, "coming so unexpectedly upon you like a ghost in the moonlight. But I am no spirit, Norine—shake hands."

He leaned across the closed gate, and took both her hands in his warm, cordial clasp. They were like ice. Her eyes were fixed almost wildly upon his face, her lips were trembling like the lips of a child about to cry.

"Won't you speak then, Norine? Have I startled you so much as that? I did not expect to see you or any one at this hour, but I had to come. Do you hear, Norry? I had to come. And now that we have met, Norine, won't you say you are glad to see me again?"

She drew away her hands suddenly—covered her face and broke into a passion of tears. Perhaps she had grown hysterical, her heart had been full before he came, and it needed only this shock to brim over. He opened the gate abruptly and came to her side.

"Speak to me, Norine! My own—my dearest, don't cry so. Look up, and say you are not sorry I have come!"

She looked up at him, forgetful of Richard Gilbert and her wedding day, forgetful of loyalty and truth.

"I thought you had forgotten me," she said. "I thought I would never see you again. And oh, I have been so miserable—so miserable!"

"And yet you are about to be married, Norine!" At that reproachful cry she suddenly remembered the New York lawyer, and all the duties of her life. She drew her hands away resolutely in spite of his resistance and stood free—trembling and white.

"You are going to be married to Richard Gilbert, Norine?"

"Yes," she said, falteringly; "and you—you are going to be married, too?"

"I?" in astonishment; "I married! Who can have told you that?"

"Mr. Gilbert."

"Then it is the first time I have ever known him—lawyer though he be—to tell a falsehood. No, Norine, I am not going to be married."

She caught her breath in the shock, the joy of the words.

"*Not* going to be married! Not going—Oh, Mr. Thorndyke, don't deceive me—don't!"

"I am not deceiving you Norine—why should I? There is but one whom I love; if she will be my wife I will marry—not unless. Can you not guess who it is, Norine? Can you not guess what I have come from New York to say before it is too late? I only heard of your projected marriage last week—heard it then by merest accident. Ah, Norine! if you knew what a shock that announcement was. Ever since I left here I have been trying to school myself to forget you, but in vain. I never knew how utterly in vain until I heard you were the promised wife of Richard Gilbert. I could stay away no longer—I felt I must tell you or die. It may seem like presumption, like madness, my coming at the eleventh hour, and you the promised bride of another man, but I had to come. Even if you refused me with scorn, I felt I must come and hear my doom from your lips. They have urged me to marry another, an heiress she is, and a ward of my uncle's—he even threatens to disinherit me if I do not. But I will be disinherited, I will brave poverty and face the future boldly so that the girl I love is by my side. Helen is beautiful, and will not say no, they tell me, if I ask, but what is that to me since I love only you. Norine, tell me I have not come too late. You don't, you can't care for this elderly lawyer, old enough to be your father. Norine, speak and tell me you care only for me."

"Only for you—only for you!" she cried, "O, Laurence, I love you with all my heart!"

There was a sound as she said it, the house door opening. In the moonlight Aunt Hetty's spare, small figure appeared in the doorway, in the silence her pleasant voice called:

"Norine! Norine! come in out of the dew dear child."

Some giant hemlocks grew near the gate—Laurence Thorndyke drew her with him into their black shadow, and stood perfectly still. Brilliant as the moonlight was, Aunt Hetty might brush against them and not see them in the leafy gloom.

"I must go," whispered Norine; "she will be here in a moment in search of me. Laurence, let me go."

"But first—I must see you again. No one knows I am here, no one must know. When does Gilbert arrive?"

"To-morrow," she answered, with a sudden shiver.

"My darling, don't fear—you are mine now, mine only. Mine you shall remain." His eyes glittered strangely in the gloom as he said it. "We cannot meet to-morrow; but we must meet to-morrow night."

"No," she faltered, "no—no. It would be wrong, dishonorable. And I dare not, we would be discovered."

"Not if you do as I direct. What time do you all retire? Half-past ten?"

"Mostly."

"Then at eleven, or half-past, the coast is sure to be clear. At eleven to-morrow night I will be here just without the gate, and you must steal out and meet me."

"Laurence!"

"You must—you will, if you love me. Are you not my wife, or going to be in a few days, which amounts to the same thing. Will Gilbert stop here?"

"I don't know. Yes, I suppose so."

"Well, even if he does it will not matter. You can steal out unheard and unobserved, can you not?"

"Yes—no. I don't know. Laurence! Laurence! I am afraid."

"Of what? Of whom? not of me, Norine?"

She shivered a little, and shrank from his side.

"It seems so strange, so bold, so wrong. I ought not, it is wicked—I don't know what to do."

"Then you don't care for me at all, Norine?"

He knew how to move her. The reproachful words went to her heart. *Care* for him! He doubted that.

"You will come," he said, that exultant gleam in his eyes again, "my loyal little girl! I have a thousand things to say to you, and we can talk uninterruptedly then. When was your wedding to be?"

"Next Thursday."

"And this is Sunday night. To-morrow afternoon Gilbert will be here. You see how little time we have to spare, Norine. You must meet me, for on Thursday you shall be my wife—not his!"

"Norry! Norry!" more loudly this time, called the voice of Aunt Hetty, still in the doorway, "where on earth is the child?"

"Let me go—let me go!" Norine cried in terror, "she will be here directly."

"You will meet me to-morrow night, promise first?"

"Yes—yes—yes! Only let me go."

He obeyed. Retreating into the shadow of the trees, he watched her glide out in the moonlit path, and up to the gate. He heard her ascend the steps, and then Aunt Hetty's voice came to him again.

"Goodness gracious, child! where have you been? Do you want to get your death, out in your bare head and the dew falling like rain?"

He could not catch Norine's faint reply. A second more, and again Miss Hester Kent was shrilly to be heard.

"Land of hope! whatever ails you. Norry? You are whiter than the dead. Oh, I know how it will be after to-night—you'll be laid up for a week."

He heard the house door close. Then he was alone with the rustling trees, and the bright, countless stars. As he stepped out into the crystal radiance, his face shone with exultant delight—alas! for Norine! *not* with happy love.

"I knew it!" he thought to himself in his triumph; "I knew I could take her from him at the very church door. Now, Richard Gilbert! whose turn is it at last—who holds the winning trump in the game? You have baffled, and foiled, and watched me many a time, notably in the case of Lucy West—when it came to old Darcy's ears through you, and he was within a hair's breadth of disinheriting me. Every dog has his day. Yours is over—mine has come. The wheel has revolved, and Laurence Thorndyke, gambler, trickster, libertine, as you paint him, is at the top. You have not spared me in the past, my good Gilbert, look to yourself now, for by all the gods I'll not spare you!"

While Mr. Thorndyke, with his hat pulled low over his brows, walked home to the obscure hotel at which he chose to stop, Norine was up in her room alone with her tumultuous heart. She had complained of a headache and gone at once. The plea was not altogether false—her brain was whirling, her heart throbbing in a wild tumult, half terror, half delight. He had come back to her, he loved her, she was going to be his wife! For over an hour she sat, hiding even in the dusk her happy face in her hands, with only this one thought pulsing through all her being—she was to be his wife!

By and by she grew calm and able to think. No thought of going to bed, or doing anything so commonplace as sleeping occurred to her. She wrapped herself in a shawl, seated herself by the window, and so for hours and hours sat motionless.

After all was love worth what she was about to give up for it—home, friends, a good man's trust, her soul's truth and honor? Was Laurence Thorndyke worth more to her than all the world beside, more than the peace of her own conscience? Richard Gilbert loved her, honored her, trusted her, she had taken his gifts, she had pledged herself to be his wife. This very day, dawning yonder over the hills of Maine, would see him here to claim her as his own forever. Was one sight of Laurence Thorndyke's face, one touch of his hand, one seductive tone of his voice sufficient to make her fling honor and truth to the winds, desert her best, her only friends, break her plighted husband's heart, and make her memory a shame and pain to them all forever? Oh, what a wretch she was, what cruel, selfish passion this love she felt must be!

The sun rose up between the fleecy clouds, filling the world with jubilant brightness, the sweet scents of sunrise in the country perfumed the warm air. Norine threw up her window and leaned out, worn and fevered with her night's vigil. That meeting under the trees seemed a long way off now, it was as if she had lived years in a few brief hours. Presently there was a rap at the door, and Aunt Hetty's voice outside spoke.

"Are you up, Norry? is your headache better, dear?"

"Much better, aunty—I'll be down directly."

"Breakfast will be ready in ten minutes," said aunty, and Norine got wearily up, and bathed her face, brushed out her tangled curls, shrinking guiltily from her own pallid face in the glass.

"How wretchedly haggard I look," she thought, drearily; "surely every one who looks at me will read my guilt in my face."

She went down stairs. Aunt Hetty nearly dropped the sweet, smelling plate of hot muffins at sight of her.

"You're whiter than a ghost, child!" she cried. "You told me you were better."

"I am better, aunty. Oh, pray don't mind my looks. Last night's headache has made me pale—I will be as well as ever after breakfast."

But breakfast was only a pretence as far she was concerned, and the day wore on and the fair, young face kept its pallid, startled look. She could do nothing, neither read or sew, she wandered about the house like a restless spirit, only shrinking from that Bluebeard's chamber, where all the wedding finery was spread. How was she to meet Mr. Gilbert, and the fleeting hours were hurrying after one another, as hours never had hurried before.

The afternoon sun dropped low, the noises in the fields grew more and more subdued, the cool evening wind swept up from the distant sea. Norine sat in the wicker chair in the garden under the old apple-tree and waited—waited as a doomed prisoner might the coming of the executioner. A book lay idle an her lap, she could not read, she sat there waiting—waiting—waiting, and schooling herself for the ordeal.

Presently, far off on the white road, rose up a cloud of dust, there came the rolling of wheels, she caught a glimpse of a carriage. She clasped her hands together and strove to steady herself. At last he was here. Out of the dusty cloud came a buggy, whirling rapidly up to the gate—out of the buggy came Richard Gilbert, his eager face turned towards her. His quick eye had espied her; she rose up to meet him, calm in the very depth of desperation. Mr. Gilbert sprang out and caught both her hands in his.

"My dear, dear girl! My own Norine! how glad I am to be with you once more! But how pale you look. Have you been ill?"

"Oh, no—that is—only my old friend, headache. Here comes Aunty Hetty and Uncle Reuben to welcome you."

She drew back, thankful for the diversion, feeling hot and cold by turns, and not daring to meet his eye. Their laughter, their gay greetings were only a confused hum in her ears, she was looking at the clump of hemlocks, and feeling—oh, such a false, treacherous guilty creature.

"How dazed you look, little girl!" her happy lover said laughing; "am I such an ogre, then, in your sight?"

He drew her hand beneath his arm, with the air of one who assumes a right, and led her to the house. They were alone together in the parlor, and she was trying to call her wandering mind to order, and listen to him and answer his questions. She could see with terror that he was watching her already with grave, troubled eyes. What was it, this pale, still change in her? Dread of her approaching marriage, maiden timidity, or worst of all—was the thought of another man haunting her still?

Tea time came and was a relief; after tea, Mr. Gilbert proposed a walk. Norine took her hat passively, and went out with him into the hushed and placid twilight. The pale primrose light was fading out of the western sky, and a rising wind was tossing the arms of the hemlocks where she stood with another lover last night.

It was a very silent walk. They strolled along the lonesome road, with the primrose light growing grayer and grayer through the velvety meadows, where the quiet cows grazed. Something of the dark shadows deepening around them seemed to steal into the man's heart, and dull it with nameless dread, but there was no voice in the rising wind, in the whispering trees, in the creeping gloom, to tell him of what was so near.

A very silent walk—the last they would ever take. The little talking done, Mr. Gilbert did himself. He told her that all his preparations for his bride, all his arrangements for her comfort were made. Their home in New York's stateliest avenue was ready and waiting—their wedding tour would be to Montreal and Niagara, unless Norine had some other choice. But she would be glad to see once more the quaint, gray, dear old Canadian town—would she not?

"Yes, she would ever be glad to see Montreal. No, she had no other choice." She shivered as she said it, looking far off with blank eyes that dare not meet his. "Niagara would do very well, all places were alike to her. It was growing cold and dark,"—abruptly this—"suppose they went home."

Something in her tone and manner, in her want of interest and enthusiasm, hurt him. More silently than they had come they recrossed the darkening fields. The moon was rising as they drew near the house, forcing its way up through dark and jagged clouds. She paused suddenly for a moment, with her pale face turned towards it. Mr. Gilbert paused, too, looking at the lowering sky.

"Listen to the wind," he said. "We will have a change to-morrow."

"A change!" she said, in a hushed sort of voice. "Yes, the storm is very near."

"And you are shivering in this raw night wind. You are white and cold as a spirit, my darling. Come let us go in."

His baggage had arrived—a trunk and valise stood in the hall as they entered. The sister and brothers sat in holiday attire in the keeping room, but very grave and quiet. The shadow that had fallen on Richard Gilbert in the twilight fields seemed to have fallen here, too.

Norine sat at the piano, her face turned away from the light, and played the melodies he asked for. From these she drifted gradually into music more in accordance with her mood, playing in a mournful, minor key, until Mr. Gilbert could endure the saddening sweetness no longer.

"Your music is very melancholy, my dear," he said quietly. "Will you not sing us something instead."

"Not to-night, I think. I find my headache has not altogether departed. If you will kindly excuse me, I will retire."

She got up as she spoke, lit a lamp, and with a brief good-night, was gone.

It was not yet ten o'clock, but there was little inducement to linger now. Mr. Gilbert owned to being rather fatigued, took his light, and departed. Before half-past ten all were in their rooms, the doors and windows secured for the night. By eleven all were asleep—all save one.

Norine sat at her window, her light shaded, her watch (one of Richard Gilbert's presents to his bride elect) open before her, gazing out into the gusty darkness, and waiting. Her hands were tightly clasped together, silent, tearless sobs shook her at times as remorse swept through her soul, and yet not for one minute did she think of withdrawing from her tryst. But she would not fly with Laurence Thorndyke— no, no! Every best impulse within her cried out she would not, she could not. She was a wretch for even thinking of it—a wretch for going to this meeting, but she would only go to say farewell forever. She loved him, but she belonged to another man; it would be better to die than to betray him. She would bid Laurence Thorndyke go to-night, and never see him more.

The threatening storm seemed drawing very near. The moon was half obscured in dense clouds; the wind tore around the gables; the trees tossed their long, green arms wildly aloft. Within the house profoundest silence reigned.

Half-past eleven! the hour of tryst; she seemed to count the moments by the dull beating of her heart. She rose up, extinguished her lamp, put on a waterproof, drawing the hood over her head, took her slippers in her hand, and opened the door. She paused and listened, half choked by the loud throbbing of her heart, by guilty, nameless dread. All was still—no sound but the surging of the trees without; no glimmer of light from any room. She stole on tiptoe along the passage, down the stairs, and into the lower hall. Noiselessly she unlocked the door, opened it, and was out in the windy dark, under the gloom of the trees. One second's pause, her breath coming in frightened gasps, then she was flitting away in the chill night wind to meet her lover. She reached the gate, leaned over it eagerly, straining her eyes through the gloom.

"Laurence!" she said, in a tremulous whisper. "Laurence, I have come."

"My own brave little girl!"

A tall figure stepped forward from beneath a tree, too warm hands clasped hers.

"Norry, you're a trump, by Jove! Come out at once. All is ready. You must fly with me to-night."

But she shrank back—shocked, terrified, yet longing with all her soul to obey.

"No, no!" she cried. "I can never go—never! never! never! O Lawrence! I have come here to bid you good-by forever!"

His answer was to laugh aloud. His face was flushed his blue eyes gleaming—Mr. Laurence Thorndyke, bold enough at all times, had primed himself with brandy for to-night's work, until he was ready to face and defy devils and men.

"Good-by forever!" he repeated. "Yes, that's so likely, my darling. Come out here, Norry—come out. I've no notion of talking with a five-barred gate between us. So old Gilbert came down to his wedding this afternoon didn't he? By Jupiter! what a row there will be to-morrow, when the cage is opened, and the bird found flown."

He laughed recklessly aloud, as he opened the gate and drew her out.

"Not if I know it, Norry. No dry-as-dust, grim, solemn owl of a lawyer for my little Canadian rosebud, old as the everlasting hills, and priggish as the devil. No, no! we'll change all that. Before morning dawns you and I will be safely in Boston, and before another night falls you'll be my blessed little wife—the loveliest bride from Maine to Florida, and I the most blissful of bridegrooms. All is ready—here are my horse and buggy—the sloop sails in an hour, and then—let them catch us who can!"

Either the excitement of his triumph, or the French brandy, had set Mr. Laurence Thorndyke half wild. He drew her with him, heedless of her struggles, her passionate protest.

"Can't go? Oh, that's all bosh, my darling! you've got to come. I love you, and you love me—(sounds like a child's valentine, don't it?)— and you don't care that for old Dick Gilbert. You won't go? If you don't I'll shoot myself before morning—I swear I will! You don't want me to shoot myself, do you? I can't live without you, Norry, and I don't mean to try. After we're married, and the honeymoon's over, I'll fetch you back to the old folks if you like, upon my sacred honor I will. Not a word now, my little angel, I won't listen. Of course you've scruples, and all that. I think the more of you for them, but you'll thank me for not listening one day. Here's the carriage—get in, get in, get in!"

He fairly lifted her in as he spoke.

Stunned, terrified, bewildered, she struggled in vain. He only laughed aloud, caught up the reins, and struck the horse with the whip. The horse, a spirited one, darted forward like a flash; there was a girl's faint, frightened scream.

"O Laurence! let me go!"

A wild laugh drowned it—they flew over the ground like the wind. Norine was gone! His exultant singing mingled with the crash of the wheels as they disappeared.

"She is won! they are gone over bush, brake and scar; They'll have fleet steeds that follow, quoth young Lochinvar."

# CHAPTER VIII.

### FLED!

r. Gilbert went to his room, went to his bed, but he did not go to sleep. He lay awake so long, tossing restlessly, that, at last, in disgust, he got up dressed himself partly, and sat down in the darkness by his open chamber window; to have it out.

What was the matter with Norine? Headache; she had said—but to eyes sharpened by deep, true love, it looked much more like heartache. The averted eyes, the faltering voice, the pallid cheeks, the shrinking form, betokened something deeper than headache. Was she at the eleventh hour repenting her marriage? Was she still in love with Laurence Thorndyke? Was she pining for the freedom she had resigned? Was there no spark of affection for him in her girl's heart after all?

"I was mad and presumptuous to dream of it," he thought. "I am thirty-six—she is seventeen. I am not handsome, nor brilliant, nor attractive to a girl's fancy in any way—she is all. Yes, she is pining for him, and repenting of her hastily-plighted troth. Well, then, she shall have it back. If I loved her tenfold more than I do, and Heaven knows to love her any better than I do mortal man cannot, still I would resign her. No woman shall ever come to me as wife with her heart in the keeping of another man. Better a thousand times to part now than to part after marriage. I have seen quite too much, in my professional capacity of marrying in haste and repenting at leisure, to try it myself. I will speak to her to-morrow; she shall tell me the truth fearlessly and frankly while it is not yet too late, and if it be as I dread, why, then, I can do as better men have done—bear my pain and go my way. Poor, pretty little Norry! with her drooping face and pathetic, wistful eyes—she longs to tell me, I know, and is afraid. It is a very tender heart, a very romantic little heart, and who is to blame her if it turns to him, young and handsome as she is herself, instead of to the grave, dull, middle-aged lawyer. And yet, it will be very hard to say good-by."

He broke down for a moment, alone as he was. A great flood of recollection came over him—the thought of parting—now—was bitter indeed. A vision rose before him—Norine as he had seen her first, standing shyly downcast in the train, her dark, childlike eyes glancing imploringly around, the sensitive color coming and going in her innocent face. She arose before him again as he had seen her later, flushed and downcast, sweet and smiling, bending over Laurence Thorndyke, with "Love's young dream" written in every line of her happy face. Again as he had seen her that day when he spoke, pale, startled, troubled, afraid to accept, afraid to refuse, and faltering out the words that made him so idiotically happy, with her little, white, handsome face, keeping its startled pallor.

"Yes," he said, "yes, yes, I see it all. She said 'yes,' because it is not in her yielding, gentle, child's heart to say no. And now she is repenting when she thinks it too late. But it is not too late; to-morrow I will speak and she will answer, and if there be one lingering doubt in her mind, we will shake hands and part. My little love! I wish for your sake Laurence Thorndyke were worthy of you, and might return; but to meet him again is the worst fate that can befall you, and in three months poor Helen Holmes will be his bride."

Hark! was that a sound? He broke off his reverie to listen. No, all was still again—only the surging of the wind in the maples.

"It certainly sounded like the opening of a door below," he thought; "a rat perhaps—all are in bed."

He was looking blankly out into the windy darkness. This time to-morrow night his fate would be decided. Would he still be in this room, waiting for Thursday morning to dawn and give him Norine, or—

He broke off abruptly again. Was that a figure moving down in the gloom to the gate? Surely not, and yet something moved. A second more, and it had vanished. Was this fancy, too? He waited, he listened. Clearly through the dusk, borne on the wind, there came to him the faint, far-off sound of a laugh.

29

"Who can it be?" he thought, puzzled. "No fancy this time. I certainly heard a laugh. Rather an odd hour and lonely spot for mirth."

He listened once more, and once more, fainter and farther off, came on the wind that laugh. Did he dream, or did a cry mingle with it? The next instant he started to his feet as the loud, rapid rush of carriage wheels sounded through the deep silence of the night. What did it mean? Had some one stealthily left the house and driven away? He rose, drew on his coat, and without his boots, quitted his room, and descended the stairs.

The house door stood ajar—some one had left them and driven away.

He walked to the gate. Nothing was to be seen, nothing to be heard. The gloomy night sky, the tossing trees, the soughing wind, nothing else far or near.

"It may have been Reuben or Joe Kent," he thought, "and yet at this time of night and in secret! And there was a cry for help, or what certainly sounded like one. No need to puzzle over it, however—to-morrow will tell. A New England farm-house is about the last place on earth to look for mysteries."

Mr. Gilbert went to bed again, and, somewhere in the small hours, to sleep. It was rather late when he awoke, and an hour past the usual breakfast time when, his toilet completed, he descended the stairs. The storm had come in pouring rain, in driving wind, in sodden earth, and frowning sky.

Aunt Hetty was alone, the table was laid for two, a delightful odor of coffee and waffles perfumed the air. She looked up from her sewing with a smile as he bade her good-morning.

"I was just wondering if you and Norry meant to keep your rooms all day. Oh, you needn't make any apology; it is as easy to wait breakfast for two as for one. The boys and me"—(they were the "boys" still to Miss Hester Kent)—"had ours at seven o'clock. Now sit right down Mr. Gilbert, and I'll go and rout out Norry, and you and her can have your breakfast sociably together. You'll have a good many sociable breakfasts alone together, I dare say, before long. Gloomy sort of day now, ain't it?"

"Norine is not down then?" the lawyer said, startled a little, yet hardly knowing why.

"Not yet. She ain't often lazy o' mornings, ain't Norry, neither. You wait, though. I'll have her down in ten minutes."

He looked at her as though to say something, changed his mind suddenly, and took seat. Miss Kent left the room. Five minutes passed. Then she came rushing down the stairs, and back to his side, all white and frightened.

"Mr. Gilbert, Norine's not in her room! Her bed was not slept in at all last night!" She sat down all at once, pressing her hand hard over her heart. "I'm," she said, panting, "I'm very foolish, I know, but it has given me a turn."

He rose to his feet. He knew it then! As well as he ever knew it in the after time, Richard Gilbert knew it all at that moment, Norine had fled.

"It was she, then, who left the house last night," he said, in a hushed voice; "and it was a man's laugh! Was it— My God! Was it—"

He stopped, turning white with the horror of that thought.

"Call your brothers," he said, his voice ringing, his face setting white and stern as stone. "We must search for her at once. At all costs we must find her—must bring her back. Quick, Miss Kent! Your brothers! I am afraid Norine has fled."

"Fled!"

"Fled—run away from home, for fear of marrying me. Don't you understand, Miss Kent? Call your brothers, I say every minute may be worth a life—or more! Quick!"

She obeyed—stunned, stupefied by the shock, the horror of her amaze. The two men rushed wildly in, frightened by their sister's incoherent words. Rapidly, clearly, Richard Gilbert told them what he had heard last night, told them even what he feared most.

"Thorndyke has come back, and either persuaded her to run away with him or forcibly abducted her. I feel sure of it. I heard him laugh, and her cry last night as plainly as I hear my own voice now. There is not a moment to be lost. On with your coats! out with the horses, and let us be off. Better she were dead than with him."

They are gone, and the woman sits alone, stunned, speechless, unable to realize it, only dumbly conscious that something awful has happened. Norine has gone! Fled on the very eve of her bridal with another man. Norine—little Norrie, who but yesterday seemed to her as a young innocent child.

The woman sits and weeps alone by her desolate hearth. The men go forth into the world, and forget their grief for the time in the excitement of the search—the men, who have the best of it always.

All his life long that miserable day remained in Richard Gilbert's memory more as a sickening dream than as a reality. He suffered afterward—horribly—to-day he was too dazed to suffer or feel. Whether found or not, Norine Bourdon was lost to him forever; dumbly he felt that, but she must be found. At all costs, she must be brought back from Laurence Thorndyke.

The two men acted passively under his orders—awed into silence by the look on his set, white face. Even to them that day remained as a dizzy dream. Now they were at the station, listening to Gilbert's rapid, lucid inquiries and description, and the clerk shook his head.

"No," he said; "so far as he could recollect, no two parties answering the description, had left by the earliest train that morning."

Then Mr. Gilbert went backward, and tried the registers of the various hotels for the name of Thorndyke. It did not appear, but in one of the lesser hotels the question was solved.

"Thar hain't ben nobody here answerin' to that air," said the Down-East innkeeper; "but thar hes ben a chap callin' himself Smith—John Smith. That may be the cove you want. Likely's not, ye know, if he's ben up to any of his larks, he would give a false name, ye know. He come Saturday night—staid Sunday and Monday, paid his bill last evenin', and made himself scarce. Shouldn't be a mite surprised, now, if he's the rooster you're after."

"Describe him," the lawyer said, briefly.

"Wal, he was a good-lookin' young fellow as ye'd wish to see. Tall and slim and genteel, city clothes, a moustache, blueish eyes, and sorter light hair—a swell young chap, sech as we ain't used to in our house."

"Thorndyke!" the lawyer muttered, between his teeth.

"He never stirred out all Sunday," pursued mine host, "until after nightfall. Then he started off afoot, and it was past eleven when he got back. All day Monday he loafed about his room the same way, and on Monday evennin', as I said, he paid his bill, got a buggy somewhere, and drove off. And I calk'late, square, he'd been a drinkin', he kinder looked and talked that way. That's all I know about Mr. John Smith."

They telegraphed along the line, but without success. Nothing satisfactory could be discovered. It was noon now—there was a train for Boston at two. Mr. Gilbert looked at his watch.

"I will not return with you," he said, decisively. "I will go on to Boston. I am positive he will take her there. Meantime, you will leave no stone unturned to track the fugitives here."

"I'll go with you to Boston," said Uncle Reuben, quietly; "if he's taken her there, my place is on the ground. Joe will do all he can here. And by the Lord! when I *do* see him, I'll make it the dearest night's work he ever did in his life."

So it was arranged. In the dismal loneliness of the pouring afternoon, Joe Kent drove back alone to Kent Hill and to the tortured woman waiting there. Who knew? thought quiet Joe. Perhaps Mr. Gilbert and Reuben had been too hasty, after all. Perhaps Norine was back.

But Norine was not back. The house was empty and desolate—Aunt Hetty sat crying alone. She had gone and left no trace behind, not one word, no note, no letter. Her clothes were all untouched, except those she had worn, and her waterproof cloak. Surely she had never meant to run away, or she would have gone differently from that, and left some line of farewell, some prayer for pardon behind. It must be as Mr. Gilbert had said—the villain had taken her by force.

And while the rainy afternoon deepened into night, the two sad, silent men sat side by side, flying along to Boston. At every station inquiries were made, but no one had seen anything of a young girl and a young man answering the description given. So many came and went always it was impossible to remember. So when night fell in lashing rain and raw east wind the lawyer and the farmer were in Boston, and no trace of runaway Norine had been found.

# CHAPTER IX.

### "MRS. LAURENCE."

t was eleven o'clock on the Wednesday morning following that eventful Monday night. In an upper room, a private parlor of a Boston hotel, seated in an easy chair, was Miss Norine Bourdon. They had arrived this morning, and in the hotel book their names were registered "Mr. and Mrs. John Laurence."

At the present moment Miss Bourdon is alone. Her dark face is very pale, her eyelids are red from much weeping; at intervals, as she sits and thinks, the lovely dark eyes fill, the childlike lips quiver, and a sob catches her breath. And yet she is not really very unhappy. Is she not with Laurence? Before another hour passes will she not be his wife? and what is the love of aunt or uncle, what the friendship of a thousand Mr. Gilberts compared to the bliss of that? Truth to tell, the first shock of consternation at her enforced flight over, Norine had found forgiveness easy. She was only seventeen, remember; she was intensely romantic; she loved him with her whole, passionate heart—a heart capable, even at seventeen, of loving, and—who was to tell?—perhaps of hating very strongly. And most girls like bold lovers. It was a very daring *coup de main*, this carrying her off, quite like something in a last century novel, and with his tender, persuasive voice in her ear, his protecting arm about her waist, with her own heart pleading for him, Norine was driven away a not unwilling captive.

"I have arranged everything, my pet," said Mr. Thorndyke; "rooms are engaged at the W—— House, Boston, and a clerical friend of mine is to perform the ceremony very much on the quiet. You don't object to being married in a hotel parlor, and by a Congregationalist minister, do you? By-and-by we'll take a run over the border and have the thing done over again in the sacred precincts of Notre Dame de Montreal, if you like. Just at present everything must be *sub rosa*, my darling. The old boy—I mean my respected uncle Darcy—will cut up deuced rough, you know, when he first comes to hear it. He expects me to marry his pet, Nellie Holmes; so does Miss Nellie, if the truth must be told. So I would have done, too, if fate and a broken limb had not thrown me upon *your* protection. And from that hour, my darling, my fate was sealed. Of all the eyes, blue, black, brown, green, or gray, for killing, wholesale slaughter, commend me to those of a fair Canadian. So you see, Norry, we will be married Wednesday morning nicely on the quiet, and we'll go to a place I've engaged, over

Chelsea way, down by the 'sad sea waves,' to spend the honeymoon. And there for one blessed month we'll forget all the uncles and aunts, all the lawyers and heiresses in Christendom, and 'do' love among the roses. You forgive me for carrying you off in this right knightly fashion—you do, don't you, Norry? Ah! I know you do; but look up, my own love, and tell me so, and so make my happiness complete."

With a little fluttering sigh Norine obeyed, clinging close to her hero's side in the darkness.

"But you'll let me write home when we are married, and tell them, Laurence, won't you? They have been so good to me, always—always, and they will think, oh yes, they will think such dreadful things of me now."

"They will forget and forgive, never fear, Norry. People always come round when they can't do anything else. Of course you shall write to them—of course you shall do for the future precisely as you wish, and I will only exist to fulfil your commands. But not just yet, you know; not until uncle Darcy relents and forgives. Because, my pet, I haven't a dollar in the world of my own, except my allowance from him, and I can't afford to offend him. But I'll soon bring him round. Let him see you once, and all will be forgiven. The man doesn't exist, old or young, who could resist *you*."

All this was very delightful, of course; and in such rose-colored, romance-flavored talk, the time sped on. Norine's spirits rose with the brisk drive in the teeth of the night gale. She was with Laurence; she was never to part from him more. All life held of rapture was said for her in that. It was rather a drawback, certainly, that she might not tell them at home of her felicity at once, but she would just drop them a line from Boston to say she was safe and well and happy, that they were not to worry about her, and to beg Mr. Gilbert's—poor Mr. Gilbert's—pardon. That much Laurence would consent to, of course. To be married in a hotel parlor, by a Congregationalist Minister was also ever so little of a drawback, to a little French Canadienne, but one must not expect unalloyed earthly happiness. And had not Laurence said they would go one day to Montreal—dear old Montreal, and be remarried in Notre Dame? Then she would visit Aunt Hetty and Uncle Reuben; then she would go to New York and plead with Mr. Darcy for her beloved husband, and Mr. Darcy would grant that pardon, and then—what then? Well, nothing then, of course, only live and be happy forever after! The sloop, in which Mr. Thorndyke had engaged passage, was ready to sail. Norine was consigned to the care of the captain's wife for the trip, and was soon so utterly prostrate with *mal de mer*, that love and Laurence were forgotten.

To tell the truth, Mr. Thorndyke was miserably sea-sick himself; but this mode of travel had been forced upon him by the exigencies of the case. The pursuers must be thrown off the track. Gilbert would surely suspect and follow; if they went by rail, he would inevitably hunt them down. So, of necessity, he chose the sloop, and with a head wind and driving rain, spent Monday night, Tuesday, and Tuesday night sea-sick and prostrate. Wednesday morning came and they were in Boston. It came in pouring rain and leaden sky, and the bleak easterly wind your Bostonian dreads. They drove to the hotel, Miss Bourdon dreadfully ashamed of her old waterproof, and ascended to their private parlor. Mr. Thorndyke ordered breakfast to be served here at once, and both partook of that repast when it came, with very excellent appetites. Mr. Thorndyke had had some more brandy, which tonic, doubtless, stimulated his appetite, his resolution and his love together. Then he put on his hat, looked at his watch, and departed on matrimonial business intent.

"I'll be off for the Reverend Jonas Maggs (his name's the Reverend Jonas Maggs) at once, and make you Mrs. Thorndyke before you eat your dinner. And I'll order a few things here—a hat, for instance, a sacque, and a few dresses and gloves. I'll be back in an hour or two at the longest. You won't be lonely, my darling, while I'm gone?"

She had answered him "no," and with a very affectionate embrace, he had left her. But in his absence she did grow lonely, did grow saddened and remorseful. What must they think of her at home? They had discovered her flight by this time—all was consternation and terror. They would wonder what had happened—why she had gone, whither, and if alone. Aunt Hetty she could see weeping and refusing to be comforted; her uncles shocked, speechless, terrified; Mr. Gilbert pale, stern, and perhaps guessing the truth. He had loved her, very truly and dearly, and Thursday next was to have been his wedding day. Oh! what a cruel, wicked, heartless, ungrateful wretch she must be now in his sight! How he would scorn and despise her—how they all would! Would they ever forgive her for this shameful flight—this cold-blooded treachery? One day she might, perhaps, come face to face with Mr. Gilbert, in the busy whirl of New York life, and how would she ever dare to meet his angry, scornful eye? As Laurence's wife, the deepest bliss life could give would be hers, but through all her life long, even in the midst of this bliss, the trail of the serpent would be over all still, in her undying shame and remorse. The ready tears of seventeen fell, until all at once Miss Bourdon recollected that Laurence would be here presently with the clergyman, and that it would never do to be married with red eyes and a swollen nose. She sprang up, bathed her face, brushed out her long silky black hair, and by the time she had made herself pretty and bright, Mr. Thorndyke's light step came flying up the stairs, three at a bound, and Mr. Thorndyke's impetuous tap was at the door.

"Come in," she said, her heart beginning to flutter, and the bridegroom came in, handsome, smiling, eager, followed by a seedy-looking personage in rusty black, and the professional "choker" of dingy white.

"Out of patience, Norine? But I could not come an instant sooner, and it is only half-past eleven. My friend, the Reverend Jonas Maggs, Miss Bourdon, soon to be transformed into Mrs. Laurence Thorndyke; and the sooner the better. Here's the ring, Norry, bought haphazard—let's see if it fits the dear little finger. So! as if you were born in it. Now then, Mr. Maggs, pity the impatience of ardent love, and get on with the ceremony."

High spirits these for a runaway match. The handsome face was flushed, the blue eyes feverishly bright, a strong odor of cigars and cognac pervaded Mr. Thorndyke's broadcloth. The Rev. Mr. Maggs coughed, a meek, clerical cough, looked furtively and admiringly at the bride, drew forth a book, and "stood at ease." Mr. Thorndyke drew Miss Bourdon up before him, the ring between his fingers, an odd sort of smile on his lips. For Norine, she had grown ashen white; now that the supreme moment had come, she was trembling from head to foot. Even to her inexperience there was something bizarre, something wrong and abnormal, in this *outre* sort of marriage. A bride without bridal dress, veil or blossoms; without bridesmaid, or friend; a bridegroom splashed with mud and rain drops, without groomsman or witness. And the Rev. Mr. Maggs, for a holy man, was as dirty and disreputable a specimen of the class as one might wish to see. She stood by his side, pale to the lips, afraid of—she knew not what. As in a dream she heard Mr. Maggs gabbling over some sort of ceremony. As in a dream she saw the ring slipped over her finger. As in a dream she saw him shut up his book with a slap, and heard him pronounce them man and wife. Then for the first time she lifted her eyes, full, clear, questioning to the face of Laurence Thorndyke. For the first time, perhaps, in his own experience of himself he shrank before their crystal clear, childishly innocent gaze. His were still full of that intolerable light of triumph—that exultant smile yet lingered on his lips.

He drew Maggs aside and slipped a crisp greenback, into his hand. Then the reverend gentleman resumed his hat, bowed to the bride, wished her joy with an unctuous smile, and slowly took himself out of the room.

"My dear little wife!" Laurence Thorndyke said. "You have made me the happiest man in America to-day. For the next four weeks, in our pretty Chelsea cottage, it shall be our business to forget that the world holds another human creature than our two selves."

"And I've paid *you* off, I think, my friend Gilbert, with compound interest." Mr. Thorndyke added, mentally, as a rider to that pretty little speech. "I'm not over and above rich this morning, but I'd give a cool hundred to see your face."

And so, while not half a mile off, Richard Gilbert and Reuben Kent were searching, with the aid of a detective officer, every hotel in Boston, a hack was rattling over the stones to Chelsea Ferry, bearing to their bridal home Laurence Thorndyke and Norine.

# CHAPTER X.

### "A FOOL'S PARADISE."

he little house was like a picture—like a doll's house, the whitest, the brightest, the trimmest, the tiniest of all tiny houses. It nestled down in a sheltered nook, with its back set comfortably against a hill. Its pretty little garden full of pretty little flowers, climbing roses and scarlet-runners all over its inviting porch, and away beyond, Chelsea beach, like a strip of silver ribbon, and the dimpling sea, smiling back the sunshine. No other house within a quarter of a mile, the dim, dark woodland rising up in the back-ground, the big, bustling, work-a-day world shut out on every hand. Could Laurence Thorndyke, if he had searched for half a lifetime, have found a more charming, more secluded spot in which to dream out Love's Young Dream?

And the dream was pretty nearly dreamed out now.

For the fourth week had come, and the days of the honey month were drawing to a close. If the truth must be told, the honey had cloyed upon Mr. Thorndyke's fastidious palate before the end of the second week, had grown distasteful ere the end of the third—had palled entirely at the beginning of the fourth. In other words, the honeymoon business and doing "love in a cottage," buried alive here, was fast becoming a most horrible bore.

"If I had been very much in love with the girl," thought Mr. Thorndyke, communing with his own heart "it might have been different—even then, though, let it have been ever so severe a case of spoons, I don't think I could have stood another week of this deadly lively sort of thing. But I wasn't very much in love. If you know yourself, Laurence Thorndyke, and you flatter yourself you do, it isn't in you to get up a *grande passion* for any body. There was Lucy West, there is Helen Holmes, here is Norine Bourdon. I don't believe you ever had more than a passing fancy for any of them, and your motto ever has been 'lightly won lightly lost.'"

He was lying upon a sofa, stretched at full length, his hands clasped behind his head, a cloud of cigar smoke half-veiling his handsome, lazy, bored face, his eyes fixed dreamily upon the sparkling sea. Down on the strip of tawny sand he could see Norine, looking like a Dresden china shepherdess in her white looped-up dress, some blue drapery caught about her, a jaunty sailor hat on her crushed dark curls, and a cluster of pink roses in her belt.

"She's very pretty, and all that," pursued this youthful philosopher and cynic, looking at her with dispassionate eyes, "but is the game worth the candle? Three weeks and two days, and I'm sick and tired to death of this place, and—alas! my pretty Norry—of you! 'Men were deceivers ever.' I suppose it was much the same in old Shakspeare's time as it is now. It is all very well to pay off Gilbert, and wipe out the old scores, but it is not at all very well to be disinherited by old Darcy. If it comes to his ears it's all up with my chance of the inheritance, and my marriage with Helen. And, upon my word, I shouldn't like to lose Helen. She's good-looking, she's good style, she can talk on any subject under Heaven, and she's twenty thousand dollars down on her wedding-day. Yes, it will never do to throw up my chances there, but how to drop quietly out of this—that's the rub. There'll be the dickens to pay with Norine, and sometimes I've thought of late, gentle as she is, much as she loves me—and she does love me, poor little soul—that she's not one of the milk-and-water sort to sit down in a corner and break her heart quietly. I wish—I wish—I wish I had left her in peace at Kent Farm!"

She was beckoning to him gaily at that moment. He shook off his disagreeable meditation, put his long limbs down off the sofa, took his straw hat, and sauntered forth to join her.

The little house—Sea View Cottage, its romantic mistress had named it, was owned by the two Miss Waddles. The two Miss Waddles were two old maids. Miss Waddle the elder, taught school in Chelsea. Miss Waddle, the younger, was literary, and wrote sensation stories for the weekly papers, poor thing. In addition, they eked out their income by taking a couple of summer boarders, for people as a rule don't become millionaires teaching school or writing for the papers. Miss Waddle, the younger, immersed in ink and romance, looked after the young man with eyes of keen professional interest.

"How grumpy he looks," thought Miss Waddle; "how radiant *she* looks. He's tired to death of it all already; she's more and more in love with him every day. The first week he was all devotion, the second week the thermometer fell ten degrees, the third week he took to going to Boston and coming home in the small hours, smelling of smoke and liquor, this fourth he yawns in her face from morning until night. And this is what fools call the honeymoon. Moonshine enough, so far as I can see, but precious little honey."

Miss Waddle stabbed her pen down in the inkstand, took a deep and vicious dip, and plunged wildly into literature once more. Mr. Thorndyke, listlessly, wearily and unutterably bored, joined the idol of his existence.

In the Chelsea cottage they were known as "Mr. and Mrs. Laurence." For Norine, she was radiantly happy—no weariness, no boredom for her. The honey grew sweeter to her taste every day; but then women as a rule have a depraved taste for unwholesome sweetmeats; the days Mr. Thorndyke found so long, so vapid, so dreary, were bright, brief dreams of bliss to her. She had written her short explanatory note home during the first week, and had given it to Laurence to post. Laurence took it, glad of an excuse over to Boston, and on the ferry-boat tore it into fifty minute fragments and cast them to the four winds of Heaven. Norine had written a second time, and a third. Her piteous little letters met the same fate. That was one drawback to her perfect Paradise—there was a second, Laurence's growing weariness of it all.

"If he should become tired of me; if he should repent his hasty marriage; if he should cease to love me, what would become of me?" she thought, clasping her hands in an agony. "Oh, mon Dieu! let me die sooner than that. I know I am far beneath him—such lovely, accomplished ladies as my darling might have married—but ah, not one of them all could ever love him better than poor Norine!"

She hid her fears; the tears she shed over their silence and unforgiveness at home were tears shed in solitude and darkness, where they might not offend or reproach him. She tried every simple little art to be beautiful and attractive in his sight. Her smiling face was the last thing he saw, let him quit her ever so often—her smiling face looked brightly and sweetly up at him let those absences be ever so prolonged. And they were growing more frequent and more prolonged every day. He took her nowhere—his own evenings, without exception now, were spent in Boston, the smallest of the small hours his universal hours for coming home. And not always too steady of foot or too fluent of speech at these comings, for this captivating young man was fonder of the rattle of the dice-box, the shuffling of the pack, and the "passing of the rosy" than was at all good for him.

"Laurence," Norine's bright voice called, "you know everything. Come and tell me what is this botanical specimen I have found growing here in the cleft of the rocks."

She held up a spray of blue blossom. Laurence looked at it languidly.

"I know everything, I admit, but I don't know that. If you had married old Gilbert now, my darling, your thirst for information might have been quenched. There isn't anything, from the laws of the nations down to the name of every weed that grows, he hasn't at his learned legal finger ends. Oh, Lord, Norry, what a long day this has been—fifty-eight hours if one."

He casts himself on the sands at her feet, pulls his hat over his eyes, and yawns long and loudly. Her happy face clouds, the dark, lovely eyes look at him wistfully.

"It is dull for you, dear," she says, tenderly, a little tremor in the soft, sweet tones; "for me the days seem all too short—I am so happy, I suppose." He glances up at her, struggling feebly with a whole mouthful of gapes.

"You *are* happy, then, Norry, are you? Almost as happy as when at home; almost as happy as if you had married that ornament of society, Richard Gilbert, instead of the scapegrace and outlaw, Laurence Thorndyke?"

She clasped her hands, always her habit when moved.

"So happy!" she said, under her breath; "so perfectly, utterly happy. How could I ever have thought of marrying any one but you, Laurence—you whom I loved from the very very first?"

"And"—he has the grace to hesitate a little—"it would make you very unhappy if we were forced to part, I suppose, Norry?"

"Part?" She starts, grows very white, and two dilated eyes turn to him. "Laurence, why do you ask me that? Unhappy? Mon Dieu! it would kill me—just that!"

He laughs a little, but uneasily, and shifts away from the gaze of the large, terrified eyes.

"Kill you? No, you're not the sort that die so easily. Don't look so white and frightened, child; I didn't mean anything, at least, not anything serious; only we have been almost a month here and it is about time I went to pay my respected Uncle Darcy a visit. He has taken to asking unpleasant questions of late—where I am, what I am doing, why I don't report myself at headquarters—meaning his house in New York. Norry, there's no help for it; I'll have to take a run up to New York."

She sits down suddenly, her hand over her heart, white as the dress she wears.

"Of course I need not stay long," Mr. Thorndyke pursues, his hat still over his eyes; "but go I must, there's no alternative. And then, perhaps, if I get a chance, I can break it to him gently—about you, you know. I hate the thought of leaving you, and all that—nobody more; but still, as I've told you, I'm absolutely depending upon him; the exchequer is running low and must be replenished. Conjugal love is a capital thing, but a fellow can't live on it. Love may come and love may go, but board goes on forever. You'll stay here with the two Waddles, do fancy work, read novels, and take walks, and you'll ever find the time slipping by until I am back. You don't mind, do you, Norine?"

"How long will you be gone?" she asks, in an odd, constrained sort of voice.

"Well, two or three weeks, perhaps. I shall have business to attend to, and—and all that. But I'll be back at the earliest possible moment, be sure of that."

She does not speak. She stands looking, with that white change in her face, over the sunny sea.

"Come, Norine!" he exclaims, impatiently, "you're not going to be a baby, I hope. If you love me, as you say you do—" She turns and looks at him, and he alters the phrase suddenly, with an uneasy laugh. "Well, *since* you love me so well, Norry, you must try and have a little common sense. Common sense and pretty girls are incompatible, I know; but really, my dear child, you can't expect that our whole lives are to be spent billing and cooing here. It would be very delicious, no doubt"—a great yawn stifles his words for an instant—"but—by Jove! who's this?"

He raises himself on his elbow, pushes back his hat, and stares hard at an advancing figure. Norine follows his glance, and sees, stepping rapidly over the sand, the small slim figure of a man.

"The—devil!" says Laurence Thorndyke.

He springs to his feet, and stands waiting. The man advances, comes near, lifts his hat to the lady, and looks with a calm glance of recognition at the gentleman. He is a pale, thin, sombre little man, not too well dressed, with keen, small, light blue eyes, and thin, decisive, beardless lips.

"Good-day, Mr. Thorndyke," he says, quietly.

"Liston—it *is* Liston!" exclaims Mr. Thorndyke, a red, angry flush mounting to his face. "At your usual insolent tricks, I see—dogging me! May I ask—"

"How I have found you out?" Mr. Liston interrupts, in the same calm, quiet voice. "I knew you were here three weeks ago, Mr. Thorndyke. I saw Maggs—the Reverend Jonas Maggs—in Boston."

He lifts his light, keen eyes for one second to Laurence Thorndyke's, then drops them to the sands. The red flush deepens on the young man's blonde face, his blue eyes flash steely fire.

"By Heaven, you have!" he exclaims, in a suppressed voice. "Has the drunken fool—"

Liston interrupts again:

"I beg your pardon, Mr. Laurence, but if you will step aside with me, I would like to say a few words to you. Meantime, here are two letters—one from your uncle, the other—"

"H'm! All right Liston!" Thorndyke says, hastily, and with a warning glance. "My uncle has sent you to hunt me up as usual, I suppose."

"As usual, Mr. Laurence. He commands your immediate presence in New York."

Again the color mounts to the young man's face, again his eyes flash angry fire.

"Do you mean to say, Liston, that you or that d—— snivelling hypocrite, Maggs—"

"Mr. Thorndyke," says Mr. Liston, interrupting for the third time, and raising his voice slightly, "I have a word to say to you in private—if the young lady will excuse you."

He bows in a sidelong sort of way to Norine, and watches her furtively beneath his drooping eyelids. She is standing very still, her eyes on one of the letters—a square, perfumed, rose-colored letter superscribed in a lady's delicate tracery, and bearing the monogram "H. H." Thorndyke thrusts both abruptly into his pocket, and draws her aside.

"Go back to the house, Norine," he says hastily. "I must hear what this fellow has to say. He's secretary—confidential clerk, valet, factotum generally, to my uncle. And I wish the devil had him before he ever found me out here!"

She obeys passively, very pale, still.

"That———snivelling hypocrite, Maggs!" she is repeating inwardly. "What a dreadful way to speak of a clergyman!"

Mr. Thorndyke rejoins Mr. Liston, a scowl on his face, his brows lowering and angry.

"Well?" he demands, savagely.

"Well," the new-comer's quiet voice repeats, "don't lose your temper, Mr. Laurence—I haven't done anything. Your uncle told me to hunt you up, and I have hunted you up—that is all."

"When did he tell you, confound him?"

"One week ago, Mr. Laurence."

"A week ago? I thought you said—"

"That I met Maggs three weeks ago? So I did. That he was beastly drunk? So he was. That he told me all? So he did. That I have kept my eyes upon you, off and on, ever since? So I have. Mr. Laurence, Mr. Laurence, I wonder you're not afraid."

A suppressed oath—no other reply from Mr. Laurence. He gnaws his mustache, and digs vicious holes with his boots in the soft sand.

"You're a bold card, Mr. Laurence," pursues Mr. Liston's monotonous voice. "You've played a good many daring games in your life, but this last daring game I think, has put the topper on the lot. I fancied mock parsons, sham marriages, and carrying off young ladies by night, went out of fashion with Gretna Green and Mrs. Radcliffe's romances. If ever Mr. Darcy hears of it, the sooner you take a rope and hang yourself, the better."

Another smothered imprecation of rage and impatience from Mr. Thorndyke. "If I only had Maggs here," he says, clenching his fist.

"You would punch his head for him—very likely. But I don't know that even that would do much good. He's got the jim-jams to-day, poor brute, the worst kind. For you, Mr. Laurence—how long before this play of yours is played out?"

"I'm going to New York to-morrow," growls Mr. Laurence Thorndyke. "I was just telling her so as you hove in sight."

"Ah! you were just telling her so—the play *is* played out, then. May I ask, Mr. Laurence, though it is none of my business, how the poor thing takes it?"

"No, you mayn't ask," replies Mr. Laurence, with ferocity, "as you say it's none of your business. Liston! look here, you're not going to turn State's evidence, are you—honor bright? You are not going to tell the old man."

His angry voice drops to a pleading cadence. Mr. Liston's shifty light eyes look up at him for a moment.

"Do I ever tell Mr. Laurence? It is late in the day to ask such a question as that.

"So it is. You're not half a bad fellow, old boy, and have got me out of no end of scrapes. Get me out of this and I'll never forget it—that I swear. One of these days you shall have your reward in hard cash—that I promise you."

"When you marry Miss Holmes? It's a bargain, Mr. Laurence—I'll try and earn my reward. What is it you want me to do?"

"I'm going to New York to-morrow," Thorndyke says, hurriedly. "I must invent some excuse for the governor, and what I say you are to swear to. And when peace is proclaimed you must come back and tell *her*. I can't do it myself—by George, I can't."

"Is that all?" asked Mr. Liston.

"You'll look after her—poor little soul! and, if she wishes it, take her to her friends. I'm sorry, sorry, sorry—for her sake and for my own. But it's rather late for all that. Liston, is Richard Gilbert in town?"

"He is in town. He has been to see your uncle. He has been speaking of this girl. My word Mr. Laurence, you'll have to do some hard swearing to prove an *alibi* this time."

"Curse the luck! Tell me what Darcy said to you Liston, word for word."

"Mr. Darcy, said this: 'Liston, go and find young Thorndyke (he never calls you young Thorndyke except when he's very far gone in anger, indeed), and fetch him to me. And hark'ee, fellow! no lying from you or him. If what I hear of him be true, I'll never look upon his false, cowardly face again, living or dead.' He was in one of his white rages, when the less said the better. That was a week ago, I had known all about you for two weeks before. I bowed, kept my own counsel, and—here I am."

"You're a trump, Liston! And he gave you this letter?"

"He gave me that letter. You'll find it considerably shorter than sweet. The other came from Miss Holmes, a few days ago—he sent that too."

"She doesn't know—"

"Not likely. She will though, if the old man finds out, and then you're cake's dough with a vengeance. How do you suppose the little one (she's very pretty, Mr. Laurence—you always had good taste), how do you suppose she will take it?"

Mr. Thorndyke's reply was a groan.

"For Heaven's sake don't ask me, Liston! It's a horrible business. I must have been mad."

"Of course—madly in love."

"Nothing of the sort—not in love at all. It was pure spite—I give you my word—not a spark of real love in the matter, except what was on her side. Gilbert was going to marry her, you know."

"I know."

"And I hate him as I hate the——"

"Prince of evil! I know *that*, too."

"You know everything that's my opinion. What a detective was lost in you, old boy. Perhaps you know why I hate him?"

"He has blocked one or two little games of yours. And he 'peached' in that affair of Lucy West."

"Liston! what an infernal scoundrel you must think me! When you recall Lucy West, I wonder you don't hate me tenfold more than I hate Gilbert."

"I do think you an infernal scoundrel," replies Mr. Liston, coolly. "As for hating—well I'm one of the forgiving sort, you know. Besides, there's nothing made by turning informer, and there is something to be made, you say, by keeping mum. Now suppose you go back to the house, and her, she's pining for you, no doubt, and tell her you're off to-morrow. I'll call for you with a light wagon about noon. Until then good-day to you."

Thorndyke seized his hand and shook it.

"I don't know how to thank you, Liston! You're the prince of good fellows. And I haven't deserved it—I know that."

He strode away. If he could only have seen the look "the prince of good fellows" cast after him!

"'You don't know how to thank me,'" he thought, with sneering scorn. "You fool! You blind, conceited, besotted fool! 'When I recall Lucy West you wonder I don't hate you!' Was there ever a time, my perfumed coxcomb, when I did not hate you? And you'll reward me, will you? Yes, I swear you shall, but not in that way. Poor little girl! how young she is, how pretty, and how innocent. She has had her fool's paradise for three weeks—it ends to-day."

---

# CHAPTER XI.

## GONE.

aurence Thorndyke strode rapidly back over the sands to where Norine stood. She had not gone into the house, she was leaning against a green mound, her hands hanging listlessly before her, the white, startled change on her face still. Laurence was going away—in an aimless sort of manner she kept repeating these words over and over, Laurence was going away!

"I've made a devil of a mess of it," thought Mr. Thorndyke, gnawing his mustache with gloomy ferocity. "What an unmitigated ass I have been in this business! Liston's right—a mock marriage is no joke. I can make my escape from her now, but the truth's got to be told, and that soon. And what is to hinder her taking her revenge and blowing me sky-high, as I deserve? One whisper of this affair, and Darcy disinherits me, Helen jilts me, and then—good Heaven above! what a fool I have been."

Yes, Mr. Thorndyke had been a fool, and was repenting in sackcloth and ashes. To gratify a passing fancy for a pretty face may be a very pleasing thing—to take revenge upon a man who has interfered with one's little plans, may also be a pleasing thing, but to cut off one's own nose to spite one's own face, is something one is apt to regret afterwards. It was Mr. Thorndyke's case. He had taken Richard Gilbert's bride from him at the very altar, as one may say, and he had gloated over his vengeance, but what was to hinder Norine Bourdon from rising, strong in her wrongs and betrayal, and ruining him for life? She was the gentlest, the most yielding of human beings now, and she loved him; but is it not those whom we have once loved best, we learn afterwards to hate most bitterly? He had cruelly, shamefully wronged and deceived her—what right had he to look for mercy in return? As he had sown, so must he reap.

She scarcely turned at his approach. How pale she was, and the large dark eyes she lifted were full of a child's startled terror.

"Norine," he abruptly began, "there is no help for it—I must go to New York to-morrow."

Her lips trembled a little.

"To-morrow," she repeated, under her breath—"so soon!"

"Rather short notice, I admit, but then you see it—it isn't for a lifetime. All husbands and wives part once in a while and survive it. Come, Norine," with irritated impatience, "don't wear that woe-begone face! I'm not to blame, I can't help it. You don't suppose I want to leave you. But here's Liston—my uncle's man. You heard him yourself. You saw the letter commanding my return."

"The letter," she repeated, looking at him; "there were two!"

"Ah—yes—two, so there were. But the other was merely a note from a friend. I leave at noon to-morrow, so see that my valise is packed, and everything all right, that's a good child. And do try to get rid of that white, reproachful face, unless you want it to haunt me like the face of a ghost."

He spoke with irritated petulance—at war with her, with himself, and his smouldering ill-temper breaking forth. It was the first time he had ever spoken sharply to her. A faint flush rose to her cheeks. She clasped both hands around his arm and looked up in his moody, discontented face with piteous imploring eyes.

"Don't be vexed, Laurence; I don't mean to reproach you, indeed, and I know you cannot help it. Only, dear, I love you so much, and—and it is our first parting, and I have been so happy here—so happy here—"

For a minute her voice broke, and she laid her face against his shoulder.

Mr. Thorndyke smothered a suppressed groan.

"O Jupiter! here it is! Tears, and scenes and hysterics. I knew how it would be, they all will do it, every chance. Norine!"—aloud and still impatient—"for pity's sake, don't cry—it's something I can't stand. Here! I'll throw my uncle, his fortune and favor, and all the hopes and ambitions of my life to the winds, and stay here, and bill and coo, all the rest of my life. If I can't go in peace I won't go at all."

She lifted her head as if he had struck her. Something in his tone, in his words, in his face, dried her tears effectually, at once and forever.

"I beg your pardon, Laurence," she said, suddenly, in an altered voice. "I won't cry any more. Shall I go and pack your valise now or leave it until to-morrow morning?"

He glanced at her uneasily. The dark, soft eyes looked far away seaward, the delicate lips had ceased to tremble, the small handsome face had grown resolutely still. What manner of woman he wondered, was this girl going to make?

"Norine! You are not offended?"

"Offended—with you, Laurence? No, that is not possible."

"You love me so much, Norine?"

"I have given you proof whether I love you or no. I am your wife."

"Yes, of course, of course!" hastily; "but Norine—see here—suppose in the future I did some great wrong—deserted you for instance—no, no! don't look at me like that—this is only a suppositious case, you know!"

The large dark eyes were fixed full upon him. He laughed in rather a flurried way, and his own shifted and fell.

37

"Go on," she said.

"Suppose I deserted you, and it was in your power to take revenge, you would hate me and take it—would you not?"

Into the dark, tender eyes there leaped a light—into the youthful, gentle face there came a glow—around the soft-cut, childlike mouth there settled an expression entirely new to Laurence Thorndyke. One little hand clenched unconsciously—she caught her breath for a second, hard.

"Yes," she said, "I would!"

The answer staggered him—literally and truly staggered him. He had not expected it—he had looked for some outbreak of love, some tender, passionate protest.

"Norine!" he cried, "you would! Do you know what you are saying? You would hate me, and ruin me for life if you could?"

She looked at him full.

"If you deserted me, would you not hate me? Would I not be ruined for life? And does not the Book of books say: 'An eye for an eye, a tooth for a tooth, a life for a life.' Yes, Laurence—if I did not go mad and die, I would hate you more then I love you now, and be revenged if I could!"

Then there was a silence. He had grown pale as herself, and stood quite motionless looking at the sea. He knew what he had to expect at last.

Norine was still clinging to his arm. He disengaged it abruptly, and without a word or look, walked away from her. A moment she stood—then two little hands clasped the arm once more, a pleading voice spoke, and the sweet, tender face of Norine looked imploringly up at him.

"Laurence—dearest Laurence! I have angered you again. But you asked me a question and I had to answer it. Forgive me."

He turned away from her resolutely.

"There is no forgiveness needed, Norine. I admire your truthful and plain-spoken spirit. Only you see I thought Norine Bourdon a loving, gentle, forgiving little soul, who cared for me so much that she was ready to forgive me seventy-times-seven, and I find, according to her own showing, she is a strong-minded woman, ready to wreak vengeance for the first wrong done her—ready for love or hatred at a moment's notice. It is well you told me—it is always best to understand one another. No, we won't have any tender scenes, if you please, Mrs. Laurence—I have found out exactly what they are worth." He pulled out his watch. "I have business over in Boston, and as it is growing late I will be off at once. If I am very late—as is likely—I must beg you will not sit up for me. Good-afternoon."

He lifted his hat ceremoniously, as to an indifferent acquaintance, and walked deliberately away.

She stood stock still where he had left her, and watched the tall, active figure out of sight. Then she sat down, feeling suddenly weak and faint, and lay back against the green mound. For a moment sea, and sky, and sands swam before her in a hot mist, and then the faintness passed away, leaving her tearless and trembling.

What did he mean?

He had talked of deserting her? Did he mean it? A hand of ice seemed to clutch her heart at the thought. No no, no! he had only been trying her—proving what her love was worth. And she had answered him like that she would hate him and be revenged. He had called her a "strong-minded woman,"—a term of bitter reproach—and no wonder. No wonder he was angry, hurt, outraged. Why had she said such a horrible thing? She hardly knew herself—the words seemed to have come to her instinctively. Were they true? She did know that either—just now she knew nothing but that Laurence had left her in anger for the first time, that he would probably not return until to-morrow morning, the fateful to-morrow that was to take him from her for—how long?

She broke down then, and laying her face against the soft, cool grass, gave way to a storm of impassioned weeping, that shook her like a reed. "The strong-minded woman" was gone, and only a child that had done wrong and is sorry—a weak girl weeping for her lost lover, remained.

The afternoon waned, the twilight fell, the wind arose chilly from the sea. And pallid as a spirit, shivering in the damp air, silent and spiritless, the younger Miss Waddle found her when she came to call her in to supper.

She drank her tea thirstily, but she could eat nothing. Immediately after the lonely meal, she hastened to her room, and throwing a shawl around her, sat down in the easy chair by the window to watch and wait. He had told her not to sit up for him—it would annoy him probably to be disobeyed, but she could not go to bed, for in the darkness and the quiet, lying down, she knew how she would toss wakefully about until she had thought herself into a fever.

Night fell. Outside the sea spread black, away until it melted into the blacker sky. The wind sighed fitfully, the stars shone frostily bright. Inside, the little piano in the parlor, played upon by the elder Miss Waddle, after her day's teaching, made merry music. In the intervals, when it was silent, the younger Miss Waddle read chapters aloud from her latest novel. Ten, eleven struck, then the parlor lights went out, doors were locked, and the Misses Waddle went up stairs to their maiden slumbers.

The pale little watcher by the window sat on, hoping against hope. He might come, and be it late or early she must be awake and waiting, to throw herself into his manly arms and implore his lordly pardon. She could never sleep more until she had sobbed out her penitence and been forgiven. But the long, dark, dragging, lonely hours wore on. One, two, three, four, and the little, white, sad face lay against the cold glass, the dark, mournful eyes strained themselves through the murky gloom to catch the first glimpse of their idol. Five! the cold gray dawn of another day crept over sea and woodland, and worn out with watching, chilled to the bone, the child's head fell back, the heavy eyelids swayed and drooped, and she lay still.

So, when two hours later Mr. Laurence Thorndyke, smelling stronger than ever of cigars and brandy, as the younger Miss Waddle's disgusted nose testified, came into the silent chamber, he found her. The pretty head, with all its dark, rippling ringlets, lay against the back of the chair, the small face looked deathly in its spent sleep. She had watched and waited for him here all night. And remembering how, over the card table and the wine bottle, his night had been passed, utterly forgetful of her, the first pang of real unselfish remorse this young gentleman had ever felt, came to him then.

"Poor little heart!" he thought; "poor little, pretty Norine. I wish to Heaven I had never heard of Gilbert's projected marriage—I wish I had never gone back to Kent Farm."

Five hours later, and white and tearless, Norine is clinging to him in the speechless pain of parting. Is there some presentiment, that she herself cannot understand, even now in her heart, that it is forever?

"Don't—*don't* look so white and wild, Norry," he is saying hurriedly. "I wish, I wish I need not leave you. Little one—little Norry, whatever happens, you—you'll try and forgive me, won't you? Don't hate me if you can help it."

She does not understand him—she just clings to him, as though death were easier than to let him go.

"Time's up, Mr. Laurence!" calls out the sharp voice of little Mr. Liston, sitting in the light wagon at the door; "if you linger five minutes more we'll lose our train."

"Good-by, Norine—good-by!"

He is glad to be called, glad to break away from the gentle arms that would hold him there forever. He kisses her hurriedly, frees himself from her clasp, and leaves her standing stricken and speechless in the middle of the floor.

"Thank Heaven that's over!" he says, almost savagely, "drive like the devil, Liston! I won't breath freely until I am out of sight of the house."

Mr. Liston obeys.

She stands where he has left her, rigid, tearless, white, listening to the rapid roll of the wheels over the gravel, over the road, growing faint and fainter, and dying out far off. Then she sinks down, and she and her lover have parted forever.

---

# CHAPTER XII.

**THE TRUTH.**

bleak autumnal afternoon, a gray, fast-drifting sky overhead, a raw wind sweeping up from the shore, the sea itself all blurred and blotted out in the chilly, creeping fog. At the parlor-window of Sea View Cottage, Norine stands looking wistfully, wearily out. Three weeks have passed since her husband left her—it is seven weeks altogether since the memorable night of her elopement. These last three, lonely weeks have wrought their sad, inevitable change. The small face has grown smaller the large dark eyes seem unnaturally large for the wan face. A sad, patient light fills them. The slight form has grown fragile, the hands that hang loosely clasped before her are almost transparent. As she stands here watching, waiting, she slips, unconsciously, her wedding ring up and down her finger. So thin that finger has grown that every now and then the ring drops loosely off altogether. Within, it is pleasant enough. A fire burns brightly in the grate, Miss Waddle's canaries bask in the heat, singing blithely, and the younger Miss Waddle sits at her desk immersed as usual, fathoms deep in ink, and romance. The inspiration of genius is evidently strong upon the younger Miss Waddle this afternoon, for her pen rushes madly along the paper, her hair is uncombed and twisted in a tight knot at the back of her head. Profound stillness reigns, the ticking of the clock the purring of puss on the rug, the chirping of the canaries, the light fall of the cinders, the sighing of the fitful wind, and the monotonous scrape, scrape, scrape, of the literary lady's pen—that is all.

At last—

"There!" cries the younger Miss Waddle, drawing a deep, intense breath of relief, "I've done with you for one day! Let the printer's devil come when he likes, I'm ready for him."

She nods at the blotted and scratched pile of MSS., wipes her pen in her hair, falls back in her chair, and looks at the clock.

"Half-past five, as I'm a sinner, and the kitchen fire not lit yet. 'Lizabeth will be home to her tea at six, as hungry as a bear. A minute ago I was writing up the sayings and doings of dukes and duchesses, now I must go and kindle the kitchen stove. Such is life—with authoresses, but a step from the sublime to the ridiculous. Mrs. Laurence, my dear child, it's of no use your straining the eyes out of your head. Whether there's a letter for you or not, my sister won't be here with it for the next half hour."

Norine clasped her hands.

"Oh!" she said, "surely, there will be a letter for me to-day."

"I hope so, I'm sure. It's uncommonly odd Mr. Laurence doesn't write, but then, as a rule, I believe men hate letter writing. Maybe he's on his way here and doesn't think it worth while—it will come out all right, depend upon it. So cheer up, Mrs. Laurence, my dear, and don't wear that woful face. You've grown as thin as a shadow during the last two weeks. You must take care or your handsome husband will be disenchanted when he sees that pallid countenance. Tell you what, Mrs. Laurence, you ought to have something to do."

"Something to do?" Norine said faintly.

"Something to do, my dear—sewing, drawing, playing, reading, writing—anything but moping about this way—waiting, waiting, waiting, and getting the horrors. It doesn't fetch him any the sooner, nor a letter from him either, and it is just killing you by inches. What a pity now," said the younger Miss Waddle, gathering up her manuscript in a heap, "that you couldn't write a story. You couldn't, I suppose?"

"I am afraid not," Norine replied, smiling. "I am not at all clever in any way. I only wish I could write stories and earn money as you do."

"Yes, it's very nice and handy," said the younger Miss Waddle, "when you're not 'respectfully declined.' *I* have been 'respectfully declined' oftener than I like to think of. But I am going to make a hit this time, if I die for it."

"Yes," said Norine, gazing in respectful awe at the smeary looking pile of writing; "what do you call it?"

"This," said the authoress, slapping her hand on the heap, "is my first novel, to run in serial form in the *Flag of the Free*. Its name is the 'Demon Dentist; or the Mystery of the Double Tooth!' What do you think of that?"

"The Demon—*what*?" asked Mrs. Laurence, rather aghast.

"'The Demon Dentist.' The title is rather a striking one, I think, and Sir Walter Scott says a good name is half the battle. And, I flatter myself, the plot is as original as the title. Lord Racer, only son of the Earl of Greenturf, the hero of the story, steals the Lemon stone, the magnificent family diamond, and hides it—where do you think? Why he goes to the Demon Dentist, gets his wisdom tooth excavated, buries it in the cavernous depths of the molar, has it cemented up again, and there it is! Search is made, but no one thinks of looking in Lord Racer's lower jaw, of course. Wilkie Collins has written a novel about a man who steals a diamond in his sleep, but I rather think my idea is a step ahead of Mr. Wilkie Collins. Finally the Demon Dentist murders Lord—oh gracious me! here's 'Lizabeth, and tea not ready."

Miss Waddle the younger jumped up in consternation, scuttled the "*Demon Dentist*," headforemost, into her desk, and made a rush for the kitchen, as Miss Waddle the elder opened the parlor door.

Norine took a step forward, her face flushing, her eyes kindling with eager hope, her breath coming quick. She did not speak a word, and one glance into Miss Waddle's pitying face answered that breathless look.

"No letter yet, Mrs. Laurence," she said very gently. "I waited for the mail."

She did not speak a word. She sat down suddenly, sick—sick to the very heart with the bitter sense of the disappointment. The flush faded from her face, the light from her eyes; she drew a long, dry, sobbing breath, folded her arms on the table and laid her face upon them.

"Poor little soul!" thought the elder Miss Waddle looking at her in silent compassion. "What brutes men are."

Miss Waddle's experience of the nobler sex was limited, but her sentiment in the main was a correct one. It was peculiarly correct in the present instance, for since that morning three weeks ago, when Laurence Thorndyke had left Sea View Cottage, not a word, not a message, not a letter had come from him. How the lonely, longing girl left in the dull little house, watched and waited, and prayed, and grew sick to the soul, as now, with disappointment, only those who have watched and waited in vain, for the one they love best on earth, can know.

Was he sick—was he dead—was he faithless. Why, why, *why* did he not write?

They were the two questions that never left the girl's mind. She lost the power to sleep or eat, a restless fever held her. She spent her days, the long, vapid, sickening days, gazing down the road he must come, the nights in wakeful, frightened thought. The one event of the twenty-four dreary hours, was the coming home of the elder Miss Waddle from Chelsea; the one hope that upheld her, the hope that each day she would bring her a letter. All this long, bleak day she had lived on that one feverish hope, and now she was here, and there was none—none!

The moments wore on. She lay there prostrate, crushed, never moving or lifting her head. Miss Waddle the elder bent over her with tears of compassion and indignation in her kindly, spinster eyes.

"Dear child," she said, "don't take on like this. Who knows what to-morrow may bring? And if it brings nothing, there isn't a man on earth worth breaking your poor heart for, as you're doing. They're a set of selfish, heartless wretches, every one—every blessed one!" said the elder Miss Waddle, vindictively; "so come along and have a cup of tea, and don't pine yourself to death for him. I daresay, if the truth were known, he's not pining much for you."

Norine lifted her face—such a sad, pathetic, patient little face.

"Don't, Miss Waddle," she said, "you mean well, I am sure, but I can't bear it. He does not intend to forget or neglect me. He is ill—I know that. He is ill, and I don't know where he is, or how to go to him. No, I don't wish any tea, a mouthful of food would choke me, I think. I will go down to the beach instead. I—I would rather be alone."

The gentle lips quivered, the gentle voice trembled over the loyal, wifely words. Not neglectful, not faithless, only ill, and unable to write—she crushed every other thought out of her heart but that. She rose, took her hat, and quitted the room. Miss Waddle looked after her, and shook her head dismally.

"Poor dear!" she thought, "only ill, indeed! Mr. Laurence, if that be his name, is a very good-looking young man, and there, it's my opinion, the young man's goodness begins and ends. He may not have deserted her, but it looks uncommonly like it. Why, he was tired of her before they were here a week."

Then Miss Waddle, the elder, went and took "tired Nature's sweet restorer, balmy"—tea, and Mrs. Laurence, with all hope and life crushed out of her fair young face, went down along the sands, where so often in the first happy days they had wandered together. Only seven weeks ago since she had left all for him—friends, home, lover, truth and honor—why, it seemed years to look back upon. She felt old and worn and tired—a horrible creeping fear clutched her heart. Why did he not write—why did he not come?

She reached the little grassy hillock and sat down, too weak and spiritless, even to walk on. Cold and gray, the twilight was falling, cold and gray spread the low lying twilight sky, cold and gray the dim sea melted into it in the distance, cold and gray like her life. It was very lonely, no human being besides herself was to be seen, not even a sea bird skimmed the sullen waters. With her hands folded in her lap, her sad, yearning eyes fixed on the dreary sea, she sat still, thinking, thinking. Why did he not write—why did he not come?

Suddenly, coming as if from the cottage, a figure appeared in view, the solitary figure of a man, moving rapidly toward her over the sands. She looked up quickly, uttered a faint cry of recognition and hope. As he had come abruptly upon them once before, Mr. Liston came abruptly upon her again. Then it had been to bear her darling away from her—now it was to bring her news of him, she knew.

She did not rise to meet him. Her heart beat so fast with alternate hope and fear that for an instant she turned faint. In that instant he was beside her. He lifted his hat.

"Mrs. Laurence?" he said, interrogatively, "they told me at the house I should find you here. They wished to call you in, but this is a better place for our meeting, so I sought you out."

She made a breathless, impatient gesture.

"You have a letter for me?" she said, hurriedly; "he sent you—he is well?"

"He sent me—yes. And he is well—oh, yes. I have a note for you, too, from him, but I will not show it to you just yet, if you will allow me. My dear young lady, I have come—he has sent me on a very hard and embarrassing errand, indeed."

Something in the man's face, in the man's tone, even more than his words, made her look quickly up. To his dying day, James Liston never forgot the haunted, terrified look in those dilating, dark eyes. She laid her hand over her fast beating heart, and spoke with an effort.

"He is well, you say?" she panted.

"He is well, Mrs. Laurence. It were better for you he were dead."

"Sir!" she cried, the light leaping to her eyes, the flush to her face; "how dare you! He is my husband—how dare you say such a thing to me!"

"He is not your husband."

The low, level, monotonous voice spoke the dreadful words, the small, light, glimmering eyes were fixed immovably upon her with a look, half-contemptuous, half-compassionate, in their depths.

She rose slowly to her feet, and stood blankly staring at him. Was the man mad?

"Not my—" she paused irresolute. Should she run away from this madman or stand her ground. "Give me my letter!" she said, angrily; "I have nothing more to say to *you*!"

"Because I tell you Laurence Thorndyke is not your husband? My child, it is true."

His tone was solemn—his face full of compassion. What a child she was, he was thinking; how she loved him. What was there about this young fellow that women should give up all that made their lives most dear, for his sake?

"I told you, Mrs. Laurence, I have been sent here on a hard and painful errand. He sent me. 'Conscience makes cowards of us all.' He is a coward as well as a villain, and he had not the courage to face you himself. You have been watching and waiting for his return, I know. Watch and wait no longer; you will never see Laurence Thorndyke again."

A cry broke from her lips—a cry that rang in his ears his life long—a cry not loud, but exceedingly bitter.

"In Heaven's name, speak and tell me what is it you mean?"

"*This*: You are not a wife—Laurence Thorndyke never married you. He deceived and betrayed you from the first; he has deserted you forever at the last. That is the task he has set me. I am but a poor diplomat to break bad news, as they call it, to any one, so I blurt out the truth at once. After all, it is the same in the end. He never meant to marry you—he never cared for you enough. He hated Richard Gilbert— that was the beginning and end of it. He hated Gilbert, Gilbert loved you, and was about to make you his wife; to revenge himself on Gilbert, he went back to Kent Hill and carried you off. He knew you loved him, and it would not be a difficult task. It seems easy enough for all women to love Laurence Thorndyke."

The last words, spoken more to himself than to her, were full of bitterness. A great stillness had fallen upon her—her eyes were fixed on his face, her own strained and fixed.

"Go on," she said, her teeth set hard.

"He took you away—how, you know best, and in Boston that mockery of marriage was gone through. Miss Bourdon the man Maggs was an actor, not a clergyman, a besotted drunkard, whom fifty dollars at any time would buy, rotten body and a filthy soul. 'She is as green as the fields she came from'; that is what Thorndyke said to Maggs, 'as innocent as her native daisies. She'll never know the difference, but she's one of the sort that will love a fellow to desperation, and all that sort of thing, and cry like a water-spout at parting, but who won't listen to a word without her wedding ring. Let her have her wedding ring—always take a short cut on a journey if you can.' So you got your wedding ring, and without license or witnesses, and by a half-drunken actor a sham ceremony was gone through. You were married to the scoundrel, for the sake of whose handsome face you gave up home and friends, and the love and honor of such a man as Richard Gilbert— one of the best and noblest men America holds to-day!"

The hand, pressed over her heart, clutched it tighter, as if in a spasm of uncontrollable pain.

"Go on," she said again.

"There's not much to tell. He brought you here, and in a week was bored to death and sick of it all. He was only too glad of the chance to go, and—he will never come back. Here is his note—read it—here is the money he gave me, to pay your board and take you back to your home in Maine. He thinks it is the best thing you can do."

With all the color stricken out of her face—dumb, still, white, tearless, and rigid, she had been standing in her awful despair. But at these last words she came back suddenly as it were from the dead.

"He said *that*?" she asked hoarsely. "He told you to take me back there—like this?"

"He did."

"My curse upon him—my curse follow him through life!"

The man before her actually recoiled. She had uplifted one arm, and in the gathering darkness of the night, she stood before him white and terrible. So, for a second—then she came back to herself, and tore open the note. Only half a dozen brief lines—the tragedies of life are ever quickly written.

"Believe all that Liston tells you. I have been the greatest scoundrel on earth to you, my poor Norine. I don't ask you to forgive me—that would not be human, I only ask you to go and—if you can—forget."

"L. T."

No more. She looked up—out over the creeping night, on the sea, over the lonely, white sands, and stood fixed and mute. The letter she had looked for, longed for, prayed for, she had got at last!

In the dead stillness that followed, Mr. Liston felt more uncomfortable, perhaps, then he had ever felt before in the whole course of his life. In sheer desperation he broke it.

"You are not angry with me, I hope, Mrs. Laurence; I am but his uncle's servant—when I am ordered I must obey. He was afraid to write all this; it would be a very damaging confession to put on paper, so he sent me. You are not angry with me?"

She put her hand to her head in a lost, dazed sort of way.

"Angry with you? Oh, no—why should I be? My head feels strange—dizzy,—I don't want to hear any more to-night. I think I will go home."

She turned slowly. He stood watching her with an anxious face. What he knew would come, came. She had walked some dozen yards, then suddenly—without warning, word or sound, she fell heavily, face downward, like a stone.

---

# CHAPTER XIII.

### MR. LISTON'S STORY

nother autumnal twilight, ghostly and gray is creeping over the Chelsea shore. In her pleasant chamber in the Chelsea cottage, Norine lies on her white bed and looks out upon it. Looks out, but sees nothing. The dark, burning, brilliant eyes might be stone blind for all they see of the windy, fast drifting sky, of the strip of wet and slippery sands, of the white-capped sea beyond. She might be stone deaf for all she hears of the wintry soughing of the wind, of the dull, ceaseless boom of the sea on the shore, or the light patter of the chill rain on the glass. She lies here as she has lain from the first—rigid—stricken soul and body.

Last evening, a little later than this, the Misses Waddle had sprung from their seats with two shrill little shrieks at the apparition of Mr. Liston entering hastily with Mrs. Laurence lying dead in his arms. Dead to all outward semblance, at first, but when they had placed her in bed, and applied the usual restoratives, the eyelids quivered, the dusk eyes opened, and with a strange, shuddering sob, she came back to life. For one instant she gazed up into the kindly, anxious faces of the spinster sisters; then memory came back with a rush. She was not

Laurence's wife; he had betrayed and cast her off; she would never look upon his face again in this world. With a low moan of agony the sisters never forgot, she turned her face to the wall and lay still. So she had lain since.

A night and a day had passed. She had neither slept nor eaten—she had scarcely moved—she lay like a stone. All night long the light had burned, all night long the sisters stole softly in and out, always to find the small, rigid figure, as they had left it; the white face gleaming like marble in the dusk; the sleepless black eyes, wild and wide. They spoke to her in fear and trembling. She did not heed, it is doubtful if she heard. In a dull, dumb trance she lay, curiously conscious of the figures flitting to and fro; of whispered words and frightened faces; of the beat of the rain on the glass; of the black night lying on the black sea, her heart like a stone in her bosom. She was not Laurence's wife—Laurence had left her for ever. These two thoughts kept beating, beating, in heart, and brain, and soul, like the ceaseless torment of the lost.

The new day came and went. With it came Mr. Liston—pale, quiet, anxious. The Misses Waddle, angry and curious, at once plied him with questions. What was it all about? What had he said to Mrs. Laurence? Where was Mr. Laurence? Was it ill news of him? And little Mr. Liston, with a face of real pain and distress, had made answer "Yes, it was ill news of Mr. Laurence. Would they please not ask him questions? He couldn't really tell. For Heaven's sake let them try and bring that poor suffering child round. He would pay every cent due them, and take her away the moment she was able to travel."

He sits in the little parlor now, his head on his hand, gazing out at the gloomy evening prospect, with a very downcast and gloomy face. He is alone, a bit of fire flickers and falls in the grate. Miss Waddle the elder is not yet at home from her Chelsea school. Miss Waddle the younger, in a glow of inky inspiration, is skurrying through a thrilling chapter of "The Mystery of the Double Tooth," and within that inner room, at which he gazes with such troubled eyes, "one more unfortunate" lies battling with woman's utter despair.

"Poor soul," Mr. Liston says inwardly. "Will she perish as Lucy West perished, while he lives and marries, is rich, courted, and happy? No, I will tell her the truth sooner, that she is his wife, that the marriage was legal, though he does not suspect it, and when Helen Holmes is his wife she shall come forward and convict him of bigamy, and my lordly Mr. Laurence, how will it be with you then!"

"Mr. Liston."

He had literally leaped to his feet with a nervous cry. He had heard no sound, but the chamber door had opened and she had come forth. Her soft French accented voice spoke his name, in the shadowy gloaming she stood before him, her face white and still, and awfully death-like. As she came forward in her white dressing gown, her loose black hair falling, her great black eyes shining she was so unearthly, so like a spirit, that involuntarily he recoiled.

"I have startled you," she said. "I beg your pardon. I did not know you were here, but I am glad you are. To-morrow I will leave this house—to-night I should like to say a few words to you."

She was very quiet, ominously quiet. She sat down as she spoke, close to the fire; her hands folded in her lap, her weird looking eyes fixed on his face. Nervously Mr. Liston got up and looked around for a bell.

"Shall I ring, I mean call, for lights. I am very glad to see you up, Miss Bour—I mean Mrs. Laurence."

"Thank you" she answered gently "and no, please—don't ask for a lamp. Such a wretch as I am naturally prefers the dark. Mr. Liston," with strange, swift abruptness, "I have lain in there, and within the last few hours I have been able to think. I believe all that you have told me. I know what I am—as utterly lost and forlorn a sinner as the wide earth holds. I know what *he* is—a greater villain than if, on the night I saw him first, he had stabbed me to the heart. All this I know. Mr. Liston, will you tell me something more. Are you Laurence Thorndyke's friend or enemy?"

In the course of his forty years of life, Mr. Liston had come across a good many incomprehensible women, but perhaps, he had never been quite so completely taken aback before. She spoke the name of her betrayer, of the man she had loved so passionately, and in one moment had lost for ever, without one tremor or falter. The sombre eyes were looking at him full. He drew nearer to her—a great exultation in his soul. This girl was made of sterner stuff than Lucy West. Laurence Thorndyke's hour had come.

"Am I Laurence Thorndyke's friend or enemy? His enemy, Miss Bourdon—his bitterest enemy on earth for the last five years."

"I thought so. I don't know why, but I thought so. Mr. Liston, what has he done to you?"

"Blighted and darkened my life, as he has blighted and darkened yours. He was hardly one-and-twenty then, but the devil was uppermost in him from his cradle. *Her* name was Lucy West, I had known her from babyhood, was almost double her age, but when I asked her to marry me she consented. I loved her well, she knew that I could take her to the city to live, that was the desire of her heart. I know now she never cared for me, but they were poor and pinched at home, and she was vain of her rose-and-milk skin, of her bright eyes and sparkling teeth.

"I was old, and small, and plain, but I could give her silk dresses and a house in town, a servant to wait upon her, and she was ready to marry me. I was then what I am now, Mr. Darcy's land steward, agent, confidential valet, all in one. Young Mr. Laurence came home from Harvard for his vacation; and full of admiration for this bright young beauty, proud and fond beyond all telling of her, I took him down with me to show him the charming little wife I was going to marry. No thought of distrusting either ever entered my mind, in my way I loved and admired both, with my whole heart. Miss Bourdon, you know this story before I tell it, one of the oldest stories the world has to tell.

"We remained a fortnight. Then I had to go back to New York. It was August, and we were to be married in October. He returned with me, stayed a week with his adopted uncle, then returned to Boston, so he said. One week later, while I was busily furnishing the pretty house I had hired for my little Lucy, came a letter from Lucy's mother. I see at this moment, Mrs. Laurence, the sunny, busy street at which I sat stupidly staring, for hours after I read that letter. I hear the shouts of the children at play, the hot, white quiver of the blazing August noon-day.

"Lucy had gone, run away from home with a young man, nobody knew who for certain, but everybody thought with the young gentleman I had brought there, Mr. Thorndyke. I had trusted her, Mrs. Laurence, as I tell you I had loved and trusted them both entirely. I sat there stupefied, I need not tell you what I suffered. Next day I went down to the village. Her mother was nearly crazed, the whole village was

43

gossiping the shameful story. He—or some one like him, had been seen haunting the outskirts of the village, she had stolen, evening after evening, to some secret tryst.

"She had left a note—'she couldn't marry old Liston,' she said; 'she had gone away with somebody she liked ten thousand times better. They needn't look for her. If he made her a lady she would come back of herself, if not—but it was no use their looking for her. Tell Mr. Liston she was sorry, and she hoped mother wouldn't make a fuss, and she was her affectionate daughter, Lucy.'

"I sat and read the curiously heartless words, and I knew just as well as if she had said so, that it was with young Laurence she had gone. I knew, too, for the first time, how altogether heartless, base, and worthless was this girl. But there was nothing to be said or done. I went back to New York, to my old life, in a stupid, plodding sort of way. I said nothing to Mr. Darcy. I sold off the pretty furniture. I waited for young Mr. Laurence to return; he did return at Christmas—handsome, high-spirited, and dashing as ever. But he rather shrank from me, and I saw it. I went up to him on the night of his arrival, and calmly asked him the question:

"'Mr. Laurence, what have you done with Lucy West?

"He turned red to his temples, he wasn't too old or too hardened to blush then, but he denied everything. Lying,—cold, barefaced lying, is one of Mr. Thorndyke's principal accomplishments.

"'He knew nothing of Lucy West—how dared I insinuate such a thing.' Straightening himself up haughtily. 'If she had run away from me, with some younger, better looking fellow, it was only what I might have expected. But fools of forty will never be wise;' and then, with a sneering laugh, and his hands in his pockets, my young pasha strolls away, and we spoke of Lucy West no more.

"That was five years ago. One winter night, a year after, walking up Grand street about ten o'clock, three young women came laughing and talking loudly towards me. It needed no second look at their painted faces, their tawdry silks, and gaudy 'jewelry,' to tell what they were. But one face—ah! I had seen it last fresh and innocent, down among the peaceful fields. Our eyes met; the loud laugh, the loud words, seemed to freeze on her lips—she grew white under all the paint she wore. She turned like a flash and tried to run—I followed and caught her in five seconds. I grasped her arm and held her fast, savagely, I suppose, for she trembled as she looked at me.

"'Let me go, Mr. Liston,' she said, in a shaking voice; 'you hurt me!'

"'No, by Heaven,' I said, 'not until you answer me half a dozen questions. The first is: 'Was it Laurence Thorndyke with whom you ran away?'

"Her eyes flashed fire, the color came back to her face, her hands clenched. She burst forth into such a torrent of words, choked with rage, interlarded with oaths, that my blood ran cold, that my passion cooled before it. She had been inveigled away by Thorndyke, there was no sham marriage here—no promise of marriage even; I will do him that justice, and in six months, friendless and penniless, she was adrift in the streets of New York. She was looking for him night and day, if ever she met him she would tear the very eyes out of his head!

"Would she go home? I asked her. I would pay her way—her mother would receive and pardon her.

"She laughed in my face. What! take *my* money—of all men! go back to the village where once she had queened it over all the girls—like this! She broke from me, and her shrill, mocking laugh came back as she ran and joined her companions. I have never seen her since.

"That is my story, Miss Bourdon. Two years have passed since that night—my dull life goes on—I serve Mr. Darcy—I watch Mr. Thorndyke. I have come to his aid more than once, I have screened his evil deeds from his uncle as I have screened this. He is to be married the first week of December to Miss Helen Holmes, a beautiful girl and an heiress. The last duty I am to perform for him is to hush up this story of yours, to restore you to your friends like a bale of damaged goods. But I think his time has come; I think it should be our turn now. It is for you and me to say whether he shall inherit his uncle's fortune—whether he shall marry Helen Holmes or not."

---

# CHAPTER XIV.

### A DARK COMPACT.

he twilight had deepened almost into darkness. Mr. Liston unconsciously, in the excitement of the tragedy of his life, told now for the first time, had risen, and was walking up and down the room. His quiet voice, never rising above its usual monotonous level, was yet full of suppressed feeling and passion. Now, as he ceased, he looked toward the still figure sitting so motionless before the smouldering fire. She had not stirred once, the fixed whiteness of her face had not altered. The large, luminous eyes looked into the dying redness in the grate, the lips were set in one tense tight line. Until last night she had been but a child, the veriest child in the tragic drama of life, the sin and shame, the utter misery of the world to her a sealed book. All at once the black, bitter page had opened, she was one of the lost herself, love, truth, honor—there were none on earth. A loathing of herself, of him, of life, filled her—an unspeakable bitterness weighed her down body and soul.

"You do not speak, Miss Bourdon," Mr. Liston said, uneasily. "You—you have not fallen asleep?"

"Asleep!" she laughed a little, strangely sounding laugh. "Not likely, Mr. Liston; I have been listening to your story—not a pleasant story to listen to or to tell. I am sorry for you, I am sorry for her. Our stories are strangely alike—we have both thrown over good and loyal men to become a villain's victim. We have no one to thank but ourselves. More or less, we both richly deserve our fate."

There was a hard, reckless bitterness in the words, in the tone. She had not shed a tear since the blow had fallen.

Mr. Liston paused in his walk and strove to read her face.

"Both?" he said. "No, Miss Bourdon. She, perhaps, but you do not. You believed yourself his wife, in all honor and truth; to you no stain of guilt attaches. But all the blacker is his dastardly betrayal of you. Without even the excuse of loving you, he forced you from home, only to gratify his brutal malice against Richard Gilbert. He told me so himself; out of his own mouth he stands condemned."

She shivered suddenly, she shrank as though he had struck her. From first to last she had been fooled; that was, perhaps, the cruelest, sharpest blow of all, to know that Laurence Thorndyke had never for one poor instant loved her, that hatred, not love, had been at the bottom of it all.

"Don't let us speak of it," she said, hoarsely. "I—I can't bear it. O Heaven! what have I done?"

She covered her face with her hands, a dry, shuddering sob shaking her from head to foot.

"If I could only die," she thought, with a pang of horrible agony and fear; "If I dared only die!"

"Listen to me, Mrs. Laurence," Mr. Liston said, steadily, and as if he read her thoughts. "Don't despair; you have something to live for yet."

"Something to live for?" she repeated, in the same stifled tones. "What?"

"Revenge."

"What?"

"Revenge upon Laurence Thorndyke. It is your right and your duty. His evil deeds have been hidden from the light long enough. Let his day of retribution come—from your hand let his doom fall."

She looked up. In the deepening dusk the man's face was set stern as stone.

"From my hand? How?"

"By simply telling the truth. Come with me to New York; come with me before Hugh Darcy and Helen Holmes, and tell your story as it stands. My word for it, there will be neither wedding nor fortune in store for Laurence Thorndyke after that."

Her black eyes lit and flashed for a moment with some of his own vengeful fire. She drew her breath hard.

"You think this?" she said.

"I know this. Stern, rigorous justice to all men is Hugh Darcy's motto. And Miss Holmes is as proud, and pure, and womanly as she is rich and beautiful. She would cast him off, though they stood at the altar."

Her lips set themselves tighter in that tense line. She sat staring steadfastly into the fire, her breast rising and falling with the tumult within.

The little clock on the mantel ticked fast and loud; the ceaseless patter, patter of the autumnal rain tapped like ghostly fingers on the pane. Down on the shore below the long, sullen breakers boomed. The man's heart beat as he waited. He had looked forward to some such hour as this, for five long years, to plot and plan his enemy's ruin. And in this girl's hands it lay to-night.

At last.

"She loves him, does she not?" She asked the question huskily.

"Do you mean Miss Holmes? Only too well, I fear, Mrs. Laurence. As I have said, it comes easily to all of you to lose your hearts to Mr. Thorndyke."

She never heeded the savage sarcasm of his tone. A tumult of temptation was warring within her.

"And she is young and gentle, and pure and good?" she went on.

"All that and more. A beautiful and gracious lady as ever drew breath."

"And I am not his wife. And you tell me she loves and trusts him. Yes! it is easy to do that! If she casts him off she will break her own heart. She at least has never wronged me—why should her life be blighted as mine and Lucy West's have been? Mr. Liston, as much as I ever loved Laurence Thorndyke, I think I hate him to-night—" her black eyes flamed up in the dusk. "I want to be revenged upon him—I will be revenged upon him, but not that way."

"Madam, I don't know what you mean."

"I mean this, Mr. Liston—and it is of no use your growing angry—I will not stab Laurence Thorndyke through the innocent girl who loves him. I have fallen very low, but not quite low enough for that. Let her marry him—I shall not lift a finger—speak a word to prevent it. She at least has never wronged me."

"No, she has never wronged you, but do you think you can do her a greater wrong than by letting her become the wife of a heartless scoundrel and libertine? I thought better of you, Miss Bourdon. Laurence Thorndyke is to escape, then, after all?"

Her eyes flashed—literally flashed in the firelight.

"No! So surely as we both live he shall not escape. But not in that way shall he be punished."

45

"Then, how——"

"Not to-night, Mr. Liston; some other time we will talk of this. When did you say the—the wedding was to take place?"

"The first week of December. They will spend the winter South. She is a Southerner by birth, although at present residing with her guardian, Mr. Darcy, in New York. I am to understand, then, you will not prevent this marriage?"

"I will not prevent it. I have had my fool's paradise—so no doubt had Lucy West, why should not Helen Holmes?"

"Very well, then, Miss Bourdon." He spoke in his customary cold, monotonous voice. "My business this evening is almost concluded. At what hour to-morrow will it be most convenient for you to leave?"

"To leave?"

"To return to your friends in Maine. Such were Mr. Thorndyke's orders. As you have no money of your own, I presume you are aware you cannot remain here. Up to the present I am prepared to pay what is due the Misses Waddle—I am to escort you in safety to Portland. After that—'the world is all before you where to choose.' Such are my master's orders."

She rose to her feet, suppressed passion in every line of her white face, in every tone of her voice.

"The coward!" she said, almost in a whisper. "The base, base, base coward! Sir, I will never go home! I will go down to the sea yonder, and make an end of it all, but home again—never!"

"Ah, I thought not!" he said quietly. "Then, Miss Bourdon, may I ask what you mean to do? You cannot stay here."

"No, I cannot stay here," she said bitterly. "I am utterly friendless and homeless to-night. I don't know what to do."

"Let me tell you. Come to New York."

"Sir!"

"Our hatred of Laurence Thorndyke is a bond between us. You shall never be friendless nor homeless while I live. I am old enough to be your father; you may trust me, and never repent it, that I swear. See here! this is what I mean to do for you. Sit down once more."

She obeyed, looking at him in wonder and doubt.

"Helen Holmes lives with Hugh Darcy. She is as dear as a daughter to him. He is one of those old, world-worn men who love to have youth and beauty about them. She reads for him his newspaper and books of poetry and romance; he is as fond of verse and fiction as a girl in her teens. She plays the piano and sings for him—he has a passion for music. Now, can you play and sing?"

"Yes."

"Then here is my plan. He is soon to lose Miss Holmes, and some one like her in her place he must have—that he told me himself. A young girl to read aloud his pet books, to play in the long winter evenings his pet music, to sing his favorite songs, to read and write his letters—to brighten the dull old house generally by her presence—to look pretty and fair and sweet always; that is what he wants. Salary is no object with him. You will have a happy home, light and pleasant work, plenty of money. Will you take it?"

"But—"

"You will suit him exactly. You are young enough, in all conscience—pretty enough, if you will pardon my saying so, to brighten even a duller house than that. You play, you sing, you can read aloud. What more do you want? You need a home. There is a home. And"—a long pause—"who can tell what may come of it?"

She was looking up, he was looking down. Their eyes met. In the darkness they could yet look at each other long and steadily for a moment. Then hers fell.

"How old is Mr. Darcy?" she asked in a subdued voice.

"He is seventy-eight, old, feeble, and easily worked upon. I say again—who knows what may come of it? To be disinherited is the only thing in heaven or earth Laurence Thorndyke is afraid of. And old men of eighty, with stubborn minds and strong resentments, do sometimes make such strange wills."

Again there was a pause. Then Norine Bourdon spoke firmly.

"I will go with you to New York."

He drew a long breath of relief.

"I thought you would. You will not repent it, Mrs. Laurence. By-the-by, would you mind leaving that name behind you?"

She looked at him inquiringly.

"You will accompany me to New York as my niece, Jane Liston. I have a niece of that name, a widow, out in Oregon. As my niece, Mrs. Jane Liston, from the country, looking for work in the city, I will introduce you to my landlady, a most respectable woman. As my niece, Jane Liston, I will present you to Mr. Darcy. We don't want Master Laurence to see our little game. If you went as Mrs. Laurence, or Miss Kent, even, he would. He will be sure to hear the name of Miss Holmes' successor.'

"But—you have forgotten—I may meet him. That"—her lips quivering—"I could not bear."

"No danger at all. You will not go there until they are off on their wedding tour. They do not return until May. In five months, judiciously made use of, great things may happen."

She rose up, with a long, weary-worn sigh.

"I am in your hands, Mr. Liston. Friendless, moneyless, helpless, I suppose I ought to thank you for this, but—I cannot. I know it is not for my sake you are doing it, but for the sake of your revenge. Say what you like of me when we go to New York; I am ready to follow where you lead. Just now I am tired—we will not talk any more. Let us say good-night."

She gave him her hand; it was like ice. He let it fall uneasily.

"And you will not fail me?" he asked.

"I shall not fail you," she answered. In what either said, it was not necessary. They understood—revenge upon Laurence Thorndyke.

"To-morrow at twelve I will call for you here to take the train for New York. You will be ready?"

"I will be ready." The door closed behind the small white figure, and he was alone.

Alone, and he had not told her the truth, that in his opinion the marriage was legal.

"Another time," he thought; "bigamy is an ugly crime. Let us wait until he marries Miss Holmes."

# CHAPTER XV.

### "A FASHIONABLE WEDDING."

nother night had passed, another day had come. At twelve sharp Mr. Liston and a hackney carriage had come for "Mrs. Laurence." Her trunks had been packed by her own-hands. Mr. Liston had settled the claim of the Misses Waddle, and white and still she had come out, shaken hands with the kindly spinsters, entered the hack, fallen back in a corner, her hand shading her eyes, and so was driven away from the Chelsea cottage forever.

"And dead and in her shroud," said the younger Miss Waddle, melo-dramatically, "she will never look more like death than she does to-day."

She had scarcely slept the night through. That pleasant cottage chamber overlooking the sea was haunted for her, full of memories that nearly maddened her to-night. With all her heart she had loved—with all her soul she had trusted. She stood here in the darkness, forsaken, deceived. She hardly knew whether it were passionate love still, or passionate hatred that filled her now. The boundary line between strong love and strong hate is but narrow at the best. A tumult that was agony filled heart and brain. He had never cared for her; never, never! Out of pure revenge upon Richard Gilbert he had mocked her with the farce of love—mocked her from first to last, and wearied of her before one poor week had ended.

"Lightly won, lightly lost," man's motto always, never more true than in her case. Without one pang he had cast her off contemptuously, glad to be rid of her, and had sent his uncle's servant to take her back to the home she had disgraced, the hearts she had broken. She clenched her hands—in the darkness she was walking up and down her room, and hoarse, broken murmurs of a woman scorned and outraged came from her lips. She could picture him even at this hour seated by the side of the girl he was so soon to marry, his arm encircling her, his eyes looking love into hers, his lips murmuring the old false vows, sealing them with the old false caresses. Face downward she flung herself upon the bed at last, wild with the remorse, the despair of her own thoughts.

"Oh," she cried; "I cannot bear it! I cannot, I cannot."

The darkness wrapped her, the deep silence of the night was around her. Up stairs the Misses Waddle slept their vestal beauty sleep, commonplace and content. A month ago she had pitied their dull, loveless, plodding lives. Ah, Heaven! to be free from this torturing pain at her heart, and able to sleep like them now. But even to her sleep came at last, the spent sleep of utter exhaustion.

The morning sun was shining brightly when she awoke. She got up feeling chilled and stiff, worn and grown old. Mechanically she bathed and breakfasted—Miss Waddle the younger gazing askance at her white cheeks and lustreless eyes. Mechanically she returned to her room, and began packing her trunks. And then, this done, she sat with folded hands by the window, looking out upon the sparkling sea, until noon and Mr. Liston should come. Her mind was a blank; the very intensity of the blow benumbed pain. Last night she had lain yonder, and writhed in her torture; to-day she felt almost apathetic—indifferent to past, present, and future. And so, pale and cold, and still, Mr. Liston had found her, so she had shaken hands, and said good-by to the Misses Waddle, and so she had been driven away from her "honeymoon paradise" to begin her life anew.

They reached New York. If Mr. Liston had indeed been the fondest of uncles, he could not have been more affectionately solicitous for the welfare and comfort of his charge. She was indifferent to it all—unconscious of it indeed, looking upon all things with dull, half-sightless eyes.

"Take good care of her, Mrs. Wilkins," he said to his landlady; "she is ailing, as you can see, and don't let her be disturbed or annoyed in my absence. She has had trouble lately, and is not like herself."

It was a shabby-genteel boarding-house, in a shabby-genteel street, close upon East Broadway. At first "Mrs. Liston" had her meals served in her room, and spent her time, for all Mrs. Wilkins could see, in sitting at the window, with idly-lying hands, gazing out into the dull street. Mr. Liston was absent the chief part of the day, and Mrs. Liston steadfastly kept her room; but in the evenings, always closely veiled, Mrs. Wilkins observed he could prevail upon her to go out with him for a walk. He was kind to her, the girl vaguely felt—she would obey him, at least; and, since she could not die and make an end of it all, why, she might as well take a little exercise for her health's sake. He was very good to her, but she felt no gratitude—it was not for her sake, but for the sake of the grudge he owed their mutual foe. Their mutual foe! Did she hate Laurence Thorndyke she wondered. There were times when her very soul grew sick with longing for the sight of his face, the tone of his voice, the touch of his hand, and the sound of his name from Mr. Liston's lips had power to thrill her to the inmost heart still.

Gradually, as the weeks passed, matters changed.

"Time, that blunts the edge of things, Dries our tears and spoils our bliss,"

was quietly at work for Norine. She came down to the public table, and the pale, spirituelle beauty of the invisible and mysterious Mrs. Liston caused a profound sensation among the boarders. Next, she took to spending the long afternoons in the dingy boarding-house parlor, playing upon the jingling, toneless boarding-house piano such melodies of mournful sweetness that Mrs. Wilkins and her handmaidens of the kitchen paused in their work, to listen, and wonder, and admire.

"That young woman has seen trouble," Mrs. Wilkins said, shaking her head. She had her own opinion—a pretty correct one—of what nature that trouble was; but her beauty and her youth were there to plead for her. She was a lady to her finger-tips, that was evident; and—most potent reason of all with Mrs. Wilkins—Mr. Liston had been her boarder and friend for the past ten years.

So December came.

How the time had gone Norine could hardly have told—it did go somehow, that was all. Trouble, remorse, despair, do not kill; she was still alive and tolerably well, could eat and sleep, play the old tunes, even sometimes sing the old songs. She looked at herself in a sort of dreary wonder in the glass. The face she saw a little paler than of old, was fair and youthful still—the bright hair glossy and abundant as ever. She had read of people whose hair turned gray with trouble; hers had passed and left no sign, only on the lips that had forgotten to smile, the eyes that never lit into gladness or hope, and the heart that lay like lead in her bosom.

The crisp, frosty December days seemed to fly, bringing with them his wedding-day. Every hour now the old agony of that night in the Chelsea cottage came back to stab her through. The seventh of December was the day—could she bear it?—and it was in her power even yet, Mr. Liston told her, to prevent it. Twice during the last fortnight she had seen him, the first time, when, closely veiled, her dress had brushed him on Broadway. He was advancing with another gentleman, both were smoking, both were laughing gayly at some good story Thorndyke seemed to be telling. Handsome, elegant, well-dressed, nonchalant, he passed her, actually turning to glance after the graceful figure and veiled face.

"That figure should belong to a pretty girl," she had heard him say. "Deuce take the veils, what do they wear 'em for. There—there's something oddly familiar about her, too."

She had turned sick and faint, she leaned against a store window for a moment, the busy street going round and round. So they had met and parted again.

The second time it was almost worse. Mr. Liston had taken her to the opera—in her passionate love of music she could forget, for a few brief hours, her pain, when, coming out, in the crush, they had come almost face to face. His bride elect was on his arm, by instinct she knew it, a tall, stylish girl, in sweeping draperies, with blonde hair, blue eyes, and a skin like pearl. He was bending his tall head over her, devotedly; both looked brilliantly handsome and happy.

"For Heaven's sake, come this way!" Liston had cried, and drawn her with him hurriedly in another direction. She had been literally unable to move, standing, white and wild, gazing upon him. Presently came the fateful wedding day. All the night preceding she lay awake, the old tempest of feeling going on within her.

Should she denounce him, or should she not, on his wedding-day? Should she take his bride from him at the very altar, and proclaim him to the world as the liar and betrayer he was, or should she wait? She could not decide. When morning came her mind was in as utter a tumult as ever.

"Have you decided?" Mr. Liston asked her. "Shall Laurence Thorndyke leave his uncle's house to-day, with his bride by his side, or as an outcast and a pauper, scorned by all? It is for you to say."

"I don't know," she answered, hoarsely. "Take me to the church—I will decide there."

He had taken her, led her in, placed her in one of the pews, and left her. His manifold duties kept him with Mr. Darcy; he would be unable to join Norine again that day.

The church filled; an hour before the ceremony it was crowded. Then they came; the bridegroom a trifle pale and nervous, as bridegrooms are wont to be, but, as usual, handsome of face and elegant of attire. Then on her guardian's arm, the bride, a dazzling vision of white satin, Honiton lace, pearl, orange blossoms, gold hair, and tender drooping face. A breathless hush fills the church—in that hush the officiating clergyman came forth—in that hush the bridal party take their places, a flock of white bridesmaids, a group of black gentlemen. And then a voice out of that great stillness speaks.

"If any here know of just cause or impediment why these two should not be joined in the bonds of matrimony, let him speak now, or forever hold his peace."

Mr. Liston turns his quiet face and watchful eyes to one particular pew, to one slender figure and veiled face. The five seconds that follow are as five centuries to the bridegroom. His face is quite white, his gloved fingers are like ice. He glances up at Liston, and then—the ceremony begins. What a horrible time it takes, Laurence Thorndyke thinks; what a horrible ordeal a fashionable public marriage is. Does a dingy hotel parlor rise before him, the rain beating on the windows, and a pale, wistful face look up at him, while a mockery of this solemn rite is being gabbled through by a tipsy actor? Is it the fair, happy, downcast face of his bride he sees or that other face as he saw it last, all white and drawn in the anguish of a last farewell?

"What God hath joined together let no man put asunder!"

It is over. He draws a long, hard breath of relief. Come what may, Helen is his wife.

They rise; they file slowly and gracefully out of the church; the bride hanging on the bridegroom's arm. Closely, very closely, they pass one particular pew wherein a solitary figure stands. She has risen with the rest; she has flung back her veil, and people who glance at her stop involuntarily and look again. The face is like stone, the dark eyes all wild and wide, the lips apart; she stands as if slowly petrifying. But the bridal party do not see her; they pass on, and out.

"Who is she?" strangers whisper. "Has she known Laurence Thorndyke?"

Then they too, go, and all is over.

The wedding party enter their carriages and are whirled away. Mr Liston sees his employer safely off, then returns hurriedly to the church. He is angry with Norine, but it is his duty to look after her, and something in her face to-day has made him afraid. There is nothing to fear, however; she is very quiet now; she sunk down upon her knees, her head has fallen forward upon the rail. He speaks to her; she does not answer. He touches her on the shoulder; she does not look up. He lifts her head—yes, it is as he feared. The edifice is almost deserted now; he takes her in his arms and carries her out into the air. For the second time in her life she has fainted entirely away.

---

# CHAPTER XVI.

### "HIS NAME IS LAURENCE THORNDYKE."

gray March afternoon is blustering itself out in the streets of New York—a slate-colored sky, fast drifting with black, rainy clouds; the wind sobs and shivers in great dusty soughs, and pedestrians bow involuntarily before it, and speed along with winking and watery eyes.

In a quiet, old-fashioned street—for there are quiet, old-fashioned streets even in New York—there stands a big, square, dingy, red brick house, set in a square of grass-grown front garden, a square of brick paving in the rear. Two slim poplars—"old maids of the forest," lift their tall, prim green heads on either side of the heavy hall door. The house looks comfortable, but gloomy, and that is precisely what it is, this dun-colored spring day, comfortable, but gloomy. There are heavy curtains of dark, rich damask draping the windows. Through the clear panes of one of the upper windows you catch the flicker and fall of a red coal fire, and the sombre beauty of a girl's face.

She stands in the large, handsome room, alone, a long, low room, with a carpet of rich, dull crimson velvet, curtains of dull crimson satin damask, papered walls, dull crimson, too. There are oil paintings in gilded frames, ponderous mahogany chairs, tables and footstools; but there is nothing bright in the apartment save the cheerful red fire. It is all dark and oppressive—not even excepting the girl. The pale face that looks gloomily out at the fast drifting sky, at the fast-fading light, is smileless and sober as all the rest. And yet it is a youthful face, a beautiful face, a face that six months ago bloomed with a childish brightness and bloom, the face of Norine Bourdon.

It is close upon four months since she entered this house, as companion, secretary, amanuensis, to Mr. Hugh Darcy. Now she stands here debating within herself whether she shall go to him to-night and tell him she must leave. She shrinks from the task. She has grown strangely old and wise in these four months; she knows something of the world—something of what it must be like to be adrift in New York, friendless and penniless, with only eighteen years and a fair face for one's dangerous dower. Friendless she will be; for in leaving she will deeply irritate Mr. Darcy, deeply anger Mr. Liston, and in all the world, it seems to Norine, there are only those two she can call friends.

And yet—friends! Can she call even them by that name? Mr. Liston is her friend and protector so long as he thinks she will aid him in his vengeance upon his enemy. Mr. Darcy—well, how long will Mr. Darcy be her friend when he discovers how she has imposed upon him? That under a false name and history she has sought the shelter of his roof—she, the cast-off of his nephew? He likes her well—that she knows; he trusts her, respects her—how much liking or respect will remain when he knows her as she is?

"And know he shall," she says, inwardly, her lips compressed. "I cannot carry on this deception longer. For the rest I would have to leave in any case—*they* return in May, and I cannot, I cannot meet them. Mr. Liston may say what he pleases, it were easier to die than to stay on and meet him again—like that."

She has not forgotten. Such first, passionate love as she gave Laurence Thorndyke is not to be outlived and trampled out in four months; and yet it is much more abhorrence than love that fills her heart with bitterness now.

"The dastard!" she thinks, her black eyes gleaming dangerously; "the coward! How dare he do it! One day or other he shall pay for it, that I swear; but I cannot meet him now. There is nothing for it but to go and tell Mr. Darcy I must leave, and take my chance in the world, quite alone."

She leaned her forehead against the cold, clear glass with a heavy heart-sick sigh. The first keen poignancy of her pain was over, but the dull, deadly sickening ache was there still, and would be for many a day. Hate him she might, long for retaliation she did, but not once could she think of him the happy husband of Helen Holmes without the very heart within her growing faint with deadly jealousy. The sound of his name, the sight of his letters, had power to move her to this day. In the drawing-room below a carefully-painted portrait of the handsome face, the bright blue eyes, the fair, waving hair, hung—a portrait so true, that it was torture only to took at it, and yet how many hours had she not stood before it, her heart full of bitterness—until burning tears filled and blinded her dark impassioned eyes.

Now he and his bride were coming home to this house, and she was expected to stay here and meet them. Expected by Mr. Darcy, who had learned to love her almost as a daughter; expected by Mr. Liston, who had told her she must confront Laurence Thorndyke in this very house, and show him to uncle and wife as he really was—a coward, a liar, a seducer.

"I cannot do it!" she said, her hands clenching together. "I cannot meet him. *Mon Dieu*, no! not yet—not yet."

She had been introduced into the house just two weeks after the marriage as "my niece from the country—Jane Liston." As Jane Liston she had remained here ever since, winning "golden opinions" from all the household. She had found Mr. Darcy a decrepit, irritable old invalid, bored nearly to death since his ward's wedding—lonely, peevish, sick. He had looked once into the pale, lovely face, and never needed to look again to like her. Trouble and tears had not marred her beauty. A little of the bloom—there never had been much—all of the sparkle, the gay brilliance that had charmed Richard Gilbert were gone; but the eighteen-year-old face was very sweet, very lovely, the dark Canadian eyes, with their unutterable sadness and pathos, wonderfully captivating; and old Hugh Darcy, with a passion for all things fair and young, had become her captive at once.

"You suit me fifty times better than Helen," he said often, drawing the dark loops of shining hair fondly through his old fingers. "Helen was a rattle pate. Never mind—matrimony will tame her down, though the lad's fond of her enough, and will make her a very good sort of husband, I dare say, as husbands go. But you, little woman, with your soft voice—you have a voice like an Æolian harp Jennie, your deft fingers, your apt ways—you are a treasure to a cross old bachelor. You are a nurse born, Jennie, child; how did I ever get along all these years without you?"

He meant it, every word, and a moonlight sort of smile, sweet and grateful, if very sad, thanked him. Once she had lifted his hand to her lips and kissed it, passionate tears filling her eyes.

"I a treasure! Oh, Mr. Darcy! You do not know what you say. I am a wretch—a wretch unworthy of your kindness and trust. But one day I shall tell you all."

He had wondered a little what she meant. "Tell him all!" What could the child have to tell? She was so young—so pathetically young to be widowed—what story lay in her life? The very oldest of all old stories, no doubt—a beloved one lost. He sighed as he thought it, bald-headed, hoary patriarch that he was. *He* had had his story and his day. The day had ended, the story was read, the book closed and put away, years and years and years ago. In the gallant and golden days of his youth he had met and loved a girl, and been (as he believed, as she told him,) loved in return. He left her to make a home and a competence—he was no millionaire in those far-off days, save in happiness—to return in a year and marry her. Eight months after there came to him his letters, his picture, his ring. A richer knight had entered the lists, and the lady was borne off no unwilling captive. A commonplace, every-day story—nothing new at all.

He took his punishment like a man, in brave silence, and the world went on, and years and riches and honors came, and a man's life was spoiled forever, that was all. As he recalls it, old, white haired, half paralyzed, now in the twilight of seventy odd years, he can remember with curious vividness how brightly the July sun shone down on the hot white pavement of the streets below, the cries of the children at play, the quivering glare of the blazing noontide, as he sat in his office and read the words that renounced him. Twenty-seven years ago, but the picture was engraven on Hugh Darcy's brain, never to be blotted out. Twenty-seven years ago, and when the fortunate rival had fallen in the battle of life, ten years later; when his feeble-souled wife had followed him to the grave, Hugh Darcy's revenge upon her had been to step forward and take the child of that marriage to his heart and home to rear him as his own son, to make his will in his favor, leaving him sole heir to a noble inheritance.

Laurence Thorndyke had sown his wild oats. Well, most young men go in for that kind of agriculture, and the seed sown had not yet begun to crop up. He was happily married, and done for, and for himself Mr. Darcy meant to keep his little "Jennie" with him always, to travel about with her this coming summer, and leave her a handsome portion at his death. "For of course," said Mr. Darcy, "she will forget the husband she has lost, and make some good man happy after I am gone."

He had settled her little romance quite to suit himself. She had crept with her quiet, gentle, womanly ways into his inmost heart—a very kindly heart in spite of life's wear and tear; very kindly, yet with a stubborn sense of justice, and of right and wrong underlying all. Kindly, yet terribly, obstinately, unforgiving to anything like immorality, deception or dishonor.

"I love the child almost better than Helen," he thought sometimes. "I don't want to lose her, and yet I should like to see her safely sheltered under a husband's wing before I go. There's Richard Gilbert now. I've often meant to introduce him to her, but somehow she always slips out of the room and the house when he sends up his card. I wonder if he's got over the loss of that girl last fall. Some men do get over that sort of thing they say. I hope Laurence had nothing to do with it. Gilbert suspected him, I know, but then—'give a dog a bad name and hang him.' Yes, my little Jennie wouldn't make half a bad wife for Dick Gilbert. I'll introduce him the very next time he comes."

Mr. Darcy sits before his study fire this chill afternoon alone. Liston left some hours ago. It is not yet dinner time, and his companion—where is she? He looks impatiently around—while he took his afternoon nap she has left him. He listens a moment to the wailing voice of the wind, sobbing in a melancholy way about the house, then reaches forth nervously, and rings the bell.

"Send Mrs. Liston here," he says to the servant who answers.

This gray twilight hour is haunted for him, with melancholy flitting faces, dead and gone. He will have Mrs. Liston in to sing and play and exorcise the ghosts. Nobody ever sang Scotch songs or played Scotch melodies half so sweetly, thinks the worn old man, as his little companion.

The door opens and she enters. Her tread, her touch, her garments, are always soft and noiseless. She comes gliding forward in the gloaming, not unlike a ghost herself. Her pale face seems almost startlingly pale in contrast with the black dress she wears. In its whiteness her great dusk eyes look bigger and blacker than ever. It strikes Mr. Darcy.

"Child," he says, "how pale you are. Come over here and let me look at you. You are more like a spirit of the twilight than a young lady of the period."

He draws her affectionately to him, and she sinks on her knees by his chair. There is no light but the dull glow of the fire; he tilts up her chin, and gazes smilingly down into the lovely sombre eyes.

"'Oh, fair, pale Margaret,'" he quotes. "Little one, what is it? You promised to tell me sometime. Why not to-night?"

"Why not to-night?" she repeats. "To-night be it, then. But first, is that a letter on the table?"

"Oh, by-the-by, yes—I nearly forgot all about it. Another letter from our mated turtle doves in Florida. I see by the postmark they are in Florida now. I have kept it for you to read, as usual."

She takes it quite calmly; she knows that big, bold chirography well, and the day comes back to her when Mr. Liston brought to the Chelsea cottage the brief, pitiless note in the same hand—her death warrant. She seats herself on a hassock near the big invalid chair, and by the light of the fire reads Laurence Thorndyke's letter.

It is the gay letter of a happy bridegroom whose bride bends over his shoulder smiling while he writes. He tells of their travels, of how well and handsome Helen is looking; that in another month for certain they will be at home. And with best love and all the kisses he can spare from Nella, he is, as ever, his affectionate nephew, Laurence Thorndyke.

She finished the letter and laid it down.

"Coming home," Mr. Darcy repeats. "Well, I am always glad to see the boy, always fond of Nella. And we will all go to Europe together in May—you to take care of the old man, my dear, and help him laugh at the turtle doves billing and cooing. And in sunny France, in fair Italy, we will see if we cannot bring back roses to these white cheeks."

The dark eyes lift, the grave young voice speaks.

"Thank you," she says. "You are always kind, Mr. Darcy, but I cannot go."

"Jennie! Cannot go?"

"I cannot go Mr. Darcy. I am sorry to leave you, more sorry than I can say, but you must get another attendant and companion. I am going away."

"Mrs. Liston?"

"I am not Mrs. Liston—my name is not Jennie—I am not Mr. Liston's niece. From first to last I have deceived you. I have come to tell you the truth to-night, although it breaks my heart to see you angry. I will tell you the truth, and then you will see that I must go. My name is not Jane Liston. It is Norine Bourdon."

There is a pause. He sits looking at her, astonishment, anger, perplexity, doubt all in his face, and yet he sees that she is telling the truth. And Norine Bourdon—where has he heard that name before? Norine Bourdon! A foreign-sounding and uncommon name, too. Where has he heard it?

"I do not wish you to blame Mr. Liston too much," the quiet voice goes on. "He is to blame, for he suggested the fraud, but I was ready enough to close with it. I had not a friend nor a home in the world that I dared turn to, and I could not face life alone. So I came here under a false name, false in everything, and broke your bread, and took your money, and deceived you. I am not what you think me; I am a girl who has been lured from her home, deceived and cast off. A wicked wretch who fled from her friends, who betrayed a good man's trust, who promised to marry him, and who ran away from him with one who betrayed her in turn. You have heard of me before—heard from Richard Gilbert of Norine Bourdon."

A faint exclamation comes from his lips.

Yes, yes, yes, he sees it all. This is *that* girl—"Norine Bourdon!" He remembers the odd French name well now.

"I will tell you my story, Mr. Darcy—my wicked and shameful story, and you shall turn me out this very night if you choose. I am the girl your friend, Richard Gilbert, honored with his respect and love; whom he asked in marriage. I loved another man, a younger, handsomer man, but he had left me, forever, I thought, and wearied of my dull country life, sad and disappointed, I accepted him. The man I loved hated Mr. Gilbert. Liston will tell you why, if you ask him. In that hatred he laid a plan of revenge. He cared nothing for me; he was betrothed to a beautiful and wealthy lady; I was but the poor little fool to whom a wise man had given his heart—what became of me did not matter. Three days before my wedding-day he came to me and urged me to fly with him. He loved me, he said; he would make me his wife; he would come for my answer the next night. I must meet him; I must go with him. At night, when they all slept, I stole from the house to meet him; not to fly with him, the good God knows—to refuse him, to forget him, to keep to my duty if my heart broke in the keeping. He had a horse and carriage waiting, and—to this day I hardly know how—he made me enter it, and drove me off. I cried out for help; it was too late; no one heard me. He soothed me with his specious promises, and perhaps I was not difficult to soothe. It was too late to go back; I thought he loved me and went on. He took me to Boston. There, next morning in the hotel, without witnesses, we were married. A man, a clergyman, he told me, came, a ceremony of some sort was gone through, we were pronounced man and wife.

"He took me with him to a cottage he had engaged by the sea shore. For three weeks he remained with me there, tired to death of me, I know now. Then he was summoned to New York to his home, and I was left. Mr. Darcy, he never came back.

"I waited for him weeks and weeks—ah, dear Heaven! what weeks those were. Then the truth was told me. His uncle's servant was in his confidence. I was deserted. I had never been his wife, not for one hour. The man who had come to the hotel was no clergyman; he was going to be married in December; I was to go back to my friends and trouble him no more. That was my fate. I had been betrayed from first to last, and he had done with me forever.

"Well, that is more than six months ago. I don't know whether hearts ever break except in books. I know I am living still, and likely to live. But not here. I have deceived you, Mr. Darcy; but I tell you the truth to-night. And to-night, if you like, I will go."

He rose slowly to his feet; swift, dark passion in his eyes—swift, heavy anger knitting his shaggy brows. He held to the arms of his chair and looked down upon her, his face set hard as iron.

"Sit there!" he ordered. "Tell me the scoundrel's name."

The dark eyes looked up at him; the gravely quiet voice spoke.

"His name is Laurence Thorndyke."

---

# CHAPTER XVII.

### A LETTER FROM PARIS.

t is a sunny summer afternoon. The New York pavements are blistering in the heat, and even Broadway looks half deserted. Up-town, brown stone mansions are hermetically sealed for the season, the "salt of the earth" are drinking the waters at Saratoga, gazing at the trembling rapids of Niagara, or disporting themselves on the beach at Long Branch. The workers of the earth still burrow in their city holes, through heat, and dust, and din, and glare, and among them Richard Gilbert.

He sits alone this stifling August afternoon, in his down-town office. The green shades that do their best to keep out the white blinding glare and fail, are closed. The windows stand wide, but no grateful breeze steals in. He sits at his desk in a loose linen coat, multitudinous documents labelled, scattered, and tied up before him. But it is a document that does not look legal, that is absorbing his attention. It is a letter, and the envelope, lying beside him on the floor, bears the French postmark. He sits and re-reads with a very grave and thoughtful face. "It is queer," he is thinking, "uncommonly queer. She must be an adventuress, and a clever one. Of course she has wheedled him into making a new will, and the lion's share will go to herself. Hum! I wonder what Thorndyke will say. Come in."

He pushes the paper away, and answers a discreet tap at the door.

"Lady and gentleman to see you, sir," announces a clerk and the lady and gentleman enter.

"Hope we don't disturb you, squire," says the gentleman, and Mr. Gilbert rises suddenly to his feet. "Me and Hetty, we thought as how it would keinder look bad to go back without droppin' in. Hot day, squire—now ain't it?"

"My dear Miss Kent—my dear Uncle Reuben, this is an unlooked-for pleasure. You in the city, and in the blazing month of August. What tempted you?"

"Well, now, blamed if I know. Only Hetty here, she's bin sorter ailin' lately, and old Dr. Perkins, he said a change would do her a heap of good, and Hetty, she'd never seen New York, and so—that's about it. Squire! we've had a letter."

He says it abruptly, staring very hard straight before him. Aunt Hetty fidgets in her chair, and Richard Gilbert's pale, worn face grows perhaps a shade paler.

"A letter," he repeats; "from *her*?"

"From her. Two letters, if it comes to that. One from this here town last Christmas—t'other from foreign parts a week ago. I want to show 'em to you. Here's number one."

He takes a letter in an envelope from his pocket, and hands it to the lawyer. It seems almost a lifetime ago, but the thrill that goes through Richard Gilbert at sight of that writing still!

"Last Christmas," he says glancing at the postmark, a shade of reproach in his tone. "And you never told me!"

"I never told you, squire. It ain't a pleasant sort of thing to talk about, least of all to you. She doesn't deserve a thought from you, Mr. Gilbert—"

The lawyer stopped him with a gesture.

"I have forgiven her long ago," he answers; "she did not care for me. Better she should fly from me before marriage than after. Thank Heaven she is alive to write at all."

He opens the note. It is very short.

"Dear Aunt Hetty—Dear Uncle Reuben—Dear Uncle Joe—if you will let me, unworthy as I am, still call you by the dear old names. This is the third time I have written since I left home, but I have reason to think you never received the first two letters. I wrote then, as I write now, to beg you on my knees for forgiveness. Oh, to see your dear faces once more—to look again on the peaceful old home. But it cannot be. What shall I say of myself? I am well—I am busy—I am as happy as I deserve, or can ever expect to be. I am safely sheltered in a good man's house. I have been to blame, but oh, not so much as you think. Some day I will come to you and tell you all. Yours,

"Norine.

"P. S.—*He* is well. I have seen him since I came to New York twice, though he has not seen me. May the good God bless him and forgive me.

"N. K. B."

Richard Gilbert read that postscript and turned away his head. He had been near her, then, twice, and had never known it. And she cared for him enough to pray for him still.

"Here's the other," said Reuben Kent; "that came a week ago."

He laid a large, foreign-looking letter on the desk, with many stamps, and an Italian postmark.

"From Florence," the lawyer said; "how can she have got there?"

It was as short as the first.

"She was well. Foreign travel had done wonders for her health and spirits. She was with kind friends. Impossible to say when she would return, but always, whether at home or abroad, she was their loving niece, Norine Bourdon."

That was all. Very gravely the lawyer handed them back.

"Well, squire," Mr. Kent said, "what do you think?"

"That I am unutterably glad, and thankful to know she is alive and well, and with friends who are good to her. It might have been worse—it might have been worse."

"You believe these letters, then?"

"Undoubtedly I believe them. She is travelling as companion, no doubt, to some elderly lady. Such situations crop up occasionally. I see she gives you no address to which to write."

"I don't know that I should care to write if she did. *You* may forgive her, squire, but by the Lord Harry! *I* aint got that far yet. If she didn't run away with young Thorndyke, what did she run away at all for?"

"Because she cared so little for me, that facing the world alone was easier than becoming my wife. We won't talk of it, Mr. Kent. How long do you remain in town?"

Uncle Reuben rose.

"We go to-day, thank fortin'. How you, all of you, manage to live in such a Babel beats me! Can't you strike work, Mr. Gilbert, and run down to see us this blazin' summer weather?"

Mr. Gilbert shook his head with a smile.

"I am afraid not. I am very busy; I find hard work does me good. Well, good-by, old friend. I am sincerely glad to have read those letters—sincerely glad she is safe and well."

Then they were gone, and Richard Gilbert sat down alone in the hot, dusty office. But the dusty office faded away, and in its place the rich greenness of meadows came, the sweet, new-mown hay scented the air, green trees and bright flowers surrounded him instead of dry-as-dust legal tomes. And fairer, brighter, sweeter than all, came floating back the exquisite face of Norine, the dark eyes gleaming, the white teeth sparkling, the loose hair blowing, the soft mouth laughing. And once she had promised to be his wife!

"Mr. Thorndyke, sir?"

The voice of his clerk aroused him. The fairy vision faded and fled, and Richard Gilbert, in his grimy office, looked grimly up into the face of Laurence Thorndyke.

"How do, Gilbert?" says Mr. Thorndyke, nodding easily; "hope I don't intrude. Was loafing down town, and thought I would just drop in and see if there was any news yet from the old man."

Mr. Thorndyke has lost none of the easy insouciance that sits upon him so naturally and becomingly. He is in faultless Broadway-afternoon- promenade costume, but he is not quite as good-looking as he used to be. His handsome face looks worn and tired, dissipated, and a trifle reckless, and the old flavor of wine and cigars hangs about him still. He draws a chair towards him, and sits astride upon it his arms folded over the back.

"The old man?" Mr. Gilbert repeats, still more grimly. "You refer to Mr. Darcy, I presume?"

"Who else. To Darcy, of course—and be hanged to him. Any news yet?"

"There is news, Mr. Thorndyke. Will you be kind enough, in talking of my old and valued friend,—and yours once,—to speak a little more respectfully?"

"A little more fiddle-dee-dee!" retorts Mr. Thorndyke. "Confound the old bloke, I say again! What business has he cutting up the way he *has* cut up ever since my marriage? I did everything I could to please him—I leave it to yourself, Gilbert, I did everything I could to please him. He wanted me to marry Helen. Well, haven't I married Helen? He wanted us to go with him to Europe in May. Didn't we come back from the South in April, to go with him in May as per agreement? And what do we find? Why, that the venerable muddle-head has started off on his own hook, with old Liston and some girl that he's taken in—adopted, or that bosh—a niece of Liston's. Started off without a word—without one blessed word of excuse or explanation to Helen or me. That's four months ago, and not a letter since. Then you talk of respect! By Jove, sir, I consider myself—Helen considers herself, shamefully treated. And here we are broiling alive in New York this beastly hot weather, instead of doing the White Mountains, or Newport, or somewhere else, where a man can get a breath of air, waiting for a letter that never comes. You've heard from him, you say—now what has the old duffer to say for himself?"

"He has nothing to say for himself. I have not heard from him. I said I had heard *of* him. How is Mrs. Thorndyke?"

"Well enough in health—devilish cross in temper. The old story—I'm a wretch, drink too much, gamble too much, spend too much, keep too late hours. Tell you what, Gilbert, matrimony's a fraud. Whilst I thought Nellie was the old man's pet and I was his heir, it was all well enough; blessed if I know what to think now. Are you going to tell me what you have heard *of* him?"

In silence, and with a face of contemptuous disgust, Mr. Gilbert takes up the French letter, points to a column, and watches him. This is what Mr. Thorndyke, with a face of horror, reads:

"I presume you know that your old friend and client, Hugh Darcy, died here two days ago. The bulk of his fortune, I hear, is left to the beautiful young widow, Mrs. Liston, whom he had legally adopted. She takes his name, and with her own rare loveliness, and Darcy's half million, Mrs. Liston-Darcy is destined to make no ordinary sensation when she returns to New York."

# CHAPTER XVIII.

**AFTER FOUR YEARS.**

"

riting again—eternally writing! One would think it was Mrs. Jellyby. Confound the scribbling, I say. "Do, for Heaven's sake, put it down, Nellie, and let us have some dinner!"

Thus—impatiently, angrily—Mr. Laurence Thorndyke to the wife of his bosom. It is five o'clock, of a brilliant summer afternoon, a stiflingly close and oppressive afternoon, in the shabby street, in the shabby tenement wherein Mr. and Mrs. Thorndyke dwell. The scene is a dingy parlor—ingrain carpet, cane chairs, fly-blown wall paper, and a lady in a soiled and torn wrapper discovered at a table rapidly writing. A child of two years, a little boy, with Laurence Thorndyke's own blue eyes and curling locks, toddles about the floor. In a basket cradle there is coiled up a little white ball of a baby. The lady jogs this cradle with her foot as she writes. A lady, young and handsome, though sadly faded, her profusion of light hair all towsy and uncombed, her brows knit in one straight frowning line. She pauses in her work for a second to glance up—anything but a loving glance, by the by—and to answer:

"I don't know Mrs. Jellyby, Mr. Thorndyke. Did she write to keep herself and her children from starving, I wonder, while her husband gambled and drank their substance? As to dinner—couldn't you manage to get that meal in the places you spend your days and nights? There is some bread and butter on the kitchen table—some tea on the kitchen stove. Joanna will give them to you if you like. You are not likely to find champagne and ortolans in a tenement house."

And then, the pretty lips setting themselves in a tight, unpleasant line, Mrs. Thorndyke goes back to her work.

She writes very rapidly, in a bold, firm hand, heedless of the child who prattles and clings to her skirts. They are law papers she is copying, in that clear, legible chirography.

For in three years it has come to this. Four tiny tenement rooms in a shabby, crowded street, soiled and torn wrappers, bread and tea dinners, one small grimy maid of all work, a drunkard and gambler instead of her brilliant bridegroom, and law papers to copy all day and far into the night, for the friend of her girlhood, Mr. Richard Gilbert, to "keep the wolf from the door."

"D—— your catlap?" says Mr. Thorndyke, with a scowl of disgust. "I say, Nellie, do stop that infernal scribble, scrabble, and send out for oysters. I haven't eaten a mouthful to-day—I had such a splitting headache this morning, and I haven't a sou left."

"And how many sous do you suppose *I* have left?" the wife demands with flashing eyes. "I paid the landlord the rent to-day, and I have to buy coal to-morrow. Oysters!" she laughs, scornfully. "I have forgotten what they are. As to your headache—probably if you had drank less whiskey last night, you would not have suffered so severely this morning. What there is in the house you are welcome to. I shall send for nothing."

The lips tighten still more—she goes resolutely on with her writing.

Mr. Thorndyke relieves his mind by an oath and a growl, as he flings himself heavily upon a lounge. His wife writes on and pays no attention. She has grown accustomed to be sworn at—it hardly affects her now.

He lies and watches her with gloomy eyes. Those three years have changed him deepening the reckless, dissipated look worn and aged him strangely. Handsome he is still, but haggard, the brilliant eyes dimmed and bloodshot, the hand tremulous, an habitual scowl on his brow.

"What does Gilbert pay you for that bosh?" he asked.

"About three times as much as he would pay any one else. You see he knew my father, and doesn't care to look on and see my father's daughter starve. Be kind enough not to talk to me, Mr. Thorndyke—I don't wish to make mistakes."

"Day has been when you liked to have me talk to you well enough," retorts, Mr. Thorndyke, with another sullen oath.

"Yes, I was a fool—no need to remind me of it. No one can regret it more than I do. Happily that day is past. *You* have cured me signally of my folly."

There is a pause. Mrs. Thorndyke immovably writes. Mr. Thorndyke lies sullenly and looks on. At last—

"She has come," he says, abruptly.

His wife lifts her eyes.

"Mrs Liston-Darcy—devil take her! And I am a going to see her to-night!"

Still that silent questioning gaze.

"I met Allison out there—*he* hasn't cut me if all the rest have; and she is to be at a party at his house. I am going."

"May I ask why? What can you possibly have to say to Mr. Darcy's heiress?"

"I shall see her, at least. They tell me she is pretty. I must own I always had a weakness for pretty and pleasant women. I must own also I never see one at home."

Her eyes flash at the sneer.

"I am quite aware, Mr. Thorndyke, of your predilection for pretty women. Haven't you paid rather dearly though for the fancy? Was the brief society of Miss Lucy West and Miss Norine Bourdon sufficient compensation for the loss of a fortune?"

He rises to his feet, his face flushing dark, angry red.

"*You* know that?" he exclaims.

She laughs contemptuously.

"I know that; I know much more than that. You did not show me the letter left by Mr. Darcy for you at his death, but you did not destroy it. That letter I have read. He states his reasons for disinheriting you plainly enough, does he not? And for my part, all I have to say is, served you right."

She rises, gathers her papers together, binds them up, and without looking at him, sweeps from the room.

"Joanna!" she calls, "look after Laurie and baby. I am going down town."

She dresses herself hastily, and in her cheap hat and muslin dress, manages somehow to look stylish and distinguished still. She takes an omnibus, rides to Wall street, and enters Mr. Gilbert's office.

Mr. Gilbert receives her with cordial kindness, takes the papers, glances over them, pronounces them well done, and gives her two crisp five-dollar greenbacks. The color comes into her pale cheeks.

"You pay me so much more than the copying is worth," she falters. "Oh, Mr. Gilbert, good, kind, faithful friend, what would become of me and my babies but for you?"

He stops her with a quick gesture.

"Hush! not one cent more than the work is justly worth. And all is gone then, Mrs. Thorndyke?"

"All! all!" she says, drearily; "long ago."

"I know that your marriage portion was squandered the first year, but Mr. Darcy left you ten thousand dollars at his death. It was left to you—*he* could not touch it. You should have kept that."

"Should have kept it! *He* could not touch it!" She laughs bitterly. "My dear Mr. Gilbert, don't you know that a married woman can be kicked or kissed into anything? I will do Mr. Thorndyke the justice to say he tried both methods while there was a dollar left. If it were not for my children I would have left him long ago—if it were not for them I could wish I were dead, Mr. Gilbert." She lays her hand upon his arm and looks up into his face with blue, glittering eyes. "I have read the letter Mr. Darcy wrote him before he died."

"You have?" the lawyer says, startled.

"I know the story of Norine Bourdon. Oh, Mr. Gilbert if you were not more angel than man you would let Laurence Thorndyke's wife and children starve before your eyes!"

"Hush!" he says again huskily, "for pity's sake, Nellie. I only wish you would take the money without the work. The betrayer of a loving and innocent girl is in the hands of God—there I leave him. But for you—do you not know that Mrs. Liston-Darcy has made a proposal to me for you?"

"For me? No. I know that she has arrived, that is all. You have seen her, then?"

"Not yet. She is coming to-day; I expect her every moment. She sent me a note telling me of it. It is this: when your life with your husband becomes unendurable—when he forces you to leave him, she is instructed to provide for you and your children. It was Mr. Darcy's wish—it is hers. A home and a competence are yours any day on that condition."

There was a tap at the door.

"Mrs. Liston-Darcy, sir," announced the clerk.

"I will go," Helen said, rising hastily. "The day when I shall be glad to accept Mrs. Darcy's offer may not be far distant. I cannot meet her now. You will send me more work to-morrow? Thank you a thousand times, and good-by."

She flitted from the room. In the outer office sat a lady dressed in a black silk walking costume, and wearing a close veil of black lace. The next instant Mrs. Thorndyke was in the street, and Mrs. Darcy was being ushered into Mr. Gilbert's sanctum.

He looked at her curiously. Rather tall, slender, graceful, elegant, that he saw, but—what was there about her that so suddenly made his pulses leap?

Still veiled, she sat down.

"I am a little late for my appointment," she began; "I was unexpectedly detained. I have not kept you waiting, I hope?"

He turned pale—he sat quite silent. He heard the voice, but not the words: his eyes were riveted upon the veil. *Who* was this woman?

"Mr. Gilbert," she said, falteringly, "I see you know me."

She lifted her veil, and sat before him revealed—Norine.

Norine! After four years—Norine. A gray, ashen pallor came over his face even to his lips. She trembled and shrank before his gaze; she covered her face with her hands and turned away.

"Forgive me!" she said, brokenly. "Oh, forgive me! If you knew how I have suffered, indeed you might."

He put his hand to his head in a dazed way for a second. Then, with a sort of shake, he aroused himself to every-day life again.

"Norine," he said, "is it indeed you? Little Norine! They told me it was Mrs. Liston-Darcy."

"It is Mrs. Darcy. I am Hugh Darcy's adopted daughter."

He stared at her bewildered.

"*You!* Her name was Jane Liston."

"Her name was Norine Bourdon. There was no Jane Liston. That was the name under which I was first introduced into Mr. Darcy's house, by which I had been known to the few of Mr. Darcy's friends whom I met, and, to save endless inquiries, it was the name published from first to last. Mr. Darcy knew all my story, knew all about me. But you, Mr. Gilbert—it is very late in the day to ask your forgiveness for the great wrong I did you four years ago, but from my heart I do ask it."

She clasped her hands together with the old gesture—the dusky eyes filled and brimmed over. But if the familiar gesture moved him, if the tears touched him, Richard Gilbert did not show it.

"I forgave you long ago, Mrs. Darcy," he said, very coldly: "pray do not think of me at all, and accept my congratulations upon your great accession of fortune."

Her head dropped, her cheeks flushed. Those three years had changed her into a beautiful, self-possessed, calm-eyed woman; but her faltering voice, her drooping head, her downcast eyes were very humble now.

"I did wrong—wrong too great for forgiveness; but if suffering can atone for sin, then surely I have atoned. Let me tell you the story of that bitter time. It is your due, and mine."

He bent his head. With lips compressed and eyes fixed upon the desk before him, he listened while she faltered forth her confession.

"I had no thought of going that night when I left the house. Oh! believe this if you can, Mr. Gilbert—no thought, as Heaven hears me, of flying with him. I was in the carriage and far away, it seems to me, before I realized it; and then—listening to his false words and promises—it seemed too late to turn back, and I went on."

She told him the story of the after-time—of all—truthfully and earnestly, up to the night of her confession to Mr. Darcy.

"He was like a man beside himself with fury," she said. "Liston came to indorse my words and tell the story of Lucy West. Then he swore a mighty oath that he would never look upon Laurence Thorndyke's face again. So, without a word, we went away—he and I, and Liston. No father could be kinder, no friend truer. I believe the blow hastened his end. We went to France, to Italy. All the time he was failing. When he knew he must die, he told me what he intended—he would make me his daughter legally and leave me all.

"Mr. Gilbert, I had vowed within myself to be revenged upon Laurence Thorndyke sooner or later. This was the beginning of my revenge. He made his will, leaving all to me, except ten thousand dollars to Helen Thorndyke, and an annuity to Liston. Three days after he died.

"What came after, you know—how Laurence Thorndyke, with all his might, sought to have that will set aside, and how signally he failed. Mr. Darcy gave his reasons to you and to him plainly and clearly. For his own crimes he was disinherited. Mr. Darcy's fortune was, and is, mine.

"For the rest, these three years I have spent wandering over Europe. I have come home to remain this summer and winter, then I go back. I have come, too, to ask your forgiveness and theirs down at home. Mr. Gilbert—it is more than I ought to ask, but,—will you not say, 'I pardon you'?"

She held out her hands imploringly, her eyes full of tears. He took them in his and clasped them for a moment, looking straight into her eyes.

"With all my heart, Norine! With all my heart I wish you well and happy!"

---

Mr. Allison's house is a stately up-town mansion, brown stone, stucco, and elegance generally; and Mr. Allison's house is all alight and alive to-night. Mrs. Allison gives a reception, and fair women and brave men muster strong; and fairest, where all are more or less fair, is the youthful and wealthy heiress of old Hugh Darcy.

Among the very latest arrivals comes Mr. Laurence Thorndyke. Time has been when bright eyes brightened, fair cheeks flushed, and delicate pulses leaped at his coming. That day is over. Time has also been when among all the golden youth of New York none were more elegant, more faultless of attire, than Laurence Thorndyke. That day also is over. Time has been when the most exclusive, most recherche doors of Fifth avenue flew gladly open at his approach. That day, likewise, is over. The places that knew him, know him no more; he is an outcast and a Bohemian; he drinks, he gambles, he is poor; his coat is gray at the seams; bistre circles surround his eyes; his haggard, handsome face tells the story of his life. Yet the old elegance and old fascination of manner, linger still. People rather stare to see him here. Mrs. Allison frowns. She has flirted desperately with him "ages" ago; but really bygones should be bygones, and Mr. Thorndyke has gone to the dogs in so pronounced a manner, and been disinherited for some dreadful doings, and, really and truly, the line must be drawn somewhere, and it is inexcusable in Mr. Allison to have asked him at all.

"No one invites him now," Mrs. Allison says, indignantly. "Both he and Helen are socially extinct. They say she takes in sewing, and lives in a dreadful tenement house away over by the East River—and with dear Mrs. Liston-Darcy here and everything! Of course it can't be pleasant for them to meet. He contested the will—if he should make a scene to-night!—good heavens! No doubt he is half-tipsy—they say he always *is* half-tipsy—and look at his dress! You ought to be ashamed of yourself, Arthur Allison, for asking him!"

"Couldn't help it, Hattie—give you my word now," responds Arthur meekly; "he as good as asked me to ask him, when he heard Mrs. Darcy was coming. And he wants to be introduced, and I've promised, and there's no use making a fuss now. He isn't tipsy, and I don't believe there will be a scene. I'll introduce him at once; the sooner it's over, the better."

He goes off uneasily, and leads Mr. Thorndyke into an inner room, where a lady sits at the piano, singing. A lady elegantly dressed in white silk, and violet trimmings, with a white perfumery rose in her black hair. Her face is averted—Mr. Thorndyke glares vindictively at the woman who has ousted him out of a fortune. She is a beautiful singer, and somehow—somehow, the sweet powerful contralto tones are strangely familiar. Can he have ever heard her before?

She finishes. Mr. Allison draws near the piano.

"Mrs. Darcy," he says, clearing his throat, "will you allow me to introduce to you Mr. Thorndyke?"

She is laughingly responding to a complimentary gentleman beside her. With that smile still on her lips she turns slowly round, lifting up her eyes. And with a gasping sound that is neither word nor cry, Laurence Thorndyke stands face to face once more with Norine.

# CHAPTER XIX.

**"WHOM THE GODS WISH TO DESTROY THEY FIRST MAKE MAD."**

orine! And like this, after four years, these two meet again.

Norine! His lips shape the word, but no sound follows. He stands before her destitute of all power to speak or move. Lost in a trance of wonder, he remains looking down upon the fair, smiling, upturned face, utterly confounded.

"I am very pleased to meet Mr. Thorndyke. By reputation I know him well."

These audacious words, smilingly spoken, reach his ear. She bows, taps her fan lightly, and makes some airy remark to her host. And still Laurence Thorndyke stands petrified. She notices, lifts her eyebrows, and ever so slightly shrugs her shoulders.

"Mr. Thorndyke does not spare me. To which of my defects, I wonder, do I owe this steady regard?"

"Norine!"

The name breaks from his lips at last. He still stands and stares.

She uplifts her graceful shoulders once more—the old French trick of gesture he remembers so well.

"I remind Mr. Thorndyke of some one, possibly," she says—impatience mingled with her "society manner," this time—"of some lady he knows?"

"Of some one I once knew, certainly, Mrs.—Ah, Darcy," he retorts, his face flushing angrily, his old insolent ease of manner returning, "I am not sure that you would call her a lady. She was a French Canadienne—her name—would you like to hear her name, Mrs. Liston-Darcy?"

"It does not interest me at all, Mr. Thorndyke."

"Her name was Norine Bourdon, and she was like—most astoundingly like *you*! So like that I could swear you were one and the same."

"Ah, indeed! But I would not take a rash oath if I were you. These accidental resemblances are so deceptive. Mr. Wentworth, if you will give me your arm, I think I will go and look at the dancers."

The last words were very marked. With a chill, formal bow to Mr. Thorndyke she took her escort's arm, and turned to move away. With that angry flush still on his face, that angry light still in his eyes, Laurence Thorndyke interposed.

"Mrs. Darcy, they are playing the 'Soldaten Lieder'. It is a favorite waltz of yours, I *know*. Will you not give it to me?"

She turned upon him slowly, a swift, black flash in her eyes that made him recoil.

"You make a mistake, Mr. Thorndyke! Of what I dance or what I do not, you can possibly know nothing. For the rest, my time of mourning for my dear adopted father has but just expired. I do not dance at all."

Then she was gone—tall, and fair and graceful as a lily. And Laurence Thorndyke drew a long breath, his face aglow with genuine admiration.

"By Jupiter!" he said; "who'd have thought it! In the language of the immortal Dick Swiveller, 'This is a staggerer!' Who'd have thought she'd have had the pluck! And who would have thought she would ever have grown so handsome?"

"You *do* know her, then, Thorndyke?" his host asked, in intense curiosity.

Mr. Thorndyke had forgotten him, but Mr. Allison was still at his elbow. His reply was a short, curious laugh.

"Know her? By Jove! I used to think so, but at this moment I am inclined to doubt it. Have you not heard her deny it, and ladies invariably tell the truth, do they not? 'These accidental resemblances are so deceptive!'" He laughed shortly. "So they are, my dear Mrs. Darcy! Yes, Allison, it's all a mistake on my part, no doubt."

He turned and swung away to escape Allison, and think his surprise out. His eyes went after her. Yes, there she was again, the centre of an admiring group of all that was best in the room. Her beautiful dark face was all alight, the black, beautiful eyes, like dusk diamonds, the waving hair most gracefully worn—by odds the most attractive woman in the rooms. Those years had changed her wonderfully—improved her beyond telling. The face, clear cut and calm as marble, the lips set and resolute, the figure matured and grown firm. About her there was all the uplifted ease, the ineffable self-poise of a woman of the world, conscious of her beauty, her wealth, and her power.

"And this is Norine—little Norry," Laurence Thorndyke thought in his trance of wonder. "I can hardly believe my own senses. I thought her dead, or buried alive down there in the wilds of Maine, and lo! here she crops up, old Darcy's heiress—beautiful, elegant, and ready to face me with the courage of a stage heroine—the woman who has done me out of a fortune. This is her revenge! And I thought her a love-sick simpleton, ready to lie down and die of a broken heart the hour I left her. By George! *how* handsome she has grown. It would be easy enough for any man to fall in love with her now."

She meant to ignore the past, utterly and absolutely ignore it—that he saw. Well, he would take his cue from her for the present, and see how the farce would play. But—was it Norine?—that self-possessed regal-looking lady! Could it be that those dark, calm, haughty eyes had ever filled with passionate tears at his slightest word of reproach? had ever darkened with utter despair at his going? Could it be that yonder beautiful, stately creature had waited and watched for him in pale anguish, night after night, his veriest slave?—had clung to him, white with direst woe, when he had seen her last? Proud, uplifted, calm—could it be?—could it be?

"Norine, surely; but not the Norine I knew—a Norine ten thousand times more to my taste. But how, in Heaven's name, has she brought this transformation about? Mrs. Jane Liston—old Liston's niece. I have it! I see it all! Liston is at the bottom of this. It is his revenge for Lucy West; and they have worked and plotted together, whilst I, blind fool, thought him my friend, and thought her too feeble, soul and body, to do anything but droop and die when I left her."

Yes, he saw it all. Like inspiration it came upon him. In his own coin he had been paid; the trodden worms had turned, and Lucy West and Norine Bourdon were avenged.

Mr. Thorndyke withdrew from every one and gave himself wholly up to the study of Mrs. Darcy. There was no scene; Mrs. Allison need not have feared it; no gentleman present "behaved himself" more quietly or decorously than Mr. Laurence Thorndyke. How wonderfully she had changed! how handsome she had grown! that was the burden of his musings. And she had loved him once—ah, yes—"not wisely, but too well." They say first love never wholly dies out. He didn't know himself; he had had so many first loves—centuries ago, it seemed to him now—they certainly had died out, wholly and entirely. But with women it was different. Had she quite outgrown the passion of her youth? And if it were not for Helen, who could tell—

He broke off, with a sudden impulse, and joined her. For a moment she was alone, in a curtained recess, wielding her fan with the languid grace of a Castilian, and watching the dancers. He came softly from behind and bent his tall head.

"Norine!"

If she had been stone-deaf she could not have sat more perfectly still and unheeding.

"Norry!"

No motion—no sign that she heard at all.

"Mrs. Darcy!"

She moved slowly now, turning her graceful shoulder and lifting the brown, tranquil eyes full to his face.

"Did you address yourself to me, Mr. Thorndyke?"

"Norine, there is no one to hear; for pity's sake have done with this farce. Norine! Norine! as though I should not know you anywhere, under any name."

"Mr. Thorndyke," Mrs. Darcy answered, her soft, sweet voice singularly calm and clear, "if you persist in this strange delusion of yours I shall be forced to throw myself upon the protection of Mr. Allison. As the disinherited nephew of the late Mr. Darcy, I have no objection to make your acquaintance; in the light of a former friend I utterly refuse to know you. I am Mrs. Darcy. If you insist upon addressing me by any other name I shall refuse to hear or answer."

There was no mistaking the tone in which it was said. His eyes flashed blue fire.

"Take care!" he said; "even you may go too far! What if I tell the world Mrs. Darcy's past?"

The dark, disdainful gaze was upon him still.

"Is that a threat, Mr. Thorndyke? I do not know you, I never have known you. If you say that I have, I am prepared to deny it, at all times, and in all places. My word will carry as much weight as yours, Mr. Thorndyke. I am not afraid of you, and if this is to be the manner of our conversation, I decline henceforth holding another."

She arose to go. He saw he had made a mistake. It was no part of his desire to make an enemy of her.

"Forgive me," he said, humbly—"forgive me, Mrs. Darcy. The resemblance is very striking; but I am mistaken, of course. You remind me of one I loved very dearly once—of one whose loss has darkened my whole life! Forgive me, and let me be your friend."

The scorn in the dark, contemptuous eyes!—it might have blighted him; but of late years Laurence Thorndyke was well used to scorn.

59

"Friend?" she said. "*No*! I do not make friends lightly. Acquaintance, if you will, for Mr. Darcy's sake—for the sake of your great disappointment pecuniarily I am willing to be that."

"It was deserved," he faltered, his eyes averted. "I have repented—Heaven knows how bitterly. That I have lost a fortune through my own misdeeds is the least of my punishment."

She turned from him, sick—sick at heart with the utter scorn she felt. As her gaze wandered away, it fell upon another face—the face of Richard Gilbert!

He was watching them. As he met her glance he bowed and walked away. A flush that Laurence Thorndyke had not for a second called there, came vividly into her pale cheeks.

"And for this craven—this hypocrite, I fled from him—spoiling my own life and his forever. Oh, fool! fool! What can he have but scorn and loathing for me now."

She arose impatiently. All at once the presence of Laurence Thorndyke had grown intolerable to her. Without a word of excuse she bent her head to him slightly and frigidly and moved away.

Mr. Thorndyke was not offended. The course he meant to pursue in regard to Mrs. Darcy was not yet quite clear. This, however, was—he would not let her easily offend him. His friend she should be. Who could tell what the future might bring forth? With all her girl's heart and strength she had loved him once. A fatuous smile came over his face as he glanced at himself in the mirror. Not so good-looking as of yore, certainly, but late hours, hard drinking, and the fierce excitement of the gaming-table had wrought the evil. He would change all that—go in for reform—total amendment of life—try sculpture and become a respectable member of society. Meantime he would see all he could of Mrs. Darcy.

By Jove! how handsome she had looked—what thoroughbred good style she was! And if—hidden under all this outward coldness—the old love still lay, how easy for him to fan the smoldering embers into bright flames. And then—?

A vision rose before him—Helen, in the shabby rooms at home, writing far into the night, to earn the bread his children ate. Whilst Helen lived, let his uncle's heiress love him never so well, what could it avail him? "There is the law of divorce," whispered the small voice of the tempter. "To the man who wills, all things are possible. Mr. Darcy's fortune, and Mr. Darcy's heiress may be yours yet. You have played for high stakes before to-night, Laurence, my boy. Play your cards with care now, and you hold the winning hand?"

From that night a change began in Laurence Thorndyke—began on the spot. Once more, that night, he had spoken to Mrs. Darcy—then it was to say farewell.

"You have told me you will accept me as an acquaintance," he said very quietly. "Life has gone hardly with me of late, and I have learned to be thankful even for small mercies. For what you have promised I thank you, and—will not easily forget it."

She bowed—gleams of scorn in her dark, brilliant eyes. So they had parted, and very grave and thoughtful Mr. Thorndyke went home.

The change began. Less drinking, less gambling, better hours. His wife looked on with suspicious eyes. She had reason to suspect. When Satan turns saint, Satan's relatives have cause to be on the alert.

"Given up gambling and going to try sculpture! Leon Saroni has given you the run of his studies, has he? I don't understand all this, Mr. Thorndyke. What new project have you in your head now?"

"Going to turn over a new leaf, Nellie. Give you my word I am," replies Mr. Thorndyke, keeping his temper with admirable patience. "Going in for legitimate industry and fame. I always felt I had a genius for sculpture. I feel it now more than ever. Soon, very soon, you may throw this beastly copying to the dogs, and we will live in comfort once more."

The wonder and incredulity of his wife's face, as she turned back to her writing, infuriated him. But he had his own reasons for standing well, even with her, just at present.

"Nellie," he said, and he stooped to kiss her, "I've been a brute to you, I know, but—you care a little for me still!"

Her face flushed, as a girl's might under her lover's first caress. Then she covered it with her hands and broke into a passion of tears.

He soothed her with caresses.

"It will be different now," he said. "Forgive the past, Nellie, if you can. I swear to do better in the future."

Forgive! What is there that a wife who loves will not forgive? On her wedding-day Helen Thorndyke had hardly been more blessed. With a glow on her cheeks and a light in her eyes, strangers there for many a day, she went back to her drudgery. And smiling a little to himself, as he lit his cigar and sauntered to his friend Saroni's studio, Mr. Thorndyke mused:

"They're all alike—all! Ready to forgive a man seventy times seven, let him do as he may. Ready to sell themselves body and soul for a kiss! And what is true of Helen shall be true of Norine."

So Mr. Thorndyke set to work, and with untiring energy, be it said. "Deserted," he meant to call this production of genius. It should tell its own story to all. The white, marble face would look up, all wrought and strained in its mortal anguish. The locked hands, the writhing figure, all should tell of woman's woe. The face he had in his brain—as he had seen it last down there in the light of the summer noon. All was at stake here—he must not—he would not fail.

And while Mr. Thorndyke chiselled marble, Mrs. Thorndyke copied her law papers. She had met Mrs. Darcy more than once in Mr. Gilbert's office, and Mr. Darcy's proposal had been laid before her. Her eyes had kindled, her face flushed as she refused.

"Leave my husband? Never! Whatever his errors, he loves me at least—has always been true to me. All other things I can forgive. Mr. Darcy meant kindly, no doubt—so do you, madame, but I refuse your offer, now and forever. I will not leave my husband."

The gravely beautiful eyes of Mrs. Darcy had looked at her compassionately.

"Loves you!" she thought—"always been true to you. Poor little fool!"

For she knew better. She and Mr. Thorndyke met often. Now that he had "gone in for" respectability and hard work, old friends came back, old doors flew open, society accepted him again. He was ever an acquisition, brilliant handsome, gay. Married, it is true, but his wife never appeared. Truth to tell, Mrs. Thorndyke had nothing to wear. Mr. Thorndyke in some way rejuvenated his wardrobe, and rose, glorious as the Phœnix, from the ashes of the shabby past. They met often, and if passionate admiration—passionate love, ever looked out of man's eyes, it looked out of his now, when they rested on Norine.

It was part of his punishment, perhaps, that the woman he had betrayed and cast off should inspire him with the one supreme passion of his life.

She saw it all, and smiled, well content. She was not perfect, by any means. Revenge she had bound herself to have. If revenge came in this shape—so let it come. Every pang he had made her suffer he should feel—as she had been scorned, so she would scorn him. For Mrs. Thorndyke—well, was it not for Mrs. Thorndyke she had been forsaken. She was his wife, at least—let his wife look to herself.

They met constantly. As yet he had never offended in words. They were friends. She was interested in his "Deserted"—she visited it in company with some acquaintances at the studio. She had praised it highly. If she recalled the resemblance to herself, in that day past and gone, no word nor look betrayed it.

"It will be a success, I am sure," she had said; "it is so true to life, that it is almost painful to look at it."

Then he had spoken—in one quick, passionate whisper.

"Norine—forgive me!"

The dark eyes looked at him, not proudly, nor coldly, nor angrily now—then fell.

His whole face flushed with rapture.

"I have something to say to you. You are never at home when I call. Norine, I implore you! let me see you alone—once."

Over her face there came a sudden change—her lips set, her eyes gleamed. What it meant he could not tell. He interpreted it to suit his hopes.

"I will see you," she said, slowly. "When will you come?"

"A thousand thanks. This evening if I may."

She bent her head and turned from him.

"Whom the gods wish to destroy they first make mad," she thought. "I know as well as you do, Mr. Thorndyke, what you are coming to say to-night, and—I shall not be the only listener."

He leaned in a sort of ecstasy against his own work. At last! she would see him—she would hear how he had repented, how he worshipped her, how the only hope that life held for him, was the one hope of winning back her love. Of Helen he never thought—never once. It seemed so easy a thing to put her away. Incompatibility of temper—anything would do. And she had the pride of Lucifer. She would never lift a finger to retard the divorce.

# CHAPTER XX.

**NORINE'S REVENGE.**

y dear Mrs. Thorndyke;—Will you come and spend the evening with me? Fetch the little people. I shall be quite alone.
"Jane Liston-Darcy."

It was not the first time such notes had come to the tenement house—not the first time they had been accepted. Laurence was always away. The late hours had begun again. The evenings at home were so dreary. It was a glimpse of the old glad life, before poverty and hard work had ground her down. Yes, she would go.

Mrs. Darcy, very simply, but very prettily dressed, welcomed her. Baby Nellie she took in her arms and kissed fondly, but little Laurie, with his father's bold, blue eyes and trick of face, she shrank from. The father she could face unmoved; the old pain actually came back when she looked at the child.

As they sat, a pretty group in the gas-light, a card was brought in. Mrs. Darcy put the baby off her lap and passed the card to Helen.

"Your husband," she said. "He begged for this interview, and—I have granted it. But I wished you to be present. Whether I do right or wrong, you shall hear what he has to say to me. You love and trust him still. You shall hear how worthy he is of it. But first—have you ever heard the name of Norine Bourdon?"

"Norine Bourdon! the girl whom Laurence—"

"Betrayed by a false marriage—for whom he was disinherited. I am she."

"You!" Helen Thorndyke recoiled.

"It was Norine Bourdon, not Jane Liston, Mr. Darcy adopted. Have you not then the right to hear what your husband has to say to me? But it shall be as you wish."

"I wish to hear," Helen answered, almost fiercely. "I *will* hear."

Norine threw open a door.

"Wait in this room. I will leave the door ajar. My maid shall take the children. And be sure of this—neither by word nor look shall I tempt your husband to say one word more than he has come to say to-night."

Helen Thorndyke passed into the inner room. Norine Darcy rang for the servant waiting without.

"Show Mr. Thorndyke up."

He came, bounding lightly and eagerly up the stairs, and entered. She arose from her seat to meet him. In full evening dress, his face slightly flushed, his blue eyes all alight with eagerness, he had never perhaps, in the days when she had adored him, looked so handsome as now.

She smiled a little to herself as she recalled that infatuation; how long ago it seemed. And for this good-looking, well-dressed, heartless libertine, she had gone near to the gates of death.

"Norine!"

He clasped the small hand, shining with diamonds, that she extended, in both his, his tone, his eyes speaking volumes.

"Good-evening, Mr. Thorndyke. Will you be seated? Quite chilly for September, is it not, to-night?"

She sank gracefully back into her easy-chair, the gas-light streaming over her dusk, Canadian loveliness. She made an effort to disengage her hand, which he still held fast, but he refused to let it go.

"No, Norine! let me keep it. Oh, love, remember it was once all mine. Norine! Norine! on my knees I implore your forgiveness for the past!"

He actually sank on one knee before her, covering the hand he held with passionate kisses. No acting here; that was plain, at least. The infatuated man meant every word he said.

"Forgive me, Norine! I know that I have sinned to you beyond all pardon, but if you knew how I have suffered, how the memory of my crime has made my whole life miserable, how, to drown the torture of memory, I fled to the wine-cup and the gambling-table, and to—"

"Marriage with Miss Helen Holmes, heiress and belle. Oh, I know it all, Mr. Thorndyke. Pray get up. Gentlemen never go on their knees nowadays except in melodrama. Get up Mr. Thorndyke; let go my hand and sit down like a rational being. I insist upon it."

"A rational being!" he repeated. "I have ceased to be that since your return. It is my madness, Norine, to love you as I never loved any women before in my life."

She laughed, toying with the fan she held.

"My dear Mr. Thorndyke, I remember perfectly well what an absolute fool I was in the days of our acquaintanceship four years ago. Even such a statement as that might have been swallowed whole. But it *is* four years ago, and—you will pardon me—I know what brilliant talent Laurence Thorndyke has for graceful fiction. To how many ladies in the course of his thirty years of life has he made that ardent declaration, I wonder?"

"You do not believe me?"

"I do not."

"Norine, I swear—"

"Hush-h-h! pray don't perjure yourself. Was it to tell me this you came here this evening, Mr. Thorndyke?"

"To tell you, Norine, what I am sure you do not know. What I never knew myself until of late, that you and you alone have ever been my wife; that our marriage *was* a marriage, legal and true—that you, not Helen, are my lawful wife. To tell you this and much more, if you will listen. From my soul I have repented of the past; how bitterly, none may know. I left you—great Heaven! I sit and wonder at my own madness now; and all the time I loved you as I never loved any one else. I married Helen Holmes—yes, I cannot deny it, but what was I to do? I was bound to her, she loved me, 'my honor rooted in dishonor stood,' and I married her. There is horrible fatality in these things. While I knelt before the altar pledging myself to her, my whole heart was back with you. I will own it—despise me more than you do already, if that be possible—I married her for her wedding dower, and because I dared not offend Mr. Darcy. Wealth so won could bring little happiness. I fled from home and her presence to drown remorse and the memory of my lost love in drink. So poverty came. I was reckless. Whether you lived or died I did not know, I dared not ask—in abandoning you I had spoiled my whole life. Then suddenly you reappeared, beautiful as a dream, so far off, so cold, so unapproachable—you my love! my love! once my very own. You held me at arm's-length—you refused to listen to a word, and all the time my heart was on fire within me. To-night I have come to speak at last. Norine, I have sinned, I have suffered, I have repented. What more can I say? I love you madly, I always loved you. Say you forgive me, or I will never rise from your feet!"

Once more he cast himself before her, real passion, its utmost abandonment, in every tone. She had let him rave on, never moving, her cold eyes fixed upon him, full of hard, contemptuous fire.

"You mean all this, Mr. Thorndyke? Yes, I see you do. And you love me—you always loved me, even when you cast me off and married Miss Holmes, really and truly?"

"Really and truly! I swear it, Norine?"

"No—don't swear, please—it's against my principles to encourage profanity. But isn't it rather late in the day to tell me all this? There is your wife—you don't care for her, of course, but still you see she *is* your wife, in the eye of the world at least. And a gentleman's wife is rather an obstacle when that gentleman makes love to another lady."

The fine irony of her tone he did not hear—the scorn of her eyes he did not see. The "madness of the gods" was upon him—blind and deaf he was going to his doom.

"An obstacle, but an obstacle easily set aside. In any case I mean to have a divorce. I never cared for her—there are times when I loathe her now. A divorce, with permission to marry again I shall obtain, and then, Norine—"

He moved as though to clasp her. With a shudder of horror and repulsion she waved him back. And still he was blind.

"And your children, Mr. Thorndyke?"

"That shall be as Helen wishes. I don't care for them—never cared for children. She may keep them if she wishes. If I had loved *her* it would be easy to love her children. You consent then, Norine? It is as I hoped. You forgive the past. You will again be my wife. Oh, darling! my whole life shall be spent in the effort to blot out the past and make you entirely happy. You love me still—say it, Norine!"

He clasped both her hands vehemently. She arose to answer. Before the words of passionate scorn on her lips could be spoken the inner door opened and Helen Thorndyke stood on the threshold.

"Great Heaven! Helen!"

He dropped Norine's hands and staggered back. For a moment he almost thought it her ghost, so white, so ghastly with concentrated passion was she. She advanced,—she tried to speak—at first the words died huskily away upon her dry lips.

"I have heard every word," she panted. "You coward! You basest of all base cowards. Though I live for a hundred years, these are the last words I shall ever speak to you. Living or dying I will never forgive you—living or dying I will never look upon your face again! Norine!"

She turned to her suddenly:

"You offered me a home and a competence once, apart from him. For his sake I refused it then—for my children's sake I ask it now. I have no hope left but in you and—Heaven."

Her head fell on Norine's shoulder with one dry, hard sob, and there lay. Norine Darcy drew her to her side, her arm clasping her closely, and so—faced Laurence Thorndyke.

"'Every dog has his day'. It is not a very elegant adage, but it is a true one. Your day has been, Mr. Thorndyke—- mine has come. For it I have hoped, and worked, for it I have let you go on—for it I have listened to the words you have spoken to-night—for it I concealed your wife yonder, that she might hear too. You love me, you say—I am glad to believe it—since a little of the torture you once made me feel you shall feel in return. For myself all memory of the past is gone. You are so utterly indifferent to me, so utterly contemptible in my sight, that I have not even hatred to give you. To me you are simply nothing. After this hour I will never see you, never speak to you. For your wife and children I will provide. You did your best to ruin me, soul and body, because you hated Richard Gilbert. I take from you wife and children, and what you value far more—fortune. I think we are quits, and as there is no more to be said, I will bid you good-night. Liston! show this gentleman to the door, and admit him here no more."

Then Mr. Liston, pale of face, soft of step, furtive of glance, appeared on the scene. Still clasping the drooping form of the outraged wife, Norine moved towards the inner room.

Thorndyke had stood quite still, his arms folded, listening to all. The game was up! A devil of fury, of disappointment, would possess him by-and-by—just now he only felt half-stunned. He turned to the door, with a harsh laugh.

"I have heard of men who murdered the women they loved, and wondered at them. I wonder no longer. By Heaven, if I had a pistol to-night you would never leave this room alive, Norine Bourdon!"

---

# CHAPTER XXI.

**"THE MILLS OF THE GODS GRIND SLOWLY, BUT THEY GRIND EXCEEDINGLY SMALL."**

 t the drawing-room window of the late Hugh Darcy's old-fashioned house, Hugh Darcy's heiress sits. It is a dreary November day, a long, lamentable blast soughs through the city streets—the two vestal poplars toss their green arms wildly aloft in the gale, and the sleety rain goes swirling before it. At all times a quiet street, it is entirely forsaken to-day. Far off comes the clatter and jangle of passing street-cars, the dull roar of the city's ceaseless life. In this by-street peace reigns.

Yet Norine sits by the window gazing steadfastly out at the wet, leaden, melancholy afternoon. In her lap some piece of flimsy feminine handicraft lies—on the table before her are strewn new books and uncut magazines. But she neither embroiders nor reads—she lies back against the crimson velvet of the old chair looking handsome and listless, her dark, thoughtful eyes, gazing aimlessly at the lashing rain. Now and then they turn from the picture without to the picture within, and she sighs softly.

A bright fire burns in the steel grate and lights ruddily the crimson-draped room. On a sofa drawn up before it, in a nest of pillows, Helen Thorndyke lies so still, so white, you might think her dead. But she is not even asleep, although she lies motionless with closed eyes. Her life seems to have come to an end. Pride she has, and it has upheld her, but love she has too, and pride cannot quite crush it out. Since that fatal September night she has been here—since that night his name has never passed her lips; these two women, whose lives Laurence Thorndyke has marred, never talk of him. She lies here and broods, broods, broods ever—of the days that are gone and can never come again.

On the floor near, little Laurie is building a house of blocks, and squat in the centre of a wool rug baby Nellie crows delightedly and watches the progress of the architect. So the minutes tick off, and it is an hour since Norine has entered the room.

In the library, before her entrance here, she has had an interview with Richard Gilbert—it is of that interview and of him she sits thinking now. Some business connected with Mr. Darcy's estate has brought him, and she has asked him, constrainedly enough, for news of Laurence Thorndyke.

"I keep Liston on his track," she said, playing nervously with her watch chain. "Helen says little, but she suffers always. And Liston's news is of the dreariest."

The strong, gray eyes of the lawyer had lifted sternly to her face. No word of censure had ever escaped his lips—what right had he? but Norine felt the steady rebuke of that firm, cold glance. He knew all, and she felt he must utterly despise her now.

"He has fallen very low," Mr. Gilbert answered, briefly, "so low that it is hardly possible for him to fall much lower. In losing his wife and children he lost his last hold on respectability, his one last hope on earth."

"He deserved to lose them," Norine said, with a flash of her black eyes.

"Perhaps so. From all I hear *you* should know best. But if stern justice is to be meted to us all, after your merciless fashion, then Heaven help us! If vengeance can gratify you, Mrs. Darcy, you may rest well content. He has sunk as low as his worst enemy could wish. But—you might have spared Helen."

Cold, cutting, the words of rebuke fell. He arose, gathering up his papers, his face set and stern. Her face drooped—she covered it with her hand, and turned away.

"She at least had never wronged you," Richard Gilbert pitilessly went on. "Have you made her any happier, Mrs. Darcy, by taking her husband from her? In spite of his myriad faults she loved him—she trusted him, and so, neither poverty, hard work, nor neglect could make her altogether miserable. *You* led him on—led him on from the first, in cold blood, working for your revenge. And when you had crazed his brain by your smiles and fair words, and allurements, you brought his wife here to overhear the passion you had labored to inspire. You madden her in turn, you take her from him, you order him from your presence like a dog. You took from him the one good angel of his life—his wife—and gave him up boldly to the devil. He has earned it all, you have your revenge, but—as I stand and look at you here, I wonder—I wonder if *you* can be Norine Bourdon."

A dry sob was her answer. He had poured forth the words, passionate reproach in his voice, passionate anger in his eyes. And she had shrank away before his just wrath like a guilty thing.

"His home is a gambler's hell—his food and drink are the liquid fire called whiskey; his associates are the scum and refuse of the city. Mrs. Darcy, I wish you joy of your work!"

"Spare me," she faltered.

Mr. Gilbert looked silently for a moment at the bowed figure, then took his hat and turned to go.

"I beg your pardon," he said, very quietly. "I had no right to speak at all. My only excuse is, that I will not so offend again. How is Helen?"

"As she always is. She says nothing; she lies and suffers in silence. Will you not see her?"

"Not to-day; it is painful to me; I can see it is painful to her, poor child. Good-afternoon, madam."

He bowed with formal coldness and was gone. So! she had had her revenge, but was the "game worth the candle" after all? Is revenge ever worth its cost, she began to wonder.

"Vengeance is mine, I will repay." Yes, yes, she was beginning to see it all? And—Christianity apart—revenge, as we wreak it, after our poor light, is so apt to recoil on ourselves.

So, Norine sits by the window now, thinking over this pleasant interview and "chewing the cud of sweet and bitter fancies." Much more bitter than sweet. Until she had lost Richard Gilbert's good opinion utterly, she had never known how she prized it.

Presently glancing back from the darkening day without, at some lustier shout than usual of Master Laurie, she finds Helen's large, mournful eyes fixed upon her. She rises, crosses over, kneels down by the sofa, and kisses tenderly the wan cheek.

"My dear," she says, "what is it?"

"Is—," she falters, "is there any news of *him*?"

"No news—only the old story. Nellie! Nellie! I begin to think I have done grievously wrong."

"How, Norine?"

"By bringing you here that night. I have been sinned against, but I have also been sinning. I had taken the fortune he prized so highly; I should have been content with that. But I was not. When I returned there was no thought of him in my mind, except the hope that we might never meet. We did meet, and when I saw his growing admiration for myself, I—Nellie, forgive me if you can—I *did* encourage it. I wonder at my own wickedness now; I am sorry, sorry, sorry. I know I should never have brought you here that night. Badly as he treated you, you were happier with him than you are now. And I parted you. Nellie, forgive me!"

Something that was almost color flushed into the pale face—something that was almost light into the blue eyes. The soft lips set themselves firmly.

"There is nothing to forgive. I thank you for having brought me here that night. Sooner or later I would have known all. And I was not his wife he said—you were—not I. 'In any case, I will have a divorce.' Have you forgotten those words? 'I never cared for her—I loathe her now—I married her for her dower.' Have you forgotten *that*? He deserved all. I don't blame you. We are only human, and I say again I am glad I know. I suffer, but no blame attaches to you for that suffering. He was treading the down-hill road before you came; he is only finishing the journey as it would have been finished in any case. I hate myself for my own misery. I hate myself that I cannot tear every thought of him out of my heart. But I think of the past, and I cannot."

She broke down suddenly, violently, passionately almost, for the first time, into wild, hysterical weeping. Norine took her in her arms, her own tears falling, and let her sob her sorrow out. The paroxysm was brief as it was stormy. She drew herself away suddenly, and buried her face, among the pillows.

"Don't mind me, please," she said; "don't talk to me. I am ashamed of my own weakness, but—"

Norine kissed her very tenderly.

"I am glad to see you cry, Nellie—anything is better than this dry, stony grief. I will take the babies down to supper, and send you up yours. And Nellie, dear, you must eat it; remember we start on a journey to-morrow."

The journey was to Kent Hill, where they were to stay over Christmas and New Year. Norine had made one flying visit already—had been clasped in Aunt Hetty's arms, had kissed Uncle Reuben's sunburnt cheek, had heard Uncle Joe's husky "Right glad to see you back, Norry," and—that was all. She took the old place, and, after one twilight talk, the past was never referred to. Truthfully and simply she told them all, not even excepting the darkest part—her own revenge bitterly repented of when too late. Now she and Helen and the children were going down for a long visit. One other guest there was to be—one who had spent every Christmas at Kent Hill during the past four years—Mr. Gilbert.

"Christmas wouldn't seem like Christmas now without him," Aunt Hetty said. "I don't believe there's his equal in wide America. A gentleman from top to toe, if there ever was one yet."

The children Aunt Hetty took to her motherly heart at once—Helen's pale lips she kissed, and Helen was at home in five minutes, as though she had known them for years. It was such a blessed, restful place—the tired heart drew a great sigh of relief, and felt half its weary load lifted off. For Norine—she was almost the Norine of old, flying up and down breezy stairways, in and out breezy rooms, the old songs rippling from her lips, until the thought of the pale, widowed wife down-stairs made her check them. Then came winter—the first fall of snow—the first gay sleighing. Little Laurie was wild with delight—even Helen's pale lips learned to smile. Kent Hill was working a transformation.

Christmas drew near, and among Norine's pleasant duties came that of decorating Mr. Gilbert's room, the old guest chamber, where he had spent so many happy, hopeful nights in the time when he had loved her. He despised her now. Ah, what a wretch she had been! He would despise her always. Well, she deserved it all; it didn't matter; but—and then a heavy sigh finished the thought. She was learning the value of what she had lost when too late.

Christmas arrived—Mr. Gilbert arrived. And Helen's wistful eyes looked into his face, and asked the question her lips were too proud to shape.

"There is no news," he said softly, as he bent over her chair; "only the old news. He is well—that is the best I can tell of him."

No more was said. Norine, proud and humble together, rather avoided him. Still they were of necessity a great deal together, indoors and out, and, in the genial glow and cheerfulness of the Christmas-time, the reserve of both melted. It began to be like old times—the bright color, the gay laugh, the light step, the sparkling eyes, the sweet singing, made Norine the very Norine of four years ago. And Mr. Gilbert—but Mr. Gilbert was ever quiet and undemonstrative; his calm, grave face told little, except that he was quietly happy; that you could see.

Christmas passed, New Year passed, Mr. Gilbert went back to New York. And suddenly a blank fell upon Kent Hill, sleighing and skating lost their zest—the weather grew colder, the dull country duller, and Mrs. Darcy, at the close of January, abruptly announced her intention of returning to New York also.

"If you are willing to come, Nellie," she said; "of course if you would rather remain—"

"I would rather go," Helen answered. "I have been happier here than I ever thought to be again, but I would rather go."

That settled it. They went. And on the second of February Mrs. Darcy donned velvet and sables, and set off for Mr. Gilbert's office. Was it altogether for Helen's sake—altogether for news of Helen's husband? Well, Mrs. Darcy did not ask herself the question, so no one else perhaps has any right to do so.

Looking very fresh, very stately, very handsome, she came like a bright vision into the lawyer's dingy office. A little desultory talk then—playing with her muff tassels, she asked the old question:

"Was there any news of him?"

"Yes," Mr. Gilbert answered this time; "there is news. He has been very ill; he has been in a hospital; some blow on the head received in a drunken brawl. I hunted him up the day he was discharged. A most pitiable object I found him—penniless, friendless, and still half dazed from the effects of the blow. I took him to a respectable boarding-house, paid a month's board in advance, and obtained the landlady's promise to look after him a little more than usual. He is there still, but gone back to the old life. I fear all hope for him is at an end."

Norine's face had fallen in her hands.

"May Heaven forgive me my share in his ruin! Oh, Mr. Gilbert! it may not be yet too late. Who knows? I will go to him—I will beg his forgiveness—he shall return to his wife and children. Give me his address"—she started impetuously to her feet, her face aglow—"I will go at once."

He gave it to her without a word, written on a slip of paper. As she took it, she paused and looked at him with clasped hands.

"Mr. Gilbert," she faltered, "if—if I do this will *you* forgive me?"

He laid his hand on her shoulder, almost as a father might, more moved than he cared to show.

"I forgive you now," he answered.

She left the house, entered her carriage, and bade the coachman drive to the address. Then with a glow of new hope, new happiness at her heart, she fell back. Yes, she would atone for her sin—she would labor with all her strength to reform Laurence Thorndyke, to win forgiveness from Heaven and her friends. Fifteen minutes brought her to the street. Before one house a crowd had collected, a suppressed murmur of infinite excitement running through the throng.

"It is the very house we are looking for, ma'am" said the coachman, opening the door.

She could not tell why, but some swift feeling of evil made her get out and join the crowd.

"What is it?" she breathlessly inquired.

"Man jumped from a three-story window and killed himself," was the answer.

She pressed forward, her hand on her heart—very pale.

"Why did he do it?" she asked.

"Del. trem., ma'am."

"Jim jams, misses."

"Delirium tremens, madam," interposed a gentlemanly man, touching his hat. "He jumped from that upper window, stark crazy, not five minutes ago. Very sad case—very sad case, indeed. A gentleman once. I knew him well. His name is Laurence Thorndyke."

# CHAPTER XXII.

## "THE WAY OF THE TRANSGRESSOR IS HARD."

he stood for a moment faint, sick, stunned, unable to speak or move; then she pressed forward, still without a word, through the throng. All made way for the beautiful, richly-robed lady with the death-white face and dilated eyes.

"Wife," one whispered, falling away.

"Not his wife—his sister," another conjectured.

"Neither," a third said. "I know her. It's Mrs. Hugh Darcy, his late uncle's adopted daughter. He has no sister, and his wife left him long ago."

It is doubtful if she heard; it is certain she never heeded. All she felt or knew was that Laurence Thorndyke lay yonder on the blood-stained flags, dying hard. She was kneeling beside him—a bleeding, mangled heap, crushed almost out of semblance of humanity.

"Laurence! Laurence!" she gasped. "Oh, Heaven! not dead! not dead!"

"Not dead, madam," a pitying voice answered—"not dead yet. I am a physician, and I tell you so. He is insensible at present, but consciousness will return. You know him?"

"Know him!" She looked into the grave, compassionate face with dazed eyes. "Know Laurence Thorndyke? What is it you intend doing with him?" she asked.

The medical man shrugged his shoulders.

"Send him to Bellevue, I suppose, unless some friend steps forward and takes charge of him. They won't want him there"—signifying the boarding-house—"again. And if he is sent to a hospital, I wouldn't give much for his chances of life."

"There is still a chance, then?"

"Well—you know the formula, 'while there's life there's hope.' With the best of care, and nursing, and medical aid, there may be one chance in a hundred for him. With hospital care and attendance, there's not a shadow."

Then for the space of five seconds a pause fell. The city street, the gaping, curious crowd around her faded away, and there arose before Norine a far different and never-to-be-forgotten picture—a desolate autumn evening; a gray, complaining sea, creeping up on its gray sands, a low, fast-drifting sky lying over it, and on the shore a girl standing, reading a few brief lines in Laurence Thorndyke's writing—lines that branded her as a thing of sin and shame for life—that broke her heart as she read. And now—her enemy lay here at her mercy. Why should she lift a finger to save him? Why not let him go to the hospital and take his chance? All that man can do to ruin a woman, body and soul, he had done—why should she lift a finger to save him now?

She thought all this in a moment of time. The tempter stood at her side and rekindled all the pain, and hatred and horror of him. Then her eyes fell upon the crushed, bleeding, senseless form at her feet, and she turned from the dark thoughts within her with horror of herself.

"Well, madam?" the voice of the medical man said, a little impatiently, "how is it to be? You evidently know this unfortunate young man—shall he be removed to the hospital, or—"

"To my house!" She rose suddenly, her self possession returning. "And I must beg of you to accompany him there. No efforts must be spared to restore him. Carry him to the carriage at once."

Men came forward, and the insensible figure was gently lifted, carried to the carriage, and laid upon the cushions.

Norine entered, and took his head in her lap. The doctor followed.

"Home!" she said to the coachman, and they drove slowly back, through the busy streets, to the quiet, red-brick mansion that for years had been Laurence Thorndyke's home.

"How should she tell Helen?" All the way that thought filled Norine.

Through her the wife had left the husband. Was Death here to separate them still more effectually? Would he ever have come to this but for her? In some way did not this horror lie at her door? In all the years that were to come could she ever atone for the wickedness she had done.

As she sat here she felt as though she were a murderess. And once she had loved this man—passionately loved him. "Fiercest love makes fiercest hate." He had cast off that love with scorn, she had vowed revenge, and verily she had had it! Of fortune, of wife and child, and now of life, it might be, she seemed to have robbed him.

"Oh, forgive me my sin!" her whole stricken soul cried out.

They reached the house, the coachman and the physician lifted the still senseless man and carried him to an upper chamber. Summoning her housekeeper to their aid, Norine left them and went in search of the wounded man's wife.

She found her in her own room lying listlessly, wearily, as usual, upon a sofa, gazing with tired, hopeless eyes at the fire, while her little children played about her. Kneeling before her, her face bowed upon the pillows, her tears falling, her voice broken and choked, Norine told the story she had come to tell. In the room above her husband lay, injured it might be unto death.

"If he dies," Norine said, her voice still husky, her face still hidden. "I shall feel, all my life-long, as though I were his murderess. If he dies, how shall I answer to Heaven and to you for the work I have done?"

Helen Thorndyke had arisen and stood holding by the sofa for support, an awful ghastliness on her face, an awful horror in her eyes. Dying! Laurence dying! and like this!

"Let me go to him!" she said, hoarsely, going blindly forward. "*You* are not to blame—he wronged you beyond all forgiveness, but I was his wife and I deserted him. The blame is mine—all mine."

She made her way to the room where they had laid him. On the threshold she paused, faint almost unto death. The yellow, wintry sunshine slanted in and filled the chamber. Upon the white bed he lay, rigid and ghastly. They had washed away the clotted blood, and the face was entirely uninjured. Worn, haggard, awfully corpse-like, it lay upon the pillows, the golden, sparkling sunshine streaming across it.

"Laurence! Laurence! Laurence!"

At that anguished cry of love and agony, all fell back before the wife. She had crossed the room, she had fallen on her knees by the bedside, she had clasped the lifeless figure in her arms, her tears and kisses raining upon the still rigid face. All was forgotten, all forgiven—the bitter wrongs he had done her. Nothing remained but the truth that she loved him still, that he was her husband, and that he lay here before her—dying.

Dying! No need to look twice in the physician's sombre countenance to see that.

"He will not live an hour," he said, in answer to Norine's agonized asking look; "it is doubtful whether he will return to consciousness at all. There is concussion of the brain, and several internal injuries—any one enough to prove his death. Mortal aid is unavailing here."

Dying! Yes, even to Norine's own inexperienced eyes the dreadful seal was yonder on the face among the pillows. His wife's arm encircled his neck, her face was hidden on his bosom, a dull, dumb, moaning sound coming from her lips. He lay there rigid—as if dead already—all unconscious of that last agonized embrace of love, and forgiveness, and remorse.

The doctor left the room, waiting without in case his services should be needed. Norine dispatched a messenger to Mr. Gilbert, another for a clergyman. He might return to reason, if only for a moment before the spirit passed away.

"He cannot—he *cannot* die like this!" she cried out, wringing her hands in her pain. "It is too dreadful!"

The doctor shook his head.

"Dreadful indeed. But 'the way of the transgressor is hard.' He will never speak on earth again."

Richard Gilbert came, almost as pale as the pale remorseful woman who met him. It was the physician who encountered and told him the story first. He entered the room. Norine stood leaning against the foot of the bed. Helen still knelt, holding her dying husband in her arms, her face still hidden on his breast. One look told him that the awful change was already at hand.

And so, with the three he had wronged most on earth around him, Laurence Thorndyke lay dying. Out of the hearts of the three all memory of those wrongs had gone, only a great awe and sorrow left. For Norine, as she stood there, the old days came back—the days that had been the most blessed of her life, when she had given him her whole heart, and fancied she had won his in return. Old thoughts, old memories returned, until her heart was full to breaking; and she hid her face in her hands, with sobs almost as bitter as the wife's own.

The moments wore on—profound silence reigned through the house. Once doctor and clergyman stole in together, glanced at the prostrate man, glanced at each other, and drew back. Priest and physician were alike powerless here. The creeping shadow that goes before was upon that ghastly face already. Death was in the midst of them. Without opening his eyes a sudden tremor ran through the senseless form from head to foot. Helen lifted her awe-struck face. That tremor shook him for a moment as though the soul were forcibly rending its way from the body. Then he stretched out his limbs and lay still.

# CHAPTER XXIII.

## "JENNIE KISSED ME."

t is a bright but chilly May day. In the luxurious sitting-room of Mrs. Liston-Darcy a coal fire is burning, and in a purple arm-chair before this genial fire Mrs. Darcy sits.

She is looking very handsome as she sits here, the brilliant morning sunshine streaming across her dusk beauty and loosely-rippling hair—very handsome in her rose-pink wrapper, with a soft drift of lace about the slim throat and wrists. Very handsome, and yet a trifle out of sorts, too; for the dark, slender brows are contracted, and the brown, luminous eyes gaze sombrely enough into the depths of the fire. She sits looping and unlooping in a nervous sort of restlessness the cord and tassels that bind her slender waist, one slippered foot beating an impatient tattoo on the hassock, her lips compressed in deep and unpleasant thought. About the room, great trunks half-packed stand; in the wardrobe adjoining, her maid is busily folding away dresses. Evidently an exodus is at hand.

"I cannot go—I shall not go until I see him," she is thinking; "it is only what I have richly earned, what my treachery of the past deserves, but it is none the less hard to bear. I cast off his love once, trampled his heart under my feet; he would be less than man to offer it again to one so treacherous and unworthy. And Nellie is an angel—who can wonder that he loves her? It is my just punishment when I have learned how good, how tender, how noble he is, to see her win him from me—when I have learned to love him with my whole heart, to see him give his to her—to lose him in my turn."

She rises with an impatient sigh and walks up and down the room, trying to crush out the bitter pain of loss—the envy and rebellion that *will* arise within her as she thinks of Helen Thorndyke the wife of Richard Gilbert.

For it has come to this—that society begins to whisper Helen will speedily doff the weeds of widowhood for the pale flowing robes of the bride.

It is the second May following Laurence Thorndyke's tragic death, one year and seven months have passed, and the most despairing of widows will not despair forever. For the last half-year, in a quiet way, Helen has been going out a good deal, and is very much admired. And yet no wife had ever grieved more deeply, passionately and truly than Helen Thorndyke in the first dark months following her husband's death. Remorse had added poignancy to her natural grief and horror of his dreadful end, and she had suffered how greatly, only Helen herself will ever know. But that is nearly two years ago, and Helen is but four-and-twenty, and

"Time, that blunts the edge of things, Dries our tears and spoils our bliss."

Time had brought its balm to her, and she could eat, drink and be merry once more. A great peace has followed that tragic time, friends surround her, and foremost and warmest among them, Richard Gilbert.

In the little cottage, presented her by Norine, where Helen and her little ones dwelt, the lawyer was a very frequent visitor. When Mrs. Thorndyke's doors closed to all others they opened to him. And there Mrs. Darcy, a daily comer, met him at least two or three times each week. It had been her wish, after Laurence Thorndyke's death, that the stricken young widow should still make her home in her house, but this Helen had refused. She wanted to be alone, to hide herself somewhere away from all eyes, and Norine had understood the feeling, and gifted her with the pretty, vine-covered cottage outside the city's noise and turmoil. There, with her babies, Helen dragged through those first miserable months, and lived down her first bitter agony of remorseful despair.

When the summer, with its fierce, beating sunshine came they left the city's scorched streets and sun-bleached parks, for the cool breezes and country sweetness of Kent Hill. Thither Richard Gilbert, by invitation, followed. The close intimacy between him and Helen never waned. The children clung to him, and crowed with delight at his coming. He seemed never to weary of their small society. Was it altogether for all their own, or a little for their mother's sake, Norine wondered, feeling her first sharp, jealous pangs. He spent a month with them, then went back. And when September, cool and delicious, came refreshingly to New York, the two handsome young widows, with the two little children, followed. In society that winter, Mrs. Liston-Darcy, the millionaire's heiress, was admired enormously. Not alone, for her bank stock; for her own bonnie black eyes and rare piquant loveliness. Many men bowed down before her, younger, handsomer, more famous men than Richard Gilbert, but her answer was to one and all the same. None of these men touched her heart, to none of them was she inclined to tell the story of her own dark past. It was a bond between herself, and Helen, and Mr. Gilbert. In spite of herself she had learned to love him, to know him, to value him. She turned her wistful eyes to his face, but those dark, lustrous looks had fooled him once—he was not the man to make himself any woman's puppet, and dance as she pulled the strings. He saw nothing but that she was rich, far beyond all riches of his, more beautiful with every passing year, surrounded by young and handsome men, ready to marry her at any moment. She had flung him off, unable to love him years ago. Was it likely that old, and gray, and grim, she could care for him now? He laughed, in a dreary sort of mockery, at the bare thought. Love and marriage had gone out of his life forever; he must be content with Helen's trust and friendship, until some more favored man bore her off, too, with her children; until they also outgrew childish loves. That the world coupled his name with hers, in *that* way, he absolutely never dreamed.

Another May had come, and Norine, wearied of it all, and full of nameless restlessness, took a sudden resolution. She would go abroad. In travel she would find change and peace, and when Helen became his wife she, at least, would not be here to see it.

69

As she walked up and down, deep in her own somber thoughts, the boudoir door opened, and Helen herself came in—she was passing these last days with her friend—came in looking tall and stately, and very fair in her trailing black dress, and most becoming widow's cap.

"Mr. Gilbert has come, Nory," she says. "Will you go down or shall he come up?"

A lovely rose pink flushes into Norine's face. She keeps it averted from Helen as she replies:

"It doesn't matter, does it?" with elaborate carelessness; "he may as well come up. I wish to speak to him on legal business. Susan, you may go for the present."

So Susan goes, and Mrs. Thorndyke returns to the drawing-room and tells Mr. Gilbert, Norine will see him up-stairs. He goes up stairs, and appears presently before the mistress of the house, rather paler than usual if she did but notice it.

"Good-morning, Mr. Gilbert," she says, coming forward with outstretched hand and a smile. "I heard from Liston you had returned to town, and sent for you at once. I hope you enjoyed your trip to Baltimore?"

"As much as one usually enjoys a flying visit, forced upon one at a most inopportune time. I went to make a will. What is this Nellie tells me? You are going to Europe?"

"Going to Europe. I am a restless, dissatisfied sort of mortal, I begin to think—never so happy as when on the wing. Mr. Darcy's death cut short my continental tour before; I shall make a prolonged one this time."

He was very grave and pale; even she noted the pallor now.

"You are looking ill," she said, drawing closer to him; "there is nothing the matter, I hope?"

"Nothing, thank you. How long do you propose remaining away?"

"Three years at the least."

There was a moment's silence. Norine broke it.

"You said just now your trip to Baltimore was to make a will. I sent for you this morning on that same errand; I am going to make my will."

He lifted his eyes and looked at her.

"Your will!" he repeated.

"My will. No, don't look anxious, dear friend; I don't think I am going to die. Only, when one intends to spend three years upon steamers and express trains, one may as well be on the safe side. If anything should happen, it is well to be able to give an account of one's stewardship. I want to provide for Helen and the children. Helen may not need any help of mine"—the steady, sweet tones shook a little—"but it belongs of right to the children. Once it was to have been all their father's. I shall only be giving them back what is rightly theirs. I wish to leave all I have to them. To-morrow, Mr. Gilbert, if you are not busy, I will go to your office and make my will."

Then there was a long, strange pause. In her own room adjoining, Helen Thorndyke sang softly as she moved about. The sweet, soft words came clearly to them as they stood there:

"Jenny kissed me when we met, Jumping from the chair she sat in. Time, you thief! who loved to get Sweets into your list, put that in. Say I'm weary, say I'm sad, Say that health and wealth have missed me. Say I'm growing old, but add— Jenny kissed me!"

Mr. Gilbert was the first to break the spell of silence.

"You are quite right," he said. "It can do no harm, only—it will be trouble taken for nothing. You will pass unscathed the fiery ordeal of steamers and express trains, and," with a smile, "one day you will marry again and make to-morrow's legal work null and void."

"I will never marry."

She said it gravely, and a little coldly. He was watching her—her eyes were steadfastly fixed upon the fire.

"Never marry?" he echoed, still smiling. "What will the honorable member from Ohio say to that?"

"You allude to Mr. More, I suppose," she said, still coldly. "I am aware gossip has coupled our names, and gossip is about as correct in this instance as it usually is."

"You are not engaged to him, then!"

"I am engaged to no one. I care nothing for Mr. More, in the way you mean. Even if I did, I still would not dream of marrying him."

"And why not?"

"Why not? You ask me that—you who know the cruel, shameful story of my past, the story I should have to tell."

"You were far more sinned against than sinning, and you have atoned."

She looked up suddenly—a swift flash of light in her eyes.

"Mr. Gilbert! *You* say that! If I could only think so, only hope I had atoned!"

"You have indeed. I say it with all my heart. Your revenge has been a noble one. You have blest and brightened the life of Helen and her children. For him—he wrought his doom with his own hand! You have atoned."

"To Helen and her children—perhaps yes," she said, her voice broken and low; "but the greatest wrong of all was not done to them. Years ago I sinned against you, beyond all forgiveness. The remorse of my life is for that. You did me so much honor, you trusted me so entirely, and I—ah! what a wretch I must have been in your eyes, what a wretch I must be still."

He arose to his feet, moved beyond all power of silence now.

"Must be still," he repeated. "Norine! *why* do you make me say this? I love and honor you beyond all women."

She gave a low cry, and stood with her hands clasped together.

"I never thought to say it—you force it from me in self-defence. I loved you then—I love you now. You have never ceased for one instant to hold your place in my heart. It is folly, I know, but folly you will not laugh at. If you wronged me, Norine—and you have—I forgive you freely, utterly, and I pray Heaven to make you happy in the love of some happier man."

She stood spell-bound—the shock of surprise was so utter, but over her face a great joy was breaking.

"And Helen?" she gasped.

"Helen?" he looked at her in wonder.

"Did you not know—can it be possible that—Mr. Gilbert, the world says Helen is to be your wife!"

His look of amaze and consternation was so great that she laughed outright—Norine's own sweet, soft laugh.

"Good Heaven!" he said. "What preposterous nonsense! Why, only yesterday Helen was urging me to speak to you—the very folly I am guilty of to-day. She was absurd enough to imagine I had still a chance left. I speedily convinced her of the contrary."

"Did you?" Norine said, a roguish smile dimpling the pretty mouth. "But then Mr. Gilbert is famous as a special pleader, and poor Nellie is so weakly credulous. I don't believe you would find it so easy to convince *me*."

"Norine!" he stood still, his face pale, his eyes startled, "for pity's sake what is it you mean? Don't let me hope only to fool me again! I—I couldn't bear that!"

She came forward, both hands eloquently outstretched, a smile quivering on her lips, tears in the dusk, lovely eyes.

"Richard, see! I love you with all my heart—I have loved you for years. Let me atone for the past—let me keep the plight I broke so long ago—let me be your wife. Life can hold no happiness half so great as that for me!"

And then, as he folded her in his arms close to the heart that would shelter her forever, Helen's happy voice came borne to them where they stood.

"Say I'm weary, say I'm sad, Say that health and wealth have missed me; Say I'm growing old, but add— Jenny kissed me!"

# SIR NOEL'S HEIR.

# CHAPTER I.

**SIR NOEL'S DEATH BED.**

he December night had closed in wet and wild around Thetford Towers. It stood down in the low ground, smothered in trees, a tall gaunt, hoary pile of gray stone, all peaks, and gables, and stacks of chimneys, and rook-infested turrets. A queer, massive, old house, built in the days of James the First, by Sir Hugo Thetford, the first baronet of the name, and as staunch and strong now as then.

The December day had been overcast and gloomy, but the December night was stormy and wild. The wind worried and wailed through the tossing trees with whistling moans and shrieks that were desolately human, and made one think of the sobbing banshee of Irish legends. Far away the mighty voice of the stormy sea mingled its hoarse bass, and the rain lashed the windows in long, slanting lines. A desolate night, and a desolate scene without; more desolate still within, for on his bed, this tempestuous winter night, the last of the Thetford baronets lay dying.

Through the driving wind and lashing rain, a groom galloped along the high road to the village at break-neck speed. His errand was to Dr. Gale, the village surgeon, which gentleman he found just preparing to go to bed.

"For God's sake, doctor," cried the man, white as a sheet, "come with me at once. Sir Noel's killed!"

Dr. Gale, albeit phlegmatic, staggered back, and stared at the speaker aghast.

"What? Sir Noel killed?"

"We're afraid so, doctor; none of us know for certain sure, but he lies there like a dead man. Come, quick, for the love of goodness, if you want to do any service!"

"I'll be with you in five minutes," said the doctor, leaving the room to order his horse, and don his hat and great coat.

Dr. Gale was as good as his word. In less than ten minutes he and the groom were flying recklessly along to Thetford Towers.

"How did it happen?" asked the doctor, hardly able to speak for the furious pace at which they were going. "I thought he was at Lady Stokestone's ball."

"He did go," replied the groom; "leastways he took my lady there; but said he had a friend to meet from London at the Royal George to-night, and he rode back. We don't, none of us, know how it happened; for a better or surer rider than Sir Noel there ain't in Devonshire; but Diana must have slipped and threw him. She came galloping in by herself about half an hour ago, all blown; and me and three more set off to look for Sir Noel. We found him about twenty yards from the gates, lying on his face in the mud, and as stiff and cold as if he was dead."

"And you brought him home and came for me?"

"Directly, sir. Some wanted to send word to my lady, but Mrs. Hilliard, she thought how you had best see him first, sir, so's we'd know what danger he was really in before alarming her ladyship."

"Quite right, William. Let us trust it may not be serious. Had Sir Noel been—I mean, I suppose he had been dining.

"Well, doctor," said William, "Arneaud, that's his *valey de chambre*, you know, said he thought he had taken more wine than prudent going to Lady Stokestone's ball, which her ladyship is very particular about such, you know, sir."

"Ah! that accounts," said the doctor, thoughtfully; "and now, William, my man, don't let's talk any more, for I feel completely blown already."

Ten minutes' sharp riding brought them to the great entrance gates of Thetford Towers. An old woman came out of a little lodge, built in the huge masonry, to admit them, and they dashed up the long winding avenue under the surging oaks and chestnuts. Five minutes more, and Dr. Gale was running up a polished staircase of black, and slippery oak, down an equally wide and black and slippery passage, and into the chamber where Sir Noel lay.

A grand and stately chamber, lofty, dark, and wainscoted, where the wax-candles made luminous clouds in the darkness, and the wood-fire on the marble hearth failed to give heat. The oak floor was overlaid with Persian rugs; the windows were draped in green velvet; and the chairs were upholstered in the same. Near the centre of the apartment stood the bed, tall, broad, quaintly carved, curtained in green damask, and on it, cold and apparently lifeless, lay the wounded man. Mrs. Hilliard, the housekeeper, sat beside him; and Arneaud, the Swiss valet, with a frightened face, stood near the fire.

"Very shocking business this, Mrs. Hilliard," said the doctor, removing his hat and gloves—"very shocking. How is he? Any signs of consciousness yet?"

"None whatever, sir," replied the housekeeper, rising. "I am so thankful you have come. We, none of us, knew what to do for him; and it is dreadful to see him lying there like that."

She moved away, leaving the doctor to his examination. Ten minutes, fifteen, twenty passed; then Dr. Gale turned to her with a very grave face.

"It is too late, Mrs. Hilliard. Sir Noel is a dead man."

"Dead!" repeated Mrs. Hilliard, trembling, and holding by a chair. "Oh, my lady! my lady!"

"I am going to bleed him," said the doctor, "to restore consciousness. He may last until morning. Send for Lady Thetford at once."

Arneaud started up. Mrs. Hilliard looked at him, wringing her hands.

"Break it gently, Arneaud. Oh, my lady! my dear lady! so young, and so pretty—and only married five months!"

The swiss valet left the room. Dr. Gale got out his lancet, and desired Mrs. Hilliard to hold the basin. At first the blood refused to flow—but presently it came in a little feeble stream. The closed eyelids fluttered; there was a restless movement, and Sir Noel Thetford opened his eyes on this mortal life once more. He looked first at the doctor, grave and pale, then at the housekeeper, sobbing on her knees by the bed. He was a young man of seven-and-twenty, fair and handsome, as it was in the nature of the Thetfords to be.

"What is it?" he faintly asked. "What is the matter?"

"You are hurt, Sir Noel," the doctor answered, sadly; "you have been thrown from your horse. Don't attempt to move—you are not able."

"I remember—I remember," said the young man, a gleam of recollection lighting up his ghastly face. "Diana slipped, and I was thrown. How long ago is that?"

"About an hour."

"And I am hurt? Badly?"

He fixed his eyes with a powerful look on the doctor's face, and that good man shrunk away from the news he must tell.

"Badly?" reiterated the young baronet, in a peremptory tone, that told all of his nature. "Ah! you won't speak, I see. I am, and I feel—I feel— Doctor, am I going to die?"

He asked the question with wildness—a sudden horror of death, half starting up in bed. Still the doctor did not speak; still Mrs. Hilliard's suppressed sobs echoed in the stillness of the vast room.

Sir Noel Thetford fell back on his pillow, a shadow as ghastly and awful as death itself, lying on his face. But he was a brave man, and the descendant of a fearless race, and except for one convulsive throe that shook him from head to foot, nothing told his horror of his sudden fate. There was a weird pause. Sir Noel lay staring straight at the oaken wall, his bloodless face awful in its intensity of hidden feeling. Rain and wind outside rose higher and higher, and beat clamorously at the windows; and still above them, mighty and terrible, rose the far-off voice of the ceaseless sea.

The doctor was the first to speak, in hushed and awe-struck tones.

"My dear Sir Noel, the time is short, and I can do little or nothing. Shall I send for the Rev. Mr. Knight?"

The dying eyes turned upon him with a steady gaze.

"How long have I to live? I want the truth."

"Sir Noel, it is very hard, yet it must be Heaven's will. But a few hours, I fear."

"So soon?" said the dying man. "I did not think—Send for Lady Thetford," he cried, wildly, half raising himself again—"send for Lady Thetford at once!"

"We have sent for her," said the doctor; "she will be here very soon. But the clergyman, Sir Noel—the clergyman. Shall we not send for him?"

"No!" said Sir Noel, sharply. "What do I want of a clergyman? Leave me, both of you. Stay, you can give me something, Gale, to keep up my strength to the last? I shall need it. Now go. I want to see no one but Lady Thetford."

"My lady has come," cried Mrs. Hilliard, starting to her feet; and at the same moment the door was opened by Arneaud, and a lady in a sparkling ball-dress swept in. She stood for a moment on the threshold, looking from face to face with a bewildered air.

She was very young—scarcely twenty, and unmistakably beautiful. Taller than common, willowy and slight, with great, dark eyes, flowing dark curls, and a colorless olive skin. The darkly handsome face, with pride in every feature, was blanched now almost to the hue of the dying man's; but that glittering bride-like figure, with its misty point-lace and blazing diamonds, seemed in strange contradiction to the idea of death.

"My lady! my lady!" cried Mrs. Hilliard, with a suppressed sob, moving near her.

The deep, dark eyes turned upon her for an instant, then wandered back to the bed; but she never moved.

"Ada," said Sir Noel, faintly, "come here. The rest of you go. I want no one but my wife."

The graceful figure, in its shining robes and jewels moved over and dropped on its knees by his side. The other three quitted the room and closed the door. Husband and wife were alone with only death to overhear.

"Ada, my poor girl, only five months a wife—it is very hard on you; but it seems I must go. I have a great deal to say to you that I can't die without saying. I have been a villain, Ada—the greatest villain on earth to you."

She had not spoken—she did not speak. She knelt beside him, white and still, looking and listening with strange calm. There was a sort of white horror in her face, but very little of the despairing grief one would naturally look for in the dying man's wife.

"I don't ask you to forgive me, Ada—I have wronged you too deeply for that; but I loved you so dearly—so dearly! Oh, my God! what a lost and cruel wretch I have been!"

He lay panting and gasping for breath. There was a draught which Dr. Gale had left standing near, and he made a motion for it. She held it to his lips, and he drank; her hand was unsteady and spilled it, but still she never spoke.

"I cannot speak loudly, Ada," he said, in a husky whisper, "my strength seems to grow less every moment; but I want you to promise me before I begin my story that you will do what I ask. Promise! promise!"

He grasped her wrist and glared at her almost fiercely.

"Promise!" he reiterated. "Promise! promise!"

"I promise," she said, with white lips.

"May Heaven deal with you, Ada Thetford, as you keep that promise. Listen now."

The wild night wore on. The cries of the wind in the trees grew louder and wilder and more desolate. The rain beat against the curtained glass; the candles guttered and flared; the wood-fire flickered and died out. And still, while hour after hour passed, Ada, Lady Thetford, in her lace and silk and jewels, knelt beside her young husband, and listened to the dark and shameful story he had to tell. She never once faltered, she never spoke nor stirred; but her face was whiter than her dress, and her great dark eyes dilated with a horror too intense for words.

The voice of the dying man sank lower and lower—it fell to a dull, choking whisper at last.

"You have heard all," he said, huskily.

"All?"

The word dropped from her lips like ice—the frozen look of blank horror never left her face.

"And you will keep your promise?"

"Yes."

"God bless you! I can die now. Oh, Ada! I cannot ask you to forgive me; but I love you so much—so much! Kiss me once, Ada, before I go."

His voice failed even with the words. Lady Thetford bent down and kissed him, but her lips were as cold and white as his own.

They were the last words Sir Noel Thetford ever spoke. The restless sea was sullenly ebbing, and the soul of the man was floating away with it. The gray, chill light of a new day was dawning over the Devonshire fields, rainy and raw, and with its first pale ray the soul of Noel Thetford, baronet, left the earth forever.

An hour later, Mrs. Hilliard and Dr. Gale ventured to enter. They had rapped again and again; but there had been no response, and alarmed they had come in. Stark and rigid already lay what was mortal of the Lord of Thetford Towers; and still on her knees, with that frozen look on her face, knelt his living wife.

"My lady! my lady!" cried Mrs. Hilliard, her tears falling like rain. "Oh! my dear lady, come away!"

She looked up; then again at the marble form on the bed, and, without word or cry, slipped back in the old housekeeper's arms in a dead faint.

---

# CHAPTER II.

### CAPT. EVERARD.

t was a very grand and stately ceremonial, that funeral procession from Thetford Towers. A week after that stormy December night they laid Sir Noel Thetford in the family vault, where generation after generation of his race slept their last long sleep. The gentry for miles around were there; and among them came the heir-at-law, the Rev. Horace Thetford, only an obscure country curate now, but failing male heirs to Sir Noel, successor to the Thetford estate, and fifteen thousand a year.

In a bed-chamber, luxurious as wealth can make a room, lay Lady Thetford, dangerously ill. It was not a brain fever exactly, but something very like it into which she had fallen, coming out of that death-like swoon. It was all very sad and shocking—the sudden death of the gay and handsome young baronet, and the serious illness of his poor wife. The funeral oration of the Rev. Mr. Knight, rector of St. Gosport, from the words, "In the midst of life we are in death," was most eloquent and impressive; and women with tender hearts shed tears, and men listened with grave, sad faces. It was such a little while, only five short months, since the wedding-bells had rung, and there had been bonfires and feasting throughout the village; and Sir Noel, looking so proud and so happy, had driven up to the illuminated hall with his handsome bride. Only five months; and now—and now.

74

The funeral was over, and everybody had gone back home—everybody but the Rev. Horace Thetford, who lingered to see the result of my lady's illness, and if she died, to take possession of his estate. It was unutterably dismal in the dark, hushed old house with Sir Noel's ghost seeming to haunt every room—very dismal and ghastly this waiting to step into dead people's shoes. But then there was fifteen thousand a year, and the finest place in Devonshire; and the Rev. Horace would have faced a whole regiment of ghosts, and lived in a vault for that.

But Lady Thetford did not die. Slowly but surely, the fever that had worn her to a shadow left her; and, by and by, when the early primroses peeped through the frost blackened earth, she was able to come down stairs—to come down feeble and frail and weak, colorless as death, almost as silent and cold.

The Rev. Horace went back to Yorkshire, yet not entirely in despair. Female heirs could not inherit Thetford—he stood a chance yet; and the pale young widow was left alone in the dreary old mansion. People were very sorry for her, and came to see her, and begged her to be resigned to her great loss; and Mr. Knight preached endless homilies on patience, and hope, and submission, and Lady Thetford listened to them just as if they had been talking Greek. She never spoke of her dead husband—she shivered at the mention of his name; but that night at his dying bed had changed her as never woman changed before. From a bright, ambitious, pleasure-loving girl, she had grown into a silent, haggard, hopeless woman. All the sunny spring days she sat by the window of her boudoir, gazing at the misty, boundless sea, pale and mute—dead in life.

The friends who came to see her, and Mr. Knight, the rector, were a little puzzled by this abnormal case, but very sorry for the mournful young widow, and disposed to think better of her than ever before. It must surely have been the vilest slander that she had not cared for her husband, that she had married him only for his wealth and title; and that young soldier—that captain of dragoons—must have been a myth. She might have been engaged to him, of course, before Sir Noel came, that seemed to be an undisputed fact; and she might have jilted him for a wealthier lover, that was all a common case. But she must have loved her husband very dearly, or she never would have been broken-hearted like this at his loss.

Spring deepened into summer. The June roses in the flower-gardens of Thetford were in rosy bloom, and my lady was ill again—very, very ill. There was an eminent physician down from London, and there was a frail little mite of babyhood lying amongst lace and flannel; and the eminent physician shook his head, and looked portentously grave as he glanced from the crib to the bed. Whiter than the pillows, whiter than snow, Ada, Lady Thetford, lay, hovering in the Valley of the Shadow of Death; that other feeble little life seemed flickering, too—it was so even a toss-up between the great rival powers, Life and Death, that a straw might have turned the scale either way. So slight being that baby-hold of gasping breath, that Mr. Knight, in the absence of any higher authority, and in the unconsciousness of the mother, took upon himself to baptize it. So a china bowl was brought, and Mrs. Hilliard held the bundle of flannel, and long, white robes, and the child was named—the name which the mother had said weeks ago it was to be called, if a boy—Rupert Noel Thetford; for it was a male heir, and the Rev. Horace's cake was dough.

Days went by, weeks, months, and to the surprise of the eminent physician neither mother nor child died. Summer waned, winter returned; the anniversary of Sir Noel's death came round, and my lady was able to walk down stairs, shivering in the warm air under all her wraps. She had expressed no pleasure or thankfulness in her own safety, or that of her child. She had asked eagerly if it were a boy or a girl; and hearing its sex, had turned her face to the wall, and lay for hours and hours speechless and motionless. Yet it was very dear to her, too, by fits and starts. She would hold it in her arms half a day, sometimes covering it with kisses, with jealous, passionate love, crying over it, and half smothering it with caresses; and then, again, in a fit of sullen apathy, would resign it to its nurse, and not ask to see it for hours. It was very strange and inexplicable, her conduct, altogether; more especially, as with her return to health came no return of cheerfulness or hope. The dark gloom that overshadowed her life seemed to settle into a chronic disease, rooted and incurable. She never went out; she returned no visits; she gave no invitations to those who came to repeat theirs. Gradually people fell off; they grew tired of that sullen coldness in which Lady Thetford wrapped herself as in a mantle, until Mr. Knight and Dr. Gale grew to be almost her only visitors. "Mariana, in the Moated Grange," never led a more solitary and dreary existence than the handsome young widow, who dwelt a recluse at Thetford Towers. For she was very handsome still, of a pale moonlight sort of beauty, the great, dark eyes and abundant dark hair, making her fixed and changeless pallor all the more remarkable.

Months and seasons went by. Summers followed winters, and Lady Thetford still buried herself alive in the gray old manor—and the little heir was six years old. A delicate child still, puny and sickly, petted and spoiled, indulged in every childish whim and caprice. His mother's image and idol—no look of the fair-haired, sanguine, blue-eyed Thetford sturdiness in his little, pinched, pale face, large, dark eyes, and crisp, black ringlets. The years had gone by like a slow dream; life was stagnant enough in St. Gosport, doubly stagnant at Thetford Towers, whose mistress rarely went abroad beyond her own gates, save when she took her little son out for an airing in the pony-phæton.

She had taken him out for one of those airings on a July afternoon, when he had nearly accomplished his seventh year. They had driven seaward some miles from the manor-house, and Lady Thetford and her little boy had got out, and were strolling leisurely up and down the hot, white sands, whilst the groom waited with the pony-phæton just within sight.

The long July afternoon wore on. The sun that had blazed all day like a wheel of fire, dropped lower and lower into the crimson west. The wide sea shone red with the reflections of the lurid glory in the heavens, and the numberless waves glittered and flashed as if sown with stars. A faint, far-off breeze swept over the sea, salt and cold; and the fishermen's boats danced along with the red sunset glinting on their sails.

Up and down, slowly and thoughtfully, the lady walked, her eyes fixed on the wide sea. As the rising breeze met her, she drew the scarlet shawl she wore over her black silk dress closer around her, and glanced at her boy. The little fellow was running over the sands, tossing pebbles into the surf, and hunting for shells; and her eyes left him and wandered once more to the lurid splendor of that sunset on the sea. It was very quiet here, with no living thing in sight but themselves; so the lady's start of astonishment was natural when, turning an abrupt angle in the path leading to the shore, she saw a man coming towards her over the sands. A tall, powerful-looking man of thirty, bronzed and handsome, and with an unmistakably military air, although in plain black clothes. The lady took a second look, then stood stock still, and gazed like one in a dream. The man approached, lifted his hat, and stood silent and grave before her.

"Captain Everard!"

"Yes, Lady Thetford—after eight years—Captain Everard once more."

The deep, strong voice suited the bronzed, grave face, and both had a peculiar power of their own. Lady Thetford, very, very pale, held out one fair jewelled hand.

"Captain Everard, I am very glad to see you again."

He bent over the little hand a moment, then dropped it, and stood looking at her silent.

"I thought you were in India," she said, trying to be at ease. "When did you return?"

"A month ago. My wife is dead. I, too, am widowed, Lady Thetford."

"I am very sorry to hear it," she said, gravely. "Did she die in India?"

"Yes; and I have come home with my little daughter."

"Your daughter! Then she left a child?"

"One. It is on her account I have come. The climate killed her mother. I had mercy on her daughter, and have brought her home."

"I am sorry for your wife. Why did she remain in India?"

"Because she preferred death to leaving me. She loved me, Lady Thetford."

His powerful eyes were on her face—that pale, beautiful face, into which the blood came for an instant at his words. She looked at him, then away over the darkening sea.

"And you, my lady—you gained the desire of your heart, wealth, and a title? Let me hope they have made you a happy woman."

"I am not happy."

"No? But you have been—you were while Sir Noel lived?"

"My husband was very good to me, Captain Everard. His death was the greatest misfortune that could have befallen me."

"But you are young, you are free, you are rich, you are beautiful. You may wear a coronet next time."

His face and glance were so darkly grave, that the covert sneer was almost hidden. But she felt it.

"I shall never marry again, Captain Everard."

"Never? You surprise me! Six years—nay, seven, a widow, and with innumerable attractions. Oh! you cannot mean it."

She made a sudden, passionate gesture—looked at him, then away.

"It is useless—worse than useless, folly, madness, to lift the veil from the irrevocable past. But don't you think, don't you, Lady Thetford, that you might have been equally happy if you had married *me*?"

She made no reply. She stood gazing seaward, cold and still.

"I was madly, insanely, absurdly in love with pretty Ada Vandeleur in those days, and I think I would have made her a good husband; better, Heaven forgive me, than I ever made my poor dead wife. But you were wise and ambitious, my pretty Ada, and bartered your black eyes and raven ringlets to a higher bidder. You jilted me in cold blood, poor love sick devil that I was, and reigned resplendent as my Lady Thetford. Ah! you knew how to choose the better part, my pretty Ada."

"Captain Everard, I am sorry for the past—I have atoned, if suffering can atone. Have a little pity, and speak of it no more!"

He stood and looked at her silently, gravely. Then he said in a voice deep and calm.

"We are both free. Will you marry me now, Ada?"

"I cannot."

"But I love you—I have always loved you. And you—I used to think you loved me."

He was strangely calm and passionless, voice and glance, and face. But Lady Thetford had covered her face, and was sobbing.

"I did—I do—I always have! But I cannot marry you. I will love you all my life; but don't, *don't* ask me to be your wife."

"As you please!" he said, in the same passionless voice. "I think it is best myself; for the George Everard of to-day is not the George Everard who loved you eight years ago. We would not be happy—I know that. Ada, is that your son?"

"Yes."

"I should like to look at him. Here, my little baronet! I want to see you."

The boy, who had been looking curiously at the stranger, ran up at a sign from his mother. The tall captain lifted him in his arms and gazed in his small, thin face, with which his bright tartan plaid contrasted harshly.

"He hasn't a look of the Thetfords. He is your own son, Ada. My little baronet, what is your name?"

"Sir Rupert Thetford," answered the child, struggling to get free. "Let me go—I don't know you!"

The captain set him down with a grim smile; and the boy clung to his mother's skirts, and eyed the tall stranger askance.

"I want to go home, mamma. I'm tired and hungry."

"Presently, dearest. Run to William, he has cakes for you. Captain Everard, I shall be happy to have you at dinner."

"Thanks; but I must decline. I go back to London to-night. I sail for India again in a week."

"So soon! I thought you meant to remain."

"Nothing is further from my intention. I merely brought my little girl over to provide her a home; that is why I have troubled *you*. Will you do me this kindness, Lady Thetford?"

"Take your little girl? Oh! most gladly—most willingly."

"Thanks. Her mother's people are French, and I know little about them; and, save yourself, I can claim friendship with few in England. She will be poor; I have settled on her all I am worth—some three hundred a year; and you, Lady Thetford, you teach her, when she grows up, to catch a rich husband."

She took no notice of the taunt; she looked only too happy to render him this service.

"I am so pleased! She will be such a nice companion for Rupert. How old is she?"

"Nearly four."

"Is she here?"

"No; she is in London. I will fetch her down in a day or two."

"What do you call her?"

"Mabel—after her mother. Then it is settled, Lady Thetford, I am to fetch her?"

"I shall be delighted. But won't you dine with me?"

"No. I must catch the evening train. Farewell, Lady Thetford, and many thanks. In three days I will be here again."

He lifted his hat, and walked away. Lady Thetford watched him out of sight, and then turned slowly, as she heard her little boy calling to her with shrill impatience. The red sunset had faded out; the sea lay gray and cold under the twilight sky; and the evening breeze was chill. Changes in sky, and sea, and land, told of coming night; and Lady Thetford, shivering slightly in the rising wind, hurried away to be driven home.

---

# CHAPTER III.

### "LITTLE MAY."

n the evening of the third day after this interview, a fly from the railway drove up the long, winding avenue leading to the great front entrance of the Thetford mansion. A bronzed military gentleman, a nurse, and a little girl, occupied the fly, and the gentleman's keen, dark eyes wandered searchingly around. Swelling meadows, velvety lawns, sloping terraces, waving trees, bright flower-gardens, quaint old fish-ponds, sparkling fountains, a wooded park, with sprightly deer—that was what he saw, all bathed in the golden halo of the summer sunset. Massive and grand, the old house reared its gray head, half overgrown with ivy and climbing roses. Gaudy peacocks strutted on the terraces; a graceful gazelle flitted out for an instant amongst the trees to look at them, and then fled in affright; and the barking of half a dozen mastiffs greeted their approach noisily.

"A fine place," thought Capt. Everard. "My pretty Ada might have done worse. A grand old place for that puny child to inherit. The staunch old warrior-blood of the Thetfords is sadly adulterated in his pale veins, I fancy. Well, my little May, and how are you going to like all this?"

The child, a bright-faced little creature, with great, restless, sparkling eyes, and rose-bloom cheeks, was looking in delight at a distant terrace.

"See, papa! See all the pretty peacocks! Look, Ellen," to the nurse, "three, four, five! Oh, how pretty!"

"Then little May will like to live here, where she can see pretty peacocks every day?"

"And all the pretty flowers, and the water, and the little boy—where's the little boy, papa?"

"In the house—you'll see him presently; but you must be very good, little May, and not pull his hair, and scratch his face, and put your fingers in his eyes, as you used to do with Willie Brandon. Little May must learn to be good."

Little May put one rosy finger in her mouth, and set her head on one side like a defiant canary. She was one of the prettiest little fairies imaginable, with her pale flaxen curls, sparkling light-gray eyes, and apple-blossom complexion; but she was evidently as much spoiled as small Sir Rupert Thetford himself.

Lady Thetford sat in the long drawing-room, after her solitary dinner, and little Sir Rupert played with his rocking-horse, and a pile of picture-books in a remote corner. The young widow lay back in the violet-velvet depths of a carved and gilded lounging-chair very simply dressed in black and crimson, but looking very fair and stately withal. She was watching her boy with a half smile on her face, when a footman entered with Captain Everard's card. Lady Thetford looked up eagerly.

"Show Captain Everard up at once."

The footman bowed and disappeared. Five minutes later, and the tall captain and his little daughter stood before her.

"At last!" said Lady Thetford, rising and holding out her hand to her old lover, with a smile that reminded him of other days—"at last, when I was growing tired waiting. And this is your little girl—*my* little girl from henceforth? Come here, my pet, and kiss your new mamma."

She bent over the little one, kissing the pink cheek and rosy lips.

"She is fair and tiny—a very fairy; but she resembles you, nevertheless, Captain Everard."

"In temper—yes," said the captain. "You will find her spoiled, and wilful, cross, and capricious, and no end of trouble. Won't she, May?"

"She will be the better match for Rupert on that account," Lady Thetford said, smiling, and unfastening little Miss Everard's wraps with her own fair fingers. "Come here, Rupert, and welcome your new sister."

The young baronet approached, and dutifully kissed little May, who put up her rosebud mouth right willingly. Sir Rupert Thetford was not tall, rather undersized, and delicate for his seven years; but he was head and shoulders over the flaxen-haired fairy, with the bright gray eyes.

"I want a ride on your rocking-horse," cried little May, fraternizing with him at once; "and oh! what nice picture-books, and what a lot!"

The children ran off together to their distant corner, and Captain Everard sat down for the first time.

"You have not dined?" said Lady Thetford. "Allow me to—" her hand was on the bell, but the captain interposed.

"Many thanks—nothing. We dined at the village; and I leave again by the seven-fifty train. It is past seven now, so I have but little time to spare. I fear I am putting you to a great deal of trouble; but May's nurse insists on being taken back to London to-night."

"It will be of no consequence," replied Lady Thetford, "Rupert's nurse will take charge of her. I intend to advertise for a nursery-governess in a few days. Rupert's health has always been so extremely delicate, that he has not even made a pretext of learning yet, and it is quite time. He grows stronger, I fancy; but Dr. Gale tells me frankly his constitution is dangerously weak."

She sighed as she spoke, and looked over to where he stood beside little May who had mounted the rocking-horse boy-fashion. Sir Rupert was expostulating.

"You oughtn't to sit that way—ask mamma. You ought to sit side-saddle. Only boys sit like that."

"I don't care!" retorted Miss Everard, rocking more violently than ever. "I'll sit whatever way I like! Let me alone!"

Lady Thetford looked at the captain with a smile.

"Her father's daughter, surely! bent on having her own way. What a fairy it is! and yet such a perfect picture of health."

"Mabel never was ill an hour in her life, I believe," said her father; "she is not at all too good for this world. I only hope she may not grow up the torment of your life—she is thoroughly spoiled."

"And I fear if she were not, I should do it. Ah! I expect she will be a great comfort to me, and a world of good to Rupert. He has never had a playmate of his own years, and children need children as much as they need sunshine."

They sat for ten minutes conversing gravely, chiefly on business matters connected with little May's annuity—not at all as they had conversed three days before by the seaside. Then, as half-past seven drew near, the captain arose.

"I must go. I will hardly be in time as it is. Come here, little May, and bid papa good-by."

"Let papa come to May," responded his daughter, still rocking. "I can't get off."

Captain Everard laughed; went over, bent down and kissed her.

"Good-by, May; don't forget papa, and learn to be a good girl. Good-by, baronet; try and grow strong and tall. Farewell, Lady Thetford, with my best thanks."

She held his hand, looking up in his sunburned face with tears in her dark eyes.

"We may never meet again, Captain Everard," she said, hurriedly. "Tell me before we part that you forgive me the past."

"Truly, Ada, and for the first time. The service you have rendered me fully atones. You should have been my child's mother—be a mother to her now. Good-by, and God bless you and your boy."

He stooped over, touched her cheek with his lips reverentially, and then was gone. Gone forever—never to meet those he left behind this side of eternity.

Little May bore the loss of her papa and nurse with philosophical indifference; her new playmate sufficed for both. The children took to one another with the readiness of childhood—Rupert all the more readily that he had never before had a playmate of his own years. He was naturally a quiet child, caring more for his picture-books, and his nurse's stories, than for tops, or balls, or marbles. But little May Everard seemed from the first to inspire him with some of her own superabundant vitality and life. The child was never, for a single instant, quiet; she was the most restless, the most impetuous, the most vigorous little creature that can be conceived. Feet, and tongue, and hands, never were still from morning till night; and the life of Sir Rupert's nurse, hitherto one of idle ease, became all at once a misery to her. The little girl was everywhere—everywhere; especially where she had no business to be; and nurse never knew an easy moment for trotting after her, and rescuing her from all sorts of perils. She could climb like a cat, or a goat; and risked her neck about twenty times per diem; she sailed her shoes in her soup, and washed her hands in her milk-and-water. She became the intimate friend of the pretty peacocks, and the big, good-tempered dogs, with whom, in utter fearlessness, she rolled about in the grass half the day. She broke young Rupert's toys, tore his picture-books, slapped his face, pulled his hair, and made herself master of the situation before she had been twenty-four hours in the house. She was thoroughly and completely spoiled. What India nurses had left undone, injudicious petting and flattery, on the homeward passage, had completed, and her temper was something appalling. Her shrieks of passion at the slightest contradiction of her imperial will rang through the house, and rent the tortured tympanums of all who heard. The little Xantippe would fling herself flat on the carpet, and literally scream herself black in the face, until, in dread of apoplexy and sudden death, her frightened hearers hastened to yield. Of course, one such victory insured all the rest. As for Sir Rupert, before she had been a week at Thetford Towers, he dared not call his soul his own. She had partially scalped him on several occasions, and left the mark of her cat-like nails in his tender visage; but her venomous power of screeching for hours at will, had more to do with the little baronet's dread of her than anything else. He fled ingloriously in every battle—running in tears to mamma, and leaving the field and the trophies of victory triumphantly to Miss Everard. With all this, when not thwarted—when allowed to smash toys, and dirty her clothes, and smear her infantile face, and tear pictures, and torment inoffensive lapdogs; when allowed, in short, to follow "her own sweet will," little May was as charming a fairy as ever the sun shone on. Her gleeful laugh made music in the dreary old rooms, such as had never been heard there for many a day, and her mischievous antics were the delight of all who did not suffer thereby. The servants petted and indulged her, and fed her on unwholesome cakes and sweetmeats, and made her worse and worse every day of her life.

Lady Thetford saw all this with inward apprehension. If her ward was completely beyond her power of control at four, what would she be a dozen years hence.

"Her father was right," thought the lady. "I am afraid she *will* give me a great deal of trouble. I never saw so headstrong, so utterly unmanageable a child."

But Lady Thetford was very fond of the fairy despot withal. When her son came running to her for succor, drowned in tears, and bearing the marks of little May's claws, his mother took him in her arms and kissed him and soothed him—but she never punished the offender. As for Sir Rupert, he might fly ignominiously, but he never fought back. Little May had the hair-pulling and face-scratching all to herself.

"I must get a governess," mused Lady Thetford. "I may find one who can control this little vixen; and it is really time that Rupert began his studies. I will speak to Mr. Knight about it."

Lady Thetford sent that very day to the rector her ladyship's compliments, the servant said, and would Mr. Knight call at his earliest convenience. Mr. Knight sent in answer to expect him that same evening; and on his way he fell in with Dr. Gale, going to the manor-house on a professional visit.

"Little Sir Rupert keeps weakly," he said; "no constitution to speak of. Not at all like the Thetfords—splendid old stock, the Thetfords, but run out—run out. Sir Rupert is a Vandeleur, inherits his mother's constitution—delicate child, very."

"Have you seen Lady Thetford's ward?" inquired the clergyman, smiling: "no hereditary weakness there, I fancy. I'll answer for the strength of her lungs at any rate. The other day she wanted Lady Thetford's watch for a plaything; she couldn't have it, and down she fell flat on the floor in what her nurse calls 'one of her tantrums.' You should have heard her, her shrieks were appalling."

"I have," said the doctor with emphasis; "she has the temper of the old demon. If I had anything to do with that child, I should whip her within an inch of her life—that's all she wants, lots of whipping. The Lord only knows the future, but I pity her prospective husband."

"The taming of the shrew," laughed Mr. Knight. "Katharine and Petruchio over again. For my part, I think Lady Thetford was unwise to undertake such a charge. With her delicate health it is altogether too much for her."

The two gentlemen were shown into the library, while the servant went to inform his lady of their arrival. The library had a French window opening upon a sloping lawn, and here, chasing butterflies in high glee, were the two children—the pale, dark-eyed baronet, and the flaxen-tressed little East Indian.

"Look," said Dr. Gale. "Is Sir Rupert going to be your Petruchio? Who knows what the future may bring forth—who knows that we do not behold the future Lady Thetford?"

"She is very pretty," said the rector, thoughtfully, "and she may change with years. Your prophecy may be fulfilled."

The present Lady Thetford entered as he spoke. She had heard the remarks of both, and there was an unusual pallor and gravity in her face as she advanced to receive them.

Little Sir Rupert was called in, May followed, with a butterfly crushed to death in each fat little hand.

"She kills them as fast as she catches them," said Sir Rupert, ruefully. "It's cruel, isn't it, mamma?"

Little May, quite abashed, displayed her dead prizes, and cut short the doctor's conference by impatiently pulling her play-fellow away.

"Come, Rupert, come," she cried. "I want to catch the black one with the yellow wings. Stick your tongue out and come."

Sir Rupert displayed his tongue, and submitted his pulse to the doctor, and let himself be pulled away by May.

"The gray mare in that team is decidedly the better horse," laughed the doctor. "What a little despot in pinafores it is."

When her visitors had left, Lady Thetford walked to the window and stood watching the two children racing in the sunshine. It was a pretty sight, but the lady's face was contracted with a look of pain.

"No, no," she thought. "I hope not—I pray not. Strange! but I never thought of the possibility before. She will be poor, and Rupert must marry a rich wife, so that if—"

She paused with a sort of shudder; then added:

"What will he think, my darling boy, of his father and mother, if that day ever comes!"

# CHAPTER IV.

### MRS. WEYMORE.

ady Thetford had settled her business satisfactorily with the rector of St. Gosport.

"Nothing could be more opportune," he said. "I am going to London next week on business, which will detain me upwards of a fortnight. I will immediately advertise for such a person as you want."

"You must understand," said her ladyship, "I do not require a young girl. I wish a middle-aged person—a widow, for instance, who has had children of her own. Both Rupert and May are spoiled—May particularly is perfectly unmanageable. A young girl as governess for her would never do."

Mr. Knight departed with these instructions, and the following week started for the great metropolis. An advertisement was at once inserted in the *Times* newspaper, stating all Lady Thetford's requirements, and desiring immediate application. Another week later, and Lady Thetford received the following communication:

"Dear Lady Thetford—I have been fairly besieged with applications for the past week—all widows, and all professing to be thoroughly competent. Clergymen's widows, doctor's widows, officer's widows—all sorts of widows. I never before thought so many could apply for one situation. I have chosen one in sheer desperation—the widow of a country gentleman in distressed circumstances, whom I think will suit. She is eminently respectable in appearance, quiet and lady-like in manner, with five years' experience in the nursery-governess line, and the highest recommendation from her late employers. She has lost a child, she tells me; and from her looks and manner altogether, I should judge she was a person conversant with misfortune. She will return with me early next week—her name is Mrs. Weymore."

Lady Thetford read this letter with a little sigh of relief—some one else would have the temper and outbreaks of little May to contend with now. She wrote to Captain Everard that same day, to announce his daughter's well being, and inform him that she had found a suitable governess to take charge of her.

The second day of the ensuing week the rector and the new governess arrived. A fly from the railway brought her and her luggage to Thetford Towers late in the afternoon, and she was taken at once to the room that had been prepared for her, whilst the servant went to inform Lady Thetford of her arrival.

"Fetch her here at once," said her ladyship, who was alone, as usual, in the long drawing-room, with the children, "I wish to see her."

Ten minutes after, the drawing-room door was flung open, and "Mrs. Weymore, my lady," announced the footman.

Lady Thetford arose to receive her new dependent, who bowed and stood before her with a somewhat fluttered and embarrassed air. She was quite young, not older than my lady herself, and eminently good-looking. The tall, slender figure, clad in widow's weeds, was as symmetrical as Lady Thetford's own, and the dull black dress set off the pearly fairness of the blonde skin, and the rich abundance of fair hair. Lady Thetford's brows contracted a little; this fair, subdued, gentle-looking, girlish young woman, was hardly the strong-minded, middle-aged matron she had expected to take the nonsense out of obstreperous May Everard.

"Mrs. Weymore, I believe," said Lady Thetford, resuming her *fauteuil*, "pray be seated. I wished to see you at once, because I am going out this evening. You have had five years' experience as a nursery-governess, Mr. Knight tells me?"

"Yes, Lady Thetford."

There was a little tremor in Mrs. Weymore's low voice, and her blue eyes shifted and fell under Lady Thetford's steady, and somewhat haughty gaze.

"Yet you look young—much younger than I imagined, or wished."

"I am twenty-seven years old, my lady."

That was my lady's own age precisely, but she looked half a dozen years the elder of the two.

"Are you a native of London?"

"No, my lady—of Berkshire."

"And you have been a widow how long?"

What ailed Mrs. Weymore? She was all white and trembling—even her hands, folded and pressed together in her lap, shook in spite of her.

"Eight years and more."

She said it with a sort of sob, hysterically choked. Lady Thetford looked on surprised, and a trifle displeased. She was a very proud woman, and certainly wished for no scene with her hired dependents.

"Eight years is a tolerable time," she said, coolly. "You have lost children?"

"One, my lady."

Again that choked, hysterical sob. My lady went on pitilessly.

"Is it long ago?"

"When—when I lost its father."

"Ah! both together? That was rather hard. Well, I hope you understand the management of children—spoiled ones particularly. Here are the two you are to take charge of. Rupert—May, come here."

The children came over from their corner. Mrs. Weymore drew May towards her, but Sir Rupert held aloof.

"That is my ward—this is my son. I presume Mr. Knight has told you. If you can subdue the temper of that child, you will prove yourself, indeed, a treasure. The east parlor has been fitted up for your use; the children will take their meals there with you; the room adjoining is to be the school-room. I have appointed one of the maids to wait on you. I trust you find your chamber comfortable."

"Exceedingly so, my lady."

"And the terms proposed by Mr. Knight suit you?"

Mrs. Weymore bowed. Lady Thetford rose to close the interview.

"You must need refreshment and rest after your journey. I will not detain you longer. To-morrow your duties commence."

She rang the bell—directed the servant who came to show the governess to the east parlor and to see to her wants, and then to send nurse for the children. Fifteen minutes after she drove away in the pony-phæton; whilst the new governess stood by the window of the east parlor and watched her vanish in the amber haze of the August sunset.

Lady Thetford's business in St. Gosport detained her a couple of hours. The big, white, August moon was rising as she drove slowly homeward, and the nightingales sang their vesper lay in the scented hedge-rows. As she passed the rectory, she saw Mr. Knight leaning over his own gate, enjoying the placid beauty of the summer evening; and Lady Thetford reined in her ponies to speak to him.

"So happy to see your ladyship. Won't you alight and come in? Mrs. Knight will be delighted."

"Not this evening, I think. Had you much trouble about my business?"

"I had applications enough, certainly," laughed the rector. "I had reason to remember Mr. Weller's immortal advice, 'Beware of widders.' How do you like your governess?"

"I have hardly had time to form an opinion. She is younger than I should desire."

"She looks much younger than the age she gives, I know; but that is a common case. I trust my choice will prove satisfactory—her references are excellent. Your ladyship has had an interview with her?"

"A very brief one. Her manner struck me unpleasantly—so odd, and shy, and nervous. I hardly know how to characterize it; but she may be a paragon of governesses, for all that. Good-evening; best regards to Mrs. Knight. Call soon and see how your *protégé* gets on."

Lady Thetford drove away. As she alighted from the pony-carriage and ascended the great front steps of the house, she saw the pale governess still seated at the window of the east parlor, gazing dejectedly out at the silvery moonlight.

"A most woeful countenance," thought my lady. "There is some deeper grief than the loss of a husband and child eight years ago, the matter with that woman. I don't like her."

No, Lady Thetford did not like the meek and submissive-looking governess, but the children and the rest of the household did. Sir Rupert and little May took to her at once—her gentle voice, her tender smile seemed to win its way to their capricious favor; and before the end of the first week, she had more influence over them than mother and nurse together. The subdued and gentle governess soon had the love of all at Thetford Towers, except its mistress, from Mrs. Hilliard, the stately housekeeper, down. She was so courteous and considerate, so anxious to avoid giving trouble. Above all, that fixed expression of settled sadness on her pale face, made its way to every heart. She had full charge of the children now: they took their meals with her, and she had them in her keeping the best part of the day—an office that was no sinecure. When they were with their nurse, or my lady, the governess sat alone in the east parlor, looking out dreamily at the summer landscape, with her own brooding thoughts.

One evening, when she had been at Thetford Towers over a fortnight, Mrs. Hilliard, coming in, found her sitting dreamily by herself, neither reading nor working. The children were in the drawing-room, and her duties were over for the day.

"I am afraid you don't make yourself at home here," said the good-natured housekeeper; "you stay too much alone, and it isn't good for young people like you."

"I am used to solitude," replied the governess, with a smile that ended in a sigh, "and I have grown to like it. Will you take a seat?"

"No," said Mrs. Hilliard. "I heard you say the other day you would like to go over the house; so, as I have a couple of hours' leisure, I will show it to you now."

The governess rose eagerly.

"I have been wanting to see it so much," she said, "but I feared to give trouble by asking. It is very good of you to think of me, dear Mrs. Hilliard."

"She isn't much used to people thinking of her," reflected the housekeeper, "or she wouldn't be so grateful for trifles. Let me see," aloud, "you have seen the drawing-room, and the library, and that is all, except your own apartments. Well come this way, I'll show you the old south-wing."

Through long corridors, up wide, black, slippery staircases, into vast, unused rooms, where ghostly echoes and darkness had it all to themselves, Mrs. Hilliard led the governess.

"These apartments have been unused since before the late Sir Noel's time," said Mrs. Hilliard; "his father kept them full in the hunting season, and at Christmas time. Since Sir Noel's death, my lady has shut herself up and received no company, and gone nowhere. She is beginning to go out more of late than she has done ever since his death."

Mrs. Hilliard was not looking at the governess, or she might have been surprised at the nervous restlessness and agitation of her manner, as she listened to these very commonplace remarks.

"Lady Thetford was very much attached to her husband, then?" Mrs. Weymore said, her voice tremulous.

"Ah! that she was! She must have been, for his death nearly killed her. It was sudden enough, and shocking enough, goodness knows! I shall never forget that dreadful night. This is the old banqueting-hall, Mrs. Weymore, the largest and dreariest room in the house."

Mrs. Weymore, trembling very much, either with cold or that unaccountable nervousness of hers, hardly looked round at the vast wilderness of a room.

"You were with the late Sir Noel then, when he died?"

"Yes, until my lady came. Ah! it was a dreadful thing. He had taken her to a ball, and riding home his horse threw him. We sent for the doctor and my lady at once; and when she came, all white and scared-like, he sent us out of the room. He was as calm and sensible as you or me, but he seemed to have something on his mind. My lady was shut up with him for about three hours, and then we went in—Dr. Gale and me. I shall never forget that sad sight. Poor Sir Noel was dead, and she was kneeling beside him in her ball-dress, like somebody turned to stone. I spoke to her, and she looked up at me, and then fell back in my arms in a fainting fit. Are you cold, Mrs. Weymore, that you shake so?"

"No—yes—it is this desolate room, I think," the governess answered, hardly able to speak.

"It *is* desolate. Come, I'll show you the billiard-room, and then we'll go up stairs to the room Sir Noel died in. Everything remains just as it was—no one has ever slept there since. If you only knew, Mrs. Weymore, what a sad time it was; but you do know, poor dear, you have lost a husband yourself."

The governess flung up her hands before her face with a suppressed sob, so full of anguish that the housekeeper stared at her aghast. Almost as quickly she recovered herself again.

"Don't mind me," she said, in a choking voice, "I can't help it. You don't know what I suffered—what I still suffer. Oh, pray, don't mind me."

"Certainly not, my dear," said Mrs. Hilliard, thinking inwardly the governess was a very odd person indeed.

They looked at the billiard-room, where the tables stood, dusty and disused, and the balls lay idly by.

"I don't know when it will be used again," said Mrs. Hilliard, "perhaps not until Sir Rupert grows up. There was a time," lowering her voice, "when I thought he would never live to be as old and strong as he is now. He was the punyist baby, Mrs. Weymore, you ever looked at—nobody thought he would live. And that would have been a pity, you know, for the Thetford estate would have gone to a distant branch of the family. As it would, too, if Sir Rupert had been a girl."

She went up stairs to the inhabited part of the building, followed by Mrs. Weymore, who seemed to grow more and more agitated with every word the old housekeeper said.

"This is Sir Noel's room," said Mrs. Hilliard, in an awe-struck whisper, as if the dead man still lay there; "no one ever enters here but me."

She unlocked it, as she spoke, and went in. Mrs. Weymore followed with a face of frightened pallor that struck even the housekeeper.

"Good gracious me! Mrs. Weymore, what is the matter? You are as pale as a ghost. Are you afraid to enter a room where a person has died?"

Mrs. Weymore's reply was almost inaudible; she stood on the threshold, pallid, trembling, unaccountably moved. The housekeeper glanced at her suspiciously.

"Very odd," she thought, "very! The new governess is either the most nervous person I ever met, or else—no, she can't have known Sir Noel in his lifetime. Of course not."

They left the chamber after a cursory glance around—Mrs. Weymore never advancing beyond the threshold. She had not spoken, and that white pallor made her face ghastly still.

"I'll show you the picture-gallery," said Mrs. Hilliard, "and then, I believe, you will have seen all that is worth seeing at Thetford Towers."

She led the way to a half-lighted room, wainscoted and antique, like all the rest, where long rows of dead and gone Thetfords looked down from the carved walls. There were knights in armor; countesses in ruffles, and powder, and lace; bishops, mitre on head and crozier in hand; and judges in gown and wig. There were ladies in pointed stomachers and jewelled fans, with the waists of their dresses under their arms, but all fair and handsome, and unmistakably alike. Last of all the long array, there was Sir Noel, a fair-haired, handsome youth of twenty, with a smile on his face, and a happy radiance in his blue eyes. And by his side, dark, and haughty, and beautiful, was my lady in her bridal-robes.

"There is not a handsomer face amongst them all than my lady's," said Mrs. Hilliard, with pride. "You ought to have seen her when Sir Noel first brought her home, she was the most beautiful creature I ever looked at. Ah, it was such a pity he was killed. I suppose they'll be having Sir Rupert's taken next and hung beside her. He don't look much like the Thetfords; he's his mother over again—a Vandeleur, dark and still."

If Mrs. Weymore made any reply, the housekeeper did not catch it; she was standing with her face averted, hardly looking at the portraits, and was the first to leave the picture-gallery.

There were a few more rooms to be seen—a drawing-room suite, now closed and disused; an ancient library, with a wonderful stained window, and a vast echoing reception-room. But it was all over at last, and Mrs. Hilliard, with her keys, trotted cheerfully off; and Mrs. Weymore was left to solitude and her own thoughts once more.

A strange person, certainly. She locked the door and fell down on her knees by the bedside, sobbing until her whole form was convulsed.

"Oh! why did I come here? Why did I come here?" came passionately with the wild storm of sobs. "I might have known how it would be! Nearly nine years—nine long, long years, and not to have forgotten yet!"

---

# CHAPTER V.

## A JOURNEY TO LONDON.

ery slowly, very monotonously went life at Thetford Towers. The only noticeable change was that my lady went rather more into society, and a greater number of visitors came to the manor. There had been a children's party on the occasion of Sir Rupert's eighth birthday, and Mrs. Weymore had played for the little people to dance; and my lady had cast off her chronic gloom, and been handsome and happy as of old. There had been a dinner-party later—an unprecedented event now at Thetford Towers; and the weeds, worn so long, had been discarded, and in diamonds and black velvet Lady Thetford had been beautiful, and stately, and gracious, as a young queen. No one knew the reason of the sudden change, but they accepted the fact just as they found it, and set it down, perhaps, to woman's caprice.

So, slowly the summer passed; autumn came and went, and it was December, and the ninth anniversary of Sir Noel's sudden death.

A gloomy, day—wet, and bleakly cold. The wind, sweeping over the angry sea, surged and roared through the skeleton trees; the rain lashed the windows in rattling gusts; and the leaden sky hung low and frowning over the drenched and dreary earth. A dismal day—very like that other, nine years ago, that had been Sir Noel's last.

In Lady Thetford's boudoir a bright-red coal-fire blazed. Pale-blue curtains of satin damask shut out the winter prospect, and the softest and richest of bright carpets hushed every footfall. Before the fire, on a little table, my lady's breakfast temptingly stood; the silver, old and quaint; the rare antique porcelain sparkling in the ruddy firelight. An easy-chair, carved and gilded, and cushioned in azure velvet, stood by the table; and near my lady's plate lay the letters and papers the morning's mail had brought.

A toy of a clock on the low marble mantel chimed musically ten as my lady entered. In her dainty morning *negligée*, with her dark hair rippling and falling low on her neck, she looked very young, and fair, and graceful. Behind her came her maid, a blooming English girl, who took off the covers, and poured out my lady's chocolate.

Lady Thetford sank languidly into the azure velvet depths of her chair and took up her letters. There were three—one, a note from her man of business; one, an invitation to a dinner-party; and the third, a big official-looking document, with a huge seal, and no end of postmarks. The languid eyes suddenly lighted; the pale cheeks flushed as she took it eagerly up. It was a letter from India from Captain Everard.

Lady Thetford sipped her chocolate, and read her letter leisurely, with her slippered feet on the shining fender. It was a long letter, and she read it over, slowly, twice, three times before she laid it down. She finished her breakfast, motioned her maid to remove the service, and lying back in her chair, with her deep, dark eyes fixed dreamily on the fire, she fell into a reverie of other days far gone. The lover of her girlhood came back to her from over the sea. He was lying at her feet once more in the long summer days, under the waving trees of her girlhood's home. Ah! how happy, how happy she had been in those by-gone days, before Sir Noel Thetford had come, with his wealth and his title, to tempt her from her love and truth.

Eleven struck, twelve, from the musical clock on the mantel, and still my lady sat, living in the past. Outside the wintry storm raged on; the rain clamored against the curtained glass, and the wind sighed among the trees. With a long sigh my lady awoke from her dream, and mechanically took up the *Times* newspaper—the first of the little heap.

"Vain, vain," she thought, dreamily; "worse than vain those dreams now. With my own hand I threw back the heart that loved me; of my own free will I resigned the man I loved. And now the old love, that I thought would die in the splendor of my new life, is stronger than ever—and it is nine years too late."

She tried to wrench her thoughts away and fix them on her newspaper. In vain! her eyes wandered aimlessly over the closely-printed columns—her mind was in India with Captain Everard. All at once she started, uttered a sudden, sharp cry, and grasped the paper with dilated eyes and whitening cheeks. At the top of a column of "personal" advertisements was one which her strained eyes literally devoured.

"If Mr. Vyking, who ten years ago left a male infant in charge of Mrs. Martha Brand, wishes to keep that child out of the work-house, he will call, within the next five days, at No. 17 Waddington Street, Lambeth."

Again and again, and again Lady Thetford read this apparently uninteresting advertisement. Slowly the paper dropped into her lap, and she sat staring blankly into the fire.

"At last!" she thought, "at last it has come. I fancied all danger was over—that death, perhaps, had forestalled me; and now, after all these years, I am summoned to keep my broken promise!"

The hue of death had settled on her face; she sat cold and rigid, staring with that blank, fixed gaze into the fire. Ceaselessly beat the rain; wilder grew the December day; steadily the moments wore on, and still she sat in that fixed trance. The ormolu clock struck two—the sound aroused her at last.

"I must!" she said, setting her teeth. "I will! My boy shall not lose his birthright, come what may."

She rose and rang the bell—very pale, but quite calm. Her maid answered the summons.

"Eliza," my lady asked, "at what hour does the afternoon train leave St. Gosport for London?"

Eliza stared—did not know; but would ascertain. In five minutes she was back.

"At half-past three, my lady; and another at seven."

Lady Thetford glanced at the clock—it was a quarter past two.

"Tell William to have the carriage at the door at a quarter-past three; and do you pack my dressing-case, and the few things I shall need for two or three days' absence. I am going to London."

Eliza stood for a moment quite petrified. In all the nine years of her service under my lady, no such order as this had ever been received. To go to London at a moment's notice—my lady, who rarely went beyond her own park gates! Turning away, not quite certain that her ears had not deceived her, my lady's voice arrested her.

"Send Mrs. Weymore to me; and do you lose no time in packing up."

Eliza departed. Mrs. Weymore appeared. My lady had some instructions to give concerning the children during her absence. Then the governess was dismissed, and she was again alone.

Through the wind and rain of the wintry storm, Lady Thetford was driven to the station in time to catch the three-fifty train to the metropolis. She went unattended; with no message to any one, only saying she would be back in three days at the farthest.

In that dull household, where so few events ever disturbed the stagnant quiet, this sudden journey produced an indescribable sensation. What could have taken my lady to London at a moment's notice? Some urgent reason it must have been to force her out of the gloomy seclusion in which she had buried herself since her husband's death. But, discuss it as they might, they could come no nearer the heart of the mystery.

# CHAPTER VI.

### GUY.

he rainy December day closed in a rainier night. Another day dawned on the world, sunless, and chilly, and overcast still.

It dawned on London in murky, yellow fog, on sloppy, muddy streets—in gloom and dreariness, and a raw, easterly wind. In the densely populated streets of the district of Lambeth, where poverty huddled in tall, gaunt buildings, the dismal light stole murkily and slowly over the crowded, filthy streets, and swarming purlieus.

In a small upper room of a large dilapidated house, this bad December morning, a painter stood at his easel. The room was bare, and cold, and comfortless in the extreme; the painter was middle-aged, small, brown, and shrivelled, and very much out at elbows. The dull, gray light fell full on his work—no inspiration of genius by any means—only the portrait, coarsely colored, of a fat, well-to-do butcher's daughter round the corner. The man was Joseph Legard, scene-painter to one of the minor city theatres, who eked out his slender income by painting portraits when he could get them to paint. He was as fond of his art as any of the great old masters; but he had only one attribute in common with those immortals—extreme poverty; for his family was large, and Mr. Legard found it a tight fit, indeed, to "make both ends meet."

He stood over his work this dull morning, however, in his fireless room, with a cheerful, brown face, whistling a tune. In the adjoining room, he could hear his wife's voice raised shrilly, and the cries of half a dozen Legards. He was used to it, and it did not disturb him; and he painted and whistled cheerily, touching up the butcher's daughter's snub nose and fat cheeks, and double chin, until light footsteps came running up stairs, and the door was flung wide by an impetuous hand. A boy of ten, or thereabouts, came in—a bright-eyed, fair-haired lad, with a handsome, resolute face, and eyes of cloudless, Saxon blue.

"Ah, Guy!" said the scene-painter, turning round and nodding good-humoredly. "I've been expecting you. What do you think of Miss Jenkins?"

The boy looked at the picture with the glance of an embryo connoisseur.

"It's as like her as two peas, Joe; or would be, if her hair was a little redder, and her nose a little thicker, and the freckles were plainer. But it looks like her as it is."

"Well, you see Guy," said the painter, going on with Miss Jenkins' left eyebrow, "it don't do to make 'em too true—people don't like it; they pay their money, and they expect to take it out in good looks. And now, any news this morning, Guy?"

The boy leaned against the window and looked out into the dingy street, his bright young face growing gloomy and overcast.

"No," he said, moodily; "there is no news, except that Phil Darking was drunk last night, and savage as a mad dog this morning—and that's no news, I'm sure."

"And nobody's come about the advertisement in the *Times*?"

"No, and never will. It's all humbug what granny says about my belonging to anybody rich; if I did, they'd have seen after me long ago. Phil says my mother was a housemaid, and my father a valet—and they were only too glad to get me off their hands. Vyking was a valet, granny says she knows; and it's not likely he'll turn up after all these years. I don't care, I'd rather go to the work-house; I'd rather starve in the streets, than live another week with Phil Darking."

The blue eyes filled with tears, and he dashed them passionately away. The painter looked up with a distressed face.

"Has he been beating you again, Guy?"

"It's no matter—he's a brute. Granny and Ellen are sorry, and do what they can; but that's nothing. I wish I had never been born."

"It is hard," said the painter, compassionately, "but keep up heart, Guy; if the worst comes, why you can stop here and take pot-luck with the rest—not that that's much better than starvation. You can take to my business shortly now; and you'll make a better scene-painter than ever I could. You've got it in you."

"Do you really think so, Joe?" cried the boy, with sparkling eyes. "Do you? I'd rather be an artist than at king—Halloo!"

He stopped short in surprise, staring out of the window. Legard looked. Up the dirty street came a Hansom cab, and stopped at their own door. The driver alighted, made some inquiry, then opened the cab-door, and a lady stepped lightly out on the curb-stone—a lady tall and stately, dressed in black, and closely veiled.

"Now who can this visitor be for?" said Legard. "People in this neighborhood ain't in the habit of having morning-calls made on them in cabs. She's coming up stairs."

He held the door open, listening. The lady ascended the first flight of stairs, stopped on the landing, and inquired of some one for "Mrs. Martha Brand."

"For granny!" exclaimed the boy. "Joe, I shouldn't wonder if it was some one about that advertisement, after all."

"Neither should I," said Legard. "There! she's gone in. You'll be sent for directly, Guy."

Yes, the lady had gone in. She had encountered on the landing a sickly young woman, with a baby in her arms, who had stared at the name she inquired for.

"Mrs. Martha Brand? Why, that's mother. Walk in this way, if you please, ma'am."

She opened a door, and ushered the veiled lady into a small, close room, poorly furnished. Over a smouldering fire, mending stockings, sat an old woman, who, notwithstanding the extreme shabbiness and poverty of her dress, lifted a pleasant, intelligent old face.

"A lady to see you, mother," said the young woman hushing her fretful baby, and looking curiously at the veiled face.

But the lady made no attempt to raise the envious screen, not even when Mrs. Martha Brand got up, dropping a respectful little servant's courtesy, and placing a chair. It was a very thick veil—an impenetrable shield, and nothing could be discovered of the face behind it but that it was fixedly pale. She sank into the seat, her face turned to the old woman behind that sable screen.

"You are Mrs. Brand?"

The voice was refined and patrician. It would have told she was a lady, even if the rich garments she wore did not.

"Yes, ma'am—your ladyship; Martha Brand."

"And you inserted that advertisement in the *Times* regarding a child left in your care, ten years ago?"

Mother and daughter started, and stared at the speaker.

"It was addressed to Mr. Vyking, who left the child in your charge; by which, I infer, you are not aware that he has left England."

"Left England, has he?" said Mrs. Brand. "More shame for him, then, never to let me know, or leave a farthing to support the boy."

"I am inclined to believe it was not his fault," said the clear, patrician voice. "He left England suddenly, and against his will; and I have reason to think will never return. But there are others interested—more interested than he could possibly be in the child, who remain, and who are willing to take him off your hands. But first, why is it you are so anxious, after keeping him all these years, to get rid of him?"

"Well, you see, your ladyship," replied Martha Brand "it is not me, nor likewise Ellen there, who is my daughter. We'd keep the lad and welcome, and share the last crust, we had with him, as we often have—for we're very poor people; but you see, Ellen, she's married now, and her husband never could bear Guy—that's what we call him, your ladyship—Guy, which it was Mr. Vyking's own orders. Phil Darking, her husband, never did like him somehow, and when he gets drunk, saving your ladyship's presence, he beats him most unmerciful. And now we're going to America—to New York, where Phil's got a brother, and work is better; and he won't fetch Guy. So your ladyship, I thought I'd try once more before we deserted him, and put that advertisement in the *Times*, which I'm very glad I did, if it will fetch the poor lad any friends."

There was a moment's pause; then the lady asked thoughtfully.

"And when do you leave for New York?"

"The day after to-morrow, ma'am—and a long journey it is for a poor old body like me."

"Did you live here when Mr. Vyking left the child with you—in this neighborhood?"

"Not in this neighborhood, nor in London at all, your ladyship. It was Lowdean, in Berkshire, and my husband was alive at the time. I had just lost my baby, and the landlady of the inn recommended me. So he brought it, and paid me thirty sovereigns, and promised me thirty more every twelvemonth, and told me to call it Guy Vyking—and that was the last as I ever saw of him."

"And the infant's mother?" said the lady, her voice changing perceptibly—"do you know anything of her?"

"But very little," said Martha Brand, shaking her head.

"I never set eyes on her, although she was sick at the inn for upwards of three weeks. But Mrs. Vine, the landlady, she saw her twice; and she told me what a pretty young creeter she was—and a lady, if there ever was a lady yet."

"Then the child was born in Berkshire—how was it?"

"Well, your ladyship, it was an accident, seeing as how the carriage broke down with Mr. Vyking and the lady, a driving furious to catch the last London train. The lady was so much hurted that she had to be carried to the inn, and went quite out of her head, raving and dangerous like. Mr. Vyking had the landlady to wait upon her until he could telegraph to London for a nurse, which one came down next day and took charge of her. The baby wasn't two days old when he brought it to me; and the poor young mother was dreadful low, and out of her head all the time. Mr. Vyking and the nurse were all that saw her, and the doctor, of course; but she didn't die, as the doctor thought she would, but got well; and before she came right to her senses, Mr. Vyking paid the doctor, and told him he needn't come back. And then, a little more than a fortnight after, they took her away, all sly and secret-like—and what they told her about her poor baby I don't know. I always thought there was something dreadful wrong about the whole thing."

"And this Mr. Vyking—was he the child's father—the woman's husband?"

Martha Brand looked sharply at the speaker, as if she suspected *she* could answer that question best.

"Nobody knew, but everybody thought so. I've always been of opinion, myself, that Guy's father and mother were gentlefolks, and I always shall be."

"Does the boy know his own story?"

"Yes, your ladyship—all I've told you."

"Where is he? I should like to see him."

Mrs. Brand's daughter, all this time hushing her baby, started up.

"I'll fetch him. He's up stairs in Legard's, I know."

She left the room and ran up stairs. The painter, Legard, still was touching up Miss Jenkins, and the bright haired boy stood watching the progress of that work of art.

"Guy! Guy!" she cried, breathlessly, "come down stairs at once. You're wanted."

"Who wants me, Ellen?"

"A lady, dressed in the most elegant and expensive manner—a real lady, Guy; and she has come about that advertisement, and she wants to see you."

"What is she like, Mrs. Darking?" inquired the painter—"young or old?"

"Young, I should think; but she hides her face behind a thick veil, as if she didn't want to be known. Come, Guy."

She hurried the lad down stairs, and into their little room. The veiled lady still sat talking to the old woman, her back to the dim daylight, and that disguising veil still down. She turned slightly at their entrance, and looked at the boy through it. Guy stood in the middle of the floor, his fearless blue eyes fixed on the hidden face. Could he have seen it, he might have started at the grayish pallor which overspread it at sight of him.

"So like! So like!" the lady was murmuring between her set teeth. "It is terrible—it is marvellous."

"This is Guy, your ladyship," said Martha Brand. "I've done what I could for him the last ten years, and, I'm almost as sorry to part with him as if he were my own. Is your ladyship going to take him away with you now?"

"No," said her ladyship sharply, "I have no such intention. Have you no neighbor or friend who would be willing to take and bring him up, if well paid for the trouble? This time the money will be paid without fail."

"There's Legard," cried the boy, eagerly. "I'll go to Legard's, granny. I'd rather be with Joe than anywhere else."

"It's a neighbor that lives up stairs," murmured Martha in explanation. "He always took to Guy, and Guy to him, in a way that's quite wonderful. He's a very decent man, your ladyship—a painter for a theatre; and Guy takes kindly to the business, and would like to be one himself. If you don't want to take away the boy, you couldn't leave him in better hands."

"I am glad to hear it. Can I see the man?"

"I'll fetch him," cried Guy, and ran out of the room. Two minutes later came Mr. Legard, in paper cap and shirt-sleeves, bowing very low to the grand, black-robed lady, and only too delighted to strike a bargain. The lady offered liberally—Mr. Legard closed with the offer at once.

"You will clothe him better, and you will educate him, and give him your name. I wish him to drop that of Vyking. The same amount I give you now will be sent you this time every year. If you change your residence in the meantime, or wish to communicate with me in any occurrence of consequence, you can address Madam Ada, post-office, Plymouth."

She rose as she spoke, stately and tall, and motioned Mr. Legard to withdraw. The painter gathered up the money she laid on the table, and bowed himself, with a radiant face, out of the room.

"As for you," turning to old Martha, and taking out of her purse a roll of crisp, Bank of England notes, "I think this will pay you for the trouble you have had with the boy during the last ten years. No thanks—you have earned the money."

She moved to the door, made a slight, proud gesture with her gloved hand, in farewell; took a last look at the golden-haired, blue-eyed, handsome boy, and was gone. A moment later, and her cab rattled out of the murky street, and the trio were alone staring at one another, and at the bulky roll of notes.

"I should think it was a dream only for this," murmured old Martha, looking at the roll with glistening eyes.

"A great lady—a great lady, surely. Guy, I shouldn't wander if that was your mother."

# CHAPTER VII.

**COLONEL JOCYLN.**

ive miles away from Thetford Towers, where the multitudinous waves leaped and glistened all day in the sunlight, as if a glitter with diamonds, stood Jocyln Hall. An imposing structure of red brick, not yet one hundred years old, with sloping meadows spreading away into the blue horizon, and densely wooded plantations down to the wide sea.

Colonel Jocyln, the lord of these swelling meadows and miles of woodland, where the red deer disported in the green arcades, was absent in India, and had been for the past nine years. They were an old family, the Jocylns, as old as any in Devon, with a pride that bore no proportion to their purse, until the present Jocyln had, all at once, become a millionaire. A penniless young lieutenant in a cavalry regiment, quartered somewhere in Ireland, with a handsome face and dashing manners, he had captivated, at first sight, a wild, young Irish heiress of fabulous wealth and beauty. It was a love match on her side—nobody knew exactly what it was on his; but they made a moonlight flitting of it, for the lady's friends were grievously wroth. Lieutenant Jocyln liked his profession for its own sake, and took his Irish bride to India, and there an heiress and only child was born to him. The climate disagreed with the young wife—she sickened and died; but the young officer and his baby-girl remained in India. In the fulness of time he became Colonel Jocyln; and one day electrified his housekeeper by a letter announcing his intention of returning to England with his little daughter Aileen "for good."

That same month of December, which took Lady Thetford on that mysterious London journey, brought this letter from Calcutta. Five months after, when the May primroses and hyacinths were all abloom in the green seaside woodlands, Colonel Joclyn and his little daughter came home.

Early on the day succeeding his arrival, Colonel Jocyln rode though the bright spring sunshine, along the pleasant high road between Jocyln Hall and Thetford Towers. He had met the late Sir Noel and his bride once or twice previous to his departure for India; but there had been no acquaintance sufficiently close to warrant this speedy call.

Lady Thetford, sitting alone in her boudoir, yawning the weary hours away over a book, looked in surprise at the card the servant brought her.

"Colonel Jocyln," she said, "I did not even know he had arrived. And to call so soon—ah! perhaps he fetches me letters from India."

She rose at the thought, her pale cheeks flushing a little with expectation. Mail after mail had arrived from that distant land, bringing her no letter from Captain Everard.

Lady Thetford descended at once. She had few callers; but was always exquisitely dressed, and ready to receive at a moment's notice. Colonel Jocyln, tall and sallow, and soldierly, rose at her entrance.

"Lady Thetford? Ah, yes! Most happy to see your ladyship once more. Permit me to apologize for this very early call—you will overlook my haste when you hear my reason."

Lady Thetford held out her white hand.

"Allow me to welcome you back to England, Colonel Jocyln. You have come to remain this time, I hope. And little Aileen is well, I trust?"

"Very well, and very glad to be released from shipboard. I need not ask for young Sir Rupert—I saw him with his nurse in the park as I rode up. A fine boy, and like you my lady."

"Yes, Rupert is like me. And now—how are our mutual friends in India?"

The momentous question she had been longing to ask from the first, but her well-trained voice spoke it as steadily as though it had been a question of the weather.

Colonel Jocyln's face darkened.

"I bring bad news from India, my lady, Captain Everard was a friend of yours?"

"Yes; he left his little daughter in my charge."

"I know. You have not heard from him lately?"

"No; and I have been rather anxious. Nothing has befallen the captain, I hope?"

The well-trained voice shook a little despite its admirable training, and the slender fingers looped and unlooped nervously her watch-chain.

"Yes, Lady Thetford, the very worst that could befall him. George Everard is dead."

There was a blank pause. Colonel Jocyln looked grave, and downcast, and sad.

"He was my friend," he said, in a low voice, "my intimate friend for many years—a fine fellow, and brave as a lion. Many, many nights we have lain with the stars of India shining on our bivouac whilst he talked to me of you, of England, of his daughter."

Lady Thetford never spoke, never stirred. She was sitting, gazing steadfastly out of the window at the sparkling sunshine, and Colonel Jocyln could not see her face.

"He was as glorious a soldier as ever I knew," the colonel went on; "and he died a soldier's death—shot through the heart. They buried him out there with military honors, and some of his men cried on his grave like children."

There was another blank pause. Still Lady Thetford sat with that fixed gaze on the brilliant May sunshine, moveless as stone.

"It is a sad thing for his poor little girl," the Indian officer said; "she is fortunate in having such a guardian as you, Lady Thetford."

Lady Thetford awoke with a start. She had been in a trance; the years had slipped backward, and she had been in her far-off girlhood's home with George Everard, her handsome, impetuous lover, by her side. She had loved him, then, even when she said no, and married another; she loved him still, and now he was dead—dead! But she turned to her visitor with a face that told nothing.

"I am so sorry—so very, very sorry. My poor little May! Did Captain Everard speak of her, of me, before he died?"

"He died instantaneously, Lady Thetford. There was no time."

"Ah, no! poor fellow! It is the fortune of war—but it is very sad."

That was all; we may feel inexpressibly, but we can only utter commonplaces. Lady Thetford was very, very pale, but her pallor told nothing of the dreary pain at her heart.

"Would you not like to see little May? I will send for her."

Little May was sent for, and came. A brilliant little fairy as ever, brightly dressed, with shimmering golden curls, and starry eyes. By her side stood Sir Rupert—the nine-year-old baronet, growing tall very fast, pale and slender still, and looking at the colonel with his mother's dark, deep eyes.

Col. Jocyln held out his hand to the flaxen-haired fairy.

"Come here, little May, and kiss papa's friend. You remember papa, don't you?"

"Yes," said May, sitting on his knee contentedly. "Oh, yes. When is papa coming home? He said in mamma's letter he would fetch me lots and lots of dolls, and picture-books. Is he coming home soon?"

"Not very soon," the colonel said, inexpressibly touched; "but little May will go to papa some day. You are mamma, I suppose?" smiling at Lady Thetford.

"Yes," nodded May, "that's mamma, and Rupert's mamma. Oh! I'm so sorry papa isn't coming home soon. Do you know," looking up in his face with big, shining, solemn eyes, "I've got a pony, and I can ride lovely; and its name is Snow-drop, because it's all white, and Rupert's is black, and *his* name is Sultan? And I've got a watch; mamma gave it to me last Christmas; and my doll's name—the big one, you know, that opens its eyes and says, 'mamma' and 'papa,' is Sonora. Have you got any little girls at home?"

"One, Miss Chatterbox."

"What's her name?"

"Aileen—Aileen Jocyln."

"Is she nice?"

"Very nice, I think."

"Will she come to see me?"

"If you wish it, and mamma wishes it."

"Oh, yes! you do, don't you, mamma? How big is your little girl—as big as me?"

"Bigger, I fancy. She is nine years old."

"Then she's as big as Rupert—he's nine years old. May she fetch her doll to see Sonora?"

"Certainly—a regiment of dolls, if she wishes."

"Can't she come to-morrow?" asked Rupert, "To-morrow's May's birthday; May's seven years old to-morrow. Mayn't she come?"

"That must be as mamma says."

"Oh, fetch her," cried Lady Thetford, "it will be so nice for May and Rupert. Only I hope little May won't quarrel with her; she does quarrel with her playmates a good deal, I am sorry to say."

"I won't, if she's nice," said May; "it's all their fault. Oh, Rupert! there's Mrs. Weymore on the lawn, and I want her to come and see the rabbits. There's five little rabbits this morning, mamma—mayn't I go and show them to Mrs. Weymore?"

Lady Thetford nodded smiling acquiescence; and away ran little May and Rupert to show the rabbits to the governess.

Colonel Jocyln lingered for half an hour or upwards, conversing with his hostess, and rose to take his leave at last, with the promise of returning on the morrow with his little daughter, and dining at the house. As he mounted his horse and rode homeward, "a haunting shape, an image gay," followed him through the genial May sunshine—Lady Thetford, fair, and stately, and graceful.

"Nine years a widow," he mused. "They say she took her husband's death very hard—and no wonder, considering how he died; but nine years is a tolerable time in which to forget. She received the news of Everard's death very quietly. I don't suppose there ever was anything really in that old story. How handsome she is, and how graceful. I wonder—"

He broke off in his musing fit to light a cigar, and see through the curling smoke dark-eyed Ada, mamma to little Aileen as well as the other two. He had never thought of wanting a wife before, in all the years of his widowhood; but the want struck him forcibly now.

"And Aileen wants a mother, and the little baronet a father," he thought, complacently; "my lady can't do better."

So next day, the earliest possible hour brought back the gallant colonel, and with him a brown-haired, brown-eyed, quiet-looking little girl, as tall, every inch, as Sir Rupert. A little embryo patrician, with pride in her infantile lineaments already, an uplifted poise of the graceful head, a light, elastic step, and a softly-modulated voice. A little lady from top to toe, who opened her brown eyes in wide wonder at the antics, and gambols, and obstreperousness, generally, of little May.

There were two or three children from the rectory, and half a dozen from other families in the neighborhood—and the little birthday feast was under the charge of Mrs. Weymore, the governess, pale and pretty, and subdued, as of old. They raced through the leafy arcades of the park and gambolled in the garden, and had tea in a fairy summer-house, to the music of plashing fountains—and little May was captain of the band. Even shy, still Aileen Jocyln forgot her youthful dignity, and raced and laughed with the best.

"It was so nice, papa!" she cried, rapturously, riding home in the misty moonlight. "I never enjoyed myself so well. I like Rupert so much—better than May, you know; May's so rude, and laughs so loud. I've asked them to come and see me, papa; and May said she would make her mamma let them come next week. And then I'm going back—I shall always like to go there."

Colonel Jocyln smiled as he listened to his little daughter's prattle. Perhaps he agreed with her; perhaps he too, liked to go there. The dinner-party, at which he and the rector of St. Gosport and the rector's wife were the only guests, had been quite as pleasant as the birthday fete. Very graceful, very fair and stately, had looked the lady of the manor, presiding at her own dinner-table. How well she would look at the head of his?

The Indian officer, after that became a very frequent guest at Thetford Towers—the children were such a good excuse. Aileen was lonely at home, and Rupert and May were always glad to have her. So papa drove her over nearly every day, or else came to fetch the other two to Jocyln Hall. Lady Thetford was ever most gracious, and the colonel's hopes ran high.

Summer waned. It was October, and Lady Thetford began talking of leaving St. Gosport for a season; her health was not good, and change of air was recommended.

"I can leave my children in charge of Mrs. Weymore," she said. "I have every confidence in her; and she has been with me so long. I think I shall depart next week. Dr. Gale says I have delayed too long."

Colonel Jocyln looked up uneasily. They were sitting alone together, looking at the red October sunset blazing itself out behind the Devon hills.

"We will miss you very much," he said, softly. "I will miss you."

Something in his tone struck Lady Thetford. She turned her dark eyes upon him in surprise and sudden alarm. The look had to be answered; rather embarrassed, and not at all so confident as he thought he would have been, Colonel Jocyln asked Lady Thetford to be his wife.

There was a blank pause. Then,

"I am very sorry, Colonel Jocyln. I never thought of this."

He looked at her, pale—alarmed.

"Does that mean no, Lady Thetford?"

"It means no, Colonel Jocyln. I have never thought of you save as a friend; as a friend I still wish to retain you. I will never marry. What I am to-day, I will go to my grave. My boy has my whole heart—there is no room in it for anyone else. Let us be friends, Colonel Jocyln," holding out her white, jeweled hand, "more, no mortal man can ever be to me."

---

89

# CHAPTER VIII.

**LADY THETFORD'S BALL.**

ears came, and years went, and thirteen passed away. In all these years, with their countless changes, Thetford Towers had been a deserted house. Comparatively speaking, of course; Mrs. Weymore, the governess, Mrs. Hilliard, the housekeeper, Mr. Jarvis, the butler, and their minor satellites, served there still, but its mistress and her youthful son had been absent. Only little May had remained under Mrs. Weymore's charge until within the last two years, and then she, too, had gone to Paris to a finishing school.

Lady Thetford came herself to the Towers to fetch her—the only time in these thirteen years. She had spent them pleasantly enough, rambling about the Continent, and in her villa on the Arno, for her health was frail, and growing daily frailer, and demanded a sunny, Southern climate. The little baronet had gone to Eton, thence to Oxford, passing his vacation abroad with his mamma—and St. Gosport had seen nothing of them. Lady Thetford had thought it best, for many reasons, to leave little May quietly in England during her wanderings. She missed the child, but she had every confidence in Mrs. Weymore. The old aversion had never entirely worn away, but time had taught her she could trust her implicitly; and though May might miss "mamma" and Rupert, it was not in that flighty-fairy's nature to take their absence very deeply to heart.

Jocyln Hall was vacated, too. After that refusal of Lady Thetford, Colonel Jocyln had left England, placed his daughter in a school abroad, and made a tour of the East. Lady Thetford he had not met until within the last year; then Lady Thetford and her son, spending the winter in Rome, had encountered Colonel and Miss Jocyln, and they had scarcely parted company since. The Thetfords were to return early in spring to take up their abode once more in the old home, and Colonel Jocyln announced his intention of following their example.

Lady Thetford wrote to Mrs. Weymore, her viceroy, and to her steward, issuing her orders for the expected return. Thetford Towers was to be completely rejuvenated—new furnished, painted, and decorated. Landscape gardeners were set at work in the grounds; all things were to be ready the following June.

Summer came and brought the absentees—Lady Thetford and her son, Colonel Jocyln and his daughter; and there were bonfires and illuminations, and feasting of tenantry, and ringing of bells, and general jubilation, that the heir of Thetford Towers had come to reign at last.

The week following the arrival, Lady Thetford issued invitations over half the county for a grand ball. Thetford Towers, after over twenty years of gloom and solitude, was coming out again in the old gayety and brilliance that had been its normal state before the present heir was born.

The night of the ball came, and with it nearly every one who had been honored with an invitation, all curious to see the future lord of one of the noblest domains in broad Devonshire.

Sir Rupert Thetford stood by his mother's side, and met his old friends for the first time since his boyhood—a slender young man, pale, and dark, and handsome of face, with dreamy, artist's eyes and quiet manners, not at all like his father's fair-haired, bright-eyed, stalwart Saxon race; the Thetford blood had run out, he was his own mother's son.

Lady Thetford, grown pallid and wan, and wasted in all those years, and bearing within her the seeds of an incurable disease, looked yet fair and gracious, and stately in her trailing robes and jewels, to-night, receiving her guests like a queen. It was the triumph of her life, the desire of her heart, this seeing her son, her idol, reigning in the home of his fathers, ruler of the broad domain that had owned the Thetford's lord for more years back than she could count.

"If I could but see her his wife," Lady Thetford thought, "I think I should have nothing left on earth to desire."

She glanced across the wide room, along a vista of lights, and flitting forms, and rich dresses, and sparkling jewels, to where a young lady stood, the centre of an animated group—a tall and eminently handsome girl, with a proud patrician face, and the courtly grace of a young empress—Aileen Jocyln, heiress of fabulous wealth, possessor of fabulous beauty, and descendant of a race as noble and as ancient as his own.

"With her for his wife, come what might in the future, my Rupert would be safe," the mother thought; "and who knows what a day may bring forth. Ah! if I dared only speak, but I dare not; it would ruin all. I know my son."

Yes, Lady Thetford knew her son, understood his character thoroughly, and was a great deal too wary a conspirator to let him see her cards. Fate, not she, had thrown the heiress and the baronet constantly together of late, and Aileen's own beauty and grace were surely sufficient for the rest. It was the one desire of Lady Thetford's heart; but she never said so to her son, who loved her dearly, and would have done a great deal to add to her happiness. She left it to fate, and leaving it, was doing the wisest thing she could possibly do.

It seemed as if her hopes were likely to be realized. Sir Rupert had an artist's and a Sybarite's love for all things beautiful, and could appreciate the grand statuesque style of Miss Jocyln's beauty, even as his mother could not appreciate it. She was like the Pallas Athene, she was his ideal woman, fair and proud, uplifted and serene, smiling on all, from the heights of high-and-mightydom, but shining upon them, a brilliant far-off star, keeping her warmth and her sweetness all for him. He was an indolent, dreamy Sybarite, this pale young baronet, who liked his rose-leaves unruffled under him, full of artistic tastes and inspirations, and a great deal too lazy ever to carry them into effect. He was an artist, and he had his studio where he began fifty gigantic deeds at once in the way of pictures, and seldom finished one. Nature had intended him for an artist, not a country squire; he cared little for riding, or hunting, or fishing, or farming, any of the things wherein country squires delight; he liked better to lie on the warm grass, with the summer wind stirring in the trees over his head, and smoke his Turkish pipe, and dream the lazy hours away. If he had been born a poor man, he might have been a clever painter; as it was, he was only an idle, listless, elegant, languid dreamer, and so likely to remain until the end of the chapter.

Lady Thetford's ball was a very brilliant affair, and a famous success. Until far into the gray and dismal dawn, "flute, violin, bassoon," woke sweet echoes in the once gloomy rooms, where so long silence had reigned. Half the county had been invited, and half the county were there; hosts of pretty, rosy girls, in laces and roses, and sparkling jewelry, baited their dainty traps, and tried "becks and nods, and wreathed smiles," for the special delectation of the handsome, courtly heir of Thetford Towers.

But the heir of Thetford Towers, with gracious greetings for all, yet walked through the rose-strewn pitfalls quite secure, while the starry face of Aileen Jocyln shone on him in its pale, high-bred beauty. He had not danced much; he had an antipathy to dancing as he had to exertion of any kind, and presently he stood leaning against a slender white column, watching her in a state of lazy admiration. He could see quite as clearly as his mother how eminently proper a marriage with the heiress of Col. Jocyln would be; he knew by instinct, too, how much she desired it; and it was easy enough, looking at her in her girlish pride and beauty, to fancy himself very much in love; and, though anything but a coxcomb, Sir Rupert Thetford was perfectly aware of his own handsome face and dreamy artist's eyes, and his fifteen thousand a year, and lengthy pedigree, and had a hazy idea that the handsome Aileen would not say no when he spoke.

"And I'll speak to-night, by Jove!" thought the young baronet, as near being enthusiastic as was in his nature, while he watched her, the brilliant centre of a brilliant group. "How exquisite she is in her statuesque grace, my peerless Aileen, the ideal of my dreams. I'll ask her to be my wife to-night, or that inconceivable idiot, Lord Gilbert Penryhn will do it to-morrow."

He sauntered over to the group, not at all insensible to the quick, bright smile and flitting flush with which Miss Jocyln welcomed him.

"I believe this waltz is mine, Miss Jocyln. Very sorry to break upon your *tête-à-tête*, Penryhn, but necessity knows no law."

A moment and they were floating down the whirling tide of the dance, with the wild, sweet waltz music swelling and sounding, and Miss Jocyln's perfumed hair breathing fragrance around him, the starry face and dark, dewy eyes, downcast a little, in a happy tremor. The cold, still look of fixed pride seemed to melt out of her face, and an exquisite rosy light came and went in its place, making her more lovely than ever; and Sir Rupert saw and understood it all, with a little complacent thrill of satisfaction.

They waltzed out of the ball-room into a conservatory of exquisite blossom, where tropic plants of gorgeous hues, and plashing fountains, under the white light of alabaster lamps, made a sort of garden of Eden. There were orange and myrtle trees oppressing the warm air with their sweetness, and through the open, French windows came the soft, misty moonlight, and the saline wind. There they stopped, looking out at the pale glory of the night, and there Sir Rupert, about to ask the supreme question of his life, and with his heart beginning to plunge against his side, opened conversation with the usual brilliancy in such cases.

"You look fatigued, Miss Jocyln. These great balls are great bores after all."

Miss Jocyln laughed frankly. She was of a nature far more impassioned than his, and she loved him; and she felt thrilling through every nerve in her body the prescience of what he was going to say; but for all that, being a woman, she had the best of it now.

"I am not at all fatigued," she said; "and I like it. I don't think balls are bores—like this, I mean; but then, certainly, my experience is very limited. How lovely the night is! Look at the moonlight, yonder, on the water, a sheet of silvery glory. Does it not recall Sorrento, and the exquisite Sorrentine landscape—that moonlight on the sea? Are you not inspired, sir artist?"

She lifted a flitting, radiant glance, a luminous smile, and then the star-like face drooped again—and the white hands took to reckless breaking off sweet sprays of myrtle.

"My inspiration is nearer," looking down at the drooping face. "Aileen—" and there he stopped, and the sentence was never destined to be finished, for a shadow darkened the moonlight, a figure flitted in like a spirit, and stood before them—a fairy figure, in a cloud of rosy drapery, with shimmering, golden curls, and dancing eyes of turquoise blue.

Aileen Jocyln started back, and away from her companion, with a faint, surprise cry. Sir Rupert, wondering and annoyed, stood staring; and still the fairy figure in the rosy gauze stood like a nymph in a stage tableau, smiling up in their faces, and never speaking. There was a blank pause of a moment, then Miss Jocyln made one step forward, doubt, recognition, delight, all in her face at once.

"It is—it is!" she cried, "May Everard!"

"May Everard!" Sir Rupert echoed—"little May!"

"At your service, monsieur. To think you should have forgotten me so completely in a decade of years. For shame, Sir Rupert Thetford!"

And then she was in Aileen Jocyln's arms, and there was an hiatus filled up with kisses.

"Oh! what a surprise." Miss Jocyln cried, breathlessly. "Have you dropped from the skies? I thought you were in France."

May Everard laughed, the mischievous laugh of thirteen years ago, as she held up her dimpled cheeks, first one and then the other, to Sir Rupert.

"Did you? So I was, but I ran away."

"Ran away! From school?"

"Something very like it. Oh! how stupid it was, and I couldn't endure it any longer; and I am so filled with knowledge now, that if I held any more, I should explode; and so when vacation began, and I was permitted to spend a week with a friend I just took French leave and came home instead. And so," folding the fairy hands, and nodding her little ringleted head, "here I am."

"But, good heavens!" cried Sir Rupert, aghast, "you never mean to say, May, you have come alone."

"All alone," said May, with another nod. "I'm used to it, you know; did it last vacation. Came across and spent it with Mrs. Weymore. I don't mind it the least; don't know what sea-sickness is; and oh! didn't some of the poor wretches suffer! Isn't it fortunate I'm here for the ball? And, Rupert, good gracious! how you've grown!"

"Thanks. I can't see that you have changed much, Miss Everard. You are the same curly-haired, saucy fairy I knew thirteen years ago. What does my lady say to this escapade?"

"Nothing. Eloquent silence best expresses her feelings; and then she hadn't time to make a scene. Are you going to ask me to dance, Rupert? because, if you are," said Miss Everard, adjusting her bracelet, "you had better do it at once, as I am going back to the ball-room, and after I once appear there, you will stand no chance amongst the crowd of competitors. But, then, perhaps you belong to Miss Jocyln?"

"Not at all," Miss Jocyln interposed hastily, and reddening a little, "I am engaged; and it is time I was back, or my unlucky cavalier will be at his wit's end to find me."

She swept away with a quicker movement than usual, and Sir Rupert laughingly gave his piquant little partner his arm. His notions of propriety were a good deal shocked; but then it was only May Everard, and May Everard was one of those exceptional people who can do pretty much as they please, and not surprise any one. They went back to the ball-room, the fairy in pink on the arm of the young baronet, chattering like a magpie. Miss Jocyln's partner found her and led her off, but Miss Jocyln was very silent and *distrait* all the rest of the night, and watched furtively, but incessantly, the fluttering pink fairy. She had reigned belle hitherto, but sparkling little May, like an embodied sunbeam, electrified the room, and took the crown and the sceptre by royal right. Sir Rupert had that one dance, and no more— Miss Everard's own prophecy was true—the demand for her was such that even the son of the house stood not the shadow of chance.

Miss Jocyln held herself aloof from the young baronet for the remaining hours of the ball. She had known as well as he the words that were on his lips when May Everard interposed; and her eyes flashed, and her dark cheeks flushed dusky red to see how easily he had been deterred from his purpose. For him, he sought her once or twice in a desultory sort of way, never observing that he was purposely avoided, wandering contentedly back to devote himself to some one else, and in the pauses to watch May Everard floating—a sunbeam in a sunny cloud—here and there, and everywhere.

---

# CHAPTER IX.

### GUY LEGARD.

"

e meant to have spoken that night; he would have spoken but for May Everard. And yet that is two weeks ago, and we have been together since, and"——Aileen Jocyln broke off abruptly, and looked out over the far spreading gray sea.

The morning was dull; the leaden sky threatening rain; the wind sighing fitfully, and the slow, gray sea creeping up the gray sands. Aileen Jocyln sat as she had sat since breakfast, aimless and dreary, by her dressing-room window, gazing blankly over the pale landscape, her hair falling loose and damp over her shoulders, a novel lying listlessly in her lap. The book had no interest—her thoughts would stray in spite of her to Thetford Towers.

"She is very pretty," Miss Jocyln thought, "with that pink and white wax-doll sort of prettiness that some people admire. I never thought *he* could, with his artistic nature; but I suppose I was mistaken. They call her fascinating; I believe that rather hoydenish manner of hers, all those dashing airs, and that 'loud' style of dress and doings, take some men by storm. I presume I was mistaken in Sir Rupert; I dare say pretty, penniless May will be Lady Thetford before long."

Miss Jocyln's short upper-lip curled rather scornfully, and she rose up with a little air of petulance, and walked across the room to the opposite window. It commanded a view of the lawn and a long wooded drive, and cantering airily up under the waving trees, she saw the young lady of whom she had been thinking. The pretty, fleet-footed pony and his bright little mistress were by no means rare visitors at Jocyln Hall; and Miss Jocyln was always elaborately civil to Miss Everard. Very pretty little May looked, all her tinselled curls floating in the breeze, like a golden banner, the blue eyes more starily radiant than ever; the dark riding-habit and jaunty hat and plume the most becoming things in the world. She saw Miss Jocyln at the window, kissed her hand, and resigned Arab to the groom. A minute more, and she was saluting Aileen with effusion.

"You solemn Aileen! to sit and mope here in the house instead of improving your health and temper by a breezy canter over the downs. Don't contradict, I know you were moping. I should be afraid to tell you how many miles Arab and I have got over this morning. And you never came to see me yesterday, either. Why was it?"

"I didn't feel inclined," Miss Jocyln answered truthfully.

"No, you never do feel inclined unless I come and drag you out by force; you sit in the house and grow yellow and jaundiced over high-church novels. I declare I never met so many lazy people in all my life as I have done since I came home. One don't mind mamma, poor thing! shutting herself up, and the sunshine and fresh air of heaven out—but for you and Rupert, and speaking of Rupert," ran on Miss Everard, in a breathless sort of way, "he wanted to commence his great picture of 'Fair Rosamond and Eleanor' yesterday—and how could he when Eleanor never came. Why didn't you—you promised?"

"I changed my mind, I suppose."

"And broke your word—more shame for you, then! Come now."

"No; thanks. It's going to rain."

"Nothing of the sort; and Rupert is so anxious. He would have come himself, only my lady is ill to-day with one of her bad headaches, and asked him to read her to sleep; and like the good boy that he is in the main, though shockingly lazy, he obeyed. Do come, Aileen, there's a dear! Don't be selfish."

Miss Jocyln rose rather abruptly.

"I have no desire to be selfish, Miss Everard. If you will wait ten minutes while I dress, I will accompany you to Thetford Towers."

She rang the bell, and swept from the room stately and uplifted. May looked after her, fidgeting a little.

"Dear me! I suppose she is offended now at that word 'selfish.' I never did get on very well with Aileen Jocyln, and I'm afraid I never shall. I shouldn't wonder if she were jealous."

Miss Everard laughed a little silvery laugh all to herself, and slapped her kid riding-boot with her pretty toy whip.

"I hope I didn't interrupt a tender declaration that night in the conservatory; but it looked like it. If I did I am sure Rupert has had fifty chances since, and I know he hasn't availed himself of them, or Aileen would never wear that dissatisfied face. I know she's in love with him, though, to be sure, she would see me impaled with the greatest pleasure if she only thought I suspected it; but I'm not so certain about him. He's a great deal too indolent, in the first place, to get up a grand passion for anybody; and I think he's inclined to look graciously on me—poor little me—in the second. You may spare yourself the trouble, my dear Sir Rupert, for a gentleman whose chief aim in existence is to smoke Turkish pipes, and lie on the grass, and write and read poetry, is not at all the sort of man I mean to bless for life.

"Tell me not of your soft sighing lovers, Such things may be had by the score; I'd rather be bride to a rover, And polish the rifle he bore."

Sang May Everard, in a gay little voice as Miss Jocyln, in a flowing riding habit, entered the room.

The two girls descended to the court-yard, mounted, and rode off. Both rode well and both looked their best on horseback, and made a wonderfully pretty picture as they galloped through St. Gosport in dashing style, bringing the admiring population in a rush to doors and windows. Perhaps Sir Rupert Thetford thought so, too, as he stood at the great front entrance to receive them with a kindling light in his artist's eyes.

"May said she would fetch you, and May always keeps her word," he said, as he walked slowly up the sweeping staircase; "besides, Aileen, I am to have the first sitting for the 'Rosamond and Eleanor' to-day, am I not? May calls me an idle dreamer, a useless drone in the busy human hive; so, to vindicate my character, and cleave a niche in the temple of fame, I am going to immortalize myself over this painting."

"You'll never finish it," said May; "it will be like all the rest. You'll begin on a gigantic scale and with super-human efforts, and you'll cool down and get sick of it before it is half finished; and it will go to swell the pile of daubed canvas in your studio now. Don't tell me! I know you."

"And have the poorest possible opinion of me, Miss Everard?"

"Yes, I have! I have no patience when I think of what you might do, what you might become, and see what you are. If you were not Sir Rupert Thetford, with a princely income, you might be a clever man. As it is—" a shrug, and a lift of the eyebrows.

"As it is!" cried the young baronet, trying to laugh and reddening violently, "I will still be a clever man—a modern Murillo. Are you not a little severe, Miss Everard; Aileen, I believe this is your first visit to my studio?"

"Yes," said Miss Jocyln, coldly and briefly. She did not like the conversation, and May Everard's familiar home-truths stung her. To her he was everything mortal man should be. She was proud, but she was not ambitious; what right had this penniless little free-speaker to come between them and talk like this?

May was flitting about like the fairy she was, her head a little on one side, like a critical canary, her flowing skirt held up, inspecting the pictures.

"'Jeannie D'Arc before her Judges,' half finished, as usual, and never to be completed; and weak—very, if it ever is completed. 'Battle of Bosworth Field,' in flaming colors, all confusion and smoke, and red ochre and rubbish, you did well not to trouble yourself any more with that. 'Swiss Peasant,' ah! that is pretty. 'Storm at Sea,' just tolerable. 'Trial of Marie Antoinette.' My dear Rupert, why will you persist in these figure paintings when you know your forte is landscape? 'An Evening in the Eternal City.' Now that is what I call an exquisite little thing? Look at the moon, Aileen, rising over these hill tops; and see those trees—you can almost feel the wind blow! And that prostrate figure—why, that looks like yourself, Rupert!"

"It is myself."

"And the other stooping—who is he?"

"The painter of that picture, Miss Everard; yes, the only thing in my poor studio you see fit to eulogize, is not mine. It was done by an artist friend—an unknown Englishman, who saved my life in Rome three years ago. Come in, mother mine, and defend your son from the two-edged sword of May Everard's tongue."

For Lady Thetford, pale and languid, appeared on the threshold, wrapped in a shawl.

"It's all for his good, mamma. Come here and look at this 'Evening in the Eternal City.' Rupert has nothing like it in all his collection, though there are the beginning of many better things. He saved your life? How was it?"

"Oh! a little affair with brigands; nothing very thrilling, but I should have been killed or captured all the same if this Legard had not come to the rescue. May is right about the picture; he painted well, had come to Rome to perfect himself in his art. Very fine fellow, Legard—a thorough Bohemian."

"Legard!"

It was Lady Thetford who had spoken sharply and suddenly. She had put up her glass to look at the Italian picture, but dropped it, and faced abruptly round.

"Yes, Legard. Guy Legard, a young Englishman, about my own age. By-the-by, if you saw him, you would be surprised by his singular resemblance to some of those dead and gone Thetfords hanging over there in the picture-gallery—fair hair, blue eyes, and the same peculiar cast of features to a shade. I was taken rather aback, I confess, when I saw it first. My dear mother—"

It was not a cry Lady Thetford had uttered—it was a kind of wordless sob. He soon caught her in his arms, and held her there, her face the color of death.

"Get a glass of water, May—she is subject to these attacks. Quick!"

Lady Thetford drank the water, and sunk back in the chair Aileen wheeled up, her face looking awfully corpse-like in contrast with her dark garments and dead black hair.

"You should not have left your room," said Sir Rupert, "after your attack this morning. Perhaps you had better return and lie down. You look perfectly ghastly."

"No," his mother sat up as she spoke and pushed away the glass, "there is no necessity for lying down. Don't wear that scared face, May—it was nothing, I assure you. Go on with what you were saying, Rupert."

"What I was saying? what was it?"

"About this young artist's resemblance to the Thetfords."

"Oh! well, there's no more to say, that is all. He saved my life, he painted that picture, and we were Damon and Pythias over again during my stay in Rome. I always do fraternize with these sort of fellows, you know. I left him in Rome, and he promised, if he ever returned to England, which he wasn't so sure of, he would run down to Devonshire to see me and my painted ancestors, whom he resembles so strongly. That is all; and now young ladies if you will take your places, we will commence the Rosamond and Eleanor. Mother, sit here by this window, if you want to play propriety, and don't talk."

But Lady Thetford chose to go to her own room; and her son gave her his arm thither, and left her lying back amongst her cushions in front of the fire. It was always chilly in those great and somewhat gloomy rooms, and her ladyship was always cold of late. She lay there looking with gloomy eyes into the ruddy blaze, and holding her hands over her painfully beating heart.

"It is destiny, I suppose," she thought, bitterly; "let me banish him to the farthest end of the earth; let me keep him in poverty and obscurity all his life, and when the day comes that it is written, Guy Legard will be here. Sooner or later, the vow I have broken to Sir Noel Thetford must be kept; sooner or later, Sir Noel's heir will have his own."

---

# CHAPTER X.

**ASKING IN MARRIAGE.**

he fire burned in Lady Thetford's room, and among piles of silken pillows my lady, languid and pale, lay, looking into the leaping flame. It was a warm summer morning, the sun blazed like a wheel of fire in a sky without a cloud, but Lady Thetford was always chilly of late. She drew the crimson shawl she wore closer around her, and glanced impatiently now and then at the pretty toy clock on the decorated chimney-piece. The house was very still; its one disturbing element, Miss Everard, was absent with Sir Rupert for a morning canter over the sunny Devon hills.

The toy clock struck up a gay little waltz preparatory to striking eleven, and my lady turned with a restless, impatient sigh among her pillows.

"How long they stay, and these solitary rides are so dangerous! Oh! what will become of me if it is too late, after all! What shall I do if he says no?"

There was a quick man's step without—a moment, and the door opened, and Sir Rupert, "booted and spurred" from his ride, was bending over his mother.

"Louise says you sent for me after I left. What is it, mother—you are not worse?"

He knelt beside her. Lady Thetford put back the fair, brown hair with tender touch, and gazed in the handsome face, so like her own, with eyes full of unspeakable love.

"My boy! my boy!" she murmured, "my darling Rupert! Oh! it is hard, it is bitter to have to leave you."

"Mother!" with a quick look of alarm, "what is it? Are you worse?"

"No worse, Rupert; but no better. My boy, I shall never be better again in this world."

"Mother—"

"Hush, my Rupert—wait; you know it is true; and but for leaving you I should be glad to go. My life has not been so happy since your father died, Heaven knows, that I should greatly cling to it."

"But, mother, this won't do; these morbid fancies are worst of all. Keeping up one's spirits is half the battle."

"I am not morbid; I merely state a fact—a fact which must preface what is to come. Rupert, I know I am dying, and before we part I want to see my successor at Thetford Towers."

"My dear mother!" amazedly.

"Rupert, I want to see Aileen Jocyln your wife. No, no; don't interrupt me, and believe me, I dislike match-making quite as cordially as you do; but my days on earth are numbered, and I must speak before it is too late. When we were abroad I thought there never would be occasion; when we returned home I thought so, too, Rupert I have ceased to think so since May Everard's return."

The young man's face flushed suddenly and hotly, but he made no reply.

"How any man in his senses could possibly prefer May to Aileen is a mystery I cannot solve; but then these things puzzle the wisest of us at times. Mind, my boy, I don't really say you do prefer May—I should be very unhappy if I thought so. I know—I am certain you love Aileen best; and I am equally certain she is a thousand times better suited to you. Then, as a man of honor, you owe it to her. You have paid Miss Jocyln such attention as no honorable gentleman should pay any lady, except the one he means to make his wife."

Lady Thetford's son rose abruptly, and stood leaning against the mantel, looking steadfastly into the fire.

"Rupert, tell me truly, if May Everard had not come here would you not before this have asked Aileen to be your wife?"

"Yes—no—I don't know. Mother!" the young man cried, impatiently, "what has May Everard done that you should treat her like this?"

"Nothing; I love her dearly, and you know it. But she is not suited to you—she is not the woman you should marry."

Sir Rupert laughed—a hard strident laugh.

"I think Miss Everard is much of your opinion, my lady. You might have spared yourself all these fears and perplexities, for the simple reason that I should have been refused had I asked."

"Rupert!"

"Nay, mother mine, no need to wear that frightened face. I haven't asked Miss Everard in so many words to marry me, and she hasn't declined with thanks; but she would if I did. I saw enough to-day for that."

"Then you don't care for Aileen?" with a look of blank consternation.

"I care for her very much, mother; and I haven't owned to being absolutely in love with our pretty little May. Perhaps I care for one as much as the other; perhaps I know in my inmost heart she is the one I should marry. That is, if she will marry me."

"You owe it to her to ask her."

"Do I? Very likely; and it would make you happy, my mother?"

He came and bent over her again, smiling down in her wan, anxious face.

"More happy than anything else in this world, Rupert."

"Then consider it an accomplished fact. Before the sun sets to-day Aileen Jocyln shall say yes or no to your son."

He bent and kissed her; then, without waiting for her to speak, wheeled round and strode out of the apartment.

"There is nothing like striking while the iron is hot," said the young man to himself with a grim sort of smile as he ran down stairs; "for good or for evil, there is no time like the present, my stately Aileen."

Loitering on the lawn, he encountered May Everard, still in her riding-habit, surrounded by three or four poodle dogs.

"On the wing again, Rupert? Is it for mamma? She is not worse?"

"No; I am going to Jocyln Hall. Perhaps I shall fetch Aileen back."

May's turquoise blue eyes were lifted with a sudden luminous, intelligent flash to his face.

"God speed you! You will certainly fetch Aileen back!"

She held out her hand with a smile that told him she knew all as plainly as he knew it himself.

95

"You have my best wishes, Rupert, and don't linger; I want to congratulate Aileen."

Sir Rupert's response to these good wishes was very brief and curt. Miss Everard watched him mount and ride off, with a mischievous little smile rippling round her rosy lips.

"My lady has been giving her idol of her existence a caudle lecture—subject, matrimony," mused Miss Everard, sauntering lazily along in the midst of her little dogs, "and really it is high time, if she means to have Aileen for a daughter-in-law; for the heir of Thetford Towers is rather doubtful that he is not falling in love with me; and Aileen is dreadfully jealous and disagreeable; and my lady is anxious, and fidgeted to death about it; and Sir Rupert doesn't want to himself if he can help it. I must be a fascinating little thing, to be sure, and I feel for him, beyond everything; at the same time Beauty," said the young lady, addressing the ugliest of the poodles with a confidential little nod, "they might all spare themselves the trouble of being tormented on the subject; because, you see, my dear little doggy, I wouldn't marry Sir Rupert Thetford if he were heir to the throne of England, much less Thetford Towers. He's a very nice young man, and a very amiable young man, and a very good-looking young man, I have no doubt; but I'm not in love with him, and never shall be; and I'm going to marry for love, or die an old maid. It seems to me a Levantine pirate, or an Italian brigand, or a knight of the road, would suit my ideas; but I suppose there is no use hoping for such fortune as that; but as for Sir Rupert—oh-h-h! good gracious!"

Miss Everard stopped with a shrill, feminine shriek. She had loitered down to the gates, where a young man stood talking to the lodge-keeper, with a big Newfoundland dog gambolling ponderously about him. The big Newfoundland made an instant dash into Miss Everard's guard of honor, with one deep, bass bark, like distant thunder, and which effectually drowned the yelps of the poodles. May flew to the rescue, seizing the Newfoundland's collar, and pulling him back with all the might of two little white hands.

"You great, horrid brute!" cried May, with flashing eyes, "how dare you! Call-off your dog, sir, this instant! Don't you see how he is frightening mine!"

She turned imperiously to the Newfoundland's master, the bright eyes flashing, the pink cheeks aflame—very pretty, indeed, in her wrath.

"Down, Hector!" called the young man, authoritatively; and Hector, like the well-trained animal he was, subsided instantly. "I beg your pardon, young lady! Hector, you stir at your peril, sir! I am very sorry he has alarmed you."

He doffed his cap with careless grace, and made the angry little lady a courtly bow.

"He didn't alarm me," replied May, testily; "he only alarmed my dogs. Why, dear me! how very odd!"

Miss Everard, looking full at the young man, had started back with this exclamation, and stared broadly. A tall, powerful looking young fellow, rather dusty and travel-stained, but eminently gentlemanly, with frank, blue eyes, and profuse fair hair, and a handsome, candid face.

"Yes, Miss May," struck in the lodge-keeper, "it is odd! I see it, too! He looks enough like Sir Noel, dead and gone, to be his own son!"

"I beg your pardon," said May, becoming conscious of her wide stare, "but is your name Legard; and are you a friend of Sir Rupert Thetford?"

"Yes, to both questions," with a smile that May liked. "You see the resemblance too, then. Sir Rupert used to speak of it. Is he at home?"

"Not just now; but he will be very soon, and I know will be glad to see Mr. Legard. You had better come and wait."

"And Hector," said Mr. Legard. "I think I had better leave him behind, as I see him eyeing your guard of honor with anything but a friendly eye. I believe I have the pleasure of addressing Miss Everard? Oh!" laughing frankly at her surprised face, "Sir Rupert showed me a photograph of yours as a child. I have a good memory for faces, and knew you at once."

Miss Everard and Mr. Legard fell easily into conversation at once, as if they had been old friends. Lady Thetford's ward was one of those people who form their likes and dislikes at first sight; and Mr. Legard's face would have been a pretty sure letter of recommendation to him the wide world over. May liked his looks; and then he was Sir Rupert's friend, and she was never particular about social forms and customs; and so they dawdled about the grounds, and through the leafy arcades, in the genial morning sunshine, talking about Sir Rupert and Rome, and art and artists, and the thousand and one things that turn up in conversation; and the moments slipped by, half hour followed half hour, until May jerked out her watch at last in a sudden fit of recollection, and found, to her consternation, it was past two.

"What will mamma say!" cried the young lady, aghast. "And Rupert; I dare say he's home to luncheon before this. Let us go back to the house, Mr. Legard. I had no idea it was half so late."

Mr. Legard laughed frankly.

"The honesty of that speech is the highest flattery my conversational powers ever received, Miss Everard. I am very much obliged to you. Ah! by Jove! Sir Rupert himself."

For riding slowly up under the sunlit trees, came the young baronet. As Mr. Legard spoke, his glance fell upon them, the young lady and gentleman advancing so confidentially, with half a dozen curly poodles frisking around them. To say Sir Rupert stared, would be a mild way of putting it—his eyes opened in wide wonder.

"Guy Legard!"

"Thetford! My dear Sir Rupert!"

The baronet leaped off his horse, his eyes lighting, and shook hands with the artist, in a burst of heartiness very rare with him.

"Where in the world did you drop from, and how under the sun do you come to be on such uncommonly friendly footing with Miss Everard?"

"I leave the explanation to Mr. Legard," said May, blushing a little under Sir Rupert's glance, "while I go and see mamma, only premising that luncheon-hour is past, and you had better not linger."

She tripped away, and the two young men followed more slowly into the house. Sir Rupert led his friend to his studio, and left him to inspect the pictures.

"Whilst I speak a word to my mother," he said; "it will detain me hardly an instant."

"All right!" said Mr. Legard, boyishly. "Don't hurry yourself on my account, you know."

Lady Thetford lay where her son had left her; lay as if she had hardly stirred since. She looked up, and half rose as he came in, her eyes painfully, intensely anxious. But his face, grave and quiet, told nothing.

"Well," she panted, her eyes glittering.

"It is well, mother. Aileen Jocyln has promised to become my wife."

"Thank God!"

Lady Thetford sunk back, her hands clasped tightly over her heart, its loud beating plainly audible. Her son looked down at her, his face keeping its steady gravity—none of the rapture of an accepted lover there.

"You are content, mother?"

"More than content, Rupert. And you?"

He smiled, and stooping, kissed the worn, pallid face. "I would do a great deal to make you happy, mother; but I would *not* ask a woman I did not love to be my wife. Be at rest; all is well with me. And now I must leave you, if you will not go down to luncheon."

"I think not; I am not strong to-day. Is May waiting?"

"More than May. A friend of mine has arrived, and will stay with us for a few weeks."

Lady Thetford's face had been flushed and eager, but at the last words it suddenly blanched.

"A friend, Rupert! Who?"

"You have heard me speak of him before," he said, carelessly; "his name is Guy Legard."

---

# CHAPTER XI.

### ON THE WEDDING EVE.

he family at Thetford Towers were a good deal surprised, a few hours later that day, by the unexpected appearance of Lady Thetford at dinner. Wan as some spirit of the moonlight, she came softly in, just as they entered the dining-room; and her son presented his friend, Mr. Legard, at once.

"His resemblance to the family will be the surest passport to your favor, mother mine," Sir Rupert said, gayly. "Mrs. Weymore met him just now, and recoiled with a shriek, as though she had seen a ghost. Extraordinary, isn't it—this chance resemblance?"

"Extraordinary," Lady Thetford said, "but not at all unusual. Of course, Mr. Legard is not even remotely connected with the Thetford family?"

She asked the question without looking at him. She kept her eyes fixed on her plate, for that fair face before her was terrible to her almost as a ghost. It was the days of her youth over again, and Sir Noel, her husband, once more by her side.

"Not that I am aware of," Mr. Legard said, running his fingers through his abundant blonde hair. "But I may be, for all that. I am like the hero of a novel—a mysterious orphan—only, unfortunately, with no identifying strawberry-mark on my arm. Who my parents were, or what my real name is, I know no more than I do of the biography of the man in the moon."

There was a murmur of astonishment—May and Rupert vividly interested, Lady Thetford white as a dead woman, her eyes averted, her hand trembling as if palsied.

"No," said Mr. Legard, gravely, and a little sadly, "I stand as totally alone in this world as a human being can stand—father, mother, brother, sister, I never have known; a nameless penniless waif, I was cast upon the world four-and-twenty years ago. Until the age of twelve I was called Guy Vyking; then the friends with whom I had lived left England for America, and a man, a painter, named Legard, took me, and gave me his name. And there the romance comes in; a lady, a tall, elegant lady, too closely veiled for us to see her face, came to the poor home that was mine, paid those who kept me from my infancy, and paid Legard for his future care of me. I have never seen her since; and I sometimes think," his voice failing, "that she may have been my mother."

There was a sudden clash, and a momentary confusion. My lady, lifting her glass with that shaking hand, had let it fall, and it was shivered to atoms on the floor.

"And you never saw the lady after?" May asked.

"Never. Legard received regular remittances, mailed, oddly enough, from your town here—Plymouth. The lady told him, if he ever had occasion to address her, which he never did have, that I know of, to address Madam Ada, Plymouth! He brought me up, educated me, taught me his art, and died. I was old enough then to comprehend my position; and the first use I made of that knowledge, was to return 'Madam Ada' her remittances, with a few sharp lines, that effectually put an end to them."

"Have you ever tried to ferret out the mystery of your birth, and this Madam Ada?" inquired Sir Rupert.

Mr. Legard shook his head.

"No, why should I? I dare say I should have no reason to be proud of my parents if I did find them; and they evidently were not very proud of me. 'Where ignorance is bliss,' etc. If destiny has decreed it, I shall know, sooner or later; if destiny has not, then my puny efforts will be of no avail. But if presentiments mean anything, I shall one day know; and I have no doubt, if I searched Devonshire, I should find Madam Ada."

May Everard started up with a cry, for Lady Thetford had fallen back in one of those sudden spasms to which she had lately become subject. In the universal consternation, Guy Legard and his story were forgotten.

"I hope what *I* said had nothing to do with this," he cried aghast; and the one following so suddenly upon the other made the remark natural enough. But Sir Rupert turned upon him in haughty surprise.

"What you said! My mother, unfortunately, has been subject to these attacks for the past two years, Mr. Legard. That will do, May; let me assist my mother to her room."

May drew back. Lady Thetford was able to rise, pallid and trembling, and, supported by her son's arm, to walk from the room.

"Lady Thetford's health is very delicate, I fear," Mr. Legard murmured, sympathetically. "I really thought for a moment my story-telling had occasioned her sudden illness."

Miss Everard fixed a pair of big, shining eyes in solemn scrutiny on his face—that face so like the pictured one of Sir Noel Thetford.

"A very natural supposition," thought the young lady; "so did *I*."

"You never knew Sir Noel?" Guy Legard said, musingly; "but, of course, you did not. Sir Rupert has told me he died before he was born."

"I never saw him," said May; "but those who have seen him in this house, our housekeeper, for instance, stands perfectly petrified at your extraordinary likeness to him. Mrs. Hilliard says you have given her a 'turn' she never expects to get over."

Mr. Legard smiled, but was very grave again directly.

"It is odd—odd—very odd!"

"Yes," said May Everard, with a sagacious nod; "a great deal, too, to be a chance resemblance. Hush! here comes Rupert. Well, how have you left mamma?"

"Better; Louise is with her. And now to finish dinner; I have an engagement for the evening."

Sir Rupert was strangely silent and *distrait* all through dinner, a darkly thoughtful shadow glooming his ever pale face. A supposition had flashed across his mind that turned him hot and cold by turns—a supposition that was almost a certainty. This striking resemblance of the painter, Legard, to his dead father was no freak of nature, but a retributive Providence revealing the truth of his birth. It came back to his memory with painfully acute clearness, that his mother had sunk down once before in a violent tremor and faintness at the mere sound of his name. Legard had spoken of a veiled lady—Madam Ada, Plymouth, her address. Could his mother—his—be that mysterious arbiter of Legard's fate? The name—the place. Sir Rupert Thetford wrenched his thoughts by a violent effort away, shocked and horrified at himself.

"It cannot be—it cannot?" he said to himself passionately; "I am mad to harbor such thoughts. It is a desecration of the memory of the dead, a treason to the living. But I wish Guy Legard had never come here."

There was one other person at Thetford Towers strangely and strongly effected by Mr. Guy Legard; and that person, oddly enough, was Mrs. Weymore, the governess. Mrs. Weymore had never even seen the late Sir Noel that any one knew of, and yet she had recoiled with a shrill, feminine cry of utter consternation at sight of the young man.

"I don't see why you should get the fidgets about it, Mrs. Weymore," Miss Everard remarked, with her great, bright eyes suspiciously keen, "you never knew Sir Noel."

Mrs. Weymore sunk down on a lounge quite white and startled.

"My dear, I beg your pardon. I—it seems strange. O May!" with a sudden sharp cry, losing self-control, "who is that young man?"

"Why, Mr. Guy Legard, artist," answered May, composedly, the bright eyes still on the alert; "formerly in 'boyhood's sunny hours,' you know, Master Guy—let me see! Yes, Vyking."

"Vyking!" repeated Mrs. Weymore with a spasmodic cry; and then dropped her white face in her hands, trembling from head to foot.

"Well, upon my word," Miss Everard said, addressing empty space, "this does cap the globe! The Mysteries of Udolpho were plain reading compared to Mr. Guy Vyking, and the effect he produces on people. He's a very handsome young man, and a very agreeable young man; but I should never have suspected he possessed the power of throwing all the elderly ladies he meets into gasping fits. There's Lady Thetford, he was too much for her, and she had to be helped out of the dining-room; and here's Mrs. Weymore going into hysterics because he used to be called Guy Vyking. I thought my lady might be the veiled lady of his story; but now I think it must have been Mrs. Weymore."

Mrs. Weymore looked up, her very lips white as ashes.

"The veiled lady? What lady? May, tell me all you know of Mr. Vyking."

"Not Vyking now—Legard," answered May; and thereupon the young lady detailed the scanty *résumé* the artist had given them of his history.

"And I'm very sure it isn't chance at all," concluded May Everard, transfixing the governess with an unwinking stare; "and Mr. Legard is as much a Thetford as Sir Rupert himself. I don't pretend to divination, of course, and I don't clearly see how it is; but it is, Mrs. Weymore; and you could enlighten the young man, and so could my lady, if either of you chose."

Mrs. Weymore turned suddenly and caught May's two hands in hers.

"May, if you care for me, if you have any pity, don't speak of this, I do know—but I must have time. My head is in a whirl. Wait, wait, and don't tell Mr. Legard."

"I won't," said May; "but it's all very strange and very mysterious, delightfully like a three-volume novel, or a sensation play. I'm getting very much interested in the hero of the performance; and I'm afraid I shall be deplorably in love with him shortly, if this sort of thing keeps on."

Mr. Legard, himself, took the matter much more coolly than any one else; smoked cigars philosophically; criticised Sir Rupert's pictures—did a little that way himself; played billiards with his host; and chess with Miss Everard, rode with that young lady, walked with her, sang duets with her, in a deep melodious bass; made himself fascinating, and took the world easy.

"It is no use getting into a gale about these things," he said to Miss Everard, when she wondered aloud at his constitutional phlegm; "the crooked things will straighten of themselves if we give them time. What is written is written. I know that I shall find out all about myself one day—like little Paul Dombey, 'I feel it in my bones.'"

Mr. Legard was thrown a good deal upon Miss Everard's resources for amusement; for, of course, Sir Rupert's time was chiefly spent at Jocyln Hall, and Mr. Legard bore this with even greater serenity than the other. Miss Everard was a very charming little girl, with a laugh that was sweeter than the music of the spheres, and hundreds of bewitching little ways; and Mr. Legard undertook to paint her portrait, and found it the most absorbing work of art he had ever undertaken. As for the young baronet, spending his time at Jocyln Hall, they never missed him. His wooing sped on smoothest wings—Colonel Jocyln almost as much pleased as my lady herself; and the course of true love in this case ran as smooth as heart could wish.

Miss Jocyln, as a matter or course, was a great deal at Thetford Towers, and saw with evident gratification the growing intimacy of Mr. Legard and May. It would be an eminently suitable match, Miss Jocyln thought, only it was a pity so much mystery shrouded the gentleman's birth. Still he was a gentleman, and with his talents, no doubt, would become an eminent artist; and it would be highly satisfactory to see May fix her erratic affections on somebody and thus be doubly out of her (Miss Jocyln's) way.

The wedding preparations were going briskly forward. There was no need of delay, all were anxious for the marriage—Lady Thetford more than anxious, on account of her declining health. The hurry to have the ceremony irrevocably over had grown to be something very like monomania with her.

"I feel that my days are numbered," she said, with feverish impatience, to her son, "and I cannot rest in my grave, Rupert, until I see Aileen your wife."

So Sir Rupert, more than anxious to please his mother, hastened on the wedding. An eminent physician, summoned down from London, confirmed my lady's own fears.

"Her life hangs by a thread," this gentleman said, confidentially, to Sir Rupert; "the slightest excitement may snap it at any moment. Don't contradict her—let everything be as she wishes. Nothing can save her, but perfect quiet and repose may prolong her existence."

The last week of September the wedding was to take place; and all was bustle and haste at Jocyln Hall. Mr. Legard was to stay for the wedding, at the express desire of Lady Thetford herself. She had seen him but very rarely since that first day; illness had compelled her to keep her room; but her interest in him was unabated, and she had sent for him to her apartment, and invited him to remain. And Mr. Legard, a good deal surprised, and a little flattered, consented at once.

"Very kind of Lady Thetford, you know, Miss Everard," Mr. Legard said, sauntering into the room where she sat with her ex-governess—Mr. Legard and Miss Everard were growing highly confidential of late—"to take such an interest in an utter stranger as she does in me."

May stole a glance from under her eyelashes at Mrs. Weymore; that lady sat nervous and scared-looking, and altogether uncomfortable, as she had a habit of doing in the young artist's presence.

"Very," Miss Everard said, dryly. "You ought to feel highly complimented, Mr. Legard, for it's a sort of kindness her ladyship is extremely chary of to utter strangers. Rather odd, isn't it, Mrs. Weymore?"

Mrs. Weymore's reply was a distressed, beseeching look. Mr. Legard saw it, and opened very wide his handsome, Saxon eyes.

"Eh?" he said, "it doesn't mean anything does it? Mrs. Weymore looks mysterious, and I'm so stupid about these things. Lady Thetford doesn't know anything about me, does she?"

"Not that *I* know of," May said, with significant emphasis on the personal pronoun.

"Then Mrs. Weymore does! By Jove! I always thought Mrs. Weymore had an odd way of looking at me! And now, what is it?"

He turned his fair, resolute face to that lady with a smile hard to resist.

"I don't make much of a howling about my affairs, you know, Mrs Weymore," he said; "but, for all that, I am none the less interested in myself and history. If you can open the mysteries a little you will be conferring a favor on me I can never repay. And I am positive from your looks you can."

Mrs. Weymore turned away, and covered her face, with a sort of sob. The young lady and gentleman exchanged startled glances.

"You can then?" Mr. Legard said, gravely, but growing very pale. "You know who I am?"

To his boundless consternation Mrs. Weymore rose up, seizing his hands and covering them with kisses.

"I do! I do! I know who you are, and so shall you before this wedding takes place. But before I tell you I must speak to Lady Thetford."

Mr. Legard withdrew his hands, his face as colorless as her own.

"To Lady Thetford! What has Lady Thetford to do with me?"

"Everything! She knows who you are as well as I do. I must speak to her first."

"Answer me one thing—is my name Vyking?"

"No. Pray, pray don't ask me any more questions. As soon as her ladyship is a little stronger, I will go to her and obtain her permission to speak. Keep what I have said a secret from Sir Rupert, and wait until then."

She turned to go, so haggard and wild-looking, that neither strove to detain her. The young man stared blankly after her as she left the room.

"At last!" he said, drawing a deep breath, "at last I shall know!"

There was a pause; then May spoke in a fluttering little voice.

"How very strange that Mrs. Weymore should know, of all persons in the world!"

"Who is Mrs. Weymore? How long has she been here? Tell me all you know of her, Miss Everard."

"And that 'all' will be almost nothing. She came down from London as nursery-governess to Rupert and me, a week or two after my arrival here, selected by the rector of St. Gosport. She was then what you see her now, a pale, subdued creature in widow weeds, with the look of one who had seen trouble. I have known her so long, and always as such a white, still shadow, I suppose that is why it seems so odd."

Mrs. Weymore kept altogether out of Mr. Legard's way for the next week or two. She avoided May also, as much as possible, and shrunk so palpably from any allusion to the past scene, that May good-naturedly bided her time in silence, though almost as impatient as Mr. Legard himself.

And whilst they waited the bridal-eve came round, and Lady Thetford was much better, not able to quit her room, but strong enough to lie on a sofa and talk to her son and Colonel Jocyln, with a flush on her cheek, and a sparkle in her eye—all unusual there.

The marriage was to take place in the village church, and there was to follow a grand ceremonial wedding-breakfast; and then the happy pair were to start at once on their blissful bridal-tour.

"And I hope to see my boy return," Lady Thetford said, kissing him fondly. "I can hardly ask for more than that."

Late in the afternoon of that eventful wedding-eve, the ex-governess sought out Guy Legard, for the first time of her own accord. She found him in the young baronet's studio, with May, putting the finishing touches to that young lady's portrait. He started up at sight of his visitor, vividly interested. Mrs. Weymore was paler even than usual, but with a look of deep, quiet determination on her face no one had ever seen there before.

"You have come to keep your promise," the young man cried—"to tell me who I am?"

"I have come to keep my promise," Mrs. Weymore answered; "but I must speak to my lady first. I wanted to tell you that, before you sleep to-night, you shall know."

She left the studio, and the two sat there, breathless, expectant. Sir Rupert was dining at Jocyln Hall, Lady Thetford was alone, in high spirits, and Mrs. Weymore was admitted at once.

"I wonder how long you must wait?" said May Everard.

"Heaven knows! Not long, I hope, or I shall go mad with impatience."

An hour passed—two—three, and still Mrs. Weymore was closeted with my lady, and still the pair in the studio waited.

# CHAPTER XII.

**MRS. WEYMORE'S STORY.**

ady Thetford sat up among her pillows and looked at her hired dependent with wide open eyes of astonishment. The pale, timid face of Mrs. Weymore wore a look altogether new.

"Listen to your story! My dear Mrs. Weymore, what possible interest can your story have for me?"

"More than you think, my lady. You are so much stronger to-day than usual, and Sir Rupert's marriage is so very near, that I must speak now or never."

"Sir Rupert," my lady said. "What has your story to do with Sir Rupert?"

"You will hear," Mrs. Weymore said, very sadly. "Heaven knows I should have told you long ago; but it is a story few would care to tell. A cruel and shameful story of wrong and misery; for, my lady, I have been cruelly wronged by one who was once very near to you."

Lady Thetford turned ashen white.

"Very near to me! do you mean—"

"My lady listen, and you shall hear. All those years that I have been with you, I have not been what I seemed. My name is not Weymore. My name is Thetford—as yours is."

A quick terror had settled down on my lady's face. Her lips moved, but she did not speak. Her eyes were fixed on the sad, set face before her, with a terrified, expectant stare.

"I was a widow when I came to you," Mrs. Weymore went on to say, "but, long before, I had known that worst widowhood, desertion. I ran away from my happy home, from the kindest father and mother that ever lived; I ran away, and was married and deserted before I was eighteen years old.

"He came to our village, a remote place, my lady, with a local celebrity for its trout-streams, and for nothing else. He came, the man whom I married, on a visit to the great house of the place. We had not the remotest connection with the house, or I might have known his real name. When I did know him, it was as Mr. Noel—he told me himself, and I never thought of doubting it. I was as simple and confiding as it is possible for the simplest village girl to be, and all the handsome stranger told me was gospel truth; and my life only began, I thought, from the hour I saw him first.

"I met him at the trout-streams fishing, and alone. I had come to while away the long, lazy hours under the trees. He spoke to me—the handsome stranger, whom I had seen riding through the village, beside the squire, like a young prince; and I was only too pleased and flattered by his notice. It is many years ago, Lady Thetford, and Mr. Noel took a fancy to my pink-and-white face and fair curls, as fine gentlemen will. It was only fancy—never at its best, love; or he would not have deserted me pitilessly as he did. I know it now; but then I took the tinsel for the pure gold, and would as soon have doubted the Scripture as his lightest word.

"My lady, it is a very old story, and very often told. We met by stealth and in secret; and weeks passed, and I never learned he was other than what I knew him. I loved with my whole foolish trusting heart, strongly and selfishly; and I was ready to give up home, and friends and parents—all the world for him. But not my good name, and he knew that; and my lady, we were married really and truly, and honestly married in a little church in Berkshire, and the marriage is recorded in the register in the church, and I have the marriage certificate here in my possession."

Mrs. Weymore touched her bosom as she spoke, and looked with earnest, truthful eyes at Lady Thetford. But Lady Thetford's face was averted, and not to be seen.

"His fancy for me was as fleeting as all his fancies; but it was strong enough and reckless enough, whilst it lasted, to make him forget all consequences. For it was surely a reckless act for a gentleman, such as he was, to marry the daughter of a village schoolmaster.

"There was but one witness to our marriage—my husband's servant—George Vyking. I never liked the man; he was crafty, and cunning, and treacherous, and ready for any deed of evil; but he was in his master's confidence and took a house for us at Windsor, and lived with us and kept his master's secrets well."

Mrs. Weymore paused, her hands fluttering in painful unrest. The averted face of Lady Thetford never turned, but a smothered voice bade her go on.

"A year passed, my lady, and I still lived in the house at Windsor, but quite alone now. My punishment had begun very early; two or three months sufficed to weary my husband of his childish village girl, and make him thoroughly repent his folly. I saw it from the first—he never tried to hide it from me; his absences grew longer and longer, more and more frequent, until at last he ceased coming altogether. Vyking, the valet, came and went; and Vyking told me the truth—the hard, cruel, bitter truth, that I was never to see my husband more.

"'It was the maddest act of a mad young man's life,' Vyking said to me, coolly, 'and he's repented of it, as I knew he would repent. You'll never see him again, mistress, and you needn't search for him, either. When you find last winter's snow, last autumn's partridges, then you may hope to find him.'

"'But I am his wife,' I said; 'nothing can undo that—his lawful, wedded wife.'

"'Yes,' said Vyking, 'his wife fast enough; but there's the law of divorce, and there's no witness but me alive. You can do your best; and the best you can do is to take it easy and submit. He'll provide for you handsomely; and when he gets the divorce, if you like, I'll marry you myself.'

"I had grown to expect some such revelation, I had been neglected so long. My lady, I don't speak of my feelings, my anguish and shame, and remorse and despair.—I only tell you here simple facts. But in the days and weeks which followed, I suffered as I never can suffer again in this world.

"I was held little better than a prisoner in the house at Windsor after that; and I think Vyking never gave up the hope that I would one day consent to marry him. More than once I tried to run away, to get on the track of my betrayer, but always to be met and foiled. I have gone down on my knees to that man Vyking, but I might as well have knelt to a statue of stone.

"'I'll tell you what we'll do,' he said, 'we'll go to London. People are beginning to look and talk about here; there they know how to mind their own business.'

"I consented readily enough. My one hope now was to find the man who had wronged me, and in London I thought I stood a better chance than at Windsor. We started, Vyking and I; but driving to the station we met with an accident, our horse ran away and I was thrown out; after that I hardly remember anything for a long time.

"Weeks passed before I recovered. Then I was told my baby had been born and died. I listened in a sort of dull apathy; I had suffered so much that the sense of suffering was dulled and blunted. I knew Vyking well enough not to trust him or believe him; but I was powerless to act, and could only turn my face to the wall and pray to die.

"But I grew strong, and Vyking took me to London, and left me in respectably-furnished lodgings. I might have escaped easily enough here, but the energy even to wish for freedom was gone; I sat all day long in a state of miserable, listless languor, heart-weary, heart-sick, worn-out.

"One day Vyking came to my rooms in a furious state of passion. He and his master had quarrelled. I never knew about what; and Vyking had been ignominiously dismissed. The valet tore up and down my little parlor in a towering passion.

"'I'll make Sir Noel pay for it, or my name's not Vyking,' he cried. 'He thinks because he's married an heiress he can defy me now. But there's law in this land to punish bigamy; and I'll have him up for bigamy the moment he's back from his wedding-tour.'

"I turned, and looked at him, but very quietly. 'Sir Noel?' I said. 'Do you mean my husband?'

"'I mean Miss Vandeleur's husband now,' said Vyking. '*You'll* never see him again, my girl. Yes, he's Sir Noel Thetford, of Thetford Towers, Devonshire; and you can go and call on his pretty new wife as soon as she comes home.'

"I turned away and looked out of the window without a word. Vyking looked at me curiously.

"'Oh! we've got over it, have we; and we're going to take it easy, and not make a scene. Now that's what I call sensible. And you'll come forward and swear Sir Noel guilty of bigamy?'

"'No,' I said, 'I never will!'

"'You won't—and why not?'

"'Never mind why. I don't think you would understand if I told you—only I won't.'

"'Couldn't you be coaxed?'

"'No.'

"'Don't be too sure. Perhaps I could tell you something might move you, quiet as you are. What if I told you your baby did not die that time, but was alive and well?'

"I knew a scene was worse than useless with this man, tears and entreaties thrown away. I heard his last words, and started to my feet with outstretched hands.

"'Vyking, for the dear Lord's sake, have pity on a desolate woman, and tell me the truth.'

"'I am telling you the truth. Your boy is alive and well, and I've christened him Guy—Guy Vyking. Don't you be scared—he's all safe; and the day you appear in court against Sir Noel, that day he shall be restored to you. Now don't you go and get excited; think it over, and let me know your decision when I come back.'

"He left the room before I could answer, and I never saw Vyking again. The next day, reading the morning paper, I saw the arrest of a pair of housebreakers, and the name of the chief was George Vyking, late valet to Sir Noel Thetford. I tried to get to see him in prison, but failed. His trial came on, his sentence was transportation for ten years; and Vyking left England, carrying my secret with him.

"I had something left to live for now—the thought of my child. But where was I to find him, where to look? I, who had not a penny in the wide world. If I had had the means, I would have come to Devonshire to seek out the man who had so basely wronged me; but as I was, I could as soon have gone to the antipodes. Oh! it was a bitter, bitter time, that long, hard struggle with starvation—a time it chills my blood even now to look back upon.

"I was still in London, battling with grim poverty, when, six months later, I read in the *Times* the awfully sudden death of Sir Noel Thetford, Baronet.

"My lady, I am not speaking of the effect of that blow—I dare not to you, as deeply wronged as myself. You were with him in his dying moments, and surely he told you the truth then; surely he acknowledged the great wrong he had done you?"

Mrs. Weymore paused, and Lady Thetford turned her face, her ghastly, white face, for the first time, to answer.

"He did—he told me all; I know your story to be true."

"Thank God! Oh, thank God! And he acknowledged his first marriage?"

"Yes; the wrong he did you was venial to that which he did me—I, who never was his wife, never for one poor moment had a right to his name."

Mrs. Weymore sunk down on her knees by the couch and passionately kissed the lady's hand.

"My lady! my lady! And you will forgive me for coming here? I did not know, when I answered Mr. Knight's advertisement, where I was coming; and when I did I could not resist the temptation of looking on his son. Oh, my lady! you will forgive me, and bear witness to the truth of my story."

"I will; I always meant to before I died. And that young man—that Guy Legard—you know he is your son?"

"I knew it from the first. My lady, you will let me tell him at once, will you not? And Sir Rupert? Oh, my lady! he ought to know."

Lady Thetford covered her face with a groan. "I promised his father on his death-bed to tell him long ago, to seek for his rightful heir—and see how I have kept my word. But I could not—I could not! It was not in human nature—not in such a nature as mine, wronged as I have been."

"But now—oh, my dear lady! now you will?"

"Yes, now, on the verge of the grave, I may surely speak. I dare not die with my promise unkept. This very night," Lady Thetford cried, sitting up, flushed and excited, "my boy shall know all—he shall not marry in ignorance of whom he really is. Aileen has the fortune of a princess; and Aileen will not love him less for the title he must lose. When he comes home, Mrs. Weymore, send him to me, and send your son with him, and I will tell them all."

---

# CHAPTER XIII.

### "THERE IS MANY A SLIP."

 room that was like a picture—a carpet of rose-buds gleaming through rich-green moss, lounges piled with downy-silk pillows, a bed curtained in lace, foamy white, plump, and tempting, fluted panels, and delicious little medallion pictures of celebrated beauties smiling down from the pink-tinted back-ground; a pretty room—Aileen Jocyln's *chambre-a-coucher*, and looking like a picture herself, in a loose, flowing morning-robe, all ungirdled, the rich, dark hair falling heavy and unbound to her waist, Aileen Jocyln lay among piles of cushions, like some young Eastern Sultana.

Lay and mused with, oh! such an infinitely happy smile upon her exquisite face; mused, as happy youth, loving and beloved, upon its bridal-eve does muse. Nay, on her bridal-day, for the dainty little French clock on the bracket, was pointing its golden hands to three.

The house was very still; all had retired late, busy with preparations for the morrow, and Miss Jocyln had just dismissed her maid. Every one, probably, but herself, was asleep; and she, in her unutterable bliss, was too happy for slumber. She arose, presently, walked to the window and looked out. The late-setting moon still swung in the sky; the stars still spangled the cloudless blue, and shone serene on the purple bosom of the far-spreading sea; but in the East the first pale glimmer of the new day shone—her happy wedding-day. The girl slid down on her knees, her hands clasped, her radiant face, glorified with love and bliss, turned ecstatically, as some faithful follower of the Prophet might, to that rising glory of the East.

"Oh!" Aileen thought, gazing around over the dark, deep sea, the star-gemmed sky, and the green radiance and sweetness of the earth, "what a beautiful, blissful world it is, and I the happiest creature in it!"

She returned to her cushions, and fell asleep; slept and dreamed dreams as joyful as her waking thoughts, and no shadow of that gathering cloud that was to blacken all her world so soon, fell upon her.

Hours passed, and still Aileen slept. Then came an imperative knock at her door—again and again, louder each time; and then Aileen started up, fully awake. Her room was flooded with sunshine, countless birds sang in the swaying green gloom of the branches, and the ceaseless sea was all aglitter with sparkling sunlight.

"Come in," Miss Jocyln said. It was her maid, she thought—and she walked over to an arm-chair, and composedly sat down.

The door opened, and Colonel Jocyln, not Fanchon, appeared, an open note in his hand, his face full of trouble.

"Papa!" Aileen cried, starting up in alarm.

"Bad news, my daughter—very bad! very sorrowful! Read that."

The note was very brief, in a spidery, female hand.

"Dear Colonel Jocyln—We are in the greatest trouble. Poor Lady Thetford died with awful suddenness this morning, in one of those dreadful spasms. We are all nearly distracted. Rupert bears it better than any of us. Pray come over as soon as you can.

"May Everard."

Aileen Jocyln sunk back in her seat, pale and trembling.

"Dead! O papa! papa!"

"It is very sad, my dear, and very shocking; and terribly unfortunate that it should have occurred just at this time. A postponed wedding is ever ominous of evil."

"Oh! pray, papa, don't think of that. Don't think of me! Poor Lady Thetford! Poor Rupert! You will go over at once, papa, will you not?"

"Certainly, my dear. And I will tell the servants, so that when our guests arrive, you may not be disturbed. Since it was to be," muttered the Indian officer under his mustache, "I would give half my fortune that it had been one day later. A postponed marriage is the most ominous thing under the sun."

He left the room, and Aileen sat with her hands clasped, and an unutterable awe overpowering every other feeling. She forgot her own disappointment in the awful mystery of sudden death. Her share of the trial was light—a year of waiting, more or less; what did it matter, since Rupert loved her unchangeably; but, poor Lady Thetford, called away in one instant from earth, and all she held most dear, on her son's wedding-day. And then Aileen, remembering how much the dead woman had loved her, and how fondly she had welcomed her as a daughter, covered her face with her hands, and wept as she might have wept for her own mother.

"I never knew a mother's love or care," Aileen thought; "and I was doubly happy in knowing I was to have one at last. And now—and now—"

It was a drearily long morning to the poor bride elect, sitting alone in her chamber, or pacing restlessly up and down. She heard the roll of carriages up the drive, the pause that ensued, and then their departure. She wondered how *he* bore it; best of all, May had said; but then he was ever still, and strong, and self-restrained. She knew how dear that poor, ailing mother had ever been to him, and she knew how bitterly he would feel her loss.

"They talk of presentiments," mused Miss Jocyln, walking wearily to and fro; "and see how happy and hopeful I was this morning, while she lay dead and he mourned. If I only dared go to him—my own Rupert."

It was late in the afternoon before Col. Jocyln returned. He strode straight to his daughter's presence, wearing a pale, fagged face.

"Well, papa?" she asked, faintly.

"My pale Aileen!" he said, kissing her fondly, "my poor, patient girl. I am sorry you must undergo this trial, and," knitting his brows, "such talk as it will make."

"Don't think of me, papa—my share is surely the lightest. But Rupert,—" wistfully faltering.

"There's something odd about Rupert; he was very fond of his mother, and he takes this a great deal too quietly. He looks like a man slowly turning to stone, with a face white and stern, and inscrutable; and he never asked for you. He sat there with folded arms, and that petrified face, gazing on his dead, until it chilled my blood to look at him. There's something odd and unnatural in this frozen calm. And, oh! by-the-by? I forgot to tell you the strangest thing—May Everard it was who told me; that painter fellow—what's his name—"

"Legard, papa?"

"Yes, Legard. He turns out to be the son of Mrs. Weymore—they discovered it last night. He was there in the room with the most dazed and mystified, and altogether bewildered expression of countenance I ever saw a man wear; and May and Mrs. Weymore sat crying incessantly. I couldn't see what occasion there was for the governess and the painter there in that room of death—and I said so to Miss Everard. There's something mysterious in the matter, for her face flushed, and she stammered something about startling family secrets that had come to light, the over-excitement of which had hastened Lady Thetford's end. I don't like the look of things, and I'm altogether in the dark. That painter resembles the Thetfords a great deal too closely for the mere work of chance; and yet, if Mrs. Weymore is his mother, I don't see how there can be anything in *that*. It's odd—confoundedly odd!"

Col. Jocyln rambled on as he walked the floor, his brows knitted into a swarthy frown. His daughter sat and eyed him wistfully.

"Did no one ask for me, papa? Am I not to go over?"

"Sir Rupert didn't ask for you. May Everard did, and I promised to fetch you to-morrow. Aileen, things at Thetford Towers have a suspicious look to-day; I can't see the light yet, but I suspect something wrong. It may be the very best thing that could possibly happen, this postponed marriage. I shall make Sir Rupert clear matters up completely before my daughter becomes his wife."

Col. Jocyln, according to promise, took his daughter to Thetford Towers next morning. With bated breath, and beating heart, and noiseless tread, Aileen Jocyln entered the house of mourning, which yesterday she had thought to enter a bride. Dark and still, and desolate it lay, the brilliant morning light shut out, unbroken silence everywhere.

"And this is the end of earth, its glory and its bliss," Aileen thought, as she followed her father slowly up stairs, "the solemn wonder of the winding-sheet and the grave."

There were two watchers in the dark room when they entered, May Everard, pale and quiet, and the young artist, Guy Legard. Even in that moment, Col. Jocyln could not repress a supercilious stare of wonder to behold the housekeeper's son in the death-chamber of Lady Thetford. And yet it seemed strangely his place, for it might have been one of those lusty old Thetfords, framed up stairs, stepped out of the canvas, and dressed in the fashion of the day.

"Very bad taste all the same," the proud old colonel thought, with a frown; "very bad taste on the part of Sir Rupert. I shall speak to him on the subject presently."

He stood in silence beside his daughter, looking down at the marble face. May, shivering drearily in a large shawl, and looking like a wan little spirit, was speaking in whispers to Aileen.

"We persuaded Rupert—Mr. Legard and I—to go and lie down; he has neither eaten nor slept since his mother died. O, Aileen! I am so sorry for you!"

"Hush!" raising one tremulous hand and turning away; "she was as dear to me as my own mother could have been. Don't think of me."

"Shall we not see Sir Rupert?" the colonel asked. "I should like to, particularly."

"I think not—unless you remain for some hours. He is completely worn out, poor fellow."

"How comes that young man here, Miss Everard?" nodding in the direction of Mr. Legard, who had withdrawn to a remote corner. "He may be a very especial friend of Sir Rupert, but don't you think he presumes on that friendship?"

Miss Everard's eyes flashed angrily.

"No, sir! I think nothing of the sort. Mr. Legard has a perfect right to be in this room, or any other room at Thetford Towers. It is by Rupert's particular request he remains."

The colonel frowned again, and turned his back upon the speaker.

"Aileen," he said, haughtily, "as Sir Rupert is not visible, nor likely to be for some time, perhaps you had better not linger. To-morrow, after the funeral, I shall speak to him very seriously."

Miss Jocyln arose. She would rather have lingered, but she saw her father's annoyed face, and obeyed him immediately. She bent and kissed the cold, white face, awful with the dread majesty of death.

"For the last time, my friend, my mother," she murmured, "until we meet in heaven."

She drew her veil over her face to hide her falling tears, and silently followed the stern and displeased Indian officer down stairs, and out of the house. She looked back wistfully once at the gray, old ivy-grown façade; but who was to tell her of the weary, weary months and years that would pass before she crossed that stately threshold again.

It was a very grand and imposing ceremonial that burial of Lady Thetford; and side by side with the heir, clad in deepest mourning, walked the unknown painter, Guy Legard. Colonel Jocyln was not the only friend of the family shocked and scandalized on this occasion. What could Sir Rupert mean? And what did Mr. Legard mean by looking ten times more like the old Thetford race than Sir Noel's own son and heir?

It was a miserable day, this day of the funeral, with a low complaining wind sighing through the yew-trees, and a dark, slanting rain lashing the sodden earth. There was a sky of lead hanging low like a pall; and it was almost dark, in the rainy gloaming, when Colonel Jocyln and Sir Rupert Thetford stood alone before the village church. Lady Thetford slept with the rest of the name in the stony vaults; the fair-haired artist stood in the porch looking at the slanting lines of rain, and Sir Rupert, with a face wan, and stern, in the dying daylight, stood face to face with the colonel.

"A private interview," the colonel was repeating; "most certainly, Sir Rupert. Will you come with me to Jocyln Hall? My daughter will wish to see you."

The young man nodded, went back a moment to speak to Legard, and then followed the colonel into the carriage. The drive was a very silent one—dark gloom lay on the faces of the two men. A vague, chilling presentiment of impending evil on the Indian officer, as he uneasily watched the young man who had so nearly been his son.

Aileen Jocyln, roaming like a restless ghost through the lonely rooms, saw them alight, and came out to the hall to meet her betrothed. She held out both hands shyly and wistfully, looking up, half in fear, in that rigid death-white face of her lover.

"Aileen!"

He took the hands, and held them fast a moment; then dropped them, and turned to the colonel.

"Now, Colonel Jocyln."

The colonel led the way into the library. Sir Rupert paused a moment on the threshold to answer Aileen's pleading glance.

"Only for a few moments, Aileen," he said, his eyes softening with infinite love; "in half an hour my fate shall be decided. Let that fate be what it may, I shall be true to you while life lasts."

With these enigmatical words, he followed the colonel into the library, and the polished oaken door closed between him and Aileen.

---

# CHAPTER XIV.

**PARTED.**

alf an hour had passed.

Up and down the long drawing-room Aileen wandered, aimlessly, restlessly, oppressed with an overwhelming dread of, she knew not what, a prescience of evil, vague as it was terrible. The dark gloom of the rainy evening was not darker than that brooding shadow in her deep, dusky eyes.

In the library Colonel Jocyln stood facing his son-in-law elect, staring like a man bereft of his senses. The melancholy half light coming wanly through the oriel window by which he stood, fell full upon the face of Rupert Thetford, white and cold, and set as marble.

"My God!" the Indian officer said, with wild eyes of terror and affright, "what is this you are telling me?"

"The truth, Col. Jocyln—the simple truth. Would to Heaven I had known it years ago—this shameful story of wrong-doing and misery!"

"I don't comprehend—I can't comprehend this impossible tale, Sir Rupert."

"That is a misnomer now, Colonel Jocyln. I am no longer *Sir* Rupert."

"Do you mean to say you credit this wild story of a former marriage of Sir Noel's? Do you really believe your late governess to have been your father's wife?"

"I believe it, colonel. I have facts and statements, and dying words to prove it. On my father's death-bed, he made my mother swear to tell the truth, to repair the wrong he had done; to seek out his son, concealed by his valet, Vyking, and restore him to his rights! My mother never kept that promise—the cruel wrong done to herself was too bitter; and at my birth she resolved never to keep it. I should not atone for the sin of my father; his elder son should never deprive *her* child of his birthright. My poor mother! You know the cause of that mysterious trouble which fell upon her at my father's death, and which darkened her life to the last. Shame, remorse, anger—shame for herself—a wife only in name; remorse for her broken vow to the dead, and anger against that erring dead man."

"But you told me she had hunted him up and provided for him," said the mystified colonel.

"Yes; she saw an advertisement in a London paper, calling upon Vyking to take charge of the boy he had left twelve years before. Now Vyking, the valet, had been transported for house-breaking long before that, and my mother answered the advertisement. There could be no doubt the child was the child Vyking had taken charge of—Sir Noel Thetford's rightful heir. My mother left him with the painter, Legard, with whom he grew up, whose name he took; and he is now at Thetford Towers."

"I thought the likeness meant something," muttered the colonel under his mustache, "his paternity is plainly enough written in his face. And so," raising his voice, "Mrs. Weymore recognized her son. Really, your story runs like a melodrama, where the hero turns out to be a duke, and his mother knows the strawberry mark on his arm. Well, sir, if Mrs. Weymore is Sir Noel's rightful widow, and Guy Legard his rightful son and heir—pray what are you?"

The colorless face of the young man turned dark red for an instant, then whiter than before.

"My mother was as truly and really Sir Noel's wife as woman can be the wife of man in the sight of Heaven. The crime was his; the shame and suffering hers; the atonement mine. Sir Noel's elder son shall be Sir Noel's heir—I will play usurper no longer. To-morrow I leave St. Gosport; the day after England, never perhaps, to return."

"You are mad," Colonel Jocyln said, turning very pale; "you do not mean it."

"I am not mad, and I do mean it. I may be unfortunate; but, I pray God, never a villain. Right is right; my brother Guy is the rightful heir—not I."

"And Aileen?" Colonel Jocyln's face turned dark and rigid as iron as he spoke his daughter's name.

Rupert Thetford turned away his changing face.

"It shall be as she says. Aileen is too noble and just herself not to honor me for doing right."

"It shall be as I say," returned Colonel Jocyln, with a voice that rang, and an eye that flashed. "My daughter comes of a proud and stainless race, and never shall she mate with one less stainless. Hear me out, young man. It won't do to fire up—plain words are best suited to a plain case. All that has passed between you and Miss Jocyln must be as if it had never been. The heir of Thetford Towers, honorably born, I consented she should marry; but, dearly as I love her, I would see her dead at my feet before she should marry one who was nameless and impoverished. You said just now the atonement was yours—you said right; go, and never return."

He pointed to the door; the young man, stonily still, took his hat.

"Will you not permit your daughter, Colonel Jocyln, to speak for herself?" he said at the door.

"No, sir. I know my daughter—my proud, high-spirited Aileen, and my answer is hers. I wish you good-night."

He swung round abruptly, turning his back upon his visitor. Rupert Thetford, without one word, turned and walked out of the house.

The bewildering rapidity of the shocks he had received had stunned him—he could not feel the pain now. There was a dull sense of aching torture upon him from head to foot—but the acute edge was dulled; he walked along through the black night like a man drugged and stupefied.

He was only conscious intensely of one thing—a wish to get away, never to set foot in St. Gosport again.

Like one walking in his sleep, he reached Thetford Towers, his old home, every tree and stone of which was dear to him. He entered at once, passed into the drawing-room, and found Guy Legard, sitting before the fire, staring blankly into the coals; and May Everard, roaming restlessly up and down, the firelight falling dully on her black robes and pale, tear-stained face. Both started at his entrance—all wet, and pale and haggard; but neither spoke. There was that in his face which froze the words on their lips.

"I am going away to-morrow," he said, abruptly, leaning against the mantel, and looking at them with quiet, steadfast eyes.

May uttered a faint cry; Guy faced him almost fiercely.

"Going away! What do you mean, Sir Rupert? We are going away together, if you like."

"No; I go alone. You remain here, it is your place now."

"Never!" cried the young artist, passionately—"never! I will go out and die like a dog, of starvation, before I rob you of your birthright!"

"You reverse matters," said Rupert Thetford; "it is I who have robbed you, unwittingly, for too many years. I promised my mother on her death-bed, as she promised my father on his, that you should have your right, and I will keep that promise. Guy, dear old fellow! don't let us quarrel, now that we are brothers, after being friends so long. Take what is your own; the world is all before me, and surely I am man enough to win my own way. Not one other word; you shall not come with me; you might as well talk to these stone walls and try to move them as to move me. To-morrow I go, and go alone."

"Alone!" It was May who breathlessly repeated the word.

"Alone; all the ties that bound me here are broken; I go alone, and single-handed, to fight the battle of life Guy, I have spoken to the rector about you—you will find him your friend and aider; and May is to make her home at the rectory. And now," turning suddenly, and moving to the door, "as I start early to-morrow, I believe I'll retire early. Good-night."

And then he was gone, and Guy and May were left staring at each other with blank faces.

The storm of wind and rain sobbed itself out before midnight; and in the bluest of skies, heralded by banners of rosy clouds, rose up the sun next morning. Before that rising sun had gilded the tops of the tallest oaks in the park, he, who had so lately called it all his own, had opened the heavy oaken door and passed from Thetford Towers, as home, forever. The house was very still—no one had risen; he had left a note to Guy, with a few brief, warm words of farewell.

"Better so," he thought—"better so! He and May will be happy together, for I know he loves her, and she him. The memory of my leave-taking shall never come to cloud their united lives."

One last backward glance at the eastern windows turning to gold; at the sea blushing in the first glance of the day-king; at the waving trees and swelling meadows, and gray, old ivy-grown front, and then he passed down the avenue, out through the massive entrance-gates, and was gone.

# CHAPTER XV.

### AFTER FIVE YEARS.

oonlight falling like a silvery veil over Venice—a crystal clear crescent in a purple sky shimmering on palace and prison, churches, squares and canals, on the gilded gondolas, and the flitting forms passing like noiseless shadows to and fro.

A young lady leaned from a window of a vast Venetian hotel, gazing thoughtfully at the silver-lighted landscape, so strange, so unreal, so dream-like, to her unaccustomed eyes. A young lady, stately and tall, with a pale, proud face, deep, dark eyes, solemn, shining, fathomless, like mountain tarns; floating dark ringlets and a statuesque sort of beauty that was perfect in its way. She was dressed in trailing robes of crape and bombazine, and the face, turned to the moonlight, was cold and still.

She turned her eyes from the moonlit canal, down which dark gondolas floated to the music of the gay gondolier's song; once, as an English voice in the piazza below, sung a stave of a jingling barcarole,

"Oh, gay we row where full tides flow And bear our bounding pinnace; And leap along where song meets song, Across the waves of Venice."

The singer, a tall young man, with a florid face, and yellow side whiskers, an unmistakable son of the "right little, tight little" island, paused in his song, as another man, stepping through an open window, struck him an airy sledge-hammer slap on the back.

"I ought to know that voice," said the last comer.

"Mortimer, my lad, how goes it?"

"Stafford!" cried the singer, seizing the outstretched hand in a genuine English grip, "happy to meet you, old boy, in the land of romance! La Fabre told me you were coming—but who would look for you so soon? I thought you were doing Sorrento?"

"Got tired of Sorrento," said Stafford, taking his arm for a walk up and down the piazza; "there's a fever there, too—quite an epidemic—malignant typhus. Discretion is the better part of valor, where Sorrento fevers are concerned. I left."

"When did you reach Venice?" asked Mortimer, lighting a cigar.

"An hour ago; and now who's here? Any one I know?"

"Lots. The Cholmonadeys, the Lythons, the Howards, of Leighwood; and, by-the-by, they have with them the Marble Bride."

"The which?" asked Mr. Stafford.

"The Marble Bride, the Princess Frostina, otherwise Miss Aileen Jocyln, of Jocyln Hall, Devonshire. You knew the old colonel, I think—he died over a year ago, you remember."

"Ah, yes! I remember. Is she here with the Howards, and as handsome as ever, no doubt?"

"Handsome to my mind, with an uplifted and unapproachable sort of beauty. A fellow might as soon love some bright particular star, etc., as the fabulously wealthy heiress of all the Jocylns. She has no end of suitors—all the best men here bow at the shrine of the ice-cold Aileen, and all in vain."

"You among the rest, my friend?" with a light laugh.

"No, by Jove!" cried Mr. Mortimer; "that sort of thing, the marble style, you know, never was to my taste. I admire Miss Jocyln immensely; just as I do that moon up there, with no particular desire ever to get nearer."

"What was that story I heard once, five years ago, about a broken engagement? Wasn't Thetford of that ilk hero of the tale? The romantic Thetford, who resigned his title and estate to a mysteriously-found elder brother, you know. The story rang through the papers and the clubs at the time like wildfire, and set the whole country talking, I remember. She was engaged to him, wasn't she, and broke off?"

"So goes the story—but who knows? I recollect that odd affair perfectly well; it was like the melo-dramas on the Surrey side of the Thames. I know the 'mysteriously found elder brother,' too—very fine fellow, Sir Guy Thetford, and married to the prettiest little wife the sun shines on. I must say Rupert Thetford behaved wonderfully well in that unpleasant business; very few men would do as he did—they would, at least, have made a fight for the title and estates. By-the-way, I wonder what ever became of him?"

"I left him at Sorrento," said Stafford, coolly.

"The deuce you did! What was he doing there?"

"Raving in the fever; so the people told me with whom he stopped. I just discovered he was in the place as I was about to leave it. He had fallen very low, I fancy; his pictures didn't sell, I suppose; he has been in the painting line since he ceased to be Sir Rupert, and the world has gone against him. Rather hard on him to lose fortune, title, home, bride, and all at one fell swoop."

"And so you left him ill of the fever? Poor fellow!"

"Dangerously ill."

"And the people with whom he is will take very little care of him. He's as good as dead. Let us go in—I want to have a look at the latest English papers."

The two men passed in, out of the moonlight, off the piazza, all unconscious that they had had a listener. The pale watcher in the trailing black robes scarcely heeding them at first, had grown more and more absorbed in the careless conversation. She caught her breath quick and hard, the dark eyes dilated, the slender hands pressed tight over the throbbing heart. As they went in off the balcony, she slid from her seat and held up her clasped hands to the luminous night sky.

"Here me, O God!" the white lips cried. "I, who have aided in wrecking a noble heart, hear me, and help me to keep my vow! I offer my whole life in atonement for the cruel and wicked past. If he dies, I shall go to my grave his unwedded widow. If he lives—"

Her voice faltered and died out, her face dropped forward on the window-sill, and the moonlight fell like a benediction on the bowed young head.

---

# CHAPTER XVI.

### AT SORRENTO.

he low light in the western sky was fading out; the bay of Naples lay rosy in the haze of the dying day; the soft, sweet wind floated over the waters; the fishing boats were coming in; and on this scene an invalid, looking from a window high up on the sea-washed cliff of Sorrento, gazed languidly.

For he was surely an invalid who sat in that window chair and gazed at the wondrous Italian sea, and that lovely Italian sky. Surely an invalid, with that pallid face, those spectral, hollow eyes, those sunken cheeks, those bloodless lips; surely an invalid, and one but very lately risen from the very gates of death, a pale shadow, worn and weak as a child.

As he sits there, where he has sat for hours, lonely and alone, the door opens, and an English face looks in—the face of an Englishman of the lower classes.

"A visitor for you, sir—just come, and a-foot; a lady, sir. She will not give her name, but wishes to see you most particular, if you please."

"A lady! To see me?"

The invalid opens his dark eyes in wonder as he speaks.

"Yes, sir; an English lady, sir, dressed in black, and a wearing of a thick veil. She asked for Mr. Rupert Thetford as soon as she see me, as plain, as plain, sir—"

The young man in the chair started, half rose, and then sunk back; an eager light lit in the hollow eyes.

"Let her come in, I will see her."

The man disappeared; there was an instant's pause, then a tall, slender figure, draped and veiled in black, entered alone.

The visitor stood still. Once more the invalid attempted to rise, once more his strength failed him. The lady threw back her veil with a sudden emotion.

"My God, Aileen!"

"Rupert!"

She was on her knees before him, lifting her suppliant hands.

"Forgive me! forgive me! I have seemed the most heartless and cruel of women. But I too, have suffered. I am base and unworthy; but, oh! forgive me, if you can."

The old love, stronger then death, shone in her eyes, plead in her passionate, sobbing voice, and went to his very heart.

"I have been so wretched, so wretched all these miserable years. While my father lived, I would not disobey his stern command, that I was never to attempt to see or hear from you, and at his death I could not. You seemed lost to me and to the world. Only by the merest accident I heard in Venice you were here, and ill—dying. I lost no time; I came hither at once, hoping against hope to find you alive. Thank God I did come. O Rupert! for the sake of the past forgive me."

"Forgive you!" and he tried to raise her. "Aileen—darling!"

His weak arms encircled her, and the pale lips pressed passionate kisses on the tear-wet face.

So while the glory of the sunset lay on the sea, and until the stars spangled the sky, the reunited lovers sat in the soft haze, as Adam and Eve may have sat in the loveliness of Eden.

"How long since you left England?" Rupert asked, at length.

"Two years ago; poor papa died in the South of France—you mustn't blame him too much, Rupert."

"My dearest, we will talk of blaming no one. And Guy and May are married? I knew they would be."

"Did you? I was so surprised when I read it in the *Times*; for you know May and I never corresponded—she was frantically angry with me. Do they know you are here?"

"No, I rarely write, and I am constantly moving about; but I know that Guy is very much beloved in St. Gosport. We will go back to England, one of these days, my darling, and give them the greatest surprise they have received since Guy Thetford learned who he really was."

He smiled as he said it—the old bright smile she remembered so well. Tears of joy filled the beautiful upturned eyes.

"And you will go back? O Rupert! it needed but this to complete my happiness."

He drew her closer, and then there was a long delicious silence, while they watched together the late-rising moon climbing the misty hills above Castellamare.

---

# CHAPTER XVII.

**AT HOME.**

nother sunset, red and gorgeous, over swelling English meadows, waving trees, and grassy terrace, lighting up with its crimson radiance the gray forest of Thetford Towers.

In the pretty, airy summer drawing-room, this red sunset streams through open western windows, kindling everything into living light. It falls on the bright-haired girlish figure, dressed in floating white, seated in an arm-chair in the centre of the room, too childish-looking, you might fancy, at first sight, to be mamma to that fat baby she holds in her lap; but she is not a bit too childish. And that is papa, tall and handsome, and happy, who leans over the chair and looks as men do look on what is the apple of their eye, and the pride of their heart.

"It's high time baby was christened, Guy," Lady Thetford—for, of course, Lady Thetford it is—was saying; "and, do you know, I am really at a loss for a name. You won't let me call him Guy, and I sha'n't call him Noel—and so what is it to be?"

"Rupert, of course," Sir Guy suggests; and little Lady Thetford pouts.

"He does not deserve the compliment. Shabby fellow! To keep wandering about the world as he does, and never to answer one's letters; and I sent him half a ream last time, if I sent him a sheet, telling all about baby, and asking him to come and be godfather, and coaxing him with the eloquence of a female Demos—, the man in the tub you know. And to think it should be all of no use! To think of not receiving a line in return. It is using me shamefully; and I don't believe I will call baby Rupert."

"Oh, yes you will, my dear! Well, Smithers, what is it?"

For Mr. Smithers, the butler, stood in the doorway, with a very pale and startled face.

"It's a gentleman—leastways a lady—leastways a lady and gentleman. Oh! here they come theirselves!"

Mr. Smithers retired precipitately, still pale and startled of visage, as a gentleman, with a lady on his arm, stood before Sir Guy and Lady Thetford.

There was a half shout from the young baronet, a wild shriek from the young lady. She sprung to her feet, and nearly dropped the precious baby.

"Rupert! Aileen!"

She never got any further—this impetuous little Lady Thetford, for she was kissing first one, then the other, crying and laughing, and talking all in a breath.

"Oh! what a surprise this is! Rupert my dear, my dear, I'm so glad to see you again! O Aileen! I never, never hoped for this! Guy, O Guy, to think it should all come right at last!"

But Guy was wringing his brother's hand, with bright tears standing in his eyes, and quite unable to reply.

"And this is the baby, May? The wonderful baby you wrote me so much about," Mr. Rupert Thetford said. "A noble little fellow, upon my word; and a Thetford from top to toe. Am I in season to be godfather?"

"Just in season. The name was to have been Rupert in any case, but a moment ago I was scolding frightfully, because you had not answered my letter, little dreaming you were coming to answer in person. And Aileen too! Oh! my dear, my dear, sit down at once and tell me all about it."

Mrs. Thetford smiles at the old impetuosity, and in very few words tells the story of the meeting and the marriage.

"Of course you remain in England?" Sir Guy eagerly asked, when he had heard the brief *résumé* of those past five years. "Of course Jocyln Hall is to be headquarters and home?"

"Yes," Rupert says, his eyes for a moment lingering lovingly on his wife, "Jocyln Hall is home. We have not yet been there; we came at once here to see the most wonderful baby of modern times—my handsome little namesake."

"It is just like a fairy tale," is all Lady Thetford can say then; but late that night, when the reunited friends were in their chambers, she lifted her golden head off the pillow, and looked at her husband entering the room. "It's so very odd, Guy," slowly and drowsily, "to think that, after all, a Rupert Thetford should be *Sir Noel's Heir*."

---

# A DARK CONSPIRACY.

n love with her—*I* want to marry her!" cried Tom Maxwell in a fine fury. "I tell you I hate her, and I hope she may die a miserable, disappointed, cantankerous old maid!"

Striding up and down the floor, his face flaming, his eyes flashing, his very coat-tail quivering with rage—a Bengal tiger, robbed of her young, could not have looked a much more ferocious object. And yet ferocity was not natural to Tom Maxwell—handsome Tom, whose years were only two-and-twenty, and who was hot-headed and fiery, and impetuous as it is in the nature of two-and-twenty to be, but by no means innately savage. But he had just been jilted, jilted in cold blood; so up and down he strode, grinding his teeth vindictively, and fulminating anathema maranathas against his fair deceiver.

"The miserable, heartless jilt! The deceitful, shameless coquette!" burst out Tom, ferociously. "She gave me every encouragement that a woman could give, until she drew me on by her abominable wiles to make a fool of myself; and then she turns round and smiles and puts her handkerchief to her eyes and is 'very sorry,'" mimicking the feminine intonation, "'and never dreamed of such a thing, and will be very happy to be my friend; but for anything further—oh! dear, Mr. Maxwell, pray don't think of it!' Confound her and the whole treacherous sex to which she belongs! But I'm not done with her yet! I'll have revenge as sure as my name is Tom Maxwell!"

"As how?" asked a lazy voice from the sofa. "She's a woman, you know. Being a woman, you can't very well call her out and shoot her, or horsewhip her, or even knock her down. A fellow may feel like that—I often have myself, after being jilted; but still it can't be did. It's an absurd law, I allow, this polite exemption of womankind from condign and just punishment; but it is too late in the day for chaps like you and me to go tilt against popular prejudices."

It was a long speech for Paul Warden, who was far too indolent generally to get beyond monosyllables. He lay stretched at full length on the sofa, languidly smoking the brownest of meerschaums, and dreamily watching the smoke curl and wreath around his head. A genial, good-looking fellow, five years Tom's senior, and remarkably clever in his profession, the law, when not too lazy to exercise it.

Tom Maxwell paused in his excited striding to look in astonishment at the speaker.

"You jilted!" he said, "You! You, Paul Warden, the irresistible!"

"Even so, *mon ami*. Like measles, and mumps, and tooth-cutting, it's something a man has to go through, willy nilly. I've been jilted and heart-broken some half-dozen times, more or less, and here I am to-night not a ha'penny the worse for it. So go it, Tom my boy! The more you rant and rave now, the sooner the pain will be over. It's nothing when you're used to it. By-the-way," turning his indolent eyes slowly, "is she pretty, Tom?"

"Of course!" said Tom, indignantly. "What do you take me for? Pretty! She's beautiful, she's fascinating. Oh, Warden! it drives me mad to think of it!"

"She's all my fancy painted her—she's lovely, she's divine," quoted Mr. Warden; "but her heart, it is another's, and it never— What's her name, Tom?"

"Fanny Summers. If you had been in this place four-and-twenty hours, you would have no need to ask. Half the men in town are spooney about her."

"Fanny. Ah! a very bad omen. Never knew a Fanny yet who wasn't a natural born flirt. What's the style—dark or fair, *belle* blonde, or *jolie* brunette?"

"Brunette; dark, bright, sparkling, saucy, piquant irresistible! Oh!" cried Tom, with a dismal groan, sinking into a chair, "it is too bad, *too* bad to be treated so!"

"So it is, my poor Tom. She deserved the bastinado, the wicked witch. The bastinado not being practicable, let us think of something else. She deserves punishment, and she shall have it; paid back in her own coin, and with interest, too. Eh? Well?"

For Tom had started up in his chair, violently excited and red in the face.

"The very thing!" cried Tom. "I have it! She shall be paid in her own coin, and I'll have most glorious revenge, if you'll only help me, Paul."

"To my last breath, Tom; only don't make so much noise. Hand me the match-box, my pipe's gone out. Now, what is it?"

"Paul, they call you irresistible—the women do."

"Do they? Very polite of them. Well?"

"Well, being irresistible, why can't you make love to Fanny Summers, talk her into a desperate attachment to you, and then treat her as she has treated me—jilt her?"

Paul Warden opened his large, dreamy eyes to their widest, and fixed them on his excited young friend.

"Do you mean it, Tom?"

"Never meant anything more in my life, Paul."

"But supposing I could do it; supposing I am the irresistible conqueror you gallantly make me out; supposing I could talk the charming Fanny into that deplorable attachment—it seems a shame, doesn't it?"

"A shame!" exclaimed poor Tom, smarting under a sense of his own recent wrong; "and what do you call her conduct to *me*? It's a poor rule that won't work both ways. Let her have it herself, hot and strong, and see how she likes it—she's earned it richly. You can do it, I know, Paul; you have a way with you among women. I don't understand it myself, but I see it takes. You can do it, and you're no friend of mine, Warden, if you don't."

"Do it! My dear fellow, what wouldn't I do to oblige you; break fifty hearts, if you asked me. Here's my hand—it's a go."

"And you'll flirt with her, and jilt her?"

"With the help of the gods. Let the campaign begin at once, let me see my fair, future victim to-night."

"But you'll be careful, Paul," said Tom, cooling down as his friend warmed up. "She's very pretty, uncommonly pretty; you've no idea how pretty, and she may turn the tables and subjugate you, instead of you subjugating her."

111

"The old story of the minister who went to Rome to convert the Pope, and returned a red-hot Catholic. Not any thanks. My heart is iron-clad; has stood too many sieges to yield to any little flirting brunette. Forewarned is forearmed. Come on, old fellow," rising from his sofa, "if 'tis done, when it is done, 'twere well 'twere done quickly.'"

"How goes the night?" said Tom, looking out; "it's raining. Do you mind?"

"Shouldn't mind if it rained pitchforks in so good a cause. Get your overcoat and come. I think those old chaps—what-do-you-call-'em, Crusaders? must have felt as I do now, when they marched to take Jerusalem. Where are we to find *la belle* Fanny?"

"At her sister's, Mrs. Walters, she's only here on a visit; but during her five weeks' stay she has turned five dozen heads, and refused five dozen hands, my own the last," said Tom, with a groan.

"Never mind, Tom; there is balm in Gilead yet. Revenge is sweet, you know, and you shall taste its sweets before the moon wanes. Now then, Miss Fanny, the conquering hero comes!"

The two young men sallied forth into the rainy, lamp-lit streets. A passing omnibus took them to the home of the coquettish Fanny, and Tom rang the bell with vindictive emphasis.

"Won't she rather wonder to see you, after refusing you?" inquired Mr. Warden, whilst they waited.

"What do I care!" responded Mr. Maxwell, moodily; "her opinion is of no consequence to me now."

Mrs. Walters, a handsome, agreeable-looking young matron, welcomed Tom with a cordial shake of the hand, and acknowledged Mr. Warden's bow by the brightest of smiles, as they were ushered into the family parlor.

"We are quite alone, this rainy night, my sister and I," she said. "Mr. Walters is out of town for a day or two. Fanny, my dear, Mr. Warden; my sister, Miss Summers, Mr. Warden."

It was a pretty, cozy room, "curtained, and close, and warm;" and directly under the gas-light, reading a lady's magazine, sat one of the prettiest girls it had ever been Mr. Warden's good fortune to see, and who welcomed him with a brilliant smile.

"Black eyes, jetty ringlets, rosy cheeks, alabaster brow," thought Mr. Warden, taking stock; "the smile of an angel, and dressed to perfection. Poor Tom! he's to be pitied. Really, I haven't come across anything so much to my taste this month of Sundays."

Down sat Mr. Paul Warden beside the adorable Fanny, plunging into conversation at once with an ease and fluency that completely took away Tom's breath. That despondent wooer on the sofa, beside Mrs. Walters, pulled dejectedly at the ears of her little black-and-tan terrier, and answered at random all the pleasant things she said to him. He was listening, poor fellow, to that brilliant flow of small talk from the mustached lips of his dashing friend, and wishing the gods had gifted him with a similar "gift of the gab," and feeling miserably jealous already. He had prepared the rack for himself with his eyes wide open; but that made the torture none the less when the machinery got in motion. Pretty Fanny snubbed him incontinently, and was just as bewitching as she knew how to his friend. It was a clear case of diamond cut diamond—two flirts pitted against each other; and an outsider would have been considerably puzzled on which to bet, both being so evenly matched.

Tom listened, and sulked; yes, sulked. What a lot of things they found to talk about, where he used to be tongue-tied. The magazine, the fashion-plates, the stories; then a wild launch into literature, novels, authors, poets; then the weather; then Mr. Warden was travelling, and relating his "hair-breadth escapes by flood and field," while bright-eyed Fanny listened in breathless interest. Then the open piano caught the irresistible Paul's eyes, and in a twinkling there was Fanny seated at it, her white fingers flying over the polished keys, and he bending above her with an entranced face. Then he was singing a delightful love-song in a melodious tenor voice, that might have captivated any heart that ever beat inside of lace and muslin; and then Fanny was singing a sort of response, it seemed to frantically jealous Tom; and then it was eleven o'clock, and time to go home.

Out in the open air, with the rainy night wind blowing bleakly, Tom lifted his hat to let the cold blast cool his hot face. He was sulky still, and silent—very silent; but Mr. Warden didn't seem to mind.

"So," he said, lighting a cigar, "the campaign has begun, the first blow has been struck, the enemy's ramparts undermined. Upon my word, Tom, the little girl is uncommonly pretty!"

"I told you so," said Tom, with a sort of growl.

"And remarkably agreeable. I don't think I ever spent a pleasanter *tête-à-tête* evening."

"So I should judge. She had eyes, and ears, and tongue for no one but you."

"My dear fellow, it's not possible you're jealous! Isn't that what you wanted? Besides, there is no reason, really; she is a professional flirt, and understands her business; you and I know just how much value to put on all that sweetness. Have a cigar, my dear boy, and keep up your heart; we'll fix the flirting Fanny yet, please the pigs!"

This was all very true; but, somehow, it wasn't consoling. She was nothing to him, Tom, of course—and he hated her as hotly as ever; but, somehow, his thirst for vengeance had considerably cooled down. The cure was worse than the disease. It was maddening to a young man in his frame of mind to see those brilliant smiles, those entrancing glances, all those pretty, coquettish, womanly, wiles that had deluded him showered upon another, even for that other's delusion. Tom wished he had never thought of revenge, at least with Paul Warden for his handsome agent.

"Are you going there again?" he asked, moodily.

"Of course," replied Mr. Warden, airily. "What a question, old fellow, from you of all people. Didn't you hear the little darling telling me to call again? She overlooked you completely, by-the-by. I'm going again, and again, and yet again, until my friend, my *fides Achates*, is avenged."

"Ah!" said Tom, sulkily, "but I don't know that I care so much for vengeance as I did. Second thoughts are best; and it struck me, whilst I watched you both to-night, that it was mean and underhand to plot against a woman like this. You thought so yourself at first, you know."

"Did I? I forget. Well, I think differently now, my dear Tom; and as you remark, second thoughts are best. My honor is at stake; so put your conscientious scruples in your pocket, for I shall conquer the fascinating Fanny or perish in the attempt. Here we are at my boarding house—won't you come in? No. Well, then, good-night. By-the-way, I shall be at the enemy's quarters to-morrow evening; if you wish to see how ably I fight your battles, show yourself before nine. By-by!"

Mr. Maxwell's answer was a deeply bass growl as he plodded on his way; and Paul Warden, running up to his room, laughed lightly to himself.

"Poor Tom! Poor, dear boy! Jealousy is a green-eyed lobster, and he's a prey to it—the worst kind. Really, Paul, my son, little black eyes is the most bewitching piece of calico you have met in your travels lately; and if you wanted a wife, which you don't, you couldn't do better than go in and win. As it is—Ah! it's a pity for the little dear's sake you can't marry."

With which Mr. Warden disrobed and went to bed.

Next evening, at half-past eight, Tom Maxwell made his appearance at Mrs. Walters, only to find his *fides Achates* there enthroned before him, and basking in the sunshine of the lovely Fanny's smiles. How long he had been there Tom couldn't guess; but he and Fanny and Mrs. Walters were just settling it to go to the theatre the following night. There was a bunch of roses, pink-and-white, his gift, Tom felt in his bones, in Fanny's hand, and into which she plunged her pretty little nose every five seconds. It was adding insult to injury, the manifest delight that aggravating girl felt in his friend's society; and Tom ground his teeth inwardly, and could have seen Paul Warden guillotined, there and then, with all the pleasure in life.

That evening, and many other evenings which succeeded were but a repetition of the first. An easy flow of delightful small talk, music, singing, and reading aloud. Yes, Paul Warden read aloud, as if to goad that unhappy Tom to open madness, in the most musical of masculine voices, out of little blue-and-gold books, Tennyson, and Longfellow, and Owen Meredith; and Fanny would sit in breathless earnestness, her color coming and going, her breath fluttering, her eyes full of tears as often as not, fixed on Paul's classic profile. Tom didn't burst out openly—he made no scene; he only sat and glowered in malignant silence—and that is saying everything for his power of self-control.

Two months passed; hot weather was coming, and Fanny begun to talk of the heat and the dust of the town; of being home-sick, for the sight of green fields, new milk, strawberry-patches, new-laid eggs, and pa and ma. It had been a very delightful two months, no doubt; and she had enjoyed Mr. Warden's society very much, and gone driving and walking with him, and let him take her to the theatre, and the opera, and played for him, and sung for him, and danced with him, and accepted his bouquets, and new music, and blue-and-gold books; but, for all that, it was evident she could leave him and go home, and still exist.

"It's all very nice," Miss Summers had said, tossing back her black ringlets; "and I have enjoyed this spring ever so much, but still I'm glad to get home again. One grows tired of balls, and parties, and the theatre, you know, after awhile, Mr. Warden; and I am only a little country-girl, and I shall be just as glad as ever for a romp over the meadows, and a breezy gallop across the hills once more. If you or Mr. Maxwell," glancing at that gloomy youth sideways out of her curls, "care much for fishing, and come up our way any time this summer, I'll try and treat you as well as you have treated me."

"But you haven't treated us well, Miss Fanny," Mr. Warden said, looking unspeakable things. "You take our hearts by storm, and then break them ruthlessly by leaving us. What sort of treatment do you call that?"

Miss Summers only laughed, and looked saucy; and danced away, leaving her two admirers standing together out in the cold.

"Well, Tom," Mr. Warden said, "and so the game's up, the play played out, the curtain ready to fall. The star actress departs to-morrow—and now, what do you think of the performance?"

"Not much," responded Tom, moodily. "I can't see that you have kept your promise. You've made love to her, I allow, *con amore,* confoundedly as if you meant it, in fact; but I don't see where the jilting comes in; I can't see where's my revenge."

"Don't you?" said Paul, thoughtfully lighting his cigar. "Well, come to think of it, I don't either. To tell you the truth, I haven't had a chance to jilt her. I may be irresistible, and I have no doubt I am, since you say so; but, somehow, the charm don't seem to work with our little favorite. Here I have been for the last two months just as captivating as I know how; and yet there's that girl ready to be off to-morrow to the country, without so much as a crack in the heart that should be broken in smithereens. But still," with a sudden change of voice, and slapping him lightly on the shoulder, "dear old boy, I don't despair of giving you your revenge yet!"

Tom lifted his gloomy eyes in sullen inquiry.

"Never mind now," said Paul Warden airily; "give me a few weeks longer. Lazy as I am, I have never failed yet in anything I have seriously undertaken; and, upon my word, I'm more serious about this matter than you may believe. Trust to your friend, and wait."

That was all Mr. Warden would deign to say.

Tom, not being able to do otherwise, took him at his word, dragged out existence, and waited for his cherished revenge.

Miss Summers left town next day, and Tom, poor, miserable fellow, felt as if the sun had ceased to shine, and the scheme of the universe become a wretched failure, when he caught the last glimmer of the lustrous black eyes, the last flutter of the pretty black curls. But his Damon was by his side to slap him on the back and cheer him up.

"Courage, old fellow!" cried Mr. Warden; "all's not lost that's in danger. Turn and turn about; your turn next."

But, somehow, Tom didn't care for revenge any more. He loved that wicked, jilting little Fanny as much as ever; and the heartache only grew worse day after day; but he ceased to desire vengeance. He settled down into a kind of gentle melancholy, lost his appetite, and his relish for Tom and Jerrys, and took to writing despondent poetry for the weekly journals. In this state Mr. Warden left him, and suddenly disappeared from town. Tom didn't know where he had gone, and his landlady didn't know; and stranger still, his bootmaker and tailor, to whom he was considerably in arrears, didn't know either. But they were soon enlightened.

Five weeks after his mysterious disappearance came a letter and a newspaper, in his familiar hand, to Tom, while he sat at breakfast. He opened the letter first and read:

In the Country.

"Dear Old Boy—I have kept my word—you are avenged gloriously. Fanny will never jilt you, nor any one else again!"

At this passage in the manuscript, Tom Maxwell laid it down, the cold perspiration breaking out on his face. Had Paul Warden murdered her, or worse, had he married her? With a desperate clutch Tom seized the paper, tore it open, looked at the list of marriages, and saw his worst fears realized. There it was, in printers' ink, the atrocious revelation of his bosom friend's perfidy.

"Married, on the fifth inst., at the residence of the bride's father, Paul Warden, Esq., of New York to Miss Fanny Summers, second daughter of Mr. John Summers, of this town."

There it was. Tom didn't faint; he swallowed a scalding cup of coffee at a gulp, and revived, seized the letter and finished it.

"You see, old fellow, paradoxical as it sounds, although I was the conqueror, I was, also, the conquered. Fanny had fallen in love with me, as you foresaw, but I had fallen in love with her also, which you didn't foresee. I might jilt her, of course, but that would be cutting off my own nose to spite my friend's face; and so—I didn't! I did the next best thing for you, though,—I married her! and I may mention, in parenthesis, I am the happiest of mankind; and as Artemus Ward remarks, 'My wife says so too.'

"Adieu, my boy. We'll come to town next week, where Fan and I will be delighted to have you call. With best regards from my dear little wife, I am, old fellow Clarence L. Cullen Mr. and Mrs. Warden did come to town next week; but Mr. Maxwell didn't call. In point of fact he hasn't called since, and doesn't intend to, and has given his friend Paul the "cut direct." And that is how Paul Warden got a wife, and Tom Maxwell his revenge.

---

# FOR BETTER FOR WORSE.

"

And all is gone?"

"Why, no, sir; no, Mr. Fletcher—not all. There's that six hundred a year, and that little place down at Dover, that you settled on your wife; you will save that out of the wreck. A trifle—a mere nothing, I am aware, out of such a noble inheritance as yours, Mr. Fletcher—but still something. Half a loaf you know, sir, is—"

He stopped abruptly at a motion of Richard Fletcher's hand. He was a lawyer, and used to this sort of thing; and not much effected by the story, he had run down from New York to tell Mr. Fletcher; his rich client had speculated rashly, and lost—a common case enough. A week ago he was worth half a million; to-night he is not worth a sixpence—that was all. There were his wife's settlements, of course; but they were his wife's—and Mr. and Mrs. Fletcher were two.

"I thought I had better let you know at once, Mr. Fletcher," the lawyer said; "it's sure to be in everybody's mouth to-morrow. And now, if I'm to catch the nine-fifty up-train, I had better be starting. Good-night, sir. Worse luck now, better next time."

"Good-night," Richard Fletcher said, mechanically. He was leaning against the low, iron gateway, his folded arms lying on its carved top, and the black shadows of the beeches shutting him in like a pall. Up the avenue colored lamps gleamed along the chestnut walks, blue, red, and green, turning the dark November night to fairy-land. The wide front of the stately mansion was all aglow with illumination, with music, and flowers, and fair women; and fairest, where all were fair, its proud young mistress, Marian Fletcher.

Two men, stragglers from the ball-room, with their cigars lighted, came down through the gloom, close to the motionless figure against the iron gate—only another shadow among the shadows—so close that he heard every word.

"Rather superb style of thing, all this," one said. "When Dick Fletcher does this sort of thing, he does do it. Wonderful luck he's had, for a poor devil, who five years ago hadn't a rap; and that wife of his—magnificent Marian—most lovely thing the sun shines on."

"Too lovely, my friend, for—she's ice."

"Ah! To her husband? Married him for his fortune, didn't she? The old story, very poor, very proud; and sold to the highest bidder. Craymore stood to win there once, didn't he?"

"It was a desperate flirtation—an engagement, the knowing ones do say; but Capt. Craymore knows better than to indulge in such a luxury as a penniless wife. So Fletcher came along, made rich by a sudden windfall, and she's Mrs. Fletcher to-night; and more beautiful and queenly than ever. I watched her dancing with Craymore half an hour ago, and—Well, I didn't envy Fletcher, if he is worth half a million. Let's go back to the house, it's beginning to rain."

"Suppose Fletcher were to lose his fortune—what then?"

"My good fellow, he would lose his wife in the same hour. Some women there are who would go with their husbands to beggary—and he's a fine fellow, too, is Fletcher; but not the lovely Marian. There, the rain begins!"

The shadow among the beeches stood stiller than stone. A long, low wind worried the trees, and the rain beat its melancholy drip, drip. Half an hour, an hour, two, passed, but the figure leaning against the iron-gate was as still as the iron itself. But slowly he stirred at last, became conscious he was dripping, and passed slowly out of the rainy gloom, and up the lamplit-avenue, and into the stately home, that, after to-night, would be his no more.

Another half-hour, and he was back in the glitter and dazzle and music of the brilliant suit of drawing-rooms, his wet garments changed, the fixed whiteness of his face telling but little of his sudden blow. He had not been missed; his radiant three months' bride shone there in diamonds, and laces, and roses resplendent—and who was to think of the rich Fletcher! "Only a clod," whom she had honored by marrying. Capt. Craymore was by her side, more fascinating than ever. How could she find time to think of any one so plebeian as the underbred rich man she had married, by his entrancing side?

But it was all over at last. The "lights were fled, the garlands dead," and Mrs. Fletcher up in her dressing-room, in the raw morning light, was under the hands of her maid. She lay back among the violet-velvet cushions, languid and lovely, being disrobed, and looked round with an irritated flush at the abrupt entrance of the master of the house. He did not often intrude; since the first few weeks of their marriage he had been a model husband, and kept his place. Therefore, Mrs. Fletcher looked surprised, as well as annoyed now.

"Do you wish to speak to me, Mr. Fletcher?" she asked, coldly; for after an evening with Capt. Craymore she was always less tolerant of her *bourgeois* husband.

"Yes—but alone. I will wait in your sitting-room until you dismiss your maid."

Something in his colorless face—something in the sound of his voice startled her; but he was gone while yet speaking, and the maid went on. "Hurry, Louise," her mistress said, briefly; and Louise coiled up the shining hair, arranged the white dressing-gown, and left her.

Marian Fletcher arose and swept into the next room. It was the daintiest *bijou* of boudoirs, all rose-silk, and silver, and filigree-work, and delicious Greuze paintings, smiling down from the fluted panels. A bright wood-fire burned on the hearth, and her husband stood against the low chimney-piece, whiter and colder than the marble itself.

"Well," she said, "what is it?"

He looked up. She stood before him in her beauty and her pride, jewels flashed on her fairy hands—a queen by right divine of her azure eyes and tinseled hair—his, yet not his; "so near, and yet so far." He loved her, how well his own wrung heart only knew.

"What is it?" she repeated, impatiently. "I am tired and sleepy. Tell me in a word."

"I can—ruin!"

"What?"

"I am ruined. All is gone. I am a beggar."

She started back, turning whiter than her dress, and leaned heavily against a chair.

"Ruined!" she repeated. "A beggar!"

"Ugly words, are they not? but quite true. I did not know it until last night; Kearstall came from town to tell me. My last grand speculation has failed, and in its failure engulfed everything. I am as poor as the poorest laborer on this estate; poorer than I was five years ago, before this fortune was left me."

There was a sort of savage pleasure in thus hideously putting things in their ugliest light. Rich or poor, she despised him alike. What need was there for him to mince matters?

"There are your settlements, your six hundred a-year and the Dover farm, that crumb of the loaf is left, and remains yours. I am sorry for you, Mrs. Fletcher—sorry that your sacrifice of youth and loveliness, on the altar of Mammon, has been in vain. I had hoped, when I married you, of winning some return for the limitless love I gave you. I know to-night how futile that hope has been. Once again, for your sake, I am sorry; for myself I do not care. The world is a wide place, and I can win my way. I give you your freedom, the only reparation for marrying you in my power to make. I leave here to-night, New York to-morrow; and so—farewell!"

She stood like a stone; he turned and left her. Once she had made a movement, seeing the white anguish of his face, as though to go to him—but she did not. He was gone, and she dropped down in the rose-and-silver glitter of her fairy-room, as miserable a woman as day ever dawned on.

A month later, and she was far away, buried alive in the Dover Cottage. All had gone; the nine days wonder was at an end; the "rich Fletcher" and his handsome wife had disappeared out of the magic whirl of society; and society got on very well without them. They had been, and they were not—and the story was told. Of all who had broken bread with the ruined man, there were not two who cared a fillip whether he were living or dead.

The December wind wailed over the stormy sea, and the wintry rain lashed the windows of the Dover Cottage. Marian Fletcher sat before the blazing fire in a long, low, gloomy parlor, and Capt. Craymore stood before her. He had but just found her out, and he had run down to see how she bore her altered fortunes. She bore them as an uncrowned queen might, with regal pride and cold endurance. The exquisite face had lost its rose-leaf bloom; the deep, still eyes looked larger and more fathomless; the mouth was set in patient pain—that was all. The man felt his heart burn as he looked at her, she was so lovely, *so* lovely. He leaned over, and the passionate words came that he could not check. He loved her. She loved him; she was forsaken and alone—why need they part?

She listened, growing whiter than a dead woman. Then she came and faced him, until the cowered soul within him shrank and quailed.

"I have fallen very low," she said. "I am poor, and alone, and a deserted wife. But Capt. Craymore, I have not fallen low enough to be your mistress. Go!"

Her unflickering finger pointed to the door. There was that in her face no man dare disobey, and he slunk forth like a whipped hound. Then as on that night when she had parted from her husband, she slipped down in her misery to the ground, and hid her face in her hands. Now she knew the man she had loved, now she was learning to know the man who had loved her. The one would drag her down to bottomless depths of blackness and infamy; the other had given up all for her—even herself—and gone forth a homeless, penniless wanderer, to fight the battle of life.

"Oh! truest and noblest!" her heart cried, in its passionate pain, "how I have wronged you! Bravest and best heart that ever beat in man's breast—am I only to know your worth when it is too late?"

115

It seemed so. Richard Fletcher had disappeared out of the world—the world she knew—as utterly as though he had never been in it. The slow months dragged drearily by; but he never came. The piteous advertisement in the *Herald* newspaper stood unanswered when the spring-buds burst; and she was alone in her worse than widowhood, in the Dover Cottage still.

With the glory of the brilliant new summer, new hope dawned for her. A tiny messenger, with Richard Fletcher's great brown eyes, smiled up in her face, and a baby head nestled against her lonely heart. Ah! she knew now how she loved baby's father, when the brown eyes, of which these were the counterpart, were lost to her forever.

So, with the great world shut out, and with only baby Richard and her two servants, life went on in the solitary cottage. The winds of winter had five times swept over the ceaseless sea, and little Richard could toddle and lisp; and in Marian Fletcher's heart hope slowly died out. She had lost him through her own fault; he, to whom she had been bound in the mysterious tie of marriage, would never look upon her cruel face again.

She sat one stormy November night, thinking very sadly of the true heart and strong love she had cast away. Her boy lay asleep before the ruddy fire; the rain and wind beat like human things against the glass. She sat looking seaward, with weary, empty eyes, so desolate—so desolate, her soul crying out with unutterable yearning for the wanderer to come back.

As she stood there gazing sadly out at the wild night falling over the wild sea, her one servant came hurriedly into the room with startled affright in her eyes.

"Oh, ma'am," she cried, "such a dreadful thing! The up-train from New York has had an accident, has fell over the embankment just below here and half the passengers are killed and wounded. The screams as I came past was awful to hear. But surely, ma'am," the woman broke off in dismay as her mistress seized her hat and shawl, "you won't go out and it raining and a blowing fit to take you off your feet. You can't do nothing, and you'll get your death."

But Mrs. Fletcher was out already, heedless of wind or rain, and making her way to the scene of the accident. "Poor souls," she was thinking, "so sudden and frightful a fate. Perhaps I can be of help to some one." For her life trouble had done this for her; made her tender of heart, and pitiful of soul to all who suffered.

A great crowd were there from Dover village as she drew near, beginning to bear away the wounded, the dying and the dead. Groans and cries of infinite misery made the rainy twilight hideous. Mrs. Fletcher shuddered, but she stooped resolutely over a man who lay almost at her feet, a man whom she might have thought dead but for the low moan that now and then came from his lips.

She bent above him timidly, her heart fluttering at something vaguely familiar in his look.

"Can I do anything for you?" she asked, "I fear you are very very badly hurt."

The eyes opened; in the dim light he half arose on his elbow. "Marian," he said, and fell back and fainted wholly away.

And so her prayers were answered after many days, and death itself seemed to have given back her husband to Marian Fletcher's arms. Over his pillow life and Death fought their sharp battle, for many long weeks, while she watched over him, and prayed beside him in what agony of remorse, and terror and passionate tenderness only Heaven and herself ever knew.

Those ceaseless, agonized prayers prevailed. In the pale dawn of a Christmas morning, the heavy brown eyes opened and fixed upon her face, no longer in delirium, but with the kindling light of recognition, and great and sudden joy.

"Marian," he said faintly, "my wife."

She was on her knees beside him, his weak head lying in her caressing arms.

"My dearest, my dearest, thank God; my own, my cherished husband, forgive your erring wife."

His face lit with a rare smile, as he looked up into the pale, tear wet, passionately earnest face.

"It is true then what I heard, what has brought me home. You have sought me. But Marian, what if I must tell you I am still poor, poor as when we parted." She shrunk away as though he had hurt her.

"I have deserved that you should say this to me," she said in a stifled voice, "I have been the basest of the base in the past—why should you think me other than heartless and mercenary still. But oh, Richard, don't you see—I love you now, so dearly and truly, my husband, that I can never have any life apart from you more. Do not talk to me of poverty—only tell me you will never leave me again." "Never again," he answered, "till death us do part. But Marian, though I am no longer the millionaire you married, I do not return to you quite a beggar. More or less I have retrieved the past, and we can begin life anew almost as luxuriously as we left it off." Her face clouded for a moment.

"Ah! I am sorry. I wanted to atone: how can I now? I have been your wife in the sunshine. I thought to show you what I could be in the shadow, and now all that is at an end. I can never show you how I have repented for—that night."

But Richard Fletcher only smiles a smile of great content. And in the silence that ensues, there comes over the snowy fields the joyful bells of the blessed Christmas morning, and in their hearts both bless God for the new life, that dawns with this holy day.

Made in the USA
Middletown, DE
07 May 2022

65465180R00066